DEMONICUS

OVERWORLD UNDERGROUND
BOOK TWO

JOHN CORWIN

ISBN- 978-1-942453-04-8

Printed in the U.S.A.

To my wonderful support group:
Alana Rock
Karen Stansbury

My amazing editors:
Annetta Ribken
Jennifer Wingard

My awesome cover artist:
Regina Wamba

Thanks so much for all your help and input!

Books by John Corwin:

The Overworld Chronicles:
Sweet Blood of Mine
Dark Light of Mine
Fallen Angel of Mine
Dread Nemesis of Mine
Twisted Sister of Mine
Dearest Mother of Mine
Infernal Father of Mine
Sinister Seraphim of Mine
Wicked War of Mine
Dire Destiny of Ours
Aetherial Annihilation
Baleful Betrayal

Overworld Underground:
Possessed By You
Demonicus

Overworld Arcanum:
Conrad Edison and the Living Curse
Conrad Edison and the Anchored World

Stand Alone Novels:
No Darker Fate
The Next Thing I Knew
Outsourced
Seventh

For the latest on new releases, free ebooks, and more, join John Corwin's Newsletter at www.johncorwin.net!

HELL ON EARTH

During a routine Custodian investigation into illegal activities by vampires, Emily Glass discovers a massive demon summoning pattern in a warehouse.

Her demon-possessed boyfriend, Tyler Rock, identifies it as a demonicus—an ancient pattern used to summon demons from different levels of hell all at the same time, with the most powerful demon devouring the souls of humans to magnify his power.

Together with the enigmatic George Glass and Mr. Sticks, they uncover a plot to create more demonicus and raise an army of demons in Eden at the cost of thousands of human souls. Unless they can stop the hellions, humanity might have a demon overlord as their new ruler.

Chapter 1

The last person I expected to see after a nice, relaxing vacation was George Walker.

I nearly dropped my purse at the sight of my enigmatic handler for the Custodians. "What's wrong?" My heart skipped a beat.

"Apologies for catching you so soon after your return, but we need your help, Miss Glass." He motioned toward a sleek black sedan. "If you don't mind, the situation is rather urgent."

Tyler wrapped his arm around my shoulders. "I don't know how you do business in the Custodians, George, but a text or a phone call would have been nice."

"I tried to reach her, but never received a response." George seemed to take no offense to Tyler's stern tone.

"It's okay." I took out my mobile and looked at it. "I put my phone on airplane mode and forgot to switch back to normal."

"What's the emergency?" Tyler asked.

George regarded him calmly. "That's for Miss Glass to know."

Tyler shrugged. "Then tell her. I promise I won't listen."

I held up my hands. "Let us put our luggage away and we'll come, George." I pointed toward his car. "Please go wait there, and I'll be down shortly."

George nodded and walked to the car.

On the way up the elevator, Tyler cornered me with a kiss. "We're not home ten seconds and you're already off on another adventure."

"Indeed." Despite all the intimate time we'd spent on holiday, I could hardly get enough of this lovely man. The thought of taking off on a Custodian mission without him left me feeling empty. "I want you to come."

"*Moi?*" A corner of his mouth lifted into a lopsided grin. "Whatever will your handler say?"

I pecked a kiss on his lips. "Absolutely nothing, if he knows what's good for him."

George raised an eyebrow when the two of us approached his car. "We're both coming," I said.

George glanced at Tyler. "Mr. Rock isn't a Custodian."

A tall man emerged from the passenger side of the car and narrowed his eyes at Tyler. Mr. Sticks didn't say a word, but it was more than obvious how he felt about me bringing a playdate.

"Does he talk?" Tyler bobbed his head toward Sticks. I had, of course, told Tyler all about the people I'd met during my work with the Custodians, including the ever-silent Mr. Sticks.

George smiled pleasantly. "He *communicates* if that's what you're asking." He turned to me. "I suppose Mr. Rock may ride along. Are you ready, Miss Glass?"

I took a deep breath and nodded. "Let's go."

Tyler ran his eyes across the sedan. "What kind of car is this?"

"A custom model," George answered.

Mr. Sticks held open the rear door and motioned me inside. I slid across the seat so Tyler could climb in beside me. The smell of new leather pleased my nose. Once Tyler was seated, George climbed into the driver seat.

Tyler leaned forward. "Who makes your custom models?"

George touched a handle on the steering column. Soundlessly, the car accelerated toward the exit. "This is the latest out of Science Academy."

"Science Academy?"

Mr. Sticks glared over his shoulder at Tyler.

"You really must attend an orientation soon," George said. "It would answer many of your basic questions."

I pulled Tyler next to me. "Let the man drive." My stomach fluttered with anxiety. Since saving Tyler from the Exorcists nearly three months earlier, I hadn't been on any missions for the Custodians. Tyler and I had taken a long overseas vacation to make sure he was safe and to give my sanity a chance to recover.

He ran a hand across the leather and looked around the car, obviously wanting to talk more about it, but finally relaxed and slung an arm over my shoulders. "Sorry, Em. I've just never seen anything like this."

"Boys and their toys." I tried to give him a serious look, but couldn't stop from smiling at his enthusiasm. "I didn't realize demons were into automobiles."

He squeezed me tight. "I acquired the taste from one of my previous hosts."

This turned Sticks's glare toward us once more.

"Perhaps it's best if you don't discuss Mr. Rock's true nature right now," George said amicably. "Mr. Sticks is a stickler when it comes to the rules and is none too happy that I promised to let Mr. Rock be."

"He's really a very nice demon," I told Sticks. "Once you get to know him."

The man shook his head and faced forward.

George pulled into traffic, drove a couple of blocks, and turned into a blind alley I'd seen him use before. Excitement replaced the anxiety. Before I'd discovered the true nature of my work for the Custodians, George had always blindfolded me before we traveled anywhere. Considering how quickly we made it across town, I knew there must be something special about the cars they used.

I wasn't disappointed.

At the press of a button, the outside of the car blurred and faded until it matched our surroundings. George pulled a lever and the car lifted from the ground, rising quickly until we were above the city. I gasped.

Tyler's hand tightened on mine. "I think I'm in love," he said.

The early morning sun hovered behind the Atlanta skyline, dividing the city into shadows crisscrossed with corridors of light. My sense of wonderment fled, replaced with worry gnawing at my insides. I didn't know what prompted this abrupt shift in my emotions. *I haven't been on a mission for a while. It's probably just nerves.*

"How much do one of these cars cost?" Tyler asked.

George pressed the accelerator and steered the car until the brass compass in the dash pointed north. "They're for official use only, I'm afraid."

"Damn." Tyler braced his elbows on the front seats and peered out of the window, much to the obvious chagrin of Mr. Sticks.

3

I contented myself to look out to the side as buildings flashed past beneath us. We soon reached a single story office building and circled overhead. A pattern of black lines across the flat roof caught my attention. They resembled burn marks, though they appeared too neat and precise to have been made by a fire. "George, what are we investigating?"

He brought the car in for a landing in a loading zone behind the building. "We received a tip that this place was being used as a cover for illegal vampire operations. We'll pose as customers and go inside while you use your special abilities to sense the truth."

A wave of heat washed across my skin from the direction of the building. I swallowed hard and nodded. "What if they catch on?"

"I have a team on standby." He looked back and smiled. "I don't anticipate any trouble. If you confirm there are vampires, we'll have to be sure they're up to illegal activities before we can raid them."

Tyler's arm tightened around my shoulders. "Don't worry, I'll protect you."

I melted into his reassuring embrace and just as quickly stiffened when I remembered there were others present. *Don't act like a frightened ninny!*

George drove the car to the front of the building and pulled into a parking space between two other cars. The warm sensation followed us the entire way, though nobody but me seemed to notice it.

Tyler slid out of the backseat. I followed and stood in the parking lot next to him. It was plain to see through the glass windows that the building lobby was empty. The sign above the door read, *Tri-Cross Blood Donations*.

Tyler chuckled. "Well, if this isn't the perfect place to run illegal vampire operations, I don't know what is."

"Technically, vampires running a blood bank isn't illegal," George said. "In fact, since vampires aren't supposed to feed directly on noms, something like this is a necessity."

I grimaced. "How awful. They're taking vital blood from normals who might need a transfusion someday."

Sticks didn't frown, which probably meant he agreed with me.

George looked at me. "Do you feel anything, Miss Glass?"

I closed my eyes and opened my senses. I sensed the low simmer of Tyler's presence, and glimpsed the brilliant white energy at the cores of Mr. Sticks and George. The radiating heat from the building intensified. I usually enjoyed warmth, but this sensation brought me no comfort. Instead, it sent chills skittering down my back.

"I don't feel vampiric auras from here," I said. "Just an odd warm feeling."

George nodded. "Let's go inside."

The moment he opened the door, a blast of rancid air hit us in the face. I staggered back, coughing and hacking and spitting. It smelled as though someone had left a truckload of eggs in the hot sun. The only one of us who didn't seem adversely affected was Tyler.

His forehead pinched and his green eyes looked deeply troubled. "This isn't good."

George pressed a handkerchief over his nose. "It's brimstone, isn't it?"

Tyler nodded. "This is the most concentrated I've ever smelled it on the mortal plane."

Mr. Sticks retrieved something from the car trunk and returned with small scraps of cloth. He placed one over his nose. The cloth spread over his nose and mouth and stuck there. George took a scrap and did the same thing. I followed his example. The moment the silky material masked my nostrils, the odor vanished.

Tyler took a scrap but stuck it in his back pocket. "I don't need it."

George raised an eyebrow. "Such high doses of brimstone fumes could harm your lungs, despite your demon soul."

"And it's such a foul odor," I added.

He gave me a hurt look. "I think it smells good." Even so, he put on the mask.

Mr. Sticks and George led the way. George stepped into an empty office in the first hallway. Scattered papers lay on the floor next to the desk. I picked up one of the papers.

I skimmed through it. "This is a shipping order to relocate blood from Los Angeles to Atlanta."

George took the document. "Interesting. This much blood would feed an army of vampires."

Sticks gave him a knowing look.

"An army?" Tyler folded his arms. "Is there something you haven't told us?"

George shook his head. "Suspicions, nothing more." He nodded toward the door. "We should continue."

After the other two men left the office, Tyler took me aside. "I get the feeling he still isn't telling you everything."

"You may be right." I sighed. "It's probably because we haven't taken that orientation yet."

He snorted. "Doubtful." We followed the others.

In the next office, coffee-stained documents littered a desk and the floor. A toppled chair, a broken mobile phone, a trace of blood— each office bore some trace of a struggle or a quick departure.

"Anything yet?" George asked me.

"I'll be sure to let you know the moment I sense anything besides this awful heat." The deeper into the building we went, the stronger the stifling heat pressed against my senses. I was tempted to dampen my sensitivity, but didn't want to miss any vital clues.

We found the body of a young man in the break room, his head tilted at a horrific angle, face terribly bruised.

George knelt next to him and ran a finger along the spine. "Neck's broken."

"Perhaps you could tell me something I didn't know the moment I saw it." I drew in a shuddering breath and took calming breaths.

"Do you sense anything from the body?" George asked.

Swallowing the bile in my throat, I knelt and touched the man's cold skin. "I don't know if my ability works on dead people."

"If he died from a broken neck, there's a good chance he's not a vampire," Tyler said.

"Agreed," George replied. "Still, it never hurts to make sure."

The blinking clock on the microwave caught my attention. I looked at the large watch on the dead man's wrist. The hands were stuck on twelve AM. "Why would this man be here at midnight?"

"True dedication," Tyler said.

George looked at the watch. "Interesting. The watch shows today's date."

I pointed to the microwave. "It looks like the power went out." I opened the microwave door and removed what had once been a frozen meal. "It looks like he was making lunch or supper."

Tyler opened the refrigerator. "I'd guess it was lunch, judging from all the food in here." He pulled several plastic containers marked

6

with names from the fridge. "When did you get the tip about this place?"

George pursed his lips. "This morning."

"Interesting timing, wouldn't you say?"

"It does raise questions." He pulled a wallet from the dead man's pocket and took out the ID. "Not many vampires carry driver's licenses." He held turned it around. "And if they do, they're usually expired."

"They don't drive cars?" I asked.

"Sure, but if they're pulled over, they can compel the police to let them go." He put the wallet into an evidence bag. "Even new vampires can do that to noms." George sighed and touched a cross-shaped pendant on his collar. "All teams move into position and secure this location. We've got at least one corpse on the premises."

A man's voice emanated from the pendant. "Sir, this is Carswell. Do you want my people to sweep for evidence?"

George replied. "Start outside and work your way in."

"Yes, sir."

Sticks stepped into the hallway and stared toward the area we hadn't yet visited. George set the evidence bag next to the corpse and followed Sticks.

Tyler's took my hand and pulled me close. "Are you okay?"

I rolled my eyes and pushed away. "I'm fine. Don't coddle me in front of the others, please."

He grinned. "Don't want to look soft in front of your part-time boss?"

"That, and there's a body in the room." I turned him to face the door. "Now, go."

"As you command."

A set of sturdy double doors guarded the last part of the building. Mr. Sticks tested them but they were locked. He solved the dilemma by spinning on a heel and smashing the door from its hinges with a powerful kick.

Tyler chuckled. "Well, if anyone's still around, they'll know we're here now." His lips curled up. The man always seemed perpetually amused by the world. Sometimes his cavalier attitude really bothered me. Today it boosted my confidence.

He'll protect me. During our long vacation, we'd dedicated an hour or so each day to learning self-defense techniques, though Tyler had taken it to an extreme and taken other martial arts classes. With his superhuman reflexes, it hadn't taken him long to pick up on the basics. I'd dedicated that time to sipping drinks by the beach.

Having encountered a vampire before, I knew there wasn't much I could realistically do to fight one. Even Tyler had barely won the fight with Stephen, a creeptastic vampire who'd nearly killed my best friend Isabel, and then tried to kill me. I'd gotten the last laugh by removing his vampiric abilities with my odd powers.

George flashed Sticks a look. "You really should work on that temper."

Sticks shrugged and went through the open door and into a black room. I followed the others inside.

It was like walking into a sauna, except the heat wasn't physical, but psychic. Grey shadows darker than the pitch black danced before my eyes. I staggered back into the hallway and breathed with relief as the heat abated. *My eyes must be playing tricks on me.*

"You just glimpsed something big, didn't you?" Tyler asked.

George turned around. "Glimpsed?"

Tyler nodded. "Yeah, that's what we call her special talent."

"Apt description." George felt along the wall. Something clicked and the lights flickered on to reveal a sprawling empty warehouse.

My mouth went dry and I wanted to run away screaming at what I saw.

Chapter 2

The black shapes I'd seen in the darkness still flitted around the room like leaves in a storm. They had no discernable shapes, but morphed from second to second. None of them looked larger than my hand. Most were like motes of dust. But what truly bothered me were the bodies.

Several slumped figures were bound together in the center of the room. I counted at least six more corpses scattered around the area.

"Jesus." Tyler's voice was rough, all traces of amusement gone.

"We need to make sure they're not alive." I took a step forward, but George quickly barred me with an arm.

"Careful," he said. "We don't know if the runes are still active."

"Runes?"

He pointed down.

A black line was burned into the concrete floor. I followed the line to a circular diagram perhaps four feet across. A body lay in the center of it. The line continued from the other side and ran to yet another diagram, this one identical in size to the first, but with a different pattern. The line ran through several such diagrams, curving in a giant circle, but it didn't stop there. Lines ran from each design and into the center to construct several slightly larger patterns, which encircled a pattern at least three times larger than the others.

Sticks's nostrils flared. He knelt and rolled a silver coin across the floor. Sparks flashed as it intersected the lines of one pattern with a body inside it, but it continued its journey all the way across the room. He rolled several more coins. Electricity arced each time one touched a pattern with a body in it except for the design in the center.

"Me either," George said. "But I think I read about something like this happening several centuries ago."

I narrowed my eyes at Sticks. "How do you hear what he's saying?"

"He said he hasn't seen anything like this." George watched as the last coin reached the other side of the room. "The runes are defused."

"It's a demonicus." Tyler hissed a breath through his teeth. "During my time in Haedaemos, I heard whispers about such a thing, but thought it was impossible to pull off something so complex."

George stepped over the outer line and walked to the nearest body. He knelt and put a hand to the neck. "This man is still alive."

I touched the fallen man. His skin was warm and I felt a pulse, but my insides felt as if someone had vacuumed them out. I didn't sense things about normal people, or if I did, I'd simply grown so accustomed to the sensation I no longer recognized it for something out of the ordinary. This man seemed normal except for the strange empty pit he evoked in my stomach.

Tyler crouched next to a woman. "This one's alive too."

I walked over and touched her. Once again, I felt a gaping void.

Mr. Sticks motioned me over to a young woman in a short skirt and knee-high boots. Her attire was far more stylish than the others'. I touched her. Her skin felt like fabric, but emitted no warmth. Her irregular pulse throbbed against my fingers. Despite the psychic heat in the room, her aura felt cold. Seconds after I touched her, I felt the squirming presence of her vampirism and nearly jerked my hand away.

Vampires unsettled me. Unlike the vampires of myth, I'd learned that the real ones still lived and breathed. I was about to release her when I sensed something else even deeper beneath the curse, which bound her to a life of drinking blood.

She, too, felt empty. I suddenly recognized the missing element. "I've glimpsed something." I rose on shaky knees. Tyler flashed to my side and steadied me. This time, I felt no shame requiring assistance.

George looked concerned. "What is it, Miss Glass?"

"These people aren't alive. Only their bodies are."

Sticks grimaced.

"Exactly," Tyler said, as if the man had spoken. "Their souls are gone."

I noticed employee badges clipped to the shirts of the men. The woman wore one at the waist of her skirt. "These people worked here." I pointed to the young woman. She looked my age, though with vampires, appearances meant little when it came to years. "She is—was—a vampire. I can still feel the aura, but her soul is gone too."

"So this was a front for the vampires." George put a finger to his chin. "It's common practice to hire noms. Vampires can tolerate sunlight to a certain degree, but they are, by nature, nocturnal." He looked at the girl. "She was probably a new convert and, as such, had low social status."

"Whatever you say." Tyler's lips attempted a smile, but faltered. It was obvious whatever had happened here bothered him a lot more than he was letting on.

"Explain this demonicus," George said.

"I don't know much." Tyler ambled toward the center of the room and the bound bodies. "I'm sure you're familiar with the nine circles of Hell."

"I've heard of them, yes." George followed him. "There is a great deal of myth about Haedaemos, but very little in the way of fact."

"There are actually thirteen circles." Tyler grabbed the leg of one of the bound bodies and unceremoniously dragged it to the side. He looked curiously at the man in the center of the bodies. "Hmm, he's got a white robe on."

"So I noticed," George said.

Sticks's gaze hardened as he watched, but he made no move to stop Tyler from moving the bodies. I decided to go check the corpses for auras while Tyler explained.

"Is there a significance to thirteen?" George asked.

Tyler pointed to the pattern in the center of the large diagram where the complex pattern connected to a series of circles with a black one at the very center. "It's all about power. The outer circles are the lesser demons, the masses. The very center represents the most powerful demons."

"Didn't you say your father was one of the powerful ones?" I asked.

"He'd like to think he's the strongest." Tyler chuckled.

"Your father is in the center?" George asked.

Tyler shook his head. "No, that's the Abyss."

"The Abyss?" he glanced at Sticks, but the other man shook his head.

"Abyssal demons are the most powerful, but they're also confined to an eternal prison." Tyler scuffed a shoe over the black circle. "There are rumors the Abyssals were once gods, tricked into creating their own prison."

"There are no gods," George said matter-of-factly. "Only demons and mortals."

A slow, condescending smile spread across Tyler's lips. "George, I'd like to politely point out that you don't know what in the hell you're talking about." He shivered. "Even during my short life I've seen enough to know there's far more to Earth than Eden and Haedaemos. We just haven't found it yet."

Mr. Sticks actually nodded.

George didn't seem to take any offense whatsoever. "Perhaps we should pray we never have to find out. I'm not certain we're equipped to handle anything more than the norm—vampires, Arcanes, lycans, and Daemos."

"Daemos?" Tyler perked with interest. "I always wondered how Baal made them."

"Baal?" I recognized that name from my religious upbringing. "Does he actually exist?"

Tyler managed a wry grin. "Yes, my father the Grand Overlord of Haedaemos."

My mouth dropped open. "Oh, dear. I'm not sure how I'll explain that one to my parents."

A commotion behind us drew our attention. A group of Custodians entered the room and stopped cold at the sight of the demonicus.

"Give us a few moments," George said. "We're still investigating."

"What is this?" asked a short stocky man. "Are these demon summoning runes?"

"Yes, Carswell."

"Sir, protocol dictates we immediately sterilize this room and contact Exorcists."

"I'm well aware of protocol, Carswell, but this is a special case."

The man opened his mouth.

"Carswell, I ordered you to give us a few moments," George said, his voice still every bit as amicable as usual. "If you can't do anything productive in the meantime, perhaps you'd like to go outside and enjoy the spring weather."

Carswell pressed a hand to his chest. "Yes, sir." He turned to his team. "Continue your sweeps outside."

Moments later, the room was empty except for the four of us.

I touched each of the bodies. All wore employee badges, two were vampires, and not a one of them still had a soul. I determined the same thing about the other bodies in the room and relayed the information to George Walker.

"In all my years, I've seen only a couple of cases of missing souls, and those were because of an incubus named Vaedaemos." Geroge cut the rope binding the bodies together. "Daemos can devour souls, but from what I've heard, the victim must agree to it."

Tyler frowned. "That's true for demons too." He shook his head. "It can't be compelled. A person has to truly give up their soul." He ran a hand through his thick hair.

"What about possession?" I asked.

"Those rules are a little easier to work around." Tyler folded his arms. "People who don't care for their bodies typically open themselves up to possession. Sometimes you can tempt your way in."

I repressed a grimace. During our vacation time, Tyler had refused to talk much about his past. What he'd told me before had been couched in generalities, but I knew he'd been a very bad boy.

"I wonder why only one person in the middle had a white robe," Tyler said. "Maybe he was part of a cult."

"Tell me more about this demonicus," George said.

Tyler opened his mouth to speak when the doors at the rear of the warehouse opened and Carswell and his group entered. The moment they stepped across the threshold, sparks flashed across the back wall like a lit fuse, racing all the way to the back right corner of the room. The floor there began to bubble like tar.

"We tripped a ward!" Carswell shouted.

"That was a demon ward," Tyler said. His eyes widened. "I hope to God your people can fight."

"Weapons free," George called.

Carswell and his people drew silver swords and formed a line just as something crawled from the inky mass on the floor.

I gasped as the creature stepped into the light. With at least a dozen legs coated in shiny black chitin, it stood as tall as a Great Dane. Each leg bristled with spiky fur and terminated in pointy spikes that clinked with every step. The monster unleashed a screech that nearly sent my skin crawling off my body.

"Oh, shit." Tyler backed away. "That's a crawler."

It skittered toward Carswell's team.

"A very descriptive name," I said in a dry tone. "What, precisely, does it do besides crawl and turn my knees to jelly?"

"Scuttles, shrieks, and devours souls."

"Can we squash it?" I asked.

"I have a better suggestion." Tyler cupped his hands to his mouth and shouted, "Run!"

"Hold your ground!" Carswell commanded his people. "Prepare to engage with lancers."

The creature closed to within several yards of the Custodians.

Carswell swung forward his arm. "Fire!"

Silver darts whistled through the air and pinged off the crawler's armor.

"You can't kill that thing with darts and swords," Tyler said. "Its armor is too tough."

Sticks removed two short rods from within his suit and raced toward the monster. He leapt, brandished the rods in each hand, and flicked them. They extended to thick staffs, each one with a curving blade at the end. The crawler shrieked and pounced. Sticks whirled his staffs and somehow knocked the creature aside in mid-air.

The crawler's claws scraped across the concrete like nails on a chalkboard, drawing sparks and making the hairs on my head stand on end. Sticks was on the creature almost immediately, staffs blurring, chitin flying as he hacked away at the tough armor.

"He's not going to win," Tyler said.

"Is there anything we can do?" George asked.

Tyler bit his lip. "Crawlers have a soft spot we might be able to exploit, but it'll be tricky."

"Just tell me what to do," George said.

"No." Tyler shook his head. "Let me try." He stepped toward the battle.

I grabbed his arm. "Are you crazy? You don't even have a weapon."

"If this works, I won't need one." He patted my hand. "I'll be fine."

Before I could argue with him, he easily slipped out of my grasp and raced toward Sticks and the crawler.

Unable to simply sit back and watch, I followed.

George moved swiftly to block my path. "Miss Glass, perhaps you should remain here."

"Out of my way." I glared at him.

"Mr. Rock possesses superhuman reflexes, which may preserve his life." He raised an eyebrow. "What if you get in the way and cause him to hesitate at a critical moment?"

I hadn't thought about that. From the way the crawler leapt back and forth like a giant jumping spider, it was likely I would get pounced if I went anywhere near it. "Fine."

"Don't worry. I have Arcanes on the way to help."

"Those are the witches and wizards?" I asked.

He returned a grim smile. "Something like that."

Tyler yelled instructions to Sticks. "Let me lure it away. I'll let it think it has me. When it goes to feed, it'll open its armor and shoot a tube at me. That's when I need you to strike, okay?"

Sticks batted aside a needle-sharp crawler leg, spun, and sliced through the appendage where he'd weakened the chitin. Sweat trickled down his forehead. He glanced at Tyler and nodded.

Tyler shouted and waved at the crawler. Sensing easier prey, it leapt toward him. Rather than fight it, Tyler backed away slowly, like a cornered animal.

I could barely stand to watch. I felt powerless. Hopeless. The man I loved was about to be devoured by a creature of Hell and I had no way of helping him short of discovering a flamethrower.

Tyler tripped and fell backward. The crawler lunged. I screamed.

He rolled side-to-side as the crawler's barbed feet tried to pin him to the ground. The shape of a human face writhed beneath the creature's armor where a spider's head might be. The face stretched into a smile. The chitin split open and a glistening black tube the size of my arm shot toward Tyler's head.

15

His hands flashed out and caught the protuberance. A round mouth lined with teeth snapped in his face. Tyler squeezed. The face within the monster shrieked in pain. Its front legs stabbed at Tyler. He narrowly dodged the thrusts.

"Now would be a good time, Sticks!" he shouted. Tyler clenched his teeth and squeezed the tube.

The crawler shuddered and screamed in pain.

Sticks flipped over the monster. His eyes locked onto the tender spot and followed up with a lightning thrust. The blade on his staff plunged deep into the opening. The face beneath the crawler's chitin unleashed a deafening shriek. Sticks braced his feet and drove the staff even deeper into the demon.

"Twist it like a blender," Tyler yelled. "Churn its insides like a frozen margarita!"

Sticks moved the staff back and forth like a rower. The other Custodians came up behind the monster and began hacking at its legs. With a final shudder, the crawler collapsed. Tyler rolled free at the last minute, hopped to his feet, and brushed off his hands.

"Anyone have hand sanitizer?" he asked, his wolfish grin back in place.

Carswell took something from a pouch on his belt and sprayed it into my boyfriend's outstretched hands.

"Thanks, man." Tyler rubbed his hands together.

I launched myself at him and squeezed him in a fierce hug. "You crazy asshole!" I backed away and pounded his chest with my fists. "What were you thinking?"

He gripped my wrists and held me at bay. "Obviously, I was thinking about a nice cold drink with the margarita comment." Tyler pecked a kiss on my nose. "You're kind of cute when you're mad, Em."

I blew out a breath. "You're lucky I don't have superhuman strength, or I'd bend you over my knee this minute." I suddenly remembered we weren't alone and felt heat creeping up my face. Thankfully, most of the others were preoccupied looking at the dead crawler.

Sticks turned around and gave Tyler a nod.

"I agree, Mr. Sticks." George looked at the dead crawler and shook his head. "Mr. Rock is no ordinary demon." He tilted his head slightly. "How did you know about the creature's weakness?"

"One of my former acquaintances told me about it," Tyler replied.

"Another demon?"

"Yeah." Tyler's voice lost its excited edge. "There are some people who summon demons and make them fight. He was unfortunate enough to be one of their favorite summons."

"Demonic gladiator matches?" George looked mildly surprised. "I've never heard of such a thing."

"They're more popular than you might think." Tyler shrugged. "You just have to pray your name never ends up in a demonomicon."

"That brings me back to my original question about the demonicus," George said. "What purpose does it serve?"

"The demonomicon is a directory of all known demon names. I heard about it from my former acquaintances. Each demon name is associated with a pattern." Tyler pointed to the different patterns on the floor. "The smaller patterns are lesser demons." He wrinkled his nose. "If they knew my pattern, it would be about that size."

"I'm sure you have a very large pattern," I mumbled.

George cast me a questioning look, but said nothing.

Tyler flashed me a smile, and I abruptly remembered everyone here except me probably had supernatural hearing. My face went hot, but I kept my head up and pretended not to care.

Tyler returned to the patterns, this time pointing out the large one in the middle. "The bigger and more complex the pattern, the more powerful the demon." He sighed and shook his head. "I'm no expert, but the size and complexity of this pattern means someone summoned a demon of epic proportions." He pointed to the soulless bodies. "And it ate all their souls for breakfast."

Chapter 3

The Custodians exchanged troubled looks. Carswell spoke. "Demons can't exist in physical form for long outside the patterns though, right?"

"What we're looking at here wasn't an ordinary summoning." Tyler waved a hand toward the bodies. "This was like the opposite of an exorcism. If I had to guess, there were other people here who invited these demons to possess them." He examined the center of the large pattern and then at the group of bound victims. His brow furrowed.

"What is it?" George asked.

"I heard rumors that if a demon devoured enough souls, it would be more powerful in the mortal plane."

"Physically?" I asked.

"Demons have their own form of magic." Tyler shuddered. "Unfortunately it requires using soul essence. I only know the basics."

I tried to grasp where this was leading. "What you're saying is we might have a powerful demon magician in this world now."

His lips pressed tight. "Judging from all these summoning patterns, we have a small army of possessed humans on the loose, and no idea what in the world they're up to."

George dropped us back at Tyler's condominium building, the Gregorian, an hour later. "I'll let you know when we need your help again, Miss Glass."

"How about you let us know what in the bloody hell is going on with the demons?" I suggested in an impolite tone.

"I was under the impression you were too busy to concern yourself with our day-to-day operations." George looked at Mr. Sticks. The other man offered a curt nod.

"Well?" I asked.

"I'd be happy to keep you apprised, but it would be beneficial if you and Mr. Rock attend the Overworld orientation classes in the meantime." He tipped his hat. "Until next time."

"Let's keep things fun next time." Tyler flashed a grin and slid out of the backseat.

I squirmed with impatience during the ride up the lift.

"Are you okay?" Tyler asked.

I narrowed my eyes. "I'm wonderful."

His lovely green eyes widened. "Was it something I did?"

The doors opened and we stepped into the foyer. His thumbprint unlocked the door to his palatial penthouse. The moment he closed the door behind us I shoved him against a wall.

"You foolish man!" I pressed my head against his chest. "I thought that thing was going to kill you."

He caressed my hand. "I'm sorry, Em. If I hadn't done something, a lot of people might have lost their souls."

Tears flooded my eyes. "I know. It was very brave."

"And sexy, right?" He tucked a finger under my chin and brought my gaze to his smoldering eyes.

"Yes," I admitted.

He swept me off my feet and carried me down the hall to the bedroom. "I think it's time we celebrated."

"I must admit, I wasn't sure if I wanted to fuck you or beat you with a cricket bat after you fought that monster."

"I wanted to tear off your clothes and take you right then." He tossed me on the bed and climbed on top of me. "I haven't decided what I'm going to do with you." He nuzzled my neck and traced my ear with his tongue.

A shiver ran through my body, leaving goose bumps in its wake. "Well, Mr. Rock, that's a difficult decision."

His tongue made its way into the hollow of my throat. "Perhaps the most difficult I've ever made." He reached a hand beneath my shirt and undid my bra clasp, then slid each strap down my arm. "I'll have to study each and every option."

"Please do." His touch was electric. I gazed into his lovely jade green eyes. They were the color of his soul—I'd seen it when he revealed to me his true nature. After a day like today, I desperately needed to feel safe. Tyler was my refuge in a world gone mad.

After a wonderful bedroom romp, we prepared a late lunch and ate on his balcony. The winter weather had given way to warm days this weekend, hinting at a possible early spring, though my British side cautioned against optimism, especially where weather was concerned.

Tyler seemed preoccupied as he sipped his wine.

"What's wrong, darling?" I touched his hand, wishing I could glimpse his every thought.

He shrugged. "When George mentioned the Daemos, it just made me think."

"About?"

"What I am." His eyes saddened. "Demon spawn—Daemos—they're a permanent part of this world. Somehow, Baal mixed demon souls and human souls to make a perfect hybrid."

"What makes you different from Daemos?" I really hadn't given it much thought, but Tyler seemed to be struggling with it.

"I'm a pure demon possessing a body." He twisted the wine glass between his fingers. "It's like I'm an invader—a foreign cell that this realm would purge if it could."

I shook my head and gripped his hand. "You belong here, Tyler." I pressed myself to him. "You belong with me."

He squeezed me and laughed. "I know. I guess I overthink things sometimes."

"You overthink things?" I pshawed. "You, sir, tend to jump first and overthink things later."

"Guilty as charged." Tyler sipped his wine. "On another subject, what would you like to do tomorrow?"

I glanced at the kitchen table where I'd piled work documents on Friday. "It's not so much about what I want to do as what I *have* to do. Our little vacation let my work pile up at OnTech."

"We can have someone else do it, Em." He leaned back in his chair. "There's no need for you to work."

I arched my eyebrows. "We've had this conversation before, Tyler. I will not be a kept woman."

"That much is obvious, what with your little jaunts with those Custodians." His voice bore a hint of condescension.

"Little jaunts? Can you really call them that especially after your hands-on experience today?"

He bit a pickle and chewed on it. "Well, today was probably more exciting than what you're used to."

"More exciting?" I almost threw the mustard bottle at him. "Every single mission has been terrifying. I was being stalked by a vampire, for God's sake."

"Yeah, and you took away his vampire mojo." He frowned. "If it's so terrifying, why do it? I mean, it's not like we don't have money."

"I don't do it for the money."

He leaned forward. "Then why do you do it?"

I dropped my sandwich on the plate. "Because I can help people."

Tyler pursed his lips. "Well, I guess that's a good enough reason."

My mood rose to a simmering anger and I was about to shout at him when I remembered a very basic fact. Tyler was a demon in a human body. True, he might perform selfless acts at times, but that didn't change the fundamental difference between him and humans. He simply didn't process emotion the same way we did.

"I'm going to ask you a question and I want you to be absolutely honest with me." I looked him directly in the eyes.

He braced his elbows on the table and rested his chin on a fist. "Go for it."

"Why did you really fight that crawler this morning?"

Tyler's smile faded.

I waited several seconds before prompting him for an answer. "Well? Why did you?"

He cleared his throat and looked down. "It seemed like an exciting challenge. Plus, I figured I could save some souls in the process." Tyler met my stony gaze. "I mean, it's the end result that matters, right?"

This time I did throw the mustard at him. "You bastard! You did it for the excitement?"

He caught the mustard bottle before it hit him and stood, holding his hands in front of him. "Emily, please. I also wanted to keep you safe."

21

John Corwin

I pressed my lips tight and took deep breaths through my nose. *He's right. What's important is that he saved lives. Otherwise, everyone there might have died.* Finally, I spoke. "It sometimes makes me wonder if you really do love me, or if you just tell me that."

Tyler wrapped his arms around me and hugged me tight. "Baby, don't say that." He kissed my forehead, my cheeks, my lips. "If there's any one thing in this world that I'm sure of, it's that I love you." His chest rose and deflated with a sigh. "I'm working hard on pinning down my other emotions, but it's like speaking another language sometimes. My demon side gets these urges to do things for stupid reasons."

"Your demon side? Aren't you demon all the way through?"

"Well, yeah, but I have human experiences and a human body, so you might say I'm just a man with a demon soul."

"Well, that doesn't sound sinister at all, does it?" I couldn't help but smile at his description. "Perhaps we should get you to church."

Tyler laughed. "Been there, done that. They tried to send me back to Haedaemos."

I kissed him and then dropped back into my seat. "You make me so emotional about the smallest things."

"I know the feeling." He poured himself another glass of wine. "If working with the Custodians and for OnTech makes you feel complete, I won't stand in your way."

"Working for the Custodians makes me feel like I'm making a difference in the world." I prodded the remains of my sandwich with a finger. "Working for OnTech makes me feel normal. Grounded. It almost makes me forget that there's a universe of hidden horrors waiting in the darkness."

"There are wonders in the Overworld too," Tyler said, a dreamy look in his eyes. "George Walker's car is definitely one of them."

"I have a feeling you'll find a way to get one, won't you?"

"It'd look great next to the Lamborghini."

I snorted in a very unladylike manner. "I'm certain it would." I stood up. "Well, I suppose I should get back to the apartment. I'm certain it's an awful mess with just Isabel around to keep it tidy."

Tyler touched my hand and shivered. "I don't want you to go, Em."

I dropped back into my seat. "I don't want to go either, but—"

22

"The thought of being here alone without you makes me feel cold." He stood and pulled me to my feet.

I pressed my cheek to his chest. "It makes me feel cold too, Tyler."

He cradled my face in his warm hands. "We saw each other nearly every hour of every day during vacation, and it made me realize how much I love having you around all the time."

"You do?" It was exactly what I wanted to hear.

"I know you're headstrong and independent, but, would you consider moving in with me?"

He looked so vulnerable and adorable, I let the question hang in the air for a long moment. Tyler was usually bold and brash, and rare moments like this were like little treasures.

I finally ended his suffering. "I'd love to."

"Yes!" His confident smile returned and he picked me up and swung me around.

I giggled and wrapped my arms around his chest. "Just don't expect me to share toothbrushes."

"We don't even need to brush our teeth anymore."

An unladylike snort burst from me. "I wouldn't go that far."

Tyler set me down and kissed me.

I'm home.

After dinner, I dug into the mound of paperwork for OnTech and read the backlog of emails on my laptop. It seemed Jack and Kevin had several more security software contracts in the works, but hadn't managed to finalize any agreements. They were hoping Tyler could help them seal the deals. His demonic aura and dashing good looks usually did the trick.

By the time I made my way through everything, I realized there was actually very little they needed me to do. I closed the laptop and pushed away the files as disappointment replaced my earlier enthusiasm. *Who am I kidding? I'm just a glorified office assistant.* Then again, maybe I could get these companies to sign the contracts.

"How's it going, hot stuff?" Tyler leaned over my shoulder and kissed my cheek.

I hid my disappointment. "Very well. I think I'm ready for Monday."

"Wow, that was fast. The way you were talking I figured you'd be working all day Sunday too."

I stood and brushed off my hands. "Nope, I'm all good."

"Great!" He brushed the back of his hand across my cheek. "In that case, I'll plan something fun tomorrow. Might as well enjoy the amazing weather."

"Can't wait." I got up and hugged him, unable to resist his boyish enthusiasm.

Cold rain the next morning washed away our plans for a hike. A phone call from a manager at one of the other companies Tyler owned put a final nail in the coffin. He ended the call, a grim look on his face.

"There's word someone is trying to steal programmers from Vermillion Unicorn," he told me.

"Is that your company that programs apps for mobile devices?"

He nodded. "Out of all the companies Hugo's father gave him for the sibling rivalry contest, this is the only one that actually performed well out of the box."

"How does someone steal programmers?"

"By offering them more money, better benefits, and so forth." He sighed. "I've spent so much time focusing on OnTech I haven't kept track of the other companies."

I folded my arms across my chest. "I'm surprised you're acting so responsibly."

"I gave what you said a lot of thought. If I'm going to be more human, I need to be responsible and figure out why I should care what happens to other people." He put on slacks and a blue button-up shirt. "Fake it 'til you make it, right?"

"I suppose." I felt a bit sad that he had to leave when we could've just spent the day cuddling inside. "I'd like to come. Perhaps it would help if I knew more about your other businesses."

He paused in the middle of buckling his belt. "Sure, if you want."

I suddenly felt very presumptuous. It wasn't as if I knew a thing about managing multi-million dollar companies. "Then again, maybe I'd just be in the way."

Tyler slipped his arms around my waist and planted a kiss on my lips. "You're never in the way."

I smiled. "Let me get ready." My phone chimed. I walked to the dresser and picked it up to see a text from George Walker.

We have two vampires in custody who might have information about the blood bank massacre. Would appreciate your help questioning them. Can pick you up in twenty minutes.

I wasn't precisely sure how I could help with an interrogation.

Tyler came up behind me. "Let me guess—George or Isabel."

"George." I showed him the text.

"Looks like we both have important business to attend today."

"I suppose so."

Tyler's driver, Joe, picked him up in a black SUV in the covered drive of the Gregorian.

Joe nodded when he saw me. "Hello, Miss Glass."

"Hey, Joe. Having a good weekend?"

"Excellent, thanks for asking."

Tyler kissed me. "I love you. Let me know when you're back."

"I will."

Tyler nipped my ear. "Until later, hot stuff." He turned and walked to the vehicle.

Joe held open the rear door for Tyler and gave me a questioning look. "Aren't you getting in?"

I shook my head. "My ride will be along shortly. Keep Tyler out of trouble, okay?"

He smiled and quickly covered it up. "Yes, ma'am." Joe climbed in the front and drove away.

George's sleek car pulled silently into the drive a few moments later. He got out and opened the passenger door for me. "Good day, Miss Glass."

"You can call me Emily."

"I prefer keeping it professional."

I groaned and slid into the front seat. "Calling me Emily won't make it any less professional. I call you George and not Mr. Walker."

George closed the door and went around to the driver's seat. "I'll consider it."

"Where's your BFF today?"

He raised an eyebrow. "I'm not familiar with that term."

"Best friend forever."

He smiled. "Ah, Mr. Sticks saw no reason to accompany me since I'm taking you to our holding facility."

"After watching him fight I know why you call him Mr. Sticks."

"Because he uses staffs?" George pulled into his favorite blind alley. "That actually has nothing to do with it. Sticks is his last name." He pressed a button and the car's exterior faded to near invisibility.

"It's a very strange last name." I peered out the window as the ground receded below. "Why doesn't he talk?"

George steered the car to the east and accelerated. "He prefers not to."

"How do you know what he's saying—telepathy?"

"Excellent guess, Miss Glass." He veered around a flock of birds and resumed course. "Mr. Sticks could talk anytime he likes, but he prefers nonverbal communication."

"He's a bit of a condescending ass, isn't he?"

George chuckled. "Yes, he is. You must admit, however, that he's very good at what he does."

"Sure, he's amazing at fighting, but he really needs to work on human relations." I ran a hand along the smooth wood trim on the dash. "Well, I suppose you should tell me what I need to know about these vampires I'm to see."

"Of course." He tapped a large glass screen on the dash. "Display dossier, subject Franco."

The image of a man with black hair, long sideburns, and a goatee filled the screen. "Subject Franco, Colombian drug lord, vampire, illegal weapons seller," a monotone voice said. "Captured by Templars two weeks ago while in pursuit of rogue Daemos Justin Slade."

George frowned. "They still haven't corrected his status."

"Whose?" I asked.

"Justin Slade's. Apparently, he helped capture Franco, his right-hand man, Marcel, and Vadaemos Slade." He stared at the rainy sky. "I'd say that means he's not a rogue Daemos."

"Daemos are the human-demon mixes, right?"

He nodded. "Something like that. They're a secretive bunch." George nodded at the dossier. "We've found evidence linking Franco to the blood bank. We think he was using it to smuggle illegal weapons into Atlanta for a vampire named Maximus. Unfortunately, he's not talking."

"How am I supposed to make him talk?"

His lips curled up. "Because you can take away that one thing he values the most."

"And that is?"

"His vampirism."

Chapter 4

My strange ability was still so new to me, I hadn't even thought of the possibility.

I swallowed a lump of fear. "I don't have to face him alone, do I?"

George shook his head. "Mr. Sticks will meet us there. He and I will accompany you."

"Can Sticks read minds with his brain?"

"I don't believe so, though he's never told me otherwise."

I felt a blush warm my face. *Goodness, I hope not!* I didn't like the idea of anyone peering into my thoughts, especially where Tyler was concerned.

George landed the car on the driveway of a large ranch. I didn't recognize the area since I was still new to Atlanta. "Where are we?"

"The Templar compound near Decatur." He drove into a large barn and down a ramp into a vast underground garage and parked. Other vehicles and objects sat nearby. Some appeared mundane while others were as exotic as George's car. Large metal boxes sat in neat rows. I thought they might be storage containers, but they had no doors.

We rode a lift down several levels and stepped into a corridor hewn into the bedrock and lined steel doors and large blacked-out windows.

"This is amazing." I ran a hand along the wall. "How large is this place?"

"Fairly extensive. The Templars use this complex to temporarily house criminals until they're transported to a prison to await trial." He motioned ahead where Sticks stood next to a window. "That's the interrogation room. I'd like you to stand behind us until I tell you otherwise."

My heart beat a little faster. "Of course."

Sticks opened the door without so much as greeting me and followed us inside. A tall man stood on the other side of the table. It was the man—no, the vampire—from the dossier. Franco.

"Who's that?" he said in a precise British accent.

"Someone who's here to ensure you cooperate," George replied in an even tone.

The vampire slashed his hand through the air. "I've nothing more to say to you, Templar."

"Technically, we're Custodians." George activated a tablet computer on the table. "We have a series of documents tying you to blood banks all across the country you've used to smuggle weapons for Maximus." He flicked the screen and it projected an image of the building we'd been in today.

I held back a gasp. I'd never seen a tablet do that before.

A cruel smiled spread across the vampire's face. "She looks like a frightened little lamb."

I stiffened and narrowed my eyes. A retort died on my lips as I remembered George's instructions.

George ignored the comment. "Tell me what you know about the employees at this facility."

Franco dropped into a chair and spoke in clipped tones. "As I said, I have nothing more to say."

George nodded at Sticks. The two of them walked around opposite sides of the table and stood behind Franco. "Last chance to cooperate."

The vampire laughed. "Or what, you'll unleash that little girl on me?"

"Precisely."

Franco crossed his arms and shook his head. "I want an advocate."

"One will be appointed to you eventually." George bound the vampire's hands to the table with a strap and placed a hand on the vampire's shoulder. "For now, you'll answer our questions."

It suddenly occurred to me that Sticks probably couldn't read minds. If he could, he would have ferreted out this vampire's secrets already.

Sticks put his hands on the opposite shoulder.

The vampire glared at them, but didn't resist. He didn't look the least bit frightened. I planned to scare the daylights out of him when my turn came.

George looked at me. "If you please."

I walked forward, keeping my eyes on Franco's threatening glare and pretending not to be scared. *If he breaks free, he'll snap my neck like a chicken's.* The cold sensation emanating from him grew stronger. To do what needed to be done, I'd have to touch him. Trying not to appear hesitant, I leaned across the table and pressed a hand to his chest.

He gave me a lascivious grin, red irises glowing. "Ah, you're here to pleasure me, is that it?" He glanced at his crotch. "I'm sure you'll find I'm more than up to the task, little girl."

Already, I felt the squirming parasitic vampirism inside him. I let the sensation grow stronger and stronger until I felt as though I could grasp it. "I'll show you pleasure," I said in a low hiss. With that, I squeezed his aura.

Franco's eyes widened into an almost comedic expression. He shouted and tried to rise, but his restraints along with Sticks and George held him fast. He wriggled and cried out. "What is that bitch doing to me?"

"She can take away your vampirism if I let her," George said, voice calm as ever. "How would you like to be mortal again, Franco?"

"She can't!" Neck muscles straining with exertion, legs flailing against the floor, he tried everything to get away.

"I can, and I will." I gave him an innocent smile. "Who's the little lamb now?" I tugged gently on the parasitic aura.

Franco's face went white as a sheet, even for a vampire. "No, please don't. I'll tell you everything." His voice cracked and it almost sounded as if he might cry.

I did my best not to gloat.

Sticks almost cracked a smile.

George nodded at me. "That will be enough, Custodian."

It occurred to me he hadn't once used my name, perhaps to protect me. I released the vampire's aura and backed away.

"The blood bank, Franco." George pointed to the hovering image of the building. "Tell me about the employees."

30

Shaking, Franco looked closely at the image. "I met with and hired four vampires for each of these operations. They oversaw the hiring of noms to assist in day-to-day operations, though none of them were supposed to know the true nature of our business."

George flicked away the image and replaced it with that of one of the dead vampires from the scene. "Like him?"

Franco's forehead pinched. "Did you kill him?"

"No, he and two other vampires were already dead when we arrived."

"Dead?" The vampire seemed genuinely confused. "How?"

"Do you remember anything in particular about this facility?"

"I don't even know where this one is," Franco said.

George projected a map and jabbed a finger near the intersection of Interstate Seventy-Five and Interstate Two Eighty-Five. "It's here."

Recognition lit Franco's gaze. "I do remember this one. We chose the location because it sat directly over a major ley line."

A what?

"Why would that matter for a gun smuggling operation?"

Franco looked at George. "The Arcanes we used to enchant the weapons and ammunition claimed it made their work much easier."

George pursed his lips. "Are there many such places?"

The vampire shrugged. "I'm no magic expert. The particular Arcanes we hired here seemed eager to secure the building, so I followed their advice."

"Do you have names for me?"

"Yes." Franco looked once again at the dead vampire. "What happened there?"

"We found several dead bodies—well, not technically dead. The bodies, in fact, were quite alive."

"But you said—"

"Their souls were devoured by demons." George watched Franco closely at this announcement.

"Demons?" Franco's eyes widened. "How could this be?"

"Who were the Arcanes?" George asked.

The vampire bit his lip. "Zad Kassus and Martin Drang."

George and Sticks looked at each other. They obviously recognized the names.

31

"Thank you, Franco. You've been most helpful." George and Sticks released the vampire's shoulders. "We'll be back if we have further questions." He paused. "Do you have their addresses?"

Franco seemed lost in thought. He looked up suddenly as if realizing the question hung in the air. "No. There might be records at the facility."

George motioned me toward the door, and the three of us left the room where the stunned vampire still stared into the distance.

Once George closed the door, I turned to him. "Who are those people he mentioned?"

"They're Arcanes, though not of the usual variety." His lips flattened. "They're battle mages and members of a society that calls themselves the Black Robe Brotherhood."

"Sounds insidious."

"Oh, they have quite a reputation. Unfortunately, they're good at covering their tracks." His affable smiled returned. "Think of them as the mafia except their thugs are highly skilled Arcanes."

I grimaced. "Definitely trouble."

"You did an excellent job, by the way." He started walking back toward the lift. "I don't believe I've ever seen a vampire so frightened."

Mr. Sticks gave me a smug look.

"Well, at least someone enjoyed the show." I stopped outside an empty cell. "What's the next move?"

"We track down Kassus and Drang." George leaned against the wall. "Are you interested in helping us?"

I had to admit it was rather exciting, much like being part of a detective show. "I'd be delighted to help."

"I'm glad to hear it, Miss Glass." He motioned toward the lift. "Let's take the levitator up a floor to the data room."

"Levitator?"

"Magical elevators." He and Sticks stepped inside. "They levitate without cables."

"How intriguing."

We traveled up two levels and entered a hallway leading to a small white room with a large desk against the far wall. The woman behind the desk stopped in the middle of a yawn and jerked upright.

"Mr. Walker, how may I help you?" she asked.

George tipped his head. "Ms. Archer, would you cull data for Zad Kassus and Martin Drang?"

"At once." She swiped her fingers across the desk and the entire surface lit up like a large tablet. She entered the names. Seconds later, icons resembling scrolls appeared on the screen.

"How quaint," I muttered.

"There's nothing quaint about this system." Ms. Archer regarded me with a raised eyebrow that reminded me uncomfortably of Sandra, the receptionist at OnTech.

"I meant the scroll icons instead of folders."

"You're obviously used to dealing with nom systems." Using her finger, she dragged the scrolls to a sphere icon and touched it. A portal opened in the corner of the desk and a marble popped out.

George took the marble. "Thank you, Ms. Archer."

She brushed a lock of hair over her ear and smiled at him. "Always a pleasure."

Judging from the look on her face, I could tell she wanted to pleasure him in more ways than one. We went back into the hallway and took it to an adjacent room. George took the marble and spun it into the air using his thumb and forefinger. Rather than falling to the ground, it hovered in place, spinning like a top. A holographic image burst from it, displaying scroll icons and pictures of people.

My mouth dropped open.

George smiled. "Miss Glass, you might have known about ASEs if you'd been to orientation."

I clamped my mouth shut. There was apparently no end to the wonders in the Overworld. I decided to schedule an orientation as soon as possible so I wouldn't look like such a fool every time they pulled a new trick from their hats.

"This is an all-seeing eye, or ASE," George explained. "We use them for surveillance and long term data storage."

"It's certainly decades ahead of what the nom world has." I reached a hand to the three-dimensional image and brushed a hand across it. It rotated to display more icons. "How do I make sense of all this information?"

"It's just like anything—you have to look." George grabbed a picture and pulled it toward him, making it larger in the process. Four men in tight-fitting black robes with tapered waists and flared hems stood outside a run-down building covered in graffiti. He traced around the first person with his finger, leaving a red circle. "This is Maulin Kassus, the leader of the brotherhood."

"What a dreadful name." I peered closer at the bald stocky man. "Are goatees a fashion statement for criminals?"

"It would seem that way." George pointed to another man next to the first. "This is his younger brother, Breth, and next to him is their cousin, Zad."

"What sort of mother would allow her children to be named Breth or Zad?" Breth and Maulin looked virtually identical with their stocky builds, bald heads, and thick goatees. Zad was thin with red hair. His facial hair was sparse and patchy. Nevertheless, he'd tried to emulate his cousins' beards and failed miserably. A tall black man stood next to him. "Is the fourth person Martin Drang?"

"Yes." George slashed a hand up and down the holographic image. It morphed into a cube. "I've given you control over a portion of the display. Use it to search for known locations and other pertinent information."

Mr. Sticks stepped to George's right.

"I certainly could've used something like this in university." I followed Sticks's example and used the section of the cube to George's left. For a long moment I stood there staring at the floating image, unsure how to do even a simple search. I found a small question mark and tapped it to display instructions.

Double-tap the display to enter a keyword search.

"Bob's your uncle."

"What was that, Miss Glass?" George glanced around the side.

"Nothing." I typed in, *Zad Kassus address.* It returned *Darkwater Consulting, The Grotto.* I tried the same for Martin and got the same result. I assumed the others probably found the same answer and wasn't sure what more I could do.

Cross-reference them with something.

I queried for their names along with the name of the blood bank, but found nothing. I did a similar search using *Atlanta.* Still nothing. On a hunch, I tried *Kassus and demon.*

Overnet results: Arcane University Demonology graduates: Zad Kassus, Rufus Cumberbatch, Ted Bandy...click here to see more.

I clicked there to see more. In the middle of a list of thirty or so names, I found Martin Drang. The roster listed everyone who'd graduated with a specialty in demonology. Not many people claimed the dubious distinction.

Resisting the desire to clap my hands with excitement, I spoke up. "It appears our mafiosos graduated from Arcane University with degrees in demonology."

George stepped to my side and read the results. "Excellent work, Miss Glass. I believe you've found evidence marking these two as prime suspects."

"The only address I found for the pair is in some place called the Grotto. They apparently work for Darkwater Consulting."

"I'm not familiar with that company." He examined the search results. "It's probably a front for the brotherhood."

We continued searching for more information, but couldn't find anything else pinning a location to either of the suspects.

George flew me in his car back to Tyler's place. Rather than drop me out front, he parked with the passenger door just above the balcony railing.

"Would you like to join us again tomorrow?" he asked.

"Unfortunately, I have my day job to attend."

"After your performance with Franco, I'm convinced you could join the Custodians full time."

"Full time?" I wasn't sure I wanted to hunt supernatural criminals all the time. "I might have a useful talent, but I can't fight, and I'm not nearly as strong as you or Mr. Sticks."

"We are not born preternaturally strong. It is a blessing given to us by the Templar Divinity."

My interest piqued. "There's a divine being who rules the Templars?"

"Perhaps." He looked toward the setting sun. "The Synod—the leading council—are the only Templars who are allowed to personally meet her. She may be myth, but the enhanced abilities are very real."

"No wonder the Templars are so efficient. A goddess looks over them." I smiled. "Perhaps that's why I sense a brilliant white ember burning at the center of most Templars. Only the wizards are different. They possess the brilliance, but it's different somehow."

"Can you touch this ember as you do with the vampires?"

I shrugged. "Perhaps. I haven't tried."

George pursed his lips. "I think we should test the extent of your abilities. I've never encountered anything like them."

"I suppose I could be a lab rat, just don't poke me with needles."

He flashed a smile. "Think about my offer to join the Custodians. The hours are long, but the pay and benefits are quite decent."

"Would I get supernatural strength?"

"Perhaps. I'd want to be sure it wouldn't interfere with your innate ability." He pressed a button. My door opened and a ramp extended over the railing to the balcony. "Have a pleasant evening, Miss Glass."

Once I was safely deposited, the door closed, leaving only a faint blur in my vision due to the car's camouflage. I entered the unlocked balcony door and froze in shock.

A strange man sitting on the couch in the den smirked back at me.

Chapter 5

"Tyler?" I called out his name, praying he was here.

The man stood. "He's not in. Do you know where he is?"

I reached into my purse for the phone. "Who are you and what are you doing in Tyler's condo?"

"I'm an old friend of...*Tyler's*." He ran a hand through thinning brown hair with a lanky arm. I wondered if he might be someone Hugo knew before he died and Tyler possessed his body. Even so, that didn't explain one thing. "How did you get in here?"

"You ask a lot of questions." He stepped forward. "Who are *you* and how did you get in here?" He looked toward the balcony. "I looked out there earlier and nobody was there."

Keeping my phone out of sight behind the counter, I sent Tyler a text. *Help! Stranger danger in your condo!*

His response came almost immediately. *Joe is dropping me off now. Be right up.*

I only had to delay this man for a moment longer.

"I know why Tyler keeps you around." He stared at me and licked his lips. "You look delicious."

"Sadly, I can't say the same about you." I eased open a drawer in the kitchen island and removed a gun Tyler kept there, careful to keep it hidden behind the backsplash. I flicked off the safety and took a deep breath to steady my nerves. "Once again, who are you and what do you want?"

A feral smile curled his lips and he walked toward me. "Perhaps *Tyler* wouldn't mind me snacking on you while I wait."

"He most definitely would." I raised the gun and aimed it at his chest. "And so would I."

He glanced at the gun as if it were a mere inconvenience. "Oh, you enjoy playing rough, do you, Emily?"

The revelation that he knew my name shook me. I gripped the gun with both hands to steady my grip. "I'll shoot your balls into oblivion if you come a step closer."

He laughed. "I'll live."

It suddenly occurred to me this man might not be normal. He could be a vampire. I opened my senses and almost immediately tasted foul burning air and a nauseating aura. It reminded me of the blood bank.

"You're a demon."

He jolted to a stop, eyebrows rising. "How could you possibly know that?" He flashed his teeth. "You're just as smart as a whip, aren't you?" Without further warning, he blurred toward me. I fired the gun. The man howled in pain and flopped to the floor, holding his knee.

I was about to fire more shots into him when the front door flew open and Tyler flashed through. He looked from me to the man on the floor. "Are you okay, babe?"

Relief flooded into me. I ran to him and hugged him tight. "He's possessed, Tyler."

Alarm flickered through his eyes. He kissed my forehead and walked to the screaming man. Without a word, he gripped the front of his shirt and jerked him off the floor. "Who the hell are you?"

Gritting his teeth and smiling, the man said, "It's good to see you again, *Grimsvokull*."

Tyler dropped the man with a thud, eliciting a grunt of pain. Eyes fierce, Tyler looked down at him. "Xasha?"

A laugh burst from the man. "Barboar. You must have lost your demonic senses, Grim."

Tyler shook his head and backed away. "Why are you here? How did you find me?"

"Oh, you were easy enough to find. Vatna just happened to be locked in a nearby cage before the Exorcists tried to send you back to Haedaemos." Grimacing, he sat up. "He saw the little trick with the soulstone and knew you weren't done."

"How did Vatna know it was me?"

"Who else has such a green glow as you, Grim?" He spat on the floor. "You and your lovely appearance and petite odor? Vatna found us the moment he was sent back to Haedaemos and told us what he'd seen."

Tyler knelt over the downed man. "He didn't know my mortal name."

"Oh, but you're a famous mortal, aren't you, precious?" He pulled a scrap of newspaper from his pocket and held up a picture. "Tyler Rock, boy millionaire."

"Fine, you found me, Barboar. I want to know why."

As they spoke, I walked behind the possessed man, ready to use the gun if he tried anything else. Unlike the pleasant heat in Tyler's aura, this demon smelled like burnt eggs. His mere presence nearly made me gag. As I closed to within a couple of feet, something flashed before my inner eye.

"Why not?" Barboar said. "You used to be a lot of fun until you turned against us."

"I didn't turn against you; I decided I was done destroying the lives of mortals."

"Bah! Mortals are nothing but cattle." His lips curled into a snarl. "Little Grimmy. The demon who cared."

I concentrated on the demon, trying to focus on the hazy image in my mind, but couldn't quite see it. Against my better judgment, I reached out a tentative finger while the possessed man was looking at Tyler and touched him.

The vision sharpened into a pattern. A word echoed through my head. *Barboarklistlsvang*. The pronunciation was bizarre, with an accent on the first and last syllables and a slight pause in the middle, almost like a chant.

"So you *do* want to play," Barboar said, looking at me.

I jerked my finger back and wiped it on the floor with disgust. "I'd rather eat a roach."

Already, the pattern was fading from my mind's eye. The name, however, was burned into memory. I looked at Tyler and wondered why I'd never sensed a pattern or a name from him.

"Maybe I'll drop you off at the Exorcists' church," Tyler said.

"I'm sure you'd like that," Barboar said. "But you know you wouldn't dare go near one yourself."

I abruptly thought of something and sent a quick text.

Tyler stood and paced. "I'd kill your body, but that would be murdering an innocent human."

"This man is hardly innocent." Barboar laughed with glee. "He's already raped two women and was thinking of killing the next one." He rubbed his hands together. "I might just sit back and let him do that while I watch."

It took all my willpower not to shoot him in the head.

"Who else is back?"

"All of us, Grimmy." Barboar licked blood from his fingers and groaned with pleasure. "I'd like to possess a vampire again. They're so carnal." He groaned and shivered. "Xasha, Vatna, and Eyja will be so happy and surprised to know I've found you."

A gust of wind blew past as the sliding glass door opened. George Walker stepped inside. "I got your message, Miss Glass." He looked at the wounded man. "Is this the demon?"

"An Exorcist?" Barboar climbed to his feet rather nimbly for a man with a gunshot wound to his lower thigh.

"I'm a Custodian." George aimed a wrist-mounted lancer at the demon. "But I'll be happy to get you to the proper authorities."

"Sorry, not interested." Barboar burst into insane laughter and reached into his pants. Grinning lewdly, he fondled his privates then withdrew his hand.

I saw something green and round in his hand. In an instant, I knew what it was. *A grenade!* His finger reached for the pin. Without thinking I pulled the trigger on the gun. A shot rang out and blood splashed from the other side of his head. Barboar's host thudded to the ground. The grenade rolled from his limp grasp and bumped against George's shoe. Sullen yellow mist filtered from the dead man's eyes and vanished into the floor.

Tyler stared at the unarmed grenade, fury burning in his eyes. "He came here just to kill me for the fun of it."

George turned his gaze to me. "Quick thinking, Miss Glass, though I'd already hit him with a lancer dart."

I looked at a silver dart protruding from the dead man's chest. With trembling hands, I placed the gun on the counter. "It was a reflex. I couldn't let him kill us."

Tyler wrapped me in his warm embrace. "It's okay, baby. I'm proud of you."

I felt no shame pressing my face to his chest and wishing the dreadful scene to go away.

George intruded on my fantasy. "Unfortunately, without a proper exorcism, the demon will be able to return in a matter of weeks, perhaps days."

"Getting rid of him wouldn't solve my problem," Tyler said. "All four of my former acquaintances are back." He looked at the corpse. "Well, three of them are still here."

"Judging from what he said earlier, I don't think they know he located you." I sucked in a breath and pulled away from him. "We need to track down each and every one of them."

"I can deliver them to the Exorcists," George said. "That should remove them from Eden for quite some time."

"But not permanently." Tyler slammed a fist on the counter. "There's only one way to get rid of them for good."

"Devouring their souls?" I said.

He waggled his hand in a so-so motion. "I don't know for sure if that works." Tyler made a face. "The other way is just as impossible. I'd have to find someone who knows a ritual of Abyssal banishment."

"I'm certain one of our Arcanes could do that," George said. "But wouldn't you need the demon's true name?"

Tyler ran a hand through his hair. "Banishment is one thing, but I want them sent into the Abyss. That's the only way to guarantee they'll never escape."

"Unfortunately, demons are not my specialty." George picked up the grenade and examined it. "I certainly hope your other acquaintances don't attack you with explosives."

"Something happened when I touched Barboar."

Tyler and George flicked their eyes my way.

"I saw a pattern and heard a name." Though I couldn't remember the pattern, I did remember the name and the precise pronunciation. "Barboarklistlsvang."

Tyler's mouth dropped open. "You sensed his true name?"

"I believe so." I tilted my head slightly. "If you ask me how, I won't be able to answer. I've never sensed any such thing from you."

George's eyebrows rose. "Impressive, Miss Glass. Your talent goes deeper than I could have imagined." He held up a finger. "We must use utmost caution, however. If people were to discover your unique abilities, you could become a target."

"I assumed that's why you didn't call me by name with Franco."

"Franco?" Tyler looked back and forth. "What are you talking about?"

I told him about my interrogation of the vampire.

"Well, sounds like you're becoming a supernatural detective." He looked at George. "I don't like knowing she was exposed to a dangerous vampire."

"Do you really think I could be in danger surrounded by Templars?" I gave him an exasperated look.

Tyler deflated. "I'm sorry. I love you, Em, and I don't want to lose you."

I suddenly felt awful.

George piled on. "It is a valid consideration, Miss Glass."

I threw up my hands. "Well, I'm sorry for pretending I'm a grown up."

Tyler chuckled.

George went to the balcony and returned with a slick shiny body bag. "If you'd be so kind, Mr. Rock."

The two of them lifted the corpse while I placed the body bag beneath it.

I heard a ding and looked toward the front door. It still hung ajar from Tyler's abrupt entrance. "Good lord, someone's coming up the lift!"

George quickly grabbed the body bag and took it outside. Tyler grabbed a nearby rug and dropped it over the puddle of blood on the floor. I rushed toward the entrance just as the lift doors slid open to reveal a police officer.

"May I help you?" I asked him.

He nodded in greeting. "Ma'am, we received reports of gunshots from several people downstairs. I just wanted to come up here and make sure everything was okay."

"Gunshots?" I pressed a hand to my heart. "I thought that noise was fireworks or something from outside."

He took out a notepad. "Describe what you heard."

"Well, I heard a loud popping noise. You don't know where it came from?"

"There are thirty tenants in the units on the floor below and I have a lot of people to interview." He shrugged. "If you hear anything else, let me know."

Tyler came out of the kitchen with a drink in his hand. "I'm sorry, did someone say something about gunshots?"

The officer's radio hissed and someone spoke. "One eighty-two officer on the scene?"

He turned away and spoke into the mic. "One eighty-five Rogers."

"Ten twelve."

"That's a negative."

The other voice spoke again. "Ten twelve."

The officer sighed and turned around. "One of our detectives is on the way and wants to ask a few questions."

My stomach went cold as ice. "A detective?"

He nodded. "Standard procedure for a gunshot report. I'm sure he wants to speak to you now instead of disturbing you again."

Less than five minutes later, the lift dinged and a short thin man with a balding head stepped into the foyer. "I've got this, Rogers."

The police officer nodded. "Want me to continue asking around on the other floors?"

"Yeah, you do that." The man turned to Tyler. "I'm Detective Long." He took out a notepad. "Mind if I have a look around?"

"A look around for what?" Tyler asked.

"For any evidence of a fired weapon."

Tyler's forehead wrinkled. "Do you plan to search every condo in this building?"

"I intend to do what's necessary to make sure nobody was injured by a bullet." The detective tried to enter the door, but Tyler stood in his way. "I'm sorry, but we're just about to sit down for dinner, and I really don't want to deal with this right now. We already gave your officer a statement."

"I'm afraid you'll have to let me in," Long said.

"Oh, you have a warrant?" Tyler took a sip of his drink and grinned at the other man's silence. "No, you don't. Now, if you'll kindly stop harassing us, we're going to eat." He nodded. "Good evening, Detective."

The other man glared at him, but didn't try to force the issue again.

Tyler closed the door in his face and listened until the lift dinged. He blew out a breath. "What in the hell was that about?"

"It was like he knew we were guilty of something," I said. "I mean, technically, we were, but still…"

"Yeah. I hope he's not really an undercover Exorcist."

I touched the amulet hanging over his chest. "My parents said they couldn't track you with this on."

He rubbed it, and tucked it under his shirt. "I just hope they're right."

We went into the den just as George reappeared from the balcony. He put the rug covering the blood into a bag then narrowed his eyes and peered around the room before walking to a small hole in the drywall. He poked a rod into the hole and withdrew a flattened slug.

"What kind of magical device did you use to get that out?" I asked.

He held up the rod. "We call this a magnet, Miss Glass."

I pursed my lips and glared at him. "Very funny."

George switched subjects. "I'll see if I can find a qualified Arcane who knows how to banish demons to the Abyss. Failing that, I believe Daemos can do it as well."

Tyler shook George's hand. "Thanks for helping us with our little emergency."

"Not a problem, Mr. Rock."

"You can call me Tyler."

"Oh no, George likes to keep things formal and professional," I said. "I'm sorry, I meant to say, Agent Walker."

"Your quick wit is always appreciated, Miss Glass." He put a bottle of blue liquid on the counter. "Use this potion to clean the blood from the floors." With that, George picked up the bag with the bloody rug and bade us farewell before getting into his invisible car and flying away.

It was a very strange day indeed when someone flying away in an invisible car was the most normal thing about it.

Tyler dropped into a chair, a melancholy look on his face.

"What's wrong?" I asked.

44

He shook his head. "Barboar just reminded me of what I am."

"How in the hell would that creature remind you of anything? You're nothing like him."

Tyler threw up his hands. "I'm a demon, Em. Somewhere deep down inside, I'm every bit as depraved and evil as that son of a bitch."

"No, you're not." I squeezed his hands. "You're special."

"Special?" He blew out a breath. "Sometimes I wonder what I really am. I'm not a Daemos, and I'm not sharing space with a human's soul. I'm in a dead man's body all by myself, pretending to be what I'm not."

"Tyler Rock, you have nothing in common with Barboar." I pressed my hands to his cheeks and made him look at me. "You are a good man, a good demon, and I happen to think you're special. Otherwise, I wouldn't be madly in love with you."

His shoulders straightened, and he gazed into my eyes. "I absolutely adore you, Em. Even if I am evil at heart, I want to be good just for you."

"Then do it." I couldn't bear the insecure look in his eyes, so I embraced him tightly and wished I never had to let go.

Barboar and Tyler's previous demon associates had left deep scars. I would do whatever it took to help him heal.

Chapter 6

I almost hugged Sandra when I saw her at work the next day, despite the arch of her imperious eyebrows. She was just so bloody normal, I wanted to kiss her. As usual, she wore a professional blouse and skirt that made her look more like an executive than a receptionist. I'd opted for jeans, a T-shirt, and flats. I'd done too much running around in high heels for this company already.

"Good morning, Sandra." I smiled and opened the box of doughnuts I'd brought with me.

Her right eyebrow climbed to the same altitude as her left. "I'm on a diet."

I was envious of her hourglass shape. "Oh, one or two won't hurt. Try the cream puffs. They're delightful."

She hesitantly took one and placed it on a napkin. "Thank you, Miss Glass."

"Emily. Remember, we're all on a first-name basis here." That had been one of Tyler's first rules, but Sandra seemed uncomfortable with such familiarity.

I walked into the programming department and left the doughnut box there. A man with a horseshoe pillow around his neck crawled from beneath a desk, nostrils flaring. Stan saw the doughnuts and grabbed two before vanishing beneath his desk again. According to Sandra, Stan's wife had kicked him out of the house so he'd lived here ever since. Unless someone complained, I wasn't going to make him sleep elsewhere.

The lift doors dinged as I walked down the hall back toward the main reception area. Jack Somers and several other programmers entered the glass doors.

"Emily!" Jack gave me a hug and pulled back. "How was vacation?" He smirked. "Or should I call it a sabbatical?"

"It was lovely." Despite the nagging worry that the Exorcists or some other Overworld agency would swoop in and take Tyler from me, the stay had been blissful. A beach, amazing sex, and wonderful food went a long way toward assuaging anxiety.

"Does Isabel know you're back yet?"

"Of course." I'd used a secure phone to stay in touch with her the entire time. "We're planning to have drinks tonight." I smirked. "We might even invite you."

"That would be so sweet."

Isabel and Jack were virtually inseparable. Then again, Tyler and I were much the same.

"The four of us should do something fun soon." I hooked my arm through his and walked with him down the hall toward the programming department. "Being in love is grand, but it certainly makes keeping up with friends difficult."

Jack stopped just outside the door to his department and regarded me seriously. He was slouching, something he rarely did. "Look, I know best friends don't spill secrets, but I really need to talk to you about something."

Worry spiked in my heart. "Are things okay between you two?"

"Things are great, but...she's been acting weird lately." He shrugged. "I dunno, secretive. She used to talk to you on the phone with me around, but while you were away, she'd go into her room." He squeezed my hand. "Emily, please tell me—is there something I should know? Am I doing something to upset Isabel?"

The worry turned to a blanket of leaden guilt. Jack didn't know about my supernatural job, or vampires, or Tyler's true nature, and Isabel was trying to keep him out of the loop. "Absolutely not, Jack. I just have some personal issues I wanted to talk to her about and felt uncomfortable with you knowing."

His slumped shoulders straightened. "Really?"

"Yes, really. She's having the time of her life with you, silly." I patted his arm. "I just can't have you knowing all our secrets. After all, sisters before misters."

He snorted. "Your secrets are safe with me, Em." A long sigh escaped him. "Wow, I feel much better now."

"I'm sure you do." I looked toward the table where I'd put the doughnut box. "Unfortunately, you missed out on the doughnuts."

Jack put the back of his hand to his forehead and pretended to swoon. "Tragic!" He looked back toward the programming department. "Well, I'd better get back there before Hinkle starts complaining about me to everyone."

I left him and met with Kevin Shale, the sales team leader so I could catch up on recent events.

"We've made some great inroads with prospective clients, but finalizing deals has been hard." He showed me a spreadsheet of companies and their software needs. "We actually had the CIO of Purple Giraffe ready to sign, but for some reason, he backed out at the last minute. Now he won't even talk to me on the phone or through email."

"That would've been worth over a hundred thousand dollars this year." I ran a finger down the list. "I don't understand why they're balking."

He blew out a breath. "None of us understand. Tony Costanzo told me his sales team went from first place during the bid process, to persona non grata."

I looked away from the computer screen. "There's too much of a pattern here for this to all be coincidence."

Kevin sat back in his chair. "I agree. Someone out there has it in for us, and they're pulling all the right strings."

I picked up the phone and called Jack's extension. "Could you come to Kevin's office, please?"

"Be right there."

The office door opened a split second later, but instead of Jack, it was Tyler. He stormed into the room, face clouded with anger. "Someone is sabotaging my companies."

Jack walked in. The smile on his face faded when he saw Tyler's mood.

"Close the door, please." I told Jack.

He gulped and shut it behind him. "Uhm, did I screw up?"

Tyler shook his head. "Have any of you noticed anything odd going on with OnTech?"

Kevin told him about the stymied sales.

"How's customer satisfaction?" I asked Jack. "Any complaints from current customers?"

He shook his head. "Nothing out of the ordinary. Janet sends out surveys to current customers, but they've all come back singing our praises."

"So none of our current customers would warn potential clients to stay away." Tyler leaned against the edge of the desk. "The same thing is happening to several other companies in my portfolio."

Cyrus Rock had given his three children several companies to manage so one could prove they deserved to inherit his riches. The original Tyler Hugo Rock—we called him Hugo—hadn't done so well managing his portfolio.

"Are they all software companies?" I asked.

"No. Vermillion Unicorn and OnTech deal with software, but I also own Alpha Construction, Ironclaw Security, Pulsar Communications, and Treat your Meat."

"Treat your Meat?" Kevin and Jack exchanged a puzzled look.

Tyler snorted. "It's a chain of massage parlors."

"They sound like brothels," I said.

"I have more companies, but I don't remember them all." Tyler's thousand-mile stare bored into the wall. "The massage parlors were doing well until a national news article claimed people had caught the Asian bird flu there. Business plummeted, even though the story was false. I'm trying to get a lawsuit off the ground, but that will take time. The other businesses are having similar issues to what Kevin said is happening to OnTech." He pushed off the desk and rounded on us. "The cyanide icing on the cake is brain drain."

"What's that?" I asked.

"Other companies are trying to lure away our top employees." He smacked a fist into his hand. "We're facing a systematic attempt to destroy the corporations I run."

Jack rubbed his neck. "Yeah, um, I was approached with a pretty sweet offer to go work for another firm just last week. I overheard Nick Reeds and Susan Daniels talking about offers they received."

"From whom?" Tyler asked.

Jack shrugged. "Some company called Trax Worldwide. I did some online research but couldn't find a lot about them. According to their website, they have their fingers in a lot of pies."

"I need to know more about them." Tyler went to the computer and gingerly pecked at the keys with two fingers.

I groaned. "You're hopeless with computers, do you know that?" I tugged him out of the chair. "Let me look them up."

Kevin and Jack pressed their lips together as if trying to suppress laughter.

The Trax Worldwide website was a minimalistic masterpiece with lots of white space and black text. They had a long list of clients, including several Fortune 500 companies. I navigated to their services page and found a laundry list of industries. They did everything from software development to construction.

I clicked on the "About" link and read aloud, "Trax was incorporated five years ago."

Jack peered at the screen "I find it very hard to believe they've grown so large in such a short period of time."

"Acquisitions and takeovers," Tyler said. "Someone with real money put together this company."

"Have the offers to employees at other companies come from Trax as well?" Kevin asked.

"I don't know, but I'm going to find out." Tyler leaned a hand against the wall. "Maybe we could get someone on the inside."

"You mean bribe someone at the company to spy on them?" Kevin didn't seem to like the idea.

"Why bribe someone when they want to hire one of my own people?" A wolfish grin spread across Tyler's face.

Jack held up his hands in front of his chest. "Uh, I'd rather not be a double agent if that's okay with you."

Tyler deflated a bit. "Yeah, I suppose it is a little risky. I'll have to figure out some other way to keep this company from bankrupting us."

"Maybe you could talk to some of our potential clients and find out why they backed out on us," Kevin said. "They won't give us time of day, but maybe someone with your clout would have better luck."

Tyler touched a hand to his chin and mused about it. "I suppose it's worth a try, but it'll take me months to individually meet with clients at every company I own."

I looked back at the list of clients Trax claimed. "Maybe we should cross reference these companies and see if any of them were potential clients for your other companies."

"Good idea." Tyler borrowed the mouse and clicked on Trax's portfolio. He scanned down the list of corporations they own and stopped at one named *The Weekly Journal*. "That's the news outlet that published the story about my massage parlors."

Kevin grunted. "I wonder who's at the top of this organization."

"I don't know, but I plan to find out." Tyler touched a finger to his chin. "Kevin, print me out a copy of your client spreadsheet and I'll see what I can find on my end."

"You got it." He sat down at the computer and brought up the document.

"Jack, I know you don't want to be a double agent, but I need some way to keep employees from abandoning ship." Tyler put a hand on Jack's shoulder. "Can you find out what the mood is like in your department and come up with some ideas?"

"I can tell you that everyone I talk to is really happy about the profit sharing arrangement." He rubbed the back of his neck. "The only person I heard complaining is Hinkle."

Kevin looked up from the computer. "Thomas Jones whines a lot too."

"Well, of course they do," I said. "They were department heads before Tyler changed everything."

"They've always been assholes," Jack admitted.

"Well, let me know if anyone seems tempted to leave," Tyler said. "OnTech won't last long without skilled programmers."

"Amen to that," Kevin said. "Without services to sell, we're dead in the water."

"I'll be in my office." Tyler looked at the client list, wrote the first number on a pad, and turned to me. "Please bring me the client printout when it's ready." He opened the door and left.

"I just need to remove the current clients from the list," Kevin said. "I'll have it ready in five minutes."

"I'll scope out the temperature of the programming department." Jack followed Tyler out.

Kevin had the printout ready a few minutes later. I took it to the door at the end of the hallway and opened it. Tyler stood behind a large wooden desk, a phone held to his ear. He motioned me over.

"I understand that he's a busy man, I'm just very surprised he doesn't have time for a quick chat with me." Tyler's fist clenched tight. "Yes, please schedule an appointment. Good day." His voice sounded as tight as his fist. He made as if to slam down the phone and stopped himself at the last minute.

I closed the door and went over to him. "I've got the list."

"I don't like being stonewalled, Emily."

"Is that what happened on your first call?"

He nodded and dropped into his chair. "It's like someone is playing keep-away just long enough to tire me out and make me give up."

"They want to starve your companies to death." I walked behind him and massaged his shoulders.

He groaned with pleasure. "Your hands are like magic, Em. I don't know what I'd do without you."

I leaned over and kissed his ear. "You'd probably grow fat and die."

In one smooth movement, he rotated the chair and swept me into his lap. "Our calisthenics sessions do keep me in shape."

"Precisely."

He nuzzled his nose against mine. "Well, perhaps we should do a little exercise right now." Tyler squeezed my breast while his tongue journeyed up my neck to my earlobe.

I groaned and shivered. "I don't think sex in your office would be appropriate workplace conduct."

His teeth nipped my neck. "It's a good thing I'm the boss." He deftly undid my jeans and slid a hand into my underpants.

My hands clenched his hair as his magical fingers danced across my clit. "Oh, God, Tyler."

There was a knock at the door.

I repressed a shriek and slid off his lap. My jeans promptly slid to my ankles, much to Tyler's amusement. Before I could pull them up, the door handle clicked. I dropped to a crouch behind the huge wooden desk and crawled into the space beneath it.

Sandra spoke. "Mr. Rock—"

"Tyler, if you please. Remember, Sandra, first names, please." His voice sounded very amused.

I couldn't pull up my jeans without bumping around and making noise, but I decided to engage in shenanigans of my own.

"Tyler." Sandra sounded very uncomfortable saying his name.

I ran a hand up Tyler's crotch and unzipped his pants slowly. I felt him stiffen in more ways than one.

"How can I help you?" Tyler's voice rose in pitch as my hand grasped his penis.

"As you know, I've been a receptionist for quite some time."

Tyler cleared his throat. "Five years, correct?"

I tried to reach him with my mouth, but there wasn't enough room beneath the desk.

"Yes. I'd like to see if there's an opportunity to expand my horizons." The sincerity in Sandra's voice made me feel guilty about diverting Tyler's attention from her request, so I released him.

"Is there some other position you'd like to apply for?"

"I'd like to be in sales." Her high heels clicked across the floor to the desk. "As you can see from previous jobs, I have sales experience. I've also been taking night classes in programming so I could better understand the services we offer."

I heard the rustle of paper. "Sandra, I'd be happy to look over your resume. I'll let you know something in a few days, okay?"

"Thank you, Mr. R—Tyler."

"Anytime."

Her heels clicked across the floor. The door clicked shut a moment later.

Tyler slid his chair back from the desk and grinned down at me. "That was fun. Why'd you stop?"

I crawled from under his desk and wriggled back into my jeans. "Because I didn't want to distract you."

"I wasn't all that distracted."

I crossed my arms. "Oh?"

He took my hand and tugged me upright. "Okay, maybe a little."

"I think it's great that employees can just come talk to you like that." I pressed my lips to his. "You're probably the most open and honest boss these people have ever had."

"It's because I'm a demon." He stood and stretched. "We're known for our honesty."

I stuck out my tongue. "Oh, yes, the very soul of honesty." But something about his comment sparked an idea. "I think I know who's behind this."

Chapter 7

Tyler raised an eyebrow. "You've had an epiphany?"

"The timing of these corporate problems is recent, correct?"

He frowned. "From what I can tell, everything started about a month ago when we were still out of town."

I nodded. "Who else has probably been around for a month? Who else would love to torture you by making you fail?"

His eyes lit. "Barboar and the other demons."

"Precisely." I put a finger to my lips. "It would seem our supernatural lives are now interfering with our normal existence."

"If you're right, then solving the demon dilemma should make these problems go away." He stood up and looked at the busy street below. "Em, we need to track them down and discover their true names. Even if I can't banish them to the Abyss, I'll be able to keep them away." He turned to me. "What I don't understand is why you can't sense my name."

"Is Barboar a weaker demon than you?"

He thought about it for a moment. "That's hard to quantify. Here in Eden we're physically about the same."

"And the others?" I asked.

"Very similar to Barboar."

"We should track down another and see if I can determine his name."

Tyler dropped back into his chair. "Eyja might be the easiest to start with."

I sat on the edge of his desk. "Why is that?"

"They all love alcohol, drugs, and partying, but Eyja is addicted to sex clubs."

"I hardly find that surprising." I gave Tyler a playful tap on the nose with my finger. "He is a demon after all."

"*She* is a demon." He snapped his teeth at my finger. "We'll need to do a little detective work."

"Do you plan to comb every sex club in the city?"

"If that's what it takes." Tyler took my hand and kissed it. "I'll do anything to stop them."

"There's one more problem."

"And that is?"

"Eyja is undoubtedly in a new body from the last time you saw her." I quirked my lips. "How will you know who she is even if we're at the right sex club?"

He chuckled. "Because I'll have you with me to find her."

I blinked at him a couple of time. "Oh yes, I'd forgotten about my ability again."

Tyler stood and ran kisses along my cheeks. "You're so cute when you're flustered."

"I'll show you flustered." My hand slid across his crotch.

He trembled. "You certainly know how to make me lose control."

"Do we start our search tonight?"

"Yes. I'll interweb search the sex clubs in the area."

I sniffed. "I think you should leave the internet searches to me, or we'll never get anywhere."

"Fine." Tyler looked all too happy to relinquish that responsibility. "I'm sure it'll be considered a proper use of office internet."

By the end of the workday, I had a list of five such clubs and showed each of them to Tyler.

He eliminated two of them right away. "Those establishments are too tame. She likes her sex a bit more on the adventurous side."

I felt a flush go up my neck. "I rather thought they were all adventurous." I caught a look from him and quickly added, "And much too risqué for me, thank you very much."

Tyler seemed to take great pleasure in my discomfort. "I'm going to enjoy this."

"Hmm, yes, I suppose you will." I did my best to conceal the smile tickling my lips.

"Well, we should go buy some clothes for tonight."

"Tonight?" I checked my phone to be sure of the day. "But it's a Monday."

"She'll still be out getting her fix."

"Why do we need to buy clothes? I have plenty of clubbing attire thanks to you."

He grinned from ear to ear. "These are sex clubs, not night clubs." Tyler raked his eyes over my body. "Yum."

My knees went weak. "Oh, dear."

He put an arm around my shoulders. "I intersearched and found some places for the proper outfits."

I kissed him on the cheek. "You mean you ran an internet search, silly."

"Sure, whatever."

Joe was waiting by the car when we exited the building. We climbed into the backseat and Tyler gave him an address on Cheshire Bridge Road. "Yes, sir." He pulled into traffic.

Butterflies fluttered in my stomach. "I can't believe we're doing this."

Tyler cupped my chin. "You want to find them, don't you?"

I nodded. "We have to find them. It's this sex club business that has me nervous."

His amused grin returned. "Out of everything we have to worry about, that's the one thing you're most worried about."

I looked down. "It just sounds so perverse."

"I suppose to some people it might be."

I immediately flicked my gaze up to his. "To some? I believe you greatly underestimate that number, sir."

"You're cute when you're indignant." Tyler pecked a kiss on my nose.

I wiped my nose with the back of my hand. "I'm dangerous when I look cute."

We soon reached a street with a string of dubious-looking establishments and an array of sex shops. Joe didn't bat an eyelash as he pulled in front of a black brick building with blacked out windows and no placard to announce its name. The parking lot was small and quite full, so Joe stopped in front of the building.

"We're here, sir." He got out and opened Tyler's door so the two of us could slide out of the back seat.

"We might be an hour or so," Tyler told Joe.

"I'll be waiting." Joe gave each of us a straight-faced nod, got back into the SUV, and drove away.

I watched the vehicle vanish into traffic. "I wonder what is going through his mind right now."

"Probably finding a parking space." Tyler took my hand. "Shall we begin?"

Steeling myself with a deep breath, I nodded. *It's for a worthy cause.* "I'm ready."

We stepped inside.

I expected a dingy, smelly room filled with whips and chains to greet me. Instead, I faced a well-lit shop with white walls, glass shelves, and a sterile feel. Indeed, there was a wall displaying a variety of whips, and shelves with every size vibrator and dildo I could imagine, plus some designs that boggled the mind. A young couple cast furtive looks at us as if they didn't wish to be seen in such a place.

Tyler stopped next to a normal sized vibrator. "Hmm, we should get some toys to play with."

I smiled sweetly. "I already have a shoebox full of them. Would you like me to demonstrate their use sometime?"

He paused, mouth open in a priceless look.

"Tyler, dear, you look positively ready to drool if you don't close your mouth."

He barked a laugh, which sent the young couple in the lube section jumping back as if a ghost had appeared. That only made him laugh louder.

I jerked on his sleeve and murmured, "You're scaring the other shoppers."

We made our way to the back where an assortment of questionable attire hung from racks. Tyler mused over a fishnet bodysuit.

"Don't even think about it," I warned. "I will not display my lady parts for everyone to see."

"I was thinking about it for home."

This brought a warm flush to my face. "Perhaps after I've had several drinks."

He ran a finger over the material. "That won't be a problem." Tyler rubbed his hands together. "For tonight, I think something like this would work." A leather dress seemed to have caught his attention.

I held it up to myself and grimaced at the length. "It barely comes down to my thighs."

He winked. "That's the point."

I removed a larger version of the same dress from the rack, but its length still left something to be desired. The rest of the "clothing" was made of similar material—leather or a disgusting rubber-like substance. We browsed for a while longer and finally settled on a leather skirt and matching top with buttons and a collar. I wasn't delighted, but at least the skirt came down a little above my knees.

Tyler chose tight pants, a shirt of the same material, and a ridiculous pair of large, tinted glasses. "To disguise my face," he explained. "She might have my description."

"Just as long as I don't have to wear a pair." I examined the pants. "Hmm, I thought the buttless chaps were far more becoming on you."

"If you'd like—"

I cut off the thought with a firm look. "I will not have your well-defined ass hanging in the breeze for all to see."

On the way out, he stopped by plastic-wrapped packages of anal plugs. I grabbed his arm and showed him firmly to the cashier.

"Those would require considerably more than alcohol for me to consider."

Tyler chuckled. "Wait, one more thing." He went to the wall of whips and chose a leather one. "Can't have a master without one of these."

"You are the master, I presume?"

He shrugged. "We'll figure that out."

We paid for the merchandise and hid the dreadful items in a brown bag. I did *not* want Joe to see them. As we climbed into the SUV, I received a text from Isabel.

Can't wait to see you for drinks tonight!

I put a hand to my forehead and showed Tyler the text. "I completely forgot. Do you think we can drop by and visit them for a bit?"

Tyler checked his watch. "Sure. Things won't get lively at the club until later anyway."

I didn't want to consider what lively entailed, but visions of leather-clad people whipping bound companions still flashed through my mind.

We went to Tyler's place, ate, and then had Joe drop us at Gronsky's, Isabel's and my favorite bar. A cold chill shivered up my spine as we walked past the alley where a vampire by the name of Stephen had assaulted Isabel and me.

Tyler seemed to know what I was thinking and rubbed my arm. "He's a mortal now. Won't be hurting anyone else."

"A man like that could still do harm."

"He's probably sitting home in his underwear, eating cheesy poofs and regretting the day he ever met you."

I pressed my head to his chest. "I certainly hope so. May he grow fat and bald so no other woman has to deal with his disgusting ass."

Isabel and Jack waved from the bar when we entered. The sight of her so happy melted my fears in a warm wave of joy. I rushed over and gave her a hug.

"So good to see you, Iz!"

She giggled. "Someone's missed me."

"Very much so." I leaned away and looked her over. She positively glowed. "Things are going well, I see."

"Jack is the best." She leaned forward and whispered conspiratorially in my ear. "Just don't tell him I said so."

"Too late," he said with a smile. He shook Tyler's hand. "Any progress on our business trouble?"

Tyler waved away the topic. "Let's save that talk for work. I just want to relax."

"You got my vote on that."

I decided now was a good time to indulge in enough alcohol to soften my inhibitions about the adventurous night ahead. My fears were something of a mystery even to me. I wasn't a complete prude when it came to sex, nor was I a stranger to pornography. During the last few months of our relationship, my ex-fiancé, Peter, had convinced me to watch such videos while we had sex.

At first, I hadn't minded, until the videos grew more disturbing— some of them filled with fake violence. I'd put a stop to his new fetish, or so I'd thought. Then I'd discovered a hidden stash of sex videos he'd made with other women, some of them recorded while we were still together.

And yet, the foundation of my anxiety about the sex clubs had nothing to do with the negative associations of the past. I simply felt embarrassed about the ordeal, even it was for a good cause.

"You're not playing around tonight," Isabel said with a laugh as I downed my third shot.

Tyler seemed amused as usual, a smile playing about his lips. "Maybe we should pace ourselves," he said. "We've got work tomorrow."

"Ugh, don't remind me." Isabel threw up her hands. "I used to love my job until they sold out to a mega-corp."

I put my drink down. "You didn't tell me about that."

"It happened while you were on vacay." She sipped her Choco-Lava rum drink. "Some big-wigs visited the office, so I had to give them a tour. Can you believe they didn't even seem to know what we did to make money?"

I bit the inside of my lip and tried to remember. "Website design, right?"

"Yep." Isabel sighed. "I got the strangest feeling they were more interested in talking to me than they were about the company."

"Yeah, because you're hot." Jack winked at her.

"Shush, you." She made a tutting noise. "Everyone knows it's because of my stunning intellect."

I nodded in agreement. "Precisely." My pronunciation was rather slurred and imprecise which was no surprise since I felt very warm, pleasant, and a touch numb.

It didn't escape Isabel's notice. "Em, I'd have to say you just achieved buzz-vana."

"Just a teensy little bit." I pinched my thumb and forefinger together to illustrate and then reached for my glass.

Tyler's hand intercepted mine. He pressed my knuckles to his lips. "Perhaps you'd like some water." He raised a hand and got Alex's attention. "Two waters please."

The bartender had them to us a moment later. "Everyone else good?"

"We're great!" I assured him.

Isabel let me take a couple of sips of water and then took me by the wrist. "Potty break. We'll be back."

Before I could resist, she guided me through the sparse Monday night crowd and to the back hall with the restrooms. She stopped outside and narrowed her eyes suspiciously at me. "Is something wrong between you and Tyler? You don't usually drink like this unless I need to kick someone's ass."

"I love you, sis." I squeezed her tight. "You've always got my back."

She extricated herself from my tight grip. "I love you too, Em. I'm worried, but I can't help if you don't tell me what's going on."

I blew a raspberry with my lips. "Demons."

She raised her eyebrows. "Demons? I thought vampires were the problem."

"Bloody fucking demons." I leaned against the wall. "Tyler's old buddies are back in this world, and we have to track one down tonight." I felt tears coming on and tried to keep them at bay. "Can you believe I have to wear a leather skirt and blouse to a sex club later?"

She snorted and covered her mouth. "You're going to a sex club?"

"It's not funny!"

"Is that where the demon will be?"

A woman exiting the bathroom gave Isabel a strange look.

"Supposedly." My insides knotted again despite the alcohol. "We're going try each place until we find her."

"Well, now your behavior makes complete sense." Isabel pretended to wipe sweat from her forehead. "Whew, I'm glad things are okay with you and Tyler."

"Our relationship is wonderful, but the demons do put a crimp in matters."

Isabel's eyes brightened as if lit by a wonderful idea. "I could buy a leather outfit and come with you."

"No, as a matter of fact, you can't." I crossed my arms and gave her a stern look. "Tyler can protect me, and he needs my ability to track down his infernal acquaintance. You could get seriously hurt if something goes wrong."

"Yes, but—"

"No buts, Iz." I gripped her hand. "Besides, what would Jack think about you going to a sex club?"

"Well, I don't have to tell him."

"Do you really want to keep things from him?"

She shook her head. "No, but I still have to since I can't tell him your and Tyler's secrets."

"Well, keeping that from him is simply a matter of Overworld policy." I was, of course, talking out of my arse, but it seemed the best way to smooth away the double standard that there were some things she had to keep from Jack.

She blew out a breath. "It really pisses me off I can't help you, Em."

"Speaking of piss, I really do have to go now." I pushed open the bathroom door and went inside.

The men didn't seem the least bit surprised by how long it took us to return, and were deep in conversation about the workplace drama. Despite his earlier assertion of staying away from work talk, Tyler seemed to be enjoying the subject.

I checked the time and realized with chagrin it was getting close to ten. "Well, I suppose we have to be going."

Tyler looked at his watch. "Wow, time flies when you're having fun."

"Can we give you a lift back to the apartment building?" I asked Isabel.

She squeezed me in a hug. "No, thanks. I'm staying at Jack's tonight. I haven't been back to the apartment since Friday." She giggled.

I felt my eyes flare with surprise. Staying over the weekend was one thing, but the weeknights were taking it to a whole new level for Isabel. "It would seem we need to brunch again quite soon. My little girl is growing up so fast and I'm just missing out on everything."

"Definitely! Let's do it this weekend, okay?"

"It's a date."

Tyler and I walked the couple to Jack's car. Joe pulled up in the SUV a moment later. Tyler opened the back door for me and slid in. "Home, please, Joe."

"Yes, sir."

Back at the penthouse, we changed into our devilish attire. I slipped on a pair of modest polka-dotted panties, which considerably increased my comfort level. This amused Tyler to no end.

He reached under the skirt and pinched my bottom. "I like the slutty girl next door look you're going for."

I ran a hand over the bulge in his leather pants and felt it swell in response. "I know how sexual conundrums turn you on, dear."

"I want to bend you over—"

"Let me stop you right there and remind you that we're on a schedule tonight, darling."

Tyler chuckled. "Oh, irony, how you wound me."

"Thankfully, blue balls is not a fatal injury." I patted his crotch gently and tried not to giggle at the desperate look on his face. "Perhaps I'll tend to your wound later."

A growl rumbled in his chest. "Oh, I think you'll have to, or I might die."

I slipped into a pair of comfortable flats and picked up the "fuck me" stiletto heels I planned to wear inside the club. "Ready when you are."

He reached into his pants, adjusted himself, and nodded. "Let's be on our way then."

We took the lift to the underground parking garage. Tyler chose a sporty coupe over his Lamborghini.

"Don't want to stick out too much," he told me.

A moment later, we were off in search of a demon.

Chapter 8

My hands trembled as we walked to the back-alley entrance of Bondage, the first club on our list. A pretty, polite girl in a corset stood behind a counter.

"Hello, are you new to Bondage?"

In more ways than one, dear.

"Yep." Tyler flashed a smile.

She gave him a quick glance, but returned her gaze to me. "I'll need you to fill out a membership form." She handed me a tablet with the form on the screen. I knew for a fact I didn't want my real name on such a document, so I entered the name of Jack's ex-girlfriend, Ana and her new sugar daddy, Bernard Paulson, along with the address I remembered from the picture Jack had shown me.

The girl took the tablet from me, her fingers and eyes lingering on me as she did. "You are so pretty."

I gulped and felt very hot all of sudden. "Oh, th-thanks. You're very pretty too."

Tyler shook and broke into a coughing fit.

"Are you okay?" I asked.

He nodded, unable to speak. I suddenly realized he was holding in laughter and rolled my eyes. "I will get you back for this," I whispered.

Tyler paid the membership and entry fees and headed for the entrance to the main part of the club. The girl handed me a slip of paper. When I took it, she leaned over the counter and murmured in my ear. "I can't fuck you when I'm working, but give me a call sometime." She bit my earlobe and moaned. "Mm, you taste so sweet."

I nearly fell over backwards with surprise. "Oh, uh, yes. It must be the bath salts."

She licked her lips and looked me up and down like a hungry wolf. I gripped Tyler's arm for support and let him guide me into the main club. Music throbbed from overhead speakers. There was a small dance floor with an equally small crowd, and a hallway lined with doors.

"She seems really nice," he said in a serious tone. "We should invite her over sometime."

"You'd like that, wouldn't you?"

"Not really." He gave me a fierce kiss. "I don't want to share you with anyone."

I bit his lower lip a little harder than usual and smiled. "Good."

He looked at the hallway. "I guess we should just walk through and see if you pick up on anything."

"That should work well enough." I wanted to get out of this place as quickly as possible. The first room was unoccupied. A bed with vinyl mattress sat in the middle. I made note of the metal bars on the headboard and the pole in the far corner. "I somewhat expected chains hanging from the ceiling, or a colorful array of handcuffs."

"It must be BYOH." He pulled on the footboard. "Sturdy. I guess you could cuff someone to just about anything in here. Maybe use a ball gag and a whip." He smacked the whip he'd brought over the palm of his hand.

I raised an eyebrow. "If anyone is to be whipped tonight, it'll have to be you."

"Fair enough." Tyler winked.

The room across the hallway was empty, and the next two were locked. A whip cracked and someone moaned. We stopped outside an open door and saw a middle-aged man, naked but for a leather thong in his mouth, being flogged by a tall, busty brunette.

"You are my little piglet," she said in a commanding voice.

The man snorted. She whipped him again and he squealed like a real pig.

My mouth dropped open and my eyes flared wide. Tyler jerked me from the doorway and led me to a set of stairs. "They probably don't want you staring in open-mouthed horror at them."

"That *was* horrifying!" I looked back toward the open door. "How absolutely humiliating for that poor man."

"It's a thing, Em. Some people want to be completely dominated." He shrugged. "It's not my cup of tea, that's for sure."

"Nor mine." I shuddered. "I would never be able to dominate someone like that."

We took the stairs down into what could only be described as a dungeon. Every manner of torture device had its place in this room of horrors. I heard moans and cries of pleasure. We walked around a wooden wall lined with leather bindings and encountered a group of people indulging in an orgy on a large padded mat.

Tyler immediately pulled me in for a kiss. His lips brushed my ear. "Don't stare, Em, or if you do, act like you're enjoying it. We don't want to look out of place."

Eyes closed, I pressed my face against his chest and drew in his scent. His presence stabilized me and melted the knot of anxiety. As those feelings faded, another sensation took their place. There was most definitely another supernatural presence in here. Unfortunately, it was not that of a demon.

It took a matter of seconds for me to spot the lovely pale woman riding cowgirl atop an overweight man with more hair than a bear. She cried out in climax and leaned down to kiss the man who seemed absolutely exhausted despite her having done all the work.

Her gaze abruptly flicked to meet mine. I offered her what I hoped was sultry smile. Instead, her head tilted to the side. She slid off the man and walked toward us, her discerning gaze on me. Fear overwhelmed my unease with her unabashed nudity. The last thing I wanted was another fight with a vampire. Tyler had barely been able to fight off Stephen, despite his martial arts training.

The vampire touched Tyler. "As I thought." She took my hand in hers and gave Tyler a severe look. "What brings a possessed into this place?"

The other participants in the orgy seemed too involved in their decadent activities to hear what she said.

"How do you know?" I asked.

Quick as a cat, her head turned to me. "You're aware of this *man's* true state?"

"Yes."

She nodded. "Well, then, that is a different matter. I do not condone the possessed using mortals without their consent."

"How can you say that after riding that poor man into the ground?" I was somewhat shocked at the directness of my own question, but held my ground.

"Did I drink his blood?"

I shrugged. "Not while I was watching."

She leaned forward, breasts dangling. "Then don't judge me."

"Fine. We'll just be on our way then."

She ran her eyes over Tyler. "Do you allow him to fuck other women?"

I shook my head. "Absolutely not. He's my"—I struggled for the terms I'd researched on the web earlier, and found the one I needed—"He's my sub and no one else's."

"He is a lovely man." She traced a fingernail down my arm.

Tyler tensed, but made no move to stop her.

"We don't share each other at all," I clarified.

The vampire sighed. "Do you allow others to watch?"

I wasn't sure how to answer that one, but decided we'd be out of place if we didn't have some kinkiness to us. "Sure. We like to watch and be watched."

She licked her lips. "I would love to watch you two."

"We're new to this club," Tyler said. "We're just looking around tonight."

She raised an eyebrow and looked to me. "Do you allow him to speak?"

I almost said, "Of course," and then remembered he was my submissive. "Did I give you permission to talk?"

Tyler pressed his lips into a line and shook his head.

"Then keep quiet."

He nodded meekly. It was so uncharacteristic of him, I almost asked if he was okay.

The woman smiled, revealing perfect white teeth, moved between us, and looped her arms into ours. "You're adorable. Welcome to my club. I am Simone, the owner."

I suddenly became acutely aware of her lithe naked body between us. "Oh, I didn't know vam—I mean, you owned this place."

She led us away from the orgy group. "I think you will find many of my kind own night establishments. It fits perfectly with our schedule."

"Yes, I suppose it does."

"You seem rather young." Simone caressed my cheek. "How long have you been in the lifestyle?"

My heart rate increased. It didn't help that I'd never met a nice vampire and expected her to snap my neck without a moment's notice. "Very new," I squeaked in a mouse-like voice.

"We're just seeing what's out there," Tyler said. He quickly realized he'd spoken without permission and looked down. "I'm sorry, mistress."

I jerked the whip from his hand and gave him a good swat on the backside. "The next time you talk out of turn, I'll make you get on your knees and beg forgiveness. Understood?"

Tyler's eyes flashed. "Absolutely, mistress." He seemed to relish the idea.

I turned back to Simone. "This is the first club we've been to."

Simone pursed her lips. "You should visit Heresy or Insurrection."

I took her hand in mine to remove it from my face and smiled. "They're on the list."

"Both have fun crowds, depending on the night." She gave my hand a gentle squeeze. "Such soft skin. Are you certain you couldn't indulge me?"

"I'm not ready for that just yet." *Or ever!*

Tyler nudged me.

"Do you have something to say, boy?" I almost smiled. *Bossing him around is fun.*

"Yes, mistress. I just wondered if there were hardcore people who come here."

Simone looked from him to me. "The members here are primarily into bondage, some whips, and group sex. If you want to see the truly debased"—she licked her lips and smiled—"then you need to go to Dante's."

I hadn't found that name when I'd searched for sex clubs. "I've never heard of it."

"I'm not surprised. You have to know where it is, much like a speakeasy."

"Well, that would explain it."

She pressed her breasts against me. "I might be persuaded to relinquish the location."

I gulped. "As I said, we don't share each other."

"I simply want to watch."

I really wanted Tyler's input on this and turned to him. "What do you think, boy?" My voice cracked a little.

His alpha-wolf grin wiped away the submissiveness. "Dante's sounds perfect."

In other words, it would probably be the most likely place to find Eyja. *Dear lord, can I do this?*

I mustered some courage and smiled at Simone. "You can watch." I turned to Tyler. "You are free to do as you wish." I was too nervous to make the first move.

Tyler moved in front of me and stroked my cheek. He ran kisses down my neck and whispered in my ear. "As you wish, mistress."

Sometime later, Tyler and I lay next to each other naked, sweaty, and completely satisfied. Once he'd gotten me in the mood, Simone's presence hadn't bothered me a bit, even when she made a show of masturbating while watching.

She softly clapped. "You are a perfect pair—poetry in motion." She leaned forward and kissed my forehead. "Perhaps in time you'll open yourself to new possibilities."

"Perhaps." I rolled over on my elbow to face her. "May I have the location now?"

"Absolutely."

We put on our clothes and left Bondage, promising Simone to come again soon, which by my definition meant never, if possible.

"It's so odd," I told Tyler as he drove us to Dante's. "It doesn't even bother me that she watched us, at least not once we got going."

"It didn't bother me either," he said.

"Yes, well I wouldn't expect so, considering your past."

He chuckled. "True. Kink is like spice."

I turned to him. "Does our sex life need spice?"

"Maybe for fun, but it's not a necessity." He shrugged. "Being with you is adventure enough."

I snorted. "I think we both bring plenty of adventure to the table."

"Sometimes, I wonder if that's a good thing." He pulled into a shopping center and parked in front of an Indian restaurant. "This is the place."

Very few patrons dined in the restaurant at this hour. I was surprised it was even open this close to midnight. We walked through a narrow alley between the restaurant and a sari shop, and down a stairway to a door. I rapped on the door in the manner prescribed by Simone. The door opened instantly.

A painfully thin woman in a skintight rubber dress motioned us in without a word. She gave me a paper membership form to fill out. Using the same information as before, I did so and handed it back.

"Two hundred, please," she said in a wispy voice.

Tyler handed her cash and slipped on his awful sunglasses.

She smiled at him. "Enjoy yourself, lovely boy."

We passed through a rubber curtain and into a room of pain.

Vinyl-padded furniture of all kinds sat in the large open room alongside crude contraptions that looked as if they belonged in a medieval dungeon. Wooden crosses, whipping poles, and even stocks had their place here. A large metal mesh bin held everything from whips and blindfolds to ball gags and rope.

A woman paddled a naked man bound and hogtied to a bed. Beyond them, a group of men took turns whipping a woman chained to a cross. Another man's arms and head were locked in stocks while a woman sodomized him with a large dildo. Those were tame in comparison to other dreadful things I saw. I did my best to avert my eyes from the couple having rough sex on a bed of nails, and tried not to vomit when I noticed two women piercing each other with large needles.

Even Tyler looked a bit pale. "Do you sense anything?" he asked in a strained voice.

"I need a moment." I bolted for the other side of a partition to get everything out of my sight.

Tyler drew me into his comforting embrace. "Breathe, baby, breathe."

At last, the nausea and shock faded, no longer overwhelming my other senses. "I don't glimpse anything right now." I looked up at him. "I'm afraid if I go back out there, I'll be too upset to detect anything."

He kissed me gently. "Wait here. I'll be right back."

I was more than happy to prolong the moment. As I sat there in silence, I felt the faint presence of at least one vampire tickling against the fringe of my senses. Tyler returned with a blindfold.

"Turn around."

I stepped back. "You want to blind me?"

"No, but at least you won't have to see anything that makes you sick." Tyler cupped my chin and kissed me. "Don't worry, I won't let you stub your toe on anything."

"That's reassuring." Despite my misgivings, his idea was rather sound. Other emotions made so much noise, they often crowded out my ability. I closed my eyes and felt him slip the blindfold over my face. "Lead the way."

He held me by an arm and led me around. I heard rattling chains, creaking leather, and the crack of whips against naked flesh with moans, screams, and giddy laughter their unsettling accompaniment. The cloying scents of sex and body odor invaded my nose while the cold sensation of a vampire grew stronger and stronger until it seemed we must be right next to one.

When the fuzzy vision of a glowing worm flashed into my inner eye, I knew we had to be just feet away. The sound of groans and heavy breathing confirmed it. As the glowing parasite squirmed, I noticed there were actually two of them. The vampires were in such close proximity to one another, I hadn't been able to realize there was more than one.

"Oh, shit," a male voice said. "I'm going to come."

The vision faded as Tyler led me away from them.

"We've covered the whole place," he said at last.

I sighed. "Well, there were two vampires having sex, but that's about it."

"Really? Where were they?"

"They were the last couple we passed."

"Well, actually it was a threesome, but that's impressive you knew there was more than one vampire." He blew out a breath. "Damn, I guess she isn't here."

"On to the next club?" I asked.

"I suppose." He didn't sound enthused.

I felt his hands on the blindfold and stopped him. "I want to keep this on until we're out of here."

71

Tyler chuckled. "I got you, babe."

As we passed by the two vampires, I stepped on something small and round. I stumbled. Tyler's firm grip on my arm held me up, but in the instant I staggered to the side, I glimpsed a burning sensation that wasn't Tyler's Beneath the odor of sweat and sex, I smelled something sickly sweet and sulfurous.

A soft and unnaturally warm hand steadied me by my other arm. "Is this little thing yours?" asked a female with a southern accent. She purred. "I'd love to taste her."

I knew without a doubt that we'd found Eyja.

Chapter 9

After regaining my balance, I lifted the blindfold and looked into crystal blue eyes made all the more striking by the woman's smooth ebony skin and frame of silky black hair.

Two exhausted male vampires lay on the bed behind her. I couldn't imagine the frenetic sexual activity that would burn through the reserves of men with supernatural strength. Though covered in a sheen of sweat, the woman looked more than ready for another round.

Even more troubling than her interest in me, I had no idea how to signal Tyler that this was Eyja. Though she was still holding my arm, I sensed no pattern or name and quickly realized I would have to touch her.

Smiling, I caressed her cheek. "You are quite lovely."

Eyja purred. "You are whipped cream on my dessert, honey." She pushed my hand down her abnormally warm skin to her chest.

My hand slipped over her generous bosom and found cold metal. I glanced down and repressed a shudder. A small chain ran between large rings piercing her nipples. While I enjoyed boobs as much as the next girl, I had no desire to play with these. Despite direct skin-to-skin contact, I hadn't glimpsed anything more about her than what I usually did about Tyler.

Tyler tensed, apparently realizing my behavior was way off from earlier.

I looked up at him. "I think we've found the perfect woman to play with, dear."

He managed an uneasy smile. "Finally."

Eyja reached out to touch him, but I intercepted her hand, afraid that when she discovered his skin was much warmer than mine, she might suspect his true nature. I slipped her finger into my mouth and bit it gently.

She hissed in pleasure. "You'll have to bite harder than that, sweetie."

I bit harder and slid her finger from my mouth as my mind searched desperately for some way to divine her true name.

Tyler leaned over and nipped my shoulder. "I saw the perfect bed further back, babe."

Another wooden partition divided this area from the next. I took Eyja's hand. "Let's go play."

She rubbed her naked body against me. "Pull me by the chain, sweetie."

The last thing I wanted to do was lead a woman by pierced nipples, but if that was what she wanted, I could just pretend she was a horse. I clasped the chain and tugged. Her nipples stretched.

She moaned and looked at Tyler. "Make yourself useful and whip me while we walk, boy."

"With pleasure." He popped her across the ass so hard, the snap startled me.

Eyja screamed with ecstasy. "Oh, god, that was good!"

In that instant, I glimpsed a pattern. It vanished too quickly for me to see. It suddenly occurred to me how we had to extricate the information from this woman. Barboar had been in extreme pain when I'd divined his secrets. Though I didn't relish the thought of torturing anyone, we'd have to do the same to Eyja.

I saw a narrow table with padded leather thongs. "Lie down," I told her. "You've been a very bad girl."

She giggled, leaned over, and kissed me. Her tongue pressed into my mouth. I was so surprised, I didn't resist as her hand ran up beneath my skirt and slapped my backside. The kiss wasn't as awful as expected, at least not until she bit my tongue hard enough to draw tears.

I jerked back and tried not to show how much it had hurt. "Facedown on the table, now!"

"Yes, mistress." She did as instructed.

Once I secured the leather straps around her wrists and ankles, I motioned Tyler over and whispered in his ear. "She has to be in pain for me to see her name and pattern."

An evil grin stretched his lips. "It's time for your punishment."

"Punish me please, master!" She cast a sultry look over her shoulder. "I need a hard spanking."

Tyler took a wooden paddle off the wall. Without warning he flicked it down with an incredibly loud smack.

Eyja shrieked with pleasure. Her pattern flashed in my head, but once again vanished.

"More!" she cried. "More!"

Tyler gripped the paddle with both hands and let her have it. I screamed with Eyja, though mine was a cry of horror.

"That was amazing," she moaned. "I'm so close to coming, master. Please, punish me more."

Tyler gave me a look of disbelief. Eyja might be a demon, but her body was that of a human. The pain should've been too much for her now.

I shook my head to let Tyler know I still hadn't seen what I needed. He looked long and hard at the paddle and seemed to come to a grim conclusion. He raised it as if to smack her one more time, then chopped it down on Eyja's arm like a machete. A bone cracked and Eyja's moans turned to a true cry of pain.

"What the fuck?" she screamed.

Eyjaphlkutarveterya! The word drowned out her screams for several seconds and the pattern flashed blue before my mind's eye. I wished I had a photographic memory, or some way to record the pattern, but the name would have to do.

I nodded at Tyler.

He pressed a hand over Eyja's mouth, muffling her screams, and removed his sunglasses. "Eyja, you should have told me you were back in town."

Tears poured down her cheeks, but her eyes flared with recognition.

"I have a surprise for you." Tyler turned to me. "Tell her."

"We have your name, Eyjaphlkutarveterya." Despite the tongue-twisting consonants, I had no problem repeating it precisely as I'd heard in my head.

She went absolutely still, face frozen in shock.

Tyler released her mouth. "What are you and the others up to? Why are you fucking with my companies?"

"Grim, please, do not exorcise me." Her lips trembled. "I am not here with the others. You know I never joined them when they tortured you."

"I do remember." Tyler narrowed his eyes. "But the timing is coincidental."

"I didn't even know they were back in Eden." She whimpered. "Please, let me be. You know I have only one pleasure in life."

As she pleaded for freedom, I realized there was something slightly different about her aura when compared to the nauseating feeling from Barboar. She seemed somehow different, though I couldn't put a finger on it.

"I have your true name, Eyja." Tyler uncuffed her uninjured arm. "If you interfere with my life I will banish you to the Abyss."

Her body trembled and sagged. "I am already cursed, Grim." Tears ran down her cheeks.

Tyler frowned. "Yes, I suppose you are." He grabbed my hand and we walked quickly for the exit. Once outside, we hopped into the car and took off.

Nausea swelled in my throat as the image of Tyler breaking Eyja's arm played back in my mind. Separating the demon from the young woman was terribly hard for me. To see the man I loved committing such violence on a bound and helpless person made me sick, even though I knew it was absolutely necessary. I opened the window and gulped fresh air to combat the feeling.

Is this the part of him that's like Barboar? I couldn't bear to think of him in the same category as that creature.

I wanted desperately to discuss my feelings with Tyler, but was afraid I might undermine his ability to do what needed to be done when we encountered the next former associate.

He touched my leg. "I'm really sorry you had to see that, Em."

I covered his hand with both of mine and shivered. "I wasn't expecting it."

"It was the only way I could cross her pain threshold." He blew out a disgusted breath. "I don't like myself right now."

I looked at him. "Do you really feel that way, or are you just saying it to make me feel better?"

He stopped at a red light and looked directly into my eyes. Pain frayed the edges of the window to his soul. "I truly mean it."

"She felt different than Barboar." I tried to put the sensation into words. "He was repulsive and putrid. She felt almost pleasant in comparison." I took out my phone and recorded Eyja's true name precisely as I heard it in my head—*Ey-JA-phlku-tar-VET-erya*. I was still amazed I could pronounce it, but like Barboar's name, once I'd glimpsed it, I'd been able to say it, at least until the impression faded from my mind.

Tyler glanced at me. "It's very odd watching you say her name."

"Do you really think she'll leave you alone?"

He bit his lip and stared at the road. "It's true she never tortured me, but she didn't try to stop the others either." His shoulders hunched into a shrug. "I think we have a good chance of her staying out of this."

"Now we just have to find the other two and get their names," I said. "I don't suppose they're also sex addicts."

Tyler shook his head. "This is going to be harder than I thought. Not only do we have to find each one, but we have to torture the information out of them."

"At least we can do something about Barboar," I suggested.

His lips formed a tight line. "We might be able to banish Barboar before he possesses another body, provided I find someone who knows how to do it right."

Thinking of Barboar and his grenade strengthened my resolve. "Let's stop Barboar first. If he comes back, he'll tell the others where we live."

Tyler's hand squeezed mine. "Agreed."

I texted George. *Any luck finding an exorcist?*

It was nearly one in the morning, so I didn't expect a response. Perhaps that was why I nearly jumped out of my seat when the phone dinged with a response.

Exorcist, yes. Abyssal banishment, no. Will let you know more tomorrow.

It occurred to me that I knew two specialists where banishing demons was concerned. I flicked through my contacts and found the number to a cell phone my father had used only once. After the Exorcists had purged Tyler, my parents revealed to me they'd used a soulstone to keep Tyler's soul from entering the rift to Haedaemos.

They'd taken Tyler and me to his condo and left us there, warning me to be careful so as not to draw the attention of the Exorcists.

I hoped this phone call wouldn't do that very thing.

The phone rang continuously and never went to voicemail. I redialed, but got the same response. "I guess my father doesn't have his cell phone anymore."

"Do you really think your parents would help us?"

I stared forlornly at my phone. "Maybe. At the very least they could point us in the right direction."

Tyler's hand tightened on my leg. "Don't worry. We'll figure this out."

I released an exasperated sigh. "I wish I felt as confident as you. Just knowing that one of your former pals could slip into your condo at any moment and kill us all isn't very reassuring."

He steered around the backside of the Gregorian and toward the parking garage. His gaze flicked to a dark sedan parked near the front of the guest parking lot. I followed his gaze and barely made out a shadowy figure in the car.

Tyler pulled into the garage and parked. "I'm almost positive that was Detective Long in that car."

I glanced back though there was no way I could see the guest parking lot. "Why would he be parked out there?"

"Maybe he's still looking into the gunshots." Tyler shrugged and got out, came around and opened my door for me. "Just what we need—cops and demons spying on us." He blew out a breath. "Maybe we should move temporarily."

"We could live in my flat," I suggested.

Tyler chuckled. "Won't it be a bit small with Isabel and Jack there?"

"I think she's been staying with him a lot." It suddenly occurred to me that Isabel and I might not be flat mates for much longer, provided our relationships went well. It was a bittersweet realization.

"I'm not certain your apartment is entirely safe either." He shifted the car into park, got out, and walked around to open my door.

"What do you mean?" I asked when he helped me out. "They don't know where I live."

"I don't exactly publicize where I live, but Barboar still found me." Tyler led me to the lift and pressed the button. "I'm worried that he and the others might know about you."

Horror stabbed me in the stomach. "What if they know and went while Isabel was there?" I took out my phone and punched in a quick text to my friend. *Don't go back to the apartment. Might be dangerous.*

I received no response, but assumed it was because she and Jack were blissfully asleep.

"I texted Joe and told him to have the security team watch this place."

That made me feel marginally better. "I still want to know how Barboar got into your condo."

Tyler nodded. "I'll have my people look around for clues tomorrow."

My feet ached from the high heels, and my skin crawled with the imaginary cooties I'd picked up from the sordid places we'd visited tonight. I wanted a hot shower and the warmth of Tyler's body against me as we drifted to sleep.

I announced my grand plan to him, and he quickly accepted.

Tyler left early the next morning for meetings with managers of his other companies as he traced what few breadcrumbs there were back to the source of his business troubles. Since two of his companies were in Charlotte, he chartered a jet.

Joe picked me up in front of the Gregorian. "Good morning, Miss Glass." He opened the back door.

"I'd like to sit in front, please."

"Sure." He opened the front door and went to the driver's side.

"Could you take me by my flat first? I need to pick up some clothes." I checked my phone for any messages from Isabel and tried not to worry at the lack of her response. I texted her again. *Are you getting my messages?*

"Is something the matter, Miss Glass?" Joe regarded me with a discerning gaze.

"Not really. I just haven't heard from Isabel today."

"Mr. Rock told me about the break-in at the condo." He stopped in front of the apartment complex. "Are you worried about the same thing happening here?"

"You're rather perceptive, aren't you?"

"That was how I survived the war." He turned off the SUV, got out, and opened my door. "I'll accompany you."

"That's really not necessary."

He ran a hand across his head. "I think it would be best."

Better safe than sorry. "Thanks."

Joe nodded. "No problem."

I jogged inside, thankful I'd worn flats, and we took the lift to my floor. I practically sprinted down the hall to the door, key in hand. It took only a cursory examination of the door handle to realize someone had forced open the door.

Joe knelt in front of it and ran his finger along the bent metal doorjamb. "Looks like they jimmied it open with a crowbar."

I twisted the knob. It turned easily—too easily. The inner mechanisms felt broken. The door opened and my heart froze with terror. The den and kitchen had been absolutely trashed. Empty cabinets hung open and all the glassware and food had been smashed and strewn all over the floor. But what truly terrified me were the crimson stains all over the carpet and the upended furniture.

The copper odor of blood filled my nostrils.

"You'd better wait here while I investigate," Joe said.

"Isabel," I croaked. Without another thought, I ran inside, Joe calling out to me to stop.

But I didn't. I couldn't. My best friend might be dead.

I checked her bedroom. It looked completely untouched, aside from some dirty clothes in the corner of the room.

My room was another story. Though nothing had been moved, a crimson pattern stained the duvet, and spattered blood streaked down the wall. I wanted to scream in sorrow and anger and horror. What had happened here?

"Shit." Joe's voice came from the hallway.

I ran to him and saw him staring at the bathtub. It was filled with blood. A blood-crusted arm dangled over the side.

A terrible scream burst from my mouth. I lunged for the tub, but Joe grabbed me.

"You can't touch it, Miss Glass. We have to call the police."

My screams drowned out whatever he said next.

He practically dragged me to the hallway and called the police. Already, other neighbors crowded the hallway, talking among themselves. I didn't know any of them.

"What happened, dear?" asked an older woman.

"We're waiting on the police," Joe said.

Another person's voice reached my ear. "Did she murder someone?"

The authorities arrived and made everyone go back into their apartments.

Agonizing sorrow held me tight in its grip. I couldn't think straight and found it difficult to answer questions a detective asked me. "Isabel," I said in a weak voice. "Please not Isabel."

"There are two bodies in there," I heard one of the blue uniforms say. "Literally a bloodbath."

"Christ Almighty." The second man shuddered. "What a world we live in."

I almost passed out when his words registered with me.

Jack and Isabel were dead.

Chapter 10

An interminable time later, a man in khakis and a polo knelt in front of me. His nametag identified him as Dudley Morgan, a lab technician. He looked back at the blue uniforms as if seeing if they were listening and turned to me.

"I just want you to know that we identified the bodies as Pat and Beth Reynolds, your next-door neighbors."

A terrible weight lifted from my chest. "It's not Jack and Isabel?"

He shook his head. "I'm not supposed to be telling you this, because of the investigation, but it looks like someone broke into your apartment and made a lot of noise. When your neighbors came to investigate, the intruder killed them."

"Why are you telling me?"

Dudley gave me a conspiratorial look. "I help George clean up messes from time to time."

Joe walked up behind Dudley, a frustrated look on his face. "I can't get a straight answer out of anyone, Miss Glass."

Dudley stood. "We'll get to the bottom of this, Miss Glass."

"Thank you so much." I was still soundly shaken and nauseous. Bitter sorrow clung to my soul as I thought about my poor neighbors. Barboar must have come to my place first while looking for Tyler. I'd left a note on the fridge with Tyler's address some time ago in case Isabel needed it. I'd been so shocked by the sight of blood, I hadn't even thought about it.

I looked at my phone and saw a text I'd meant to send to Tyler. *Jack and Isabel are dead.* I apparently hadn't hit the send button. I erased the text and sent him a longer one with details about the apartment break-in.

I'm cancelling my meetings and coming straight home. Tyler replied.

No! Barboar did this before he came to your place. I'm safe. You need to find out who's behind the business problems. I'm going to work. Or at least I planned to once the police told me I could.

There was a long pause before his next text. *Fine, but let me know at the first sign of trouble. Love you.*

A familiar figure exited. "We meet again, Miss Glass." Detective Long seemed awfully pleased with himself. "Where you were yesterday?"

Joe put himself between us. "Hasn't she been through enough today without an interrogation?"

He gave Joe a pointed look. "I need to ask her a few questions before she's free to go."

I tucked my phone in my purse and took a deep breath. "I stayed at my boyfriend's condo the night before and went to work all day. After work, he and I went for drinks with friends."

He jotted something on a notepad. "I suppose they can corroborate that?"

"Surely you don't think I committed this gruesome crime?"

"You tracked bloody footprints all over a crime scene, Miss Glass." His upper lip curled. "Either you had something to do with it, or you completely polluted the evidence by tromping inside."

My other emotions vanished in a flare of anger. "I thought my friend was in there!"

His eyes narrowed. "How well do you know Pat and Beth Reynolds?"

I decided to play stupid since Dudley shouldn't have told me anything. I pinched my brow. "Not at all. Who are they?"

"Have you noticed any suspicious activity on your premises before? Do you have any enemies? Where were you last night? Does Tyler Rock know Pat and Beth Reynolds?" He rained question after question on me for nearly an hour while Joe stood by and watched helplessly.

I played ignorant about everything. I couldn't simply tell him about Barboar or Tyler's other enemies. When he asked me for the names of people who could corroborate my whereabouts on the day in question, I gave him Jack, Isabel, and Tyler's.

He tapped a pen to his lips. "You can go, but—"

"Don't leave town?" I said sweetly.

His face darkened. "Don't get smart with me, Miss Glass. I can make things difficult for you during the investigation whether you're guilty or not."

Joe sprang off the wall. "Is that a threat?"

Detective Long raised an eyebrow and looked at the taller man. "I do what it takes to make someone cooperate." He turned and went back inside the apartment.

"Asshole." Joe flinched. "I'm sorry, Miss Glass, it was unprofessional of me to say that."

I touched his arm. "He is an asshole Joe. I think being truthful and forthright is very professional."

He blew out a breath. "Would you like me to take you home?"

"No, I'd much prefer to go to work."

The moment I entered the lobby at work, I went to the programming department, found Jack, and motioned him aside. "Why hasn't Isabel answered my texts today?"

Jack blinked. "Why hello to you too, Emily."

I huffed. "This is a serious question."

"She left her phone at my place." He shrugged. "I noticed it when I was leaving."

Even though I knew Isabel wasn't dead, I still sagged with relief and leaned against the wall for support. "There's been an incident."

Jack's face went white. "Is Isabel okay?"

I waved away his concern. "Yes, she's fine. Our apartment, on the other hand, is uninhabitable."

He frowned. "Water damage?"

"If only." I told him what I'd found. By the time I finished, Jack was the one leaning on the wall for support.

"Holy shit, Em." He stared in horror at me. "What if we'd been there?"

"I don't even want to think about it." I took a moment to calm the churning in my stomach and to figure out what I should tell Jack. I decided it was best not to tie it to Tyler.

"Do the cops know why this happened?"

I shook my head. "No." That much was true.

Jack ran a shaking hand through his hair. "I gotta go see Isabel right now." He looked up. "Is that okay?"

"I'm not your boss."

Demonicus

"Yeah, well, Tyler is." He didn't need to qualify the statement further.

"Sure. I'll cover for you." I gripped his hands. "Hug her for me too, okay?"

He pressed the heels of his hands into red eyes. "I will."

I walked him to the lift. Sandra raised an eyebrow but said nothing as he left. I went to check in with Kevin, but he was out meeting with clients. Since I was officially the assistant to Kevin and Jack, their absences left me with very little to do. I knew I should do something productive, but my late night combined with the horrific morning left me feeling drained. I walked down the back hall and sneaked into the stairwell so I could sit down and rest my eyes a moment. I walked down a couple of flights of stairs and sat on the floor in a most unladylike manner. My office would have been far more preferable, but it lacked privacy. The last thing I wanted was for the others to see me napping on the job.

The thud of a closing door echoed down the stairwell a moment after I closed my eyes. I remained still, listening closely for someone descending. Instead, I heard voices speaking in half whispers.

"They're both out. Can you install the software?"

"Yeah, I need you to watch the hallway outside Kevin's office, then we'll move to Jack's."

"Not a problem." A pause. "What about the bitch?"

"She's not in either. I walked around the office and didn't see her. It's the perfect time to do this." His whisper broke into a full voice that I instantly recognized. I knew who the other person was by association.

Thomas Jones and George Hinkle.

When I'd first met Thomas, I'd fallen for him fast, primarily because he was possessed by Tyler at the time. Without my wonderful demon controlling him, Thomas Jones was a complete ass. Hinkle, the former head of the programming department, was nearly his twin brother, at least in spirit. They'd been profoundly displeased with the change in management, and with their demotions.

I'd wanted to fire them, but Tyler believed in giving everyone a second chance. His instincts were wrong with these two.

I almost marched up the stairs to confront them, but instantly thought better of it. It sounded like they planned to install malicious

85

software on Jack and Kevin's computers, but I didn't know more than that.

"This is gonna make us rich and bankrupt that stupid bitch and her boyfriend at the same time," Jones said.

"Let's do this now," Hinkle said. "I don't know how much time we have."

My face grew hot at Jones's words, but I knew it'd be better to find out what they were doing before making accusations. The stairwell door clicked open and shut again. I took off my flats and ran barefooted up the stairs. I peeked through the door and saw the pair turn the corner in the back hall toward Kevin's office.

I crept to the corner and peeked around it. Jones leaned casually against a wall in the corridor, facing toward the other end of the hall. I didn't see a way to spy on Hinkle, so I turned around and went to Jack's office. The programming department was nearly empty since it was lunchtime, offering an easy opportunity for Jones and Hinkle to do what they needed to do.

I searched high and low for a hiding place, but there was nowhere to conceal myself. I examined the webcam on Jack's monitor, but didn't know how I could activate it without Hinkle realizing it was on. It then occurred to me that I had the perfect spy device. I took out my phone, turned on its video recording feature, and propped it on a shelf behind and to the side of the computer monitor. From that angle and height, it should have a good view of Hinkle's activities.

I quickly left the office and hid inside one of the cubicles near the back of the room. I could peer over the edge of the divider and have a clear view of Jack's office through the open door. Moments later, Jones and Hinkle came around the corner from the back hallway with furtive looks on their faces. I resisted the urge to hurl a stapler at Jones as he took up a position outside Jack's office.

Jones's attempts to act casual as he kept lookout were almost comical. He twitched from side to side like a nervous cat and finally had the sense to walk to the corner where he could look down the highly trafficked hallway from the lift and the break room.

Janet exited the break room. Jones flinched and looked ready to make a run for Hinkle when Janet appeared to have second thoughts about going back to her desk and went back inside the room, probably for a doughnut or two.

Hinkle, meanwhile, tapped on the keyboard of Jack's computer. I didn't know how the man was accessing the computer without a password. He might be a right arse, but he knew his way around a computer. For all I knew, he'd written a program specifically for the scheme he and Jones had hatched. A moment later, he pocketed something that looked like a jump drive and left Jack's office, a smug look on his face.

Jones nearly jumped through the ceiling when Hinkle tapped him on the shoulder. He jerked a thumb over his shoulder and the pair vanished into the back hallway.

I dashed into Jack's office and picked up my phone. The computer monitor displayed the login screen and didn't look as if anyone had tampered with it. I went back to my office, closed the door and the blinds, and played the recorded video.

In the recording, Hinkle slid a jump drive into a port on Jack's computer and powered it off. When it restarted, lines of text ran across the screen for several seconds. The login screen appeared for an instant before changing to the desktop. Hinkle clicked on skull-shaped icon with the mouse, and a black window appeared with more lines of text in it. When he was done, he restarted the computer again, took the jump drive, and left.

I still don't know what he did.

Presumably, the Hinkle had installed spyware so, as Jones had said in the stairwell, they would become rich. They could steal all the source code for the software from Jack's computer, and download other valuable market information from Kevin's workstation. For a moment, I considered the possibility that these two were the saboteurs after Tyler's other companies.

While Jones and Hinkle were obviously devious and determined, I didn't see how they could possibly be the root cause for the other issues. For one, they couldn't afford to hire employees from the other companies, nor could they be the ones running Trax. A more likely possibility existed—they were moles for the other corporation. Finding disaffected employees and hiring them to undermine a company was nothing new. Jones and Hinkle fit the profile perfectly.

Well, two can play at that game.

I waited until the lunch rush was over and enjoyed a meal in solitude. My phone chimed several times in a row with texts from Isabel.

OMG I'm so sorry I missed your texts! I'm fine boo! Love you girl!

I couldn't help but be a bit angry with her even though it wasn't her fault. *Don't you ever forget your phone again, missy!*

Jack returned half an hour later, a smirk on his face.

"Well, someone got lucky." I meant it as a joke, but Jack winked.

"Nothing like some afternoon delight."

"Yes, well I have some afternoon discontent for you as well." I took him back to my office and closed the door.

Jack sat on the edge of my desk. "What happened while I was gone?"

"It appears Hinkle and Jones are working against our best interests." I showed him the video.

Jack's fist clenched with white-knuckled intensity. "That piece of shit. I'm going to push his face into a toilet bowl until he drowns."

"Not with these water-efficient commodes," I replied dryly. "Can you identify the program he installed on your computer?"

He looked at the phone for a moment. "Can I upload the video to your computer? I don't dare do it on mine."

"Of course." I got up and let him do what he needed.

It didn't take him long to upload the video. With my large high-resolution monitor, we were able to make out some of the text, though it did nothing to help me identify it.

"Hah, just what I thought." Jack pushed back from the desk. "He downloaded a program to exploit holes in the computer security, and then installed a canned spy application to my computer."

"Canned?" I asked.

"He purchased the software." Jack pshawed. "When he was our pit boss, he didn't do a lick of programming. Hell, when I checked his workstation after Tyler put me in charge, I recovered his deleted browser history and found he'd spent most his time browsing porn and watching cat videos."

I chuckled. "I don't suppose the internet is good for much else."

"Yeah, not really." Jack pursed his lips. "I think we need to fight fire with fire."

"Are you going to hack his computer?"

He shook his head. "No, I don't think there's anything worth knowing on his computer. We need to install spyware on Hinkle and Jones's mobile phones."

"How will we accomplish that?"

"Wish I knew. I don't program apps for phones." Jack frowned. "Guess it's time I learned."

"That could take months." This swiftly mounting crisis might upend the company in far less time.

Chapter 11

Jack and I conjured a few more ideas to combat information theft. Kevin returned from his sales meetings and we informed him about everything. Like Jack, he was ready to throw the traitors out a window.

When he'd calmed down, Kevin came up with a wonderful idea. "We should put fake software on Jack's computer so if they steal it, it won't do them any good."

"That's an excellent idea." Jack took over my computer once again and began moving files. "Since I'm moving things across the network from a different computer, the spy program on my computer won't record it."

"It only records information when you're physically using the workstation?" Kevin asked.

Jack nodded. "I'm going to introduce a few bugs into the source code of our latest products along with some spyware of our own. That way whoever steals it will be infecting their computer at the same time."

"Brilliant!" I leaned over Jack's shoulder and watched him work. It didn't take long for me to grow bored. "How long will it take to do this?"

"A few hours at least." He gave me an apologetic look. "You don't mind if I use your computer, do you?"

I shook my head. "Not at all."

"I'll see what I can do to get Jones's cell phone. Maybe we can put some spyware on it." Kevin stood up. "Let me know if there's anything else I can do to help. Since my computer is probably bugged, I might be able to put some fake sales reports on there."

"Thanks, Kevin." I checked the time and noticed it was nearly five. The day had flown by. "Use my computer as long as you need," I told Jack. "I'm going to head home."

He looked at his phone. "I'm almost done for now. I promised Isabel we'd go by your apartment to pick up more of her things, if the cops let us in."

I shook my head. "Look, if she needs any essentials, she should buy them. I don't want her anywhere near that place until it's deemed safe."

He shuddered. "From the way you described the scene, it sounds like someone tried to summon a demon with a blood ritual."

My eyes flared with surprise.

He apparently took my expression for disgust. "Sorry, I'm a huge nerd when it comes to paranormal and freaky stuff."

"Well, this certainly tops the freaky list."

Tyler arrived home soon after Joe dropped me off. He squeezed me in a tight hug the moment he saw me. "God, Em. I can't believe what happened at your apartment."

I melted in his embrace and said nothing for a while. Unfortunately, we had all too much unpleasantness to discuss.

"Let's get out of the house for dinner tonight," he suggested.

I kissed his cheek. "That sounds wonderful."

Tyler took me out to a great hamburger place in the Highlands. After my first sip of beer, I felt ready to unload the day's events on him, starting with Hinkle and Jones.

"I'm not surprised." He popped a tater tot in his mouth and chewed.

I paused with the beer bottle at my lips. "You're not? Then why the bloody hell didn't you fire them a long time ago?"

"I didn't have a good reason." He ate another tot. "Now I do."

"Can you wait until after we've spied on them a while?"

He nodded. "I like your counterintelligence plan. If we're lucky, it'll lead us up the ladder to the culprits."

"Do you still think your demon friends are the ones behind this?"

"They're high on my list." Tyler picked at the label on his beer bottle. "I'm still figuring out how to find the others."

"If we'd been smart about it, we could have followed Eyja back to them."

He snapped his fingers. "That's it. We have her true name. That means someone with skills might be able to track her."

A man in a hat and dark glasses slid into the seat next to me. "That's correct, Mr. Rock."

I nearly jumped out of my chair. Fortunately, I recovered my wits and realized my father, ridiculous as he looked, had just unexpectedly showed up. I lowered my voice. "Dad, what are you doing here?"

"You called, angel, so I came." He took one of my tater tots and ate it.

I challenged him with an eyebrow. "You didn't answer the phone."

"You're the only person who has the number, and I knew you wouldn't call unless it was urgent."

"Is everything okay?" Tyler asked him. "You look tense."

Dad looked around the dining area and took off his sunglasses. "There is a rift in the Exorcists. A man by the name of Albert Montjoy convinced a majority of our people that the Divinity has a higher purpose for them." A frown dragged down the corners of his mouth. "They are hunting those who refused to follow."

"Hunting?" My voice rose a little higher than intended.

Dad sighed. "I'm afraid so. Thankfully, your mother and I saw this coming months ago and were prepared."

"When I rescued Tyler from your former friends, I overheard someone talking about a person named Daelissa." I watched his face for a reaction.

He simply nodded. "She's supposedly the messenger of the Divinity, but I eavesdropped on her talking to Montjoy once, and am convinced she's the one in charge." Dad shuddered. "Not only is she insane, but she uses a form of magic I've never seen before."

"How so?" Tyler looked very interested.

I interrupted before the conversation veered off course. "I'm sorry to hear about your job, or whatever it was you had with them, but we have some demon problems we hope you can help us with."

Dad perked up, eyes alert. He held up a hand and twisted it. A moment later, another figure in a baseball cap and sunglasses sat down next to Tyler.

"Mum?" I had to admit she still looked lovely as ever, even in sports attire.

"Don't sound so shocked, dear." She lowered the sunglasses. "Clear?"

Dad nodded. "They were just about to explain why Emily called me."

Mum looked at me. "Very well, let's hear it."

"Well, hello to you, too, Mum." I blew out a breath. "One of Tyler's former acquaintances by the name of Barboar paid us a visit the other day." I told them the entire story.

When Dad heard the part about the apartment, his face darkened. "I'll do whatever is possible to send them back to Haedaemos."

"Yes," Mum said in a dry tone. "We can't have Tyler's childhood friends threatening you with grenades or murdering your neighbors."

I touched Dad's hand. "Actually, we want to banish them to the Abyss."

"That's impossible without their true names."

"I have two of them."

Dad stared blankly at me for a moment. "I don't know how you got them, but that's excellent." He paused. "Are you certain the names are accurate?"

I replayed the recording of the two names I'd learned.

"You've already spoken their true names?" Mum gave me a disbelieving look. "Demons can sense when their true name is spoken no matter where they are. You, of all people, should know to use caution when dabbling with dangerous creatures."

"I wasn't dabbling, Mum!" I spoke in a loud hiss, not eager to get into an argument with her in the middle of the restaurant.

Dad turned to Tyler. "They're lesser demons, correct?"

He nodded. "Yes."

"That gives us plenty of time, provided we can capture the ones in hosts right now."

"Can we take care of Barboar immediately?" I asked.

Dad waggled his hand. "It takes time to prepare for an Abyssal banishment. By the time we're ready for Barboar, he might be back in another host. In order to banish the others, we first need to exorcise them and send their spirits to Haedaemos."

I nodded eagerly. "You can do that?"

"Yes, dear," Mum said. "But we need to use the arch at the Church of the Divinity."

"You can't just tie them to a bed and do it the old-fashioned way?"

"Hardly." Mum tsked. "Emily, you don't even know enough to separate fact from fantasy in the supernatural world. Have you been to an orientation yet?"

I didn't want to answer her question. "Fine, let's use the arch in the church." The last time I'd been there had been a nightmarish attempt to rescue Tyler from the Exorcists and I wasn't eager to return.

Dad destroyed what little hope I had right away. "Montjoy controls the church."

"We'd have to infiltrate the church when it's not in use," Mum added. "A most difficult task."

"Why not just kill the host bodies?" Tyler said. "Or use their patterns?"

"I don't remember the exact patterns," I said.

"I find it hard to believe you remember such complex names so precisely, and cannot recall the accompanying patterns." Mum shook her head slowly. "You need to train your mind, Emily. This world is harsh and deadly—nothing like the fantasyland you grew up in."

"Fantasyland?" I sputtered for some sort of comeback, but my life had been pretty easy for the most part, at least until Peter. Everything about the Overworld, however, made that pale in comparison. "I'm trying to learn, Mum."

"Emily, you are a grown woman." Mum reached across the table and gripped my hands. "As such, you need to stop speaking to us like you're a child."

I almost jerked my hands free. "What are you talking about?"

"Only a little girl still calls her parents *Mummy* and *Daddy*." She said the endearments in a contemptuous tone. "Now, back to the matter at hand—we don't have their patterns, so the only course of action is to kill the hosts and use their true names for a banishment."

I was still too stung by her words to respond.

Tyler's hand gripped my leg. "If we capture them, Emily can get their patterns again." He gave Mum—Victoria—a steady look. "She's pretty amazing."

My father, Patrick, looked from Victoria to me. "I suppose that will work."

"I'll have to draw the pattern," I said. "Judging from the complexity of the ones in the demonicus, it'll probably take me hours."

Victoria's eyes snapped toward me. "Demonicus? Where?"

It occurred to me we hadn't mentioned the Custodian investigation.

Tyler beat me with an answer. "Yes, someone inscribed a massive demonomicus, complete with soul offerings and everything needed to allow a greater demon into this world."

"Why didn't you mention this earlier?" Victoria stood. "We need to see the demonicus."

"It would seem things are worse than I thought." Patrick popped the remaining tater tots from my tray into his mouth. "Let's go."

"Now?" I asked.

He nodded grimly. "*Now*." Once outside, Patrick pointed to a black sedan that resembled the ones I'd seen in the Templar compound. "I'll drive."

Tyler walked over to Joe where he sat in the SUV and talked to him for a moment. Then he came over and climbed into the back seat of the sedan.

I gave Patrick the address. He took out his phone and put it in a notch on the dashboard, then spoke the address. The phone's GPS drew him a route, and he took off.

"Can this car fly?" I asked.

"I'm afraid this one is limited to ground travel." He patted the dash. "On the upside, it's aether powered, so it doesn't need gas."

Victoria turned around in her seat. "How did you discover this demonicus?"

I'd never told my parents about my side job, primarily because they'd vanished soon after helping me rescue Tyler. *Now is as good a time as any.* "I'm working with the Custodians."

Patrick hissed in a breath. "You're doing what?"

"Yes, I've been working with them ever since I met Tyler." I repressed a groan. "I'm only doing it part time, though."

"Perhaps," Victoria said in a condescending voice, "but part-time can get you permanently killed."

"They're very protective of me." I crossed my arms and glared back at her. "And I get to do something to help people."

"You're untrained, ignorant of dangers, and have only a marginal skill at detecting supernatural entities." Victoria tutted. "You should leave this sort of work to the professionals."

My face turned red hot and it took everything I had not to call my mother a bitch right then and there. *She'll never change.* She'd always been harsh on my brother, Phillip, and me. He was still going to university at Oxford and very rarely heard from them, according to him. "We're not all perfect like you, *Victoria*." I sometimes wished her twin sister, Lydia, had been my mother. She was meek and sweet—the polar opposite of this ice queen.

"I never proclaimed to be perfect, dear." She seemed not the least bit irked by my tone. "But if you plan to be the Custodian's supernatural detector, you should be able to protect yourself."

"She can do more than detect," Tyler said. "She literally ripped the vampirism from a vampire and made him mortal again. She saw the patterns and true names of those demons."

Victoria raised an eyebrow. "Can you take a demon spirit from a mortal body?"

I shrugged. "My abilities are still something of a mystery to me."

Patrick glanced back at Tyler. "You and I need to have a talk about the danger you're putting my daughter into."

I gripped my father's arm. "Are you serious? It's *my* decision to work with the Custodians. It's *my* decision to help Tyler track down the true names of Barboar and the others. Not his. Not yours."

Tyler smirked. "In case you hadn't noticed, Emily doesn't always listen to my suggestions."

I looked at Victoria. "Not unlike someone else in this car."

She raised an eyebrow, but offered no retort.

We reached the offices of Tri-Cross Blood Donations and parked in front of the dark and foreboding building. I waited for Tyler and Patrick to lead the way. Police tape and chains barred the door. My father retrieved a pair of bolt cutters from the trunk of the car and made short work of the padlock.

The warm emanations I'd felt during my first visit to this building were absent. Victoria tossed a glowing sphere into the air to light our way into the back warehouse. Once we reached the wide open space,

Patrick turned on the lights and surveyed the charred patterns etched into the concrete floor.

"Wow." He scratched his chin. "I've heard about demonicus, but never saw one." He retrieved the glowing ball and snuffed it before putting it into his pocket. "Give us a few minutes to make sense of it." He and Victoria knelt next to one of the smaller patterns in the outer ring.

I walked in the opposite direction so I could cool off after the "conversation" with Victoria. The soulless bodies were gone, presumably taken by the Custodians. As I looked down at one of the patterns, an identical image flashed before my eyes and a name echoed in my mind. I staggered and stared at it a moment longer.

Tyler was at my side in an instant. "What's wrong, Em?"

I pointed to the pattern. "That's Barboar's pattern. I knew it the instant I saw it."

Tyler motioned my parents over. "Over here, please."

The pair looked up from the middle pattern and walked over.

"What is it," Victoria asked.

"I recognize this pattern," I replied. "It's Barboar's."

My father took out his phone and snapped a picture, then labeled it with the name. "Recognize any others?"

I walked the perimeter but didn't find any others. I looked at Tyler. "I guess Eyja was being truthful about not being here with the others."

"Well, we've got that going for us," Tyler said.

Patrick stopped at each pattern and took a picture. "I'll record the rest of these in case you happen to sense more."

Taking out my phone, I followed his example and also took pictures.

"The big one in the middle poses a problem," my father said. "I need an overhead shot to make sure I have the angles perfect."

Tyler pointed to a set of stairs leading up a catwalk and to an office on the far wall. "I could reach the metal rafters and shimmy out to the middle. That should do the trick."

Patrick handed him his phone. "Sounds like a plan."

I gave him my phone as well. "Don't break your neck."

He pecked me on the cheek. "Wouldn't dream of it."

The rest of us stepped outside the large pattern in the middle and watched Tyler climb the stairs and use the catwalk railing to reach the metal beam overhead. Biceps bulging, he easily swung himself hand-over-hand along the length of the rafter and positioned himself directly above the large diagram. Clenching his legs against the ridges, he hung upside down. His hair gel defied gravity, making him look like a suave secret agent homing in on secret documents.

A little sigh escaped my mouth as I watched his supple body work.

My father groaned. "Enjoying your eye candy?"

I chuckled. "He is rather pleasing to the eye."

Victoria raised an eyebrow, but made no other comment.

Dust sprinkled down from the rafters. Tyler sneezed, and I feared it might dislodge him. He winked at my look of alarm and retrieved the phones from his pocket. Using each one in turn, he snapped the pictures and made his way back to the catwalk.

"Here you go." He handed back our phones then dusted his pants.

Dad looked at the picture and grunted. "Excellent. I'll run these against our database and see if any match what we have in our records."

"What do you think the demonicus was for?" I asked.

"To summon a greater demon," Victoria said. "The outer patterns are for the lesser demons to occupy their hosts. Once completed, they create a circuit, which allows a greater order of demons, possibly knights, to enter their hosts. The middle would be reserved for another of much higher magnitude."

"Possibly even a demon lord," Patrick said. "Whoever it was devoured the souls of those people bound in the middle, though I'm not sure why they were tied up."

"Yes, the process must be entirely voluntary," Victoria said. "It is perplexing."

I drew upon my limited knowledge of demon summoning. "I didn't think demons could leave their patterns when they were summoned."

"That is true of normal summonings," Victoria said. "A demonicus is not used to summon demons for temporary use, but to give them corporeal form so they can live in this realm on their own."

"It's a whole new ball game," Tyler added.

"Fools who are absolutely willing to give up their soul to a demon are, fortunately, rare." Victoria tapped a finger to her chin. "If someone changes their mind, they are no longer willing, and thus immune."

"Is it the same for possession?" I asked.

Patrick shook his head. "There's a much lower threshold for that."

I knelt and examined the crimson stains at the outer edge of the burn marks. "Why is there blood?"

"Probably to strengthen the circuity," Patrick said. "They apparently used something to etch the pattern into the concrete and then outlined it in blood. I don't know if it was a necessity, or just being overly cautious."

"Losing control of such a large summoning would be disastrous," Victoria said.

"How many soulless bodies were there?" Patrick asked.

"Thirteen," I replied. "One in each of the middle diagrams, and seven in the center."

"That's a lot of zealots," he said.

Victoria abruptly crumpled to her knees.

My father gripped her arm. "What's wrong?"

"Despair," she said in a rasping voice. "Foreboding."

He helped her to her feet and she leaned on his arm for support.

I didn't want to act concerned, but ice queen or not, she was still my mother. "Are you okay?"

"I think she just had a premonition," Patrick said.

I narrowed my eyes at them. "What's that supposed to mean?"

"You're able to sense supernaturals." Victoria patted Patrick's arm and stood upright, regaining her stiff posture. Sometimes I get a feeling about the future."

"You see the future?"

She shook her head. "No. Unfortunately, this ability is little more than a gauge about the tests that lay ahead. In this case, I have never felt such crippling despair." Her lower lip trembled, but she quickly stilled it.

We all turned and looked at the demonicus.

It was a harbinger of the horrors to come.

Chapter 12

I did a quick count of the circles in the pattern and calculated some troubling numbers. *Thirteen lessers, six greaters, one demon lord.* My mouth dropped open in horror. "Just how bad is a demon lord?"

"Bad enough." Patrick gritted his teeth. "This incursion couldn't have come at a more perfect time. With Montjoy leading the Exorcists, there's no one to counter these demons."

Tyler fingered the amulet at his neck that protected him from detection by the Exorcists. "Much as I want to avoid your organization, I'd have to agree with you." He tucked away the amulet. "The important question we need to ask is *why* the demons wanted to come here in the first place. They're not very good at cooperation unless someone more powerful is forcing them."

"Agreed." Victoria frowned. "There's little more to be gained by remaining here. I think Patrick and I need to research solutions."

"To this and our other problems." Patrick turned off the lights and reactivated the glowball to guide us outside to the car. "We still don't know what to do with ourselves now that we're without the Exorcists."

"The answer will come in time, Patrick." Victoria gave him a severe look before getting into the car.

The rest of us piled in.

"Maybe you could join the Custodians," I suggested. "I'm sure someone with your skills would be valuable."

Patrick nodded. "We've given it some thought. The Templars might take us in." His eyes caught on something off to the side of the road. He slowed and stopped.

"What is it?" I asked.

"Demons affect this world simply by being here." He got out of the car and held the glowball over a patch of yellowed grass.

The rest of us got out and looked. The grass was dying in a straight line as far back as I could see.

Tyler knelt. "Look at the insects."

That was the last thing I wanted to do, but I looked closer and saw dead earthworms and other bugs twitching or lying dead. "Demons caused this?"

Victoria spat on the ground. "A demon lord caused it."

Patrick nodded.

I looked across the road to a stretch of woods. "Why don't we just follow this trail all the way to the demons?"

"That might work for a while, but once we're further into the city"—Patrick scuffed a foot on the pavement—"there won't be enough vegetation to work with."

I hovered a hand over the dying grass, but my extra sense detected nothing. "Of course it couldn't be that easy."

We got back in the car and resumed travelling back into town.

My mind traveled in circles as it attempted to divine why so many demons had invaded our realm now, of all times. If the powers that be in Haedaemos were so interested in conquering Earth—Eden—why wait until now to do so? The religious part of me wanted to cling to old admonitions—*Humanity will pay the price for sin and iniquity.* The more informed part of me knew it had little to do with that.

With the Exorcists running off to do their own thing, all the vampire activity the Templars were fighting, and now a demon incursion, it seemed the supernatural world was undergoing some sort of upheaval. That didn't bode well at all for us mere mortals. I thought of Tyler and my parents. The possibility of losing them sent a shock of pain into my stomach. I wanted to hug my mother and father right then, but thinking of Victoria's earlier words stung those emotions back into submission.

I wanted to talk to my parents like any child would, but Victoria began to speak to Patrick about people they could contact for more information regarding the demonicus, ignoring me.

I haven't seen her in months! I'd thought my mother had softened a little after her help with Tyler, but it was apparent that change had been short lived.

"Stop trying to do it on your own, and let the Custodians help," I said in a disgusted voice.

"We are quite capable—" Victoria started to say.

"I don't care how capable you are. You don't have the resources to pull this off." I leaned forward and met her eyes. "The Custodians do."

"We'll consider it," she said.

Patrick pulled into the semi-circular drive of the Gregorian. Everyone but my mother got out of the car. My father crushed me in a bear hug and whispered, "Despite what your mother says, I still like you calling me Dad." He kissed my cheek. "See you later, kiddo." He nodded at Tyler. "Keep her safe."

Tyler didn't hesitate with his reply. "Always."

"Goodbye, dear," Victoria said from inside the car. "We'll speak soon."

I didn't respond and went inside. It had been a long day, and I was ready for bed.

Calling George Walker was first on my list of priorities when I walked into work the next day, but Jack intercepted me on the way to my office.

"I finished putting the bugged software on my workstation," he said. "The only thing is, I don't know how I'm going to do any work."

"You could use my computer."

He shook his head. "If Hinkle sees me working over here, he'll suspect I know something is wrong with my workstation."

"Good point." I went into my office and dropped into the chair. "In other words, we need to find out what's going on quickly, before it kills productivity."

Jack took a seat on the other side of my desk. "I hope you don't mind, but I called a friend of mine to give the office a thorough sweep for bugs and surveillance equipment."

A chill touched my heart. "I hadn't even considered the possibility."

"It didn't occur to me at first either."

I leaned forward. "When is he coming?"

"Tonight after everyone leaves."

My eyes flicked around the room. I hadn't decorated the office much, but cameras and audio devices were easy to hide. "Well, if they've got them in my office, then we're already bolloxed."

"In this part of the world, we say 'screwed'." Jack smiled. "When the thought hit me, I took a good look in your office last night and didn't find anything. I think we're safe in here."

"Let's hope so."

"I downloaded some other tracing software we might be able to use to find out where the information is going." Jack took a jump drive from his shirt pocket. "I just need to put it on my computer and disguise it as new software."

I pushed away from my desk. "Well, if you need to use my computer for that, go ahead." I walked to the door. "I need to make an important phone call."

Jack was already sitting down as I left. "This won't take long."

Jack's suspicions ignited my paranoia, so I took the lift down to the lobby and made my phone call from there.

George answered on the first ring. "I'm sorry it's taken me some time to get back to you, Miss Glass, but we've been swamped. There was an attack on a Templar convoy in Bogota, Colombia, and we've had to devote considerable resources to cleaning it up."

"An attack in Colombia?" It reminded me of Franco, the weapons dealing vampire.

"Vampires aided by battle mages. They nearly killed Thomas Borathen and abducted Justin Slade." He yawned. "Pardon me, I haven't had a chance to sleep."

I revisited my thoughts from last night. *Major upheaval in the supernatural world.* "George, have there been many other attacks like this recently?"

"There have been other unrelated incidents, yes."

"Are incidents like this common?"

He paused. "No, not at all. Most of the time we have to cover up accidental supernatural exposure, but nothing as intentional as this."

"I think these events might be related." I wasn't sure why I felt so certain. "The Exorcists have started following a new leader named Albert Montjoy, causing a large split in their faction."

"I wasn't aware of this. Then again, the Exorcists broke from the Templars a long time ago." He paused. "Was there something else?"

"Yes, the huge demon summoning." I wished he were in front of me instead of on the phone. "Surely it's no coincidence that happened right after the Exorcists decided to follow Montjoy and Daelissa."

George's voice grew very serious. "Did you just say Daelissa?"

"Yes. I think I pronounced it correctly."

"I will be back in Atlanta tomorrow evening. Let's not discuss this further over the phone."

"Okay, but wait." I said the words quickly so he wouldn't hang up. "Tyler and I want to do the orientation class. What do we need to do?"

"I will text you directions." I heard muffled conversation as he spoke to someone else. "Until tomorrow, Miss Glass." He ended the call.

I knew I should go back up to the office, but I felt agitated and restless. I could almost see a pattern to all this madness, but it eluded me like an itch between my shoulder blades. I walked down the street to a coffee shop, ordered a coffee and bagel sans the cream cheese. George's text blinked on my phone a moment later with a very strange address.

Phipps Plaza, lower parking deck, rear entrance, red parking zone, five PM today. Code word: cold gravy

A ritzy shopping mall seemed a bizarre place to hold a secret orientation about a supernatural society, but there were things about this strange Overworld I'd probably never understand. I hoped Tyler would be back in Atlanta in time to go. I sent him a text to which he quickly replied.

I'll be back by then. Will they be serving snacks? ;)

I snorted and responded. *I'm sure they'll have blood candy for vampires and cupcakes topped with soul frosting for demons, dear. :P*

I'm afraid cupcakes will ruin my figure.

I wanted to call him and hear his reassuring voice and almost sent him a text saying as much, but put down the phone and chewed on my bagel instead. Thoughts cluttered my mind, but I couldn't put them in any order that made sense. There was something afoot in the Overworld, but I simply lacked the knowledge to piece it together. I hoped George might make more sense of it all.

So lost in my thoughts was I, that I nearly bumped into Detective Long on his way out of the office tower.

"I've been looking for you," he said.

Fear made my heart jump. Was he here to arrest me? *Of course he isn't, you ninny!* I hadn't done anything wrong.

"I need to ask you some questions." He held a folder and briefcase in one and motioned to a nearby bench. We sat down.

Steeling myself, I nodded. "Go ahead."

"How was your relationship with your neighbors?"

"Non-existent." I'd occasionally seen my neighbors in the hallway, but hadn't said much other than a quick greeting on my way in or out.

"Can you elaborate?" he said.

"On what?" I looked at him for a moment. "I almost never spoke with them."

"Are you aware your neighbors filed noise complaints against you?"

"Why would they do that?" Isabel and I were always very quiet. "We never threw any parties or had guests."

He returned a dubious look. "According to the concierge at your apartment building, your neighbors reported you for excess noise on several occasions. The concierge also remembers you entering the building late one night, dripping wet and, to quote him, 'Obviously high on drugs, judging from her appearance.'" The detective paused as if to let his words sink in before he spoke again.

I didn't let him continue. "Firstly, we were never warned or told of any noise complaints, so the concierge must be confusing us with someone else. Secondly, I had an accident with a bottled water on the night I returned wet." It was a lie, of course. I'd doused myself with holy water after discovering Tyler's true nature. "How the concierge on duty that night could equate being wet to being high is simply beyond my comprehension." I resisted the urge to jab him in the chest with a finger as one might do with a saber during a fencing match. "Are you somehow implying that I murdered my neighbors because of a noise complaint?"

"Not precisely." He displayed a complaint form with my apartment complex's letterhead. "This is a report of an altercation between Tyler Rock and your neighbors, the Reynolds."

Mr. Rock pounded on the Reynold's door and yelled at them. He said they needed to leave his girlfriend alone or he'd kill them. They shouted a lot and Miss Glass had to pull him away.

I tried to take the document from him, but he tucked it back into the folder.

"Who wrote that?" I asked.

"One of your other neighbors."

"Which in particular?" I resisted the urge to snatch the folder from him. "It's an outright lie."

"I'll need a statement as to your whereabouts Saturday night."

My mind raced over recent events. *We found the demonicus Saturday, right?* Sunday had been Franco and Barboar. So much had happened in such a short period of time it was a big blur. I certainly couldn't tell him about what we'd really been doing, but coming up with an elaborate lie wouldn't do either. "We stayed in that night, if you must know."

He wrote that down. "I'll need a written statement from you and Mr. Rock."

"I can certainly write that down."

A smug look crossed his face. "What were you and Mr. Rock doing the night of the gunshot in his building?"

My heart went cold. *Is he somehow tying these events together?* I knew how they were related, but surely, he had no idea. He was desperately grasping at straws. "Oh, something quite dreadful—we were talking about what to eat for dinner."

"Isn't it true Mr. Rock has violent tendencies?"

I flinched at the sudden question. "Absolutely not."

"How many arguments did he have with your neighbors?"

"None!"

"Who fired the gun?"

I almost fumbled the answer. "I have no bloody idea and that's the last question I'm answering."

He tucked the folder into a briefcase. "Let's go up to Mr. Rock's office so I can get written statements from the two of you."

"Tyler isn't here."

He checked the time. "When do you expect him?"

"I'm not sure. He's out of town on business."

The detective looked around as if he were expecting something or someone and frowned. "The sooner he meets with me the better." It sounded almost like a threat. "Otherwise I might have to get a warrant to search his condominium."

Anger surged and I very nearly said something nasty. It then occurred to me that the detective's bizarre accusations might not be his fault. Suspicion replaced the anger. I opened my senses and took a good long look at Detective Long. Unfortunately, there seemed to be no supernatural influence on him I could detect. Then again, if he was under a spell, I might not be able to glimpse it.

I noticed a twitch in his eye as I stared him down, and a bead of sweat caught in the wrinkles of his forehead. If those weren't signs that he was nervous about something, I didn't know what was. I'd nearly overlooked that there might be a non-supernatural reason for his behavior.

"He and I don't have time for your games, Detective."

The detective picked up the folder and stood. "Then I suggest you ask him yourself. It will be much cleaner if I don't have to get a warrant. That could cause embarrassing publicity for Mr. Rock."

I remained sitting. "Who is putting you up to this, Detective?"

He stiffened. "Nobody puts me up to anything, Miss Glass. I'm doing my job." He leaned closer, a snarl curling his lip. "I want permission by tomorrow, or I'll bring a warrant with me next time."

"I'd be very surprised if you could get a warrant on such thin evidence."

He smirked. "Then expect to be surprised." He turned on his heel and marched to an illegally parked sedan.

The coffee must have perked up my presence of mind, because I had the sense to look into the vehicle to see if anyone else was with him. It was empty.

My phone chimed with a text message from Jack. *Go to a news website now!*

I did as he commanded. A photo of Tyler and me stood beneath a stunning headline: *Gruesome Murders at Home of Rock's Fiancé.*

Chapter 13

I immediately called Tyler and went to voicemail. Hands shaking, I read the story on my phone and then watched a live stream of Brandon Rock leaving a building and being mobbed by reporters.

"Mr. Rock, where is your brother?" One reporter asked. "Does he have any comment on the murders?"

A blood vessel stood out from Brandon's forehead and he wheeled on the reporter. "As I've told the countless reporters who have called me today, I have no comment on the matter."

A woman shouted a question above the noise. "Have police tied his fiancé to the murders?"

My stomach went ice cold.

Brandon gave her a look of disbelief. "What sort of wild accusation is that?"

The rest of the reporter mob grew quiet as they listened to the woman speak.

"According to witness statements, Tyler was seen threatening her neighbors after they complained about excessive noise from his fiancé's apartment." She smirked as if relishing the attention of the crowd. "These are the very same people who were found dismembered in her bathtub."

A troubled look passed over Brandon's face. "I've heard nothing of this." He looked around at the cameras. "I'm sure my brother had nothing to do with this. He's overcome his past problems and wouldn't jeopardize his future with such nonsense." Brandon nodded to some other men in suits around him and they cleared a path to a waiting limo. He briskly walked to it and climbed inside while the reporters continued shouting at him.

A reporter turned to face the camera. "It appears there may be more to this developing story than we first thought. Is it possible Tyler Rock and his fiancé are involved with these murders?"

The scene switched back to a studio where a man and woman behind a news desk debated several possibilities, all of which were completely absurd, the least of which was that I was engaged to Tyler. The noise of car doors opening and shutting took my attention from the phone.

Three news vans were parked at the curb. A reporter looked at a small mirror and applied fresh makeup while a man unpacked a large camera. Other news crews began to do the same. I might have stared longer if it didn't suddenly occur to me that they were here to see Tyler or me.

Thankful the bench was far enough from the entrance of the building to avoid being seen by the reporters, I got up and walked toward a nearby information kiosk. I hid behind it while the reporters set up an ambush for me. One reporter tried to go inside the building, but was quickly ushered out by security.

I called Jack. "I can't get back inside the building. There must be six reporting crews down here."

"Damn. Bad news travels fast." He clicked his tongue. "Maybe you should go back to Tyler's until this shit storm blows over."

"I don't think it will." I peered from behind the kiosk and wondered how long it would take for the reporters to give up and leave. "Besides, they're probably waiting at Tyler's place too."

"True." He blew out a breath. "I didn't know you and Tyler were engaged."

"We're not. They seem to be fabricating everything from the depths of their wildest dreams." Just thinking about it made me seethe. "Some woman claimed there were witness reports of Tyler threatening our neighbors after a noise complaint."

"Tyler's only been over to your place what, three or four times?" Jack said. "And I can't imagine him threatening anyone."

"Neither he nor I even spoke to any of my neighbors, much less threatened them." I turned and leaned against the kiosk. "The investigating detective just confronted me a moment ago with all sorts of absurd accusations."

"Something smells wrong with this entire situation." He made a thoughtful noise. "What if whoever wants to sabotage the company is doing the same thing to Tyler's image? I mean, if stockholders don't have faith in a CEO, the stock plummets and makes it easier to do a hostile takeover."

"The possibility occurred to me. I even checked for signs of—" I'd almost said something about demonic influence but caught myself at the last minute. "I mean, he seemed nervous. I wonder if someone is paying him to do this."

"There's a video clip with that woman you mentioned," Jack said. "It's the one where she told Brandon Rock that Tyler was seen threatening your neighbors." He sighed. "It's getting tons of views right now."

"What news organization was she with?" I asked.

"I'm checking."

I looked out at the reporters once again. A man on the other side of the kiosk looked up. Recognition lit his eyes and I belatedly saw the ID badge from the BBC hanging around his neck.

"Emily Glass?" He asked.

I nearly bolted like a startled deer, but another thought hit me. "What in the world is the BBC doing here?"

He seemed surprised by my question. "Are you Emily—"

"Again, I ask you, what is the BBC doing here?"

He chuckled. "Well, bit of a strange thing, but Emily Glass—you—are originally from England and we do report news from the U.S."

I stared at him for a moment. "I will give you and only you an interview if you can meet me around the corner."

"I'd be delighted."

"Good. Meet me there in five minutes." I turned and walked away, thoughts whirling in my mind. I heard a faint voice and realized I'd forgotten Jack was still on the line.

"Emily?"

"I'm still here. It looks as though I'll be giving the BBC an exclusive."

"Oh really?" he seemed excited. "I can't seem to find which organization that woman is with, but I found another video with reporters tossing questions at Tyler's sister, Arianna Rock. A man there asked her questions nearly identical to what the woman said."

"How very interesting."

"Yep. Reporters couldn't reach Cyrus Rock for comment, so I don't have any video of that." Keys tapped in the background. "I sent you links for the videos."

I reached the rendezvous corner and concealed myself lest other reporters come my way. "Keep searching for information on that man and woman. There's something dodgy about those two."

"I will divine the depths of their bolloxed dodginess."

I snorted. "That's not how you use those words, Jack."

"I'll get back to you soon. Good luck with the interview!" He disconnected.

A shock of panic raced through me as I realized I hadn't looked into a mirror to make sure I was presentable. Using my phone's selfie camera, I checked my makeup and made sure my eyebrows passed muster.

I peeked around the corner and saw the reporter coming my way with his cameraman. Much to my relief, no one else was following them. When they came around the corner, I put on my best smile and projected as much confidence as possible.

The reporter shook my hand. "I'm David Cornwall, and this is my cameraman Brent Wilkins."

Abandoning my forced American accent, I smiled and greeted him. "A pleasure, Mr. Cornwall and Mr. Wilkins. It's a pleasure hearing proper English."

The two men chuckled. "It can be rather trying on the soul, Miss Glass," David said. "Are you comfortable interviewing here, or should we adjourn somewhere else?"

"This will be quite all right, if Mr. Wilkins thinks the lighting is favorable," I replied.

"The lighting is splendid," Brent said. "I think it will do justice to your lovely features."

"You are too kind." I nearly shed a tear. "It's so wonderful to witness proper manners again."

David smiled. "Indeed, Miss Glass."

"Will this be live or recorded?" I asked.

"Our camera transmits to our van around the corner," Brent replied. "It will be live, but with a five second delay."

David motioned to Brent. "Ready when you are, Mr. Wilkins."

The cameraman counted down. "Three, two—" He held up one finger and then pointed it at David who stood in front of me. "Today we have the privilege of interviewing Miss Emily Glass, fiancé to millionaire Tyler Rock, and a former British citizen." He turned to me. "Miss Glass, there has been a storm of rumors surrounding the incident at your apartment, but we have yet to hear anything from you or Mr. Rock. Would you be so kind as to tell us the particulars?"

A surge of terror skittered through me as I imagined how many people were watching and I froze for an instant. *Don't do this now, you ninny!* Somehow, I managed to speak. "I'd be delighted." I forced my lips into a smile. "First, I should clarify that Tyler and I are not engaged. We're dating."

David smiled pleasantly. "Duly noted, Miss Glass."

His smile chased away some of my jitters and I was finally able to arrange my scattered thoughts. "It's one of many false rumors I've seen on the news today." I paused a second to let that sink in. "Joe and I went by my apartment to pick up some of my personal items. When we opened the door, we encountered a nightmare." I detailed the crime scene down to every remembered detail. "We immediately called the police, of course."

"What of the accounts claiming you and Tyler feuded with your neighbors?" David asked.

"In the few months I've lived here, I've never once met my neighbors aside from seeing them on occasion in the hallway. My roommate and I have never held a party, nor have we ever been up late at night shouting." I smiled. "Our wild nights consisted of eating Nutella with a spoon and talking about the day's events."

"So there is no truth to the claims that you were the subject of noise complaints, or that Mr. Rock threatened your neighbors?" David asked.

I shook my head. "Absolutely not. In fact, when I saw the interviews with Arianna and Brandon Rock, I immediately wondered where those news reporters had gotten such terrible information. When I tried to look up who they were, or which news organizations they represented, I couldn't find anything." Keeping my expression as pleasant as possible, I shook my head. "It's almost as if they were intentionally spreading malicious rumors."

"Interesting," David said. "We'll look into that as well, Miss Glass."

I considered broaching the subject of the issues Tyler was having with his companies and adding that this latest incident might be a part of a broader effort to financially damage him, but decided not to. I didn't want to sound like a conspiracy nutter.

"We here at the BBC want to thank you for this exclusive opportunity, Miss Glass," David said.

"The pleasure was mine," I said.

David turned to the camera. "This is David Cornwall, live from Atlanta, Georgia."

Brent made a cutting motion and lowered the camera.

I turned to David. "Will you really check into those videos I mentioned, Mr. Cornwall?"

"Absolutely. It wouldn't be the first time someone planted people in a mob of reporters." He tilted his head slightly. "Do you think someone might be doing this to financially harm Mr. Rock?"

I shrugged. "Bad PR would certainly be an effective weapon."

"Indeed." He shook my hand. "Perhaps you should hire a taxi, Miss Glass. I suspect other reporters will descend upon this place within minutes."

I nodded. "A good day to you both." I hailed a nearby taxi and instructed it to drop me at a Vietnamese restaurant down the road. Though I wasn't terribly hungry thanks to the bagel, I decided it was lunchtime anyway.

Tyler called me when I had a mouthful of noodles. I gulped and answered. "Have you heard?"

His voice was grim. "Yes. I've hired a PR firm to start damage control already. Any problems on your end?"

His mention of a PR firm made me feel uneasy. Not because I thought the firm might do a poor job, but because I'd just gone on live television and possibly said something counterproductive. "Um, nothing too bad, though a horde of reporters descended on the office today."

"I'd expect so."

"Yes, well, I hope I didn't bollox things up, but I gave an interview to the BBC." I winced in anticipation of his anger.

"What did you tell them?" Tension filled his voice.

I told him.

"Good. That's the same story we're going with."

I swirled the noodles in my bowl with a chopstick. "It's not a story. It's the truth." I stabbed a piece of meat. "Detective Long also visited me shortly before the media storm began. He made similar accusations to those I heard on the news—about you threatening the neighbors, and them reporting us for noise violations." I growled. "We know those are lies."

"Those may be lies, but public perception is easily molded by the media." He released a loud breath. "We might be able to push back, but damage has already been done. Stocks in companies I own have fallen across the board."

"Your former demon acquaintances must be determined to torture you in every way possible."

"Now I know why Barboar murdered your neighbors," Tyler said.

I almost agreed with him, but something about the demon angle didn't make sense to me. "If he intended to use those murders in a long-term plan to bring down your business empire, then why did he intend to kill us with a grenade?"

Tyler remained silent a moment. "You're right. I never knew Barboar or the others to be long-term planners. They were like little kids looking for instant gratification. That's what usually separates the lesser demons from the greater ones."

"It's possible Barboar committed the murders as part of a long-term plan, but couldn't resist the temptation to kill you when he had the chance."

"Possibly," Tyler said. "Another demon might have commanded him to follow a more complex plan, but why would my financial destruction be of any interest to a greater demon?"

"We've been so involved in the supernatural world that we haven't even considered more mundane miscreants." It didn't take much imagination to name two of them. "Brandon and Arianna would both benefit from destroying you financially."

"And both of them are capable of masterminding such a devious plan." He grunted. "I think the murders just happened to play right into their hands. In cases like this, the police don't usually release all the information to the public."

I pounced on the conclusion. "An inside person leaked the information to Brandon or Arianna."

"An instant public relations nightmare was born," Tyler finished. "We have to figure out who the inside man is."

"I believe that would be Detective Long." I told him how the man had acted while questioning me. "His assertions were patently ridiculous."

"Yes, but when that man and woman dropped the bombs about threats and feuding with the neighbors, it sparked a blaze." A beep sounded at his end. "Hold on a moment."

I chewed on a slice of beef during the wait.

"This just keeps getting worse," he said. "The videos with Brandon and Arianna's interviews are going viral according to the PR firm."

"Isn't there something they can do about it?"

"Not immediately." He sounded hopeless. "My company stocks are tanking. If we don't turn this around soon, Brandon or Arianna will be able to buy them for pennies on the dollar."

Chapter 14

I lost my appetite and pushed away the bowl of noodle soup. "Then I suppose we'll just have to find out who Detective Long reports to."

"Yes, we will." Steel edged his voice. "I'll see you later, babe."

I suddenly remembered our appointment. "We have an Overworld Orientation class today at five. Will you be back by then?"

"Yeah, I'm about to leave for the airport right now. I'll see you at home."

I ended the call and stared at the cooling bowl of soup, praying for inspiration. If an epiphany lurked somewhere in my mind, it twisted and tumbled in a maelstrom of anxiety, anger, and random thoughts.

I called Joe and asked him to pick me up.

I climbed into the SUV and saw his worried face. "There are a lot of reporters outside the Gregorian, Miss Glass." He scratched his cheek and looked over at me. "I'll see if I can sneak you into the garage."

"Surely they're not blocking it as well."

"Hard to say, but if you duck under my jacket, I don't think they'll see you." He reached behind him and picked up his wadded jacket. "Maybe you should ride in the back."

"That's a good idea." I climbed back between the front seats and buckled myself into the rear.

Reporters packed the sidewalk in front of the Gregorian. A line of security personnel held them at bay to keep them off the driveway. I ducked behind the seats and covered myself with the jacket, feeling very much like a fugitive. We made it through without incident. I peered between the front seats. The garage entrance looked clear.

116

Joe opened the gates with a fob and drove inside. He stopped near the elevator, got out, and opened my door. "I've got to go to the airport and pick up Mr. Rock."

I was tempted to go with him, but decided my time might be better spent searching for more information on Detective Long. "Thanks Joe."

"No problem." He drove away.

Just as I turned toward the elevator, I felt a warm sensation pressing against my face. I quickly ducked behind a car and nearly fell over thanks to my high heels. Footsteps sounded from the direction of a niche directly across from the elevator. I peered through the car windows to see who it was.

Two men with chiseled jaws and dashing good looks stepped forward. They might have been fashion models except for the flames dancing in their eyes.

"I know I heard the gate closing," the one with lustrous blond hair said.

The other man ran a hand through his stylishly coiffed brown hair. "It did, Xasha."

Since I'd seen Eyja and Barboar was hopefully still dead, that meant the other man must be Vatna.

"I can't believe our little Grim has been hiding from us all this time," Xasha said in a sneering tone. "We had so much fun together."

"After what he did to us, I want to prolong his suffering." Vatna snapped his teeth together. "He won't escape me again."

I suddenly saw quite clearly that Tyler's former acquaintances weren't pursuing him just for the fun of it. They were out for revenge.

Tyler, what did you do to them?

I hoped for their conversation to continue, but Vatna motioned toward his right.

The pair walked to the opposite side of the parking deck, eyes alert, and vanished behind the central area with private closed garages where Tyler kept his most expensive cars. I briefly considered making a run for the elevator, but since I didn't have a clear idea of where the demons were, I remained where I was. I closed my eyes and tried to determine their location by the sound of their footsteps and the hot spots on my senses. They most definitely emitted unpleasant auras, different from Eyja's or Tyler's.

My supernatural senses proved quite useful. The heat tickling my extra sense had grown fainter and it seemed to be coming from somewhere to my left, which meant the demons were near the backside of the garage. I slipped off my heels and judged the distance to the elevators.

I can make it.

Before I could move, an intense smoldering sensation warmed my backside. I spun around almost expecting to see the demons right behind me. Instead, I watched as the pedestrian gate opened and a tall muscular man entered. This man radiated heat even from this distance, drowning out the sensations of the other demons with a nauseating emanation.

"Why are you here?" He spoke in a low threatening voice.

Vatna and Xasha stepped into view.

"Checking the perimeter, sir," Vatna said.

"The perimeter is several hundred yards that way." The man pointed behind him without looking. Though his voice didn't rise with anger, it seethed with dark power that chilled me to the very core. "Astra saw you leave and come over here."

"I'm sorry, Karak, we thought this was part of the patrol." Xasha's voice trembled.

Karak's hand flashed to Xasha's throat and lifted him from the ground. Eyes blazing with orange light, the big man spoke. "You lessers are weak and pitiful. If it would not degrade me, I would devour you myself." His other fist rammed Vatna in the stomach.

Vatna doubled over with a loud oof, and fell to his knees. "Please, Karak, have mercy."

"I have no mercy for the likes of you." Karak dropped Xasha. "Only the will of the master preserves you." He pointed back outside the gate. "Now, go."

The two underlings ran away like whipped hounds. Karak's burning eyes raked the garage. They seemed to hesitate when they looked in my direction, but it might have been my imagination. Even so, my bones turned to jelly. If I hadn't already been crouching, I would have fallen down. The demon turned and walked outside and the gate clanged shut behind him.

Common sense told me to make for the elevator. Curiosity made me pause. Why were they supposed to be patrolling a perimeter?

What was several hundred yards away in the direction indicated by Karak?

I left my high heels where they were and went after Karak. I hit the button for the pedestrian gate and closed it quietly behind me.

How did he open the gate in the first place?

For that matter, how had Vatna and Xasha gotten inside? How had Barboar slipped inside the day he'd tried to blow us up?

It must be some form of demon magic.

I spotted the unmistakable figure of Karak walking down the street behind the Gregorian. A woman jogging down the street with her dog shrieked as her dog yelped and tried to race away.

She stumbled after him calling his name. "Juno, stop! Bad girl!"

Karak didn't even spare her a glance. A bird on the power lines above the street went still and fluttered to the ground seconds after the demon passed beneath it.

I gulped and remembered Dad's warning about the ill effects of powerful demons on this world. "Why am I following this monster?"

A tiny portion of common sense prevailed. I texted Tyler. *Your demon friends came to visit. I'm following them.* I didn't expect an answer from him since his plane hadn't landed yet. Following a greater demon definitely wasn't one of my brighter notions, so I decided to let George know as well.

Found greater demon named Karak. Following him to construction site behind Gregorian.

After walking a few blocks, Karak went through a gate in the chain link fence around the site of a new condominium complex. A banner wrapped around the fence, blocking a view of the inside. All I could see were the naked concrete columns and metal beams rising into the air behind it. I waited until the intense sensation of Karak's presence faded a little before peeking through a crack between the gate and a post.

Though I couldn't see anyone, I felt four distinct pinpoints of heat in addition to the blaze that was Karak. One of those pinpoints grew closer to my right side. I quickly reversed course and went across the street to a bus stop, where I sat down and tried to look innocent. Considering my business attire and lack of shoes, I probably looked a little strange to most people.

A woman in a cute blue skirt and blouse seemed to be the source of the demonic emanations. Her eyes seemed far too watchful and wary to be someone out for an afternoon stroll. She stopped outside the gate and checked a watch on her wrist. Another source of heat came into range from my left.

A man wearing a T-shirt with the words, *Tri-Cross Bloodbank, Donate Today!* came into view. He nodded at the woman and they spoke for a moment. The woman showed him her watch. His forehead creased with what seemed worry.

Her eyes hardened. She pushed open the gate and motioned him inside. Her companion hesitated, but finally complied.

"Now, what was that all about?" I murmured to myself. I squeezed shut my eyes and concentrated on the fading emanations. It felt as though all the demons were inside the fence, though I wasn't certain. I snapped a picture of the construction zone and sent it to George.

He still hadn't answered my first text, which led me to believe he was still quite busy with events in Colombia. My ability didn't include foresight of the future, but I didn't need that to tell me something major was happening at this construction site, and I needed to find out what it was.

What I should do is return home and wait for Tyler.

Yes, that made the most sense. Plus, I couldn't exactly wander into a construction zone without any shoes. I got up and briskly walked the four blocks back to the Gregorian and used my fob to enter the pedestrian gate. After retrieving my shoes, I took the elevator back to the penthouse and changed into yoga pants and a T-shirt.

"You're going to go back down there, aren't you?" I asked myself. "Who do you think you are?" Apparently, I thought of myself as a highly trained agent, because I put on socks and tennis shoes.

I've got to see what's inside that fence.

I nearly slapped a palm to my forehead when a smarter notion occurred to me. *You're in the penthouse, you ninny!* I stepped onto the balcony and walked around to the east side, which offered me a clear view into the construction zone. Work crews had excavated an area spanning several acres. A wide concrete foundation with cement columns and metal beams occupied the center, but little else had been done. The original builder had gone bankrupt some time ago, according to Tyler, and nobody else had stepped up to finish the work.

I hadn't given the eyesore much thought.

Despite my nearly unobstructed view, I didn't see a single person anywhere inside the construction area. I retrieved a pair of binoculars from the upstairs closet and returned to my vantage point. Scanning the area revealed no signs of the possessed. Just as I was about to give up, I spotted a set of stairs leading down into a trench on the north side of the building.

"They're in the basement." I nearly danced with excitement. What if I'd just discovered the secret hideout of the demons?

My phone chimed.

GO HOME RIGHT NOW! Tyler's text left little wiggle room for me to do anything except obey him and stay put. Before I could text him back, he called.

"Yes, dear?"

Tyler cut straight to the point. "Emily, where are you?"

"I'm at the condo."

"Thank god." He blew out a long breath. "What in the world possessed you to follow demons?"

I chuckled. "Very nice pun."

"I wasn't trying to be funny." Anger weighed down his words.

His tone made me angry. "Well, if you must know, Vatna and Xasha were waiting in the garage when Joe dropped me off. Thankfully, I felt their presence and hid."

"Damn it. They must have seen me on the news."

"Yes, well, a rather large chap named Karak showed up and nearly made them soil their knickers."

Tyler went silent for a long moment. When he spoke, it was a harsh whisper. "Did you say Karak?"

"Yes, why?"

"Oh, shit."

My anger melted to sharp anxiety. "Is Karak bad?"

"He's a demon lord for Domathus, one of the most powerful overlords in Haedaemos." He sucked in a breath. "Times like this, I wish I could pick up the phone and ask Baal what in the hell is going on down there."

John Corwin

"Well, I suppose the long-distance rates to Hell are rather unreasonable."

"Babe, I want you to stay put. I'll be home in half an hour."

Though I was a bit irritated at his commanding tone, it was also a bit of a turn-on. "I will."

"Love you."

"Love you too." I ended the call and returned to spying on the construction zone.

Just as I was growing bored, four figures walked up the stairs. I recognized Vatna and Xasha, along with the other two unnamed possessed. They left by the same gate. Vatna jabbed his finger at a woman several times, as if he were wielding a knife. I wondered if that was Astra, the tattletale. She didn't seem the least bit intimidated and squared her shoulders at him.

Xasha dragged the other man away. Obviously, Vatna wasn't happy he'd been ratted out.

The possessed continued their patrols, once turning away a raggedly clothed man with a shopping cart who tried to enter the premises by one of the five gates I counted. I looked for other ways into the underground section, and saw another staircase on the south side.

A text from George blinked on my phone. *Do not engage. Will return today.*

I didn't see how he'd return today, even if he did have a flying car. Then again, he probably had other means of transport at his disposal.

"There you are."

I jumped and nearly lost the binoculars over the side of the building.

Tyler grinned and swept me into his arms. "Up to no good, I see."

Taking a deep breath to calm myself, I pecked him on the nose. "I'm spying on the demons."

He looked at my yoga pants and up to my T-shirt. "Were you really planning on sneaking over there in that outfit?"

"Yes, why?"

He snorted. "Definitely super-spy material."

I lightly slapped him on the shoulder. "Tyler, don't you dare make fun of my spy outfit."

122

He nodded toward the balcony. "Why don't you show me where the demons are?"

I handed him the binoculars and pointed him toward the building. "The two male model lookalikes walking around are Xasha and Vatna."

"Hmm, yeah, I see who you're talking about." He tsked. "They always did like to pose as pretty boys."

"George said he's returning from Colombia today," I informed him.

"Guess this is about to turn into a major operation." Tyler lowered the binoculars. "I wonder what in the world they're doing in there."

"Maybe it's the demon headquarters," I suggested.

He seemed to mull it over. "I doubt it. This place seems too exposed."

"Yes, but it's abandoned and they can hide underground." I waved a hand at the surroundings. "What better place to hide than right in the middle of everything?"

"These are demons, Em." He shook his head. "My kind don't enjoy living like beggars when they're on the mortal plane. A demon as powerful as Karak could probably commandeer just about any house he wants without anyone figuring it out, and yet, he's slumming it in an abandoned construction site."

"Fine, if you say so." I wished I knew more about the magical world so I could make an educated guess. It was with some chagrin I realized we probably wouldn't make it to our orientation class today.

There was only one way to find out what those demons were up to, and that meant sneaking into the viper's nest.

Chapter 15

"I know it's early, but, I'm starving." Tyler went into the kitchen and rummaged in the fridge, seemingly unconcerned about the demonic activities transpiring a few blocks away.

My stomach rumbled at the thought of food, and I decided to take a break. "I could eat something as well."

We made sandwiches and took a bottle of white wine onto the balcony. I picked up the binoculars from the table.

Tyler rolled his eyes. "Can we please give the spying a short rest?"

Reluctantly, I put them back down. "I do believe I missed my calling in life."

He chuckled. "I'm sure Her Majesty's secret service would love to have you."

"Do you doubt my abilities?"

"Not for a minute." He chased a bite of turkey sandwich with a gulp of wine. "Have you told your parents about the demons?"

I suddenly felt quite foolish. "In all the excitement, I suppose I forgot." I quickly sent my father a text.

"How did things go in Charlotte today?" I asked.

Tyler wrinkled his nose. "Not well. Some of the clients I spoke to said they couldn't make any decisions until the legal cloud hanging over my head went away."

I dropped the remains of my sandwich on the plate. "Whoever is behind this must be enjoying themselves right now."

"They won't be laughing when I'm done with them."

We finished eating. Just as I returned from putting the plates in the kitchen, I felt a rush of wind and saw a ripple in the air just off the balcony. A door opened, revealing the interior of George Walker's company car, hovering in the air.

He walked down a ramp extending from the bottom of the car. "Good afternoon, Miss Glass, Mr. Rock." He nodded at each of us in turn. "It sounds like there's been quite a development today."

"How in the world did you get here so quickly?" I waved away my own question. "Never mind. I want you to look at something." I took him by the sleeve of his suit jacket and led him around the balcony so he could see the construction site. Using the binoculars, I pointed out the lesser demons prowling the fence. "I haven't seen that Karak fellow again, but you'll definitely know him when you see him." I held my hands far apart. "He's big as a moose."

Tyler snorted. "Interesting description."

I amended my description. "Well, more like a bear, to be honest." I nodded my head toward the car. "Where's Mr. Sticks?"

"Still in Colombia." He set down the binoculars. "I tried to free up more resources, but we are in full scandal cover-up mode down there."

"Sounds exciting," Tyler said.

"Yes, I suppose it has that element, though the attempted assassination of a Templar commander by a coordinated vampire assault has thrown the Overworld political situation into turmoil." George brushed a bit of dust from his lapel. "It was done in such an open and blatant manner, that we'll be lucky to keep it contained."

"Luckily, you have us," I said. "I believe the three of us could, um, what's that word—"

"Infiltrate?" Tyler suggested.

"Yes." I nodded my head sharply. "We'll infiltrate the construction site and find out what's going on."

My phone chimed. I took it out and read a text from Dad. *We're on the way.*

I smiled. "Make that five of us."

George raised an eyebrow. "Who are the other two?"

"My parents."

"I take it they are still active with the Exorcists?" he asked.

I waggled my head in a so-so manner. "Not precisely. As I said on the phone, they didn't like where Montjoy was taking the organization." I thought back to my earlier conversation with him. "Who is Daelissa? My father seems to think she has something to do with this Templar Divinity of yours."

"Yes, well the last two weeks have been full of shocking revelations." George's calm demeanor cracked with a slight eye twitch. "The Divinity is apparently a Seraphim named Daelissa."

His statement took a moment to process. "Did you just say she's a Seraphim, as in angel?"

"Precisely." His eye twitched again. "Thomas Borathen has accepted this assertion as fact, while other Templar commanders are adhering to the Synod's official line that the Divinity is an all-knowing, all-seeing goddess."

"But, an angel?" Clearly, George had lost his mind. "What is one of God's messengers doing on Earth?"

"Honey, I think you need to remember that religion and reality don't always mix." Tyler wrapped an arm around my shoulder. "I'm living proof of that."

Shaking my head to clear the confusion, I still found it difficult to reconcile what I'd been taught all my life with the notion that an angel from Heaven walked among us and apparently was up to no good.

"I simply haven't had the time to delve deeper into the matter of the Divinity, but the political ramifications are quite clear." George folded his arms and looked into the distance. "The Templars may well split into two or more camps—one side supporting the Divinity, the other opposing her. Coupled with the other shockwaves passing through the Overworld, this latest disruption couldn't have been better timed."

"That's what I was trying to tell you earlier." I wished I'd taken the time to make a flow chart, but settled for an oral argument. "The timing of this demon incursion is no coincidence. It must have something to do with everything else that's happening."

"Agreed," Tyler said. "Now that you've given me a clearer picture, I'm positive something major is going down."

"What do you know about Seraphim?" I asked Tyler.

He shook his head. "Nothing. I'm a young demon, so if our kind has had dealings with them in the past, I haven't heard about it."

I pinched my forehead. "Not even in history class?"

"We don't go to school in Haedaemos." He clenched his hand. "Knowledge is the ultimate form of power there, and it's not freely traded."

126

"From what little I've heard, the Seraphim are from another realm," George said. "The legends say there are several different realms, but the only one we've proven to exist is the Gloom."

"That doesn't sound very inviting," I said.

"It's a very strange place—a reflection of Eden completely devoid of life except for creatures we call minders." He took out his phone and showed me a picture of a flying jellyfish. "We use them to guard the Obsidian Arch at La Casona."

I raised an eyebrow. "Dare I even ask why you use these things to guard an arch?"

"The arch is how I traveled here so quickly." He flicked to the image of a massive black arch in the middle of a silver circle. "These facilitate instant travel from one arch to another."

That reminded me of another unfortunate subject. "I suppose we won't make it to the orientation class tonight."

George checked his watch. "You still have an hour to make it to the location I gave you."

I gave him an incredulous look. "Surely, you're joking. I'm not going to an orientation class when there are more important things to deal with."

"Yeah, George." Even Tyler looked a bit nonplussed. "You can't go running in there by yourself."

George gave us a very even stare. "I think this operation would work better if I go with your parents, Miss Glass. They are, after all, seasoned Exorcists who know how to handle themselves. If we require your particular skills, I will let you know."

"Oh, no you don't, George Walker." I set my arms akimbo and glared at him. "I found these demons, and I refuse to let you sideline me." I spared one of my arms to motion at Tyler. "Besides, we have a vested interest in making sure some of those demons are handled in a specific way."

"Abyssal banishment," Tyler said. "I want them gone from my life forever."

George didn't look swayed by either my stern look or argument. "I think it best if your parents and I take a look around first, Miss Glass. We have no idea what intentions the demons have, and it would be much easier for a small group to infiltrate the construction site undetected. I am trained in such matters, and suspect your parents have had some Templar training as well."

I couldn't argue with him there. "I still plan to reschedule the orientation class."

"The sooner you take it, the better." Steel rang in George's voice. "There are a great many simple things I must explain to you which take up valuable time. Today's class is the first of five you must attend."

"Five classes?" And here I'd been thinking one class was too much. "How long are they?"

"One or two hours each." He looked at something on his phone. "If you miss tonight's you'll have to wait another week to start them."

Tyler's phone rang. He answered it. "Yes, please send them right up." He gave me a meaningful look. "Your parents have arrived."

George gave his suit another inspection. "This will be interesting."

As if discussing angels and demons wasn't interesting enough. I checked my own attire and decided the yoga pants and shirt would simply have to be enough.

"Had you planned to infiltrate the construction site in your exercise clothes, Miss Glass?" George's face showed no emotion, but I just knew he was chortling on the inside.

"It's much better than a business skirt, wouldn't you agree?"

"Absolutely." He revealed a faint smile. "It's much easier to run for your life in athletic gear."

The elevator in the secure foyer dinged. Tyler hit a button next to the front door. The magnetic lock disengaged with a buzz and a click, and he opened it.

My mother stepped off the elevator ahead of my father. The mane of her ponytail swayed in a businesslike manner as she strode forward. She offered a polite smile to Tyler. "Mr. Rock." She nodded at me. "Emily."

I was a bit stung by her cool reception even thought we'd just seen each other the night before. I nodded back. "Mum—Victoria."

Patrick embraced me and kissed my head. "Hey there, angel."

At least someone knows how to greet their child properly.

Victoria approached, held me at arms' length, and looked me up and down. "Exercise clothes. I'm glad to see you're taking steps to

128

keep your lovely figure from vanishing now that you're living the posh life."

"Mother!" I almost pushed her away. "Do you think I've been eating like a slob all this time?"

"I do know your fondness for Nutella, dear." She obviously had nothing more to say on the subject and turned to George. "Who's this fine-looking young man?"

He stepped forward, hand extended. "Agent George Walker. Pleased to meet you."

"Victoria Glass." She motioned to my father. "This is my husband, Patrick."

My father turned to George. "You must be the Custodian."

"I am." George didn't look tense, but something about his posture made me think he was ready to spring into action if my parents seemed the least bit threatening. He probably didn't trust Exorcists. "Emily has told me a bit about you, but I'd be interested in knowing more."

Victoria, as usual, took charge. "First, I'd like to know precisely what's going on."

I told them about the suspicious activities down the block.

"Karak?" Dad said when he heard the name. "I read an Exorcist scroll on the greater demon, Domathus, several years ago, and Karak was named as his second."

Victoria tapped her chin. "I broke into the secure Exorcist archives after our departure from them and found mention of another demonicus used nearly two thousand years ago."

I gave my mother a shocked look. "You hacked the Exorcist computers?"

She pshawed. "Computers? The Exorcists still use scrolls for almost everything, child. Patrick and I physically broke into the vault with the help of another Exorcist who left the order after Montjoy took control. We were able to use modern technology to record anything of interest."

"Impressive," George said. "The Templars would dearly love to know where the legendary Vault of the Exorcists is hidden."

"It isn't just one vault," Victoria said. "There are dozens of them scattered about the world. This particular one is buried deep beneath the Church of the Divinity." She held up a cautionary finger. "Just because I told you its location doesn't mean you can easily find it."

"Details would be much appreciated," George said.

"I'm sure they would." Victoria flashed a smile. She walked into the kitchen and looked over the wine rack. "What a lovely selection." She turned to Tyler. "I believe good wine facilitates good planning, don't you agree?"

Tyler flashed a wide smile. "Absolutely, Victoria. Help yourself."

"I believe this nineteen-seventy cabernet will start things off nicely." She opened a drawer in search of a cork remover.

George turned to me and made a polite observation. "Your mother is quite assertive."

"I believe 'dominating' is the word you're looking for," I replied.

"Yes, I believe that is more precise." He checked his watch. "You should leave now if you're to get to your class."

Patrick raised an eyebrow. "Class?"

"Orientation." I pretended to yawn. "Boring."

He returned a stern expression. "And absolutely necessary."

"Yes, but—"

"No buts, young lady." Patrick turned to Victoria. "It appears Emily and Tyler have to attend Overworld Orientation today."

"*Emily*." Victoria sounded very disappointed. "You really shouldn't put it off."

"We can start next week." I jabbed a finger toward the demon hideout. "After we take care of the demons."

"Yes, well, whatever the demons are up to, I'm certain it won't happen before late tonight." She poured two glasses of wine and gave George a querying look.

"I suppose I can indulge," he said.

Victoria poured the third glass.

"What about *our* wine?" I felt rather indignant being treated like this in Tyler's house.

Tyler wrapped an arm around my shoulder. "Let's give the experts some time to talk. We'll go to class and come right back."

George looked at Tyler with a discerning gaze. "If you're to make it on time, I suppose you'll need to take my car." He withdrew a silver cross from his pocket and handed it to him. "I take it you know how to drive a car?"

Tyler's eyes lit with excitement. "Of course, but not a flying one."

"Well, it handles precisely the same in the way." He took Tyler to the car, felt around with his hand, and located the invisible door handle to open the door. He pointed to the controls. "Use this joystick to control the pitch and roll."

"Just like a jet," Tyler said. "Easy enough."

"Yes, well, when you're ready to set down, deactivate the levitation by pressing this button." He pointed out the one in particular. "The blue button beneath it will deactivate the camouflage."

Tyler slapped George on the back. "George, this is the best present anyone's ever given me."

"Why don't you bloody kiss him so we can be on our way?" I said, irritated as ever that we were being forced to go to this class. Then again, Tyler would go no matter what since George bribed him with his flying car.

Tyler lifted me up to the railing since the ramp hadn't deployed. I shrieked with fright since the invisible exterior of the car made it look like I was about to be tossed into thin air. George had parked the car right up against the balcony railing, making it nearly impossible to fall from this side. I slid inside and across the seat to the passenger side. Tyler climbed in after me.

He waved to the others. "We'll be back soon."

"Be careful not to use all the aether charge," George said. "Also, you might want to park it in the parking deck when you return."

"You got it." Tyler closed the door. "Buckle your seatbelt, babe."

I gripped his hand. "Don't you dare get us killed, Tyler."

"Wouldn't dream of it." He eased forward the car and steered it around a nearby building. Once we were out of sight of the Gregorian, he punched it.

My head bounced against the headrest as we streaked forward. "Slow down!"

Tyler dodged between buildings, his face lit with excitement. "Sure, babe." He didn't slow down much.

I knew from experience his supernaturally enhanced reflexes allowed him to drive on the ground with impeccable precision. I just hoped it translated to flying a car as well. A scant handful of minutes later, he landed the car in an empty truck delivery area behind Phipps Plaza, and deactivated the camouflage.

"I love this car." Tyler ran a hand adoringly along the dash. "I want one so bad."

"Perhaps you can make love to it later." I squeezed his forearm. "For now, can we please get to the meeting location?"

He ran a hand along my leg. "Maybe we could break in the back seat."

I looked at him, horrified. "Are you out of your mind? For all we know, there are cameras in this car."

Tyler chuckled. "I'll bet George would like to see a video."

"No, he would not!" I pointed ahead. "Go, now."

"Now you just sound like your mother." He still wore a grin as he navigated us to the rear entrance of the parking deck. A red-striped zone stood out to the right of the entrance, so he steered that way and parked.

A man in a fancy valet uniform complete with a captain's hat, suit jacket, and white gloves, knocked on the window.

Tyler lowered it. "Yes?"

"Sir, I'm sorry, but you can't park here," the valet said.

"We're supposed to park here."

The other man waited expectantly.

I finally remembered the last part of the instructions. "Cold gravy."

The valet nodded. "Very well, you may proceed."

Tyler looked confused. "Proceed where?"

"Straight ahead." He pointed to the concrete wall in front of us. Large red letters proclaimed, *No Parking At Any Time*. "Just take my word for it, and drive forward."

"George is gonna be pissed if I scratch this car," Tyler muttered, but he eased forward anyway.

Much to our surprise, the nose of the car went straight through the wall.

"What the hell?" Tyler hit the brakes and stared at it for second. "Something tells me this is going to be interesting."

I knew without a doubt, he was right.

Chapter 16

We continued straight through the immaterial wall and followed a long winding ramp until we arrived at a parking deck hundreds of feet beneath the surface. A wild variety of vehicles occupied the parking spaces. Tyler slowed down to gawk at a dark yellow Bugatti speckled with black leopard spots.

"Please don't tell me you want one of those too," I said.

He shrugged. "I don't have enough garage space for one right now."

I looked around the vast cavern and felt my jaw fall open when they settled upon a giant black arch towering in the middle. "Look at the size of that thing."

Tyler whistled. "Must be one of those Obsidian Arches George showed us."

"And what's that doing over there?" I pointed to a huge wooden barn. Elephants, giraffes, and other animals wandered the confines of fenced-in areas around the building.

"A stable?" Tyler snorted. "I knew this was going to be interesting, but I feel like I just stepped into la-la land."

"Me too."

After parking, we walked over to an information booth.

"Where is the orientation class?" I asked the woman behind the counter.

"They're gathering at the stables," she said brightly, and pointed toward the barn.

I spotted a group of people with confused expressions meandering near the elephant pen. "Thanks."

A young boy at the edge of the crowd tugged on his mother's dress. "But, Mom, what if—what if—a vampire bit a werewolf? Would the werewolf drink blood then? Would he be a vampwolf?"

"I don't know, son." She blew out an exasperated breath and met my eyes. "My husband just had to go and get himself good and drunk and bitten by vampires." She threw up her hands. "Now look where we are."

The supposed husband looked down. "I swear, baby, It ain't my fault!"

The woman looked at Tyler, her expression turning a bit dreamy. "What did you do to end up here?"

"I'm possessed by a demon," Tyler replied with a deadpan look.

Her husband made a sign of the cross. "What in tarnation? This Overworld ain't no place for decent folk. Get thee behind me, Satan!"

"Shut up, Ellis." The woman cuffed him on the back of the head and smiled at Tyler.

"Mom." The little boy tugged on her dress. "Mom. Mom!"

"What?" she shouted at her kid.

"W-what if a demon got bitten by a vampire and a werewolf? Would he be a demon blood-drinking wolf? Would he be invulnerable? Would he be a vampwolfdemon?"

"He would eat the souls of little children." I smiled reassuringly at him.

The boy didn't seem the least bit worried. "Cool!"

"Can we leave?" Ellis asked his wife. "I don't want nothing to do with none of this stuff, least of all no demons."

I looked around at the other Overworld newbies. A man in an expensive business suit spoke with another fellow wearing a ragged T-shirt and cargo pants. A group of college-aged girls whispered to each other and looked around with wide eyes. It seemed there were people from every walk of life present here. I wondered if these were all the people in the Atlanta area who'd been exposed to the supernatural, or if they'd been sent here from other parts of the world as well.

A gentleman in a loose black robe approached the groups, a weary look on his face. He clapped his hands. "Welcome, everyone, I am Desmond, your guide to the Overworld."

Ellis raised his hand. "Do we have to do this? I swear I ain't gonna tell nobody nothing."

"If you think this will be too much stress due to religious objections, or a cognitive inability to process new things, then you are welcome to undergo our mind-wiping process." Desmond's lips curled into a faint smile. "There are only a few negative side effects of the process."

"Like what?"

"Impairment of motor coordination and a possible loss of other brain functionality."

Ellis seemed to think about it long and hard. His wife rolled her eyes and knocked him on the back of the head. "We're not having our minds wiped, you moron!" She tapped a finger on her chin as if reconsidering. "Actually, can you make him forget we're married?"

There were quite a few chuckles and snorts of amusement from the group.

Desmond nodded seriously. "Oh, we can do all sorts of things."

"Fine, I'll go through the stupid classes," Ellis whined.

"In that case, let's get started." Desmond retrieved a long pointy cap from within his robes and put it on. "If you get lost, just look for my hat."

Tyler laughed softly. "I guess robes and wizard hats are in fashion in these parts."

"How unfortunate." I tried to imagine Tyler wearing something so outlandish, and had to admit he'd probably look rather dashing in just about anything.

Desmond stepped onto a podium. "You are now standing in the Grotto way station. It is called a way station because this large black arch behind me is a method of transportation here in the Overworld." He pointed to the yellow and black striped circle guarding the silver band surrounding the arch. "At no time are you to cross this barrier unless you are the one traveling."

"Why not?" the businessman asked.

"Obsidian Arches open gateways to other arches all around the world. Sometimes, cracks in the fabric of reality accidentally open, forming a rift into a realm we call the Gloom." Desmond paused as if to let that sink in. "Suffice it to say, you don't want to end up there. The only way out is for us to send in a Templar rescue team."

Several people tried to ask questions at once, but Desmond held up a hand. "Please keep the questions to a minimum. We have a lot to cover today. Now, if you'll please follow me." He stepped off the platform and walked toward a pair of large wooden doors several hundred feet behind us. "On the other side of these doors you'll find an entire city we call the Grotto."

"An underground city?" Ellis's little boy seemed really excited by the prospect.

Desmond continued. "This city exists inside what we call a pocket dimension."

Tyler and I exchanged confused looks. I resisted the urge to grill Desmond for more information. Other group members blurted questions.

Our teacher ignored them all. "We don't know who made the arches or the pocket dimensions. There are hundreds of them located all around the world, each with its own Obsidian Arch way station."

I tried to imagine so many worlds hidden within our world. How the Overworld had managed to keep them secret for so long was amazing.

Desmond opened the doors to reveal a cobblestone road leading past quaint shops. We followed him inside. Gasps took flight all around as people looked up to see blue skies overhead.

A group of well-dressed people with pale skin walked past.

"Fresh meat," one of them said with a laugh, and flashed fangs at us.

The young girls shrieked and jumped behind some of the men.

"Don't worry. Vampires aren't allowed to attack you," Desmond said.

"Yeah, because they all follow the rules," Tyler muttered.

I bared my teeth at the bloodsuckers and wished I could defang each and every one of them.

Desmond led the group along winding streets, giving tidbits of history like a tour guide as we passed different parts of the Grotto. We eventually ended up in a large grassy park in a more modern section of town. The glass on some buildings rippled like water, gaining the immediate interest of Tyler.

We stopped outside two large buildings. One was made of white glass blocks, which blinked into transparency at times like windows. The building across the street seemed to be made entirely of the liquid glass material. Two robed men shouted insults at each other in the middle of the street, while crowds of onlookers urged them on.

"How fortunate," Desmond said, stopping on the sidewalk near the altercation. "It appears MagicSoft and Orange have released their new flagship arcphones to the public today."

"Arcphone?" someone asked.

"Yes, much like the smartphones you use, but these incorporate magic as well."

"Well, now I know where to get one like George's," I murmured.

"Which is better?" asked the businessman.

"I think we'll find out momentarily," Desmond said as the two shouting men charged each other, fists flailing.

Within minutes, both men fell to the ground panting without a clear victor in sight.

"I suppose that means it's a personal preference," I observed dryly.

"More or less," Desmond replied. He stepped around the exhausted fighters and led us into a brown two-story building down the street. The first room, a small auditorium, seemed to be our final destination.

"For the rest of this week, we'll meet here," Desmond informed us. "If you have any trouble finding it, simply get on one of the town trolleys I showed you and instruct it to take you to the Overworld Orientation Complex."

Tyler and I took seats near the back of the room. Ellis's wife gazed longingly at Tyler, but thankfully sat down near the front.

"I'll begin the class with basic terms that will help you adjust to your new life," Desmond said. He laid a tablet computer on the table in the front of the room. A few flicks of his finger later, it projected the three-dimensional words *Overworld Orientation* into the air, drawing gasps and looks of disbelief from most of those present.

I felt a bit smug, having already seen my father's phone do the same thing.

"How many of you here have supernatural abilities?" Desmond asked.

Tyler made as if to raise his hand, but I stopped him.

He wrinkled his forehead. "Why not?"

"I don't want to talk about our private business in front of these people." I shrugged. "Besides, George wants to keep my ability secret."

One of the college girls raised her hand, a sad look on her face.

"What's your name, young lady?" Desmond asked the girl.

"Angela."

"What's your supernatural ability?"

"I got turned into a vampire."

Desmond nodded. "Was it personal choice, or were you turned against your will?"

"Someone gave me this stuff to drink at a party, and it turned me into a vampire." A tear trickled down her cheek. "Then they tried to kidnap me and take me to Colombia, but my friends tazed him and sprayed his eyeballs with pepper spray and saved me."

I scowled. It sounded like the potion vampires had used in high schools to turn the students.

"Anyone else?" Desmond said, looking around. When no one answered, he swiped his hand across the holographic image to display two words and went on to explain them. "Supernatural beings are sometimes referred to as supers. Normal people are often referred to as noms."

"Noms? What kind of stupid name is that?" Ellis asked.

Desmond didn't answer him, and moved on. "There are many kinds of supernatural beings in the Overworld. The most common by far are vampires. Contrary to what you've read, vampires will not turn to dust if staked in the heart, nor do they burst into flame in the sun. They do drink blood, and they easily sunburn." He looked at the girl. "I'm afraid you'll have to wear plenty of sunblock during sunny days."

Her eyes flared. "I can't go to the beach anymore?"

"I'm afraid it just won't be the same."

She burst into tears.

"I feel awful for the poor dear," I told Tyler.

He wrapped an arm around my shoulders. "Well, why don't you offer to help her?"

I felt a smile stretch my lips. "Oh, Tyler. That's such a sweet and wonderful idea." *He is nothing like Barboar.*

Despite the crying girl, our teacher pushed on. "Other supernatural types are lycans, often referred to as werewolves, felycans—feline shifters—Daemos, demons, and Arcanes." He switched to images of the various kinds, and showed videos of a man changing into a large wolf followed by images of a woman turning into a black panther. Everyone was absolutely enthralled by the spectacle.

"Daemos, or demon spawn, are something of an enigma," Desmond said. "They are able to shift into demonic forms, and can also summon minions from the netherworld." The image of a huge black dog with glowing yellow eyes appeared. "Hellhounds are the most common form."

"What's the difference between a demon and a Daemos?" someone asked.

"Excellent question." Desmond tapped a finger on his chin. "Daemos are part demon, part human. As such, the human half of their soul is rooted here while the demon half resides in Haedaemos— the demon realm. They are something of a hybrid creature. Daemos must also feed on the soul essence of humans to maintain their supernatural attributes."

Ellis scratched his head and looked ready to ask a question, but a stern look from Desmond kept him quiet.

"Demons, on the other hand, have no physical body. They are, in essence, a soul or spirit being." He flicked to an image of a creature with a massive deformed mouth and abnormally short body standing on a pattern drawn on concrete. "This is a summoned demon in its natural form. The pattern allows an Arcane to summon a demon."

I shivered. "Looks awful."

"Do they possess people too?" a woman near the front asked.

He nodded.

The woman asked another question. "Wouldn't that make them like Daemos?"

Desmond shook his head. "No, because the possessing demon isn't combining its soul with the human's—it's simply taking control. They also don't need to feed on soul essence like Daemos, but they do corrupt the body they're in. Demons are parasites, no matter the form."

I stood up to tell Desmond just how wrong he was about that, but Tyler quickly pulled me back down. "He's wrong!" I hissed.

Tyler shrugged. "Maybe. At least I know what makes me different from Daemos."

I wanted to argue the point further, but Desmond continued to elaborate about Daemos.

"A male Daemos is an incubus, and a female is a succubus." Desmond switched to an image displaying a very attractive male and female. "They are able to seduce just about anyone they wish and feed on their soul essence."

I shuddered. "Just what we need—supernatural sexual predators."

"Last, but not least, we reach the Arcanes," Desmond said. "That is what I am."

"You mean like wizards and warlocks?" Ellis asked.

"What if a vampire bit a witch?" his kid asked. "And then a lycan bit the witch? Would she still be able to fly a broom?"

Desmond blinked a couple of times. "Will you two please hush?" He produced a wand. "Or must I force the issue?"

Ellis and his boy clamped their lips shut, eyes wide with fear.

Tyler snorted and covered his mouth.

"Now, as I was saying, Arcanes are the magic users." He glared at Ellis. "Terms like wizard, warlock, sorcerer, mage, and witch refer to different kinds of magical practitioners." Desmond cleared his throat. "Witches and warlocks prefer natural magic and potions. Wizards and sorcerers are archaic terms rarely used, though they formerly referred to Arcanes with great elemental control. Mages are Arcanes who have achieved mastery of the arcane arts in at least two fields."

"What about magicians?" someone asked.

Desmond scowled. "That is an insulting term to true Arcanes. I suggest you never use it again."

The businessman raised his hand. "Are there any other kinds of supers?"

"There are various forms of leechers, gnomes, and even trolls. We don't know much about them because they haven't been seen in centuries." He tapped a finger to his chin. "There are dryads near Arcane University in Queens Gate, though we've never found them elsewhere, and I once met a woman who could tell what kind of powers a person had simply by being near them."

My heart seemed to freeze in place. "Was this at Arcane University as well?" I asked.

"Yes, in the Fairy Gardens." Desmond clicked his tongue. "We really must push on if we're to cover all the material today."

Tyler squeezed my hand and leaned over as Desmond droned on in the background. "According to George, you're the only person he's ever met with your ability."

I felt shocked and elated. "My God, it would be amazing to meet someone else with my special senses."

"I think we need to ask Desmond about it more after class."

"Yes, but not tonight." I couldn't stop thinking about Karak and his minions. "We need to get back so we can help George."

Desmond finally wrapped up about forty minutes later and quickly left the room before anyone could bombard him with questions. I stopped the vampire girl as she and her friends walked toward the exit.

"May I speak with you alone for a moment?" I asked her.

She and her friends stared longingly at Tyler.

I snapped my fingers. "Hello?"

"Oh, yes, sorry." She looked at her friends. "Be right back."

They were too busy adoring Tyler to respond.

I remembered the girl's name from earlier. "Angela, right? I'm Emily."

"Nice to meet you," she said in a shy voice.

I decided not to beat around the bush. "Do you really want to be rid of your vampirism?"

"More than anything." Her lower lip quivered. "I hate being different and not being able to go to the beach is just awful."

"Well, perhaps I can help you."

Her eyes brightened. "How?"

"I have the ability to remove your vampirism."

"Oh my God, that's so cool." She turned to her friends as if to tell them, but I stopped her.

"You can't tell anyone I did it." I leaned toward her. "My ability is a secret."

She nodded solemnly. "I totally understand."

"Excellent." I checked the time on my phone. "I don't have time to do it today, but perhaps sometime this week after one of our classes."

Angela giggled and hugged me. "I can't wait. Oh my God, my parents won't ever have to know I was a vampire."

"You haven't told them yet?"

She shook her head. "How am I supposed to tell them something like that?"

I didn't know what to say.

Angela looked at Tyler. "You have the dreamiest boyfriend ever."

"Yes, well don't be fooled, his super power is charm."

She sighed. "It totally works."

Tyler wore his trademark amused grin as the girls talked to him. He looked at me the moment I drew near. A dreamy look came into his eyes, and it was like the other girls weren't even there. I couldn't help but smile.

"Ready, babe?" He took my hand and kissed it.

The girls sighed in unison.

I nodded. "Let's go."

After a quick joyride in George's flying car, we arrived back at the Gregorian and parked in the underground deck. Nerves aflutter, I could hardly wait to ask George and my parents what they'd decided to do about the demons.

The condo was empty when we went inside. Tyler and I looked around, but found no sign of the others.

He snatched a scrap of paper from the table and showed it to me.

We're going inside the construction area. Be back soon.

My parents were in enemy territory.

Chapter 17

I went from being furious to sick with worry in a matter of seconds. True, they'd told me their intentions, but I hadn't expected them to actually go inside. Snatching the binoculars, I went to the balcony and peered at the construction site. Unfortunately, it was almost dark and I had only the street lamps to see by.

Unless the possessed had changed clothes, I didn't see them on patrol among the sparse foot traffic near the fence.

"We've got to go after them," I told Tyler.

"Let me change into something more appropriate." He glanced at me. "Are you sticking with the yoga pants?"

"Yes, now go change!" I shooed him away.

He returned moments later in dark jeans and T-shirt. "I'm ready."

We took the lift down to the parking deck and headed outside. Just as we were crossing the street, I saw George and my parents strolling our way as if out for a casual evening walk.

I stormed up to them. "Did you really go in there without us?"

Victoria raised an eyebrow. "Darling, we are the seasoned professionals and you the rank amateur. Do you truly think for a second that we'd need to wait for you?"

I was furious, mainly because I knew she was right.

Tyler put a hand on my shoulder, but looked at my mother. "Find anything useful?"

George nodded. "Karak and his minions are preparing another demonicus."

"We have to stop them, right?" I asked.

"Indeed." He crossed his arms. "Zad Kassus and Martin Drang are inside, drawing the demonicus while Karak instructs them."

"It's a very curious arrangement," Victoria said. "Demons do not usually share such sensitive information about their patterns."

"They couldn't do it without the help of Arcanes," Patrick said.

"Those are no ordinary Arcanes," George said. "Kassus and Drang are battle mages of the highest order."

"With degrees in demonology, right?" I still found it hard to believe such words came from my lips.

"Precisely." George took out his phone—arcphone—and tapped on it. "There's a confluence of powerful ley lines running beneath the construction site."

"That explains the location," Victoria said.

I paced back and forth and stopped. "Just like the blood bank?"

George nodded. "In that case, there was only one major ley line beneath it."

I glanced at the phone. "Do you have a map of these things?"

"Of course." He handed me the phone.

The map on the display looked like a mess of tangled yarn. "How in the world do you see anything in this mess?"

"You can adjust the filters to show ley lines of varying magnitudes." He scrolled to a series of checkboxes with numbers next to them.

I unchecked all the smaller ones and left only the four largest categories. Even then, it was hard to see everything on the small screen. "How do you project the image?"

"You don't want to do that here in the open," George said.

It seemed now wasn't the time to do this, so I handed back his phone. "What's the plan for stopping Karak from using the new demonicus?"

"I'm waiting to see if any Templar reinforcements are available," George said. "We counted thirteen possessed down there."

"Karak, his four knights, and eight lessers," Patrick said.

"So, the knights are the ones in between greater and lesser?" I asked.

"There is no accepted standard of demon classifications," Victoria said. "The Exorcists have long used feudal terms. The Templars adopted a numerical system two centuries ago."

"The thing is, ninety-nine percent of the demons we deal with are lessers," Patrick said. "Incursions by demons as powerful as Karak are virtually unheard of because they have a great deal of power to lose if they're caught and purged by Exorcists."

"Lessers, by definition, hold very little power in the demon realm which is why the mortal world holds such an allure for them." Victoria pursed her lips. "This second demonicus would not only raise another group of lessers and knights, but also another demon lord like Karak."

"Which means Domathus is exerting his influence in a big way." Tyler's forehead pinched. "I wonder if Baal or any of the other demon overlords know about this."

"According to our sources, Domathus achieved near parity with Baal some time ago," Victoria said.

"Sources?" Tyler looked puzzled.

"We have demonic informants." Patrick grinned at Tyler's expression. "That's one way we find possessed people so quickly. We also like to keep an eye on the power structure of the underworld."

"I suggest we return to Mr. Rock's penthouse to await word from the Templars," George said.

"Prudent idea," Victoria agreed.

Since it seemed there was little else we could do at the moment, I shrugged and headed back.

Victoria uncorked another bottle of wine when we arrived. This time, I made sure to procure glasses for Tyler and myself.

George took out his phone and projected a ley line map of the area. Several of the largest ones crisscrossed in one location.

I pointed them out. "Where's that?"

"That would be the Grotto way station," George said. He adjusted the settings and a translucent view of the city appeared over the ley lines.

I traced a large vein running north. "Where is the blood bank?"

George touched a spot on the map and highlighted it. Then he traced the same line down into midtown where five other lines crossed and highlighted the area there. "That is the construction site."

I zoomed out and looked at the junction. From there, each of the other five lines continued onward across the nation and presumably the world.

"This is odd," George said, peering at the five-line junction. "I'm almost certain there were only three ley lines there before."

"Surely, you're mistaken." Victoria leaned forward in her chair. "One cannot simply create new ley lines."

"You're quite right." George fiddled with the map. The image blinked away, replaced by another that looked identical except where there had been five lines, there were now only three. "And yet, there are now two extra ley lines."

My father exchanged a look of concern with my mother. "That's impossible. Are you sure your map is correct?"

"Yes, the spell powering this application is tied into the ley line grid used by the arcphone communication system." George switched back to the previous map. "This is the most current image."

"Notice how the two new lines are only a few miles long," Victoria said.

Patrick frowned and shook his head.

Even George looked uncertain.

I didn't understand much about ley lines, but seeing our resident Overworld experts stumped tightened my stomach with apprehension. "Are you certain there's no way to create ley lines?"

"Let me ask a specialist," George said. He flicked away the map and dialed a number using the holographic keypad.

"Zuba speaking," a voice said without an accompanying image.

"Professor, this is George Walker with the Custodians. We need some information and hoped you might be able to provide it."

"Of course. How can I help you?"

"Is there anything in the historical archives about ley lines being created?"

"Hold on." The holographic image of the keypad flickered away, replaced by the live feed of a young man in a gray robe. "It's odd you would ask me this since several new ley lines just appeared."

"In Atlanta?" George asked.

Zuba shook his head. "No, in southern Colombia beneath the city of El Dorado."

George's lips pressed together. "What created them?"

"I spoke with one of the Arcanes in the City of Angels—"

I couldn't help but interrupt. "Los Angeles?"

"No, this is a place with a similar name in Colombia. Legend has it, El Dorado was once ruled by angels." He chuckled. "It's all a myth, of course."

"Of course." Knowing what I knew now, I wasn't so sure.

146

Zuba continued. "As I was saying, one of the Arcanes went on an expedition to apprehend the notorious demon spawn, Vadaemos Slade. During their adventure, they were chased by ley worms."

"I'm sorry, but are we still talking about myths?" Victoria said.

"Ley worms aren't mythical," Zuba said. "On the other hand, though we know they exist, we still don't know a lot about them except that they're attracted to ley lines and possibly feed off them."

"Are you suggesting the ley worms actually make ley lines?" Patrick asked.

"Let me show you something." Zuba vanished, replaced by a map of glowing lines. "Before the Vadaemos expedition, there were seven major ley lines beneath El Dorado." A red circle appeared around the cluster. The image changed and three new lines appeared, though none of them were as long as the original seven. "You can clearly see the new additions."

"That's exactly what's happened here," Victoria said.

"How large are ley worms?" I asked Zuba.

The map flickered away to reveal the professor. "Let me show you." He picked up a small orb I recognized as an ASE and spun it. A dim image appeared. Screeching wails like those of infants sent shivers down my spine. A bright glowing orb shot into the air, revealing a large cavern. The ground swarmed with shiny black monsters eerily resembling toddlers.

Before I could proclaim my horror, the audio rumbled and a gargantuan snake plowed through the masses. Its long lean muzzle bore spikes and shiny red scales. Massive parietal eyes gleamed with an inner light. This creature was no worm.

"It's a bloody dragon!" I shouted.

The video vanished, replaced by Zuba. "The expedition managed to capture this footage."

"Just before they were all killed?" I asked.

"Improbable as it seems, they escaped." Zuba shook his head slowly.

Tyler chuckled. "In other words, we have giant underground dragons that can create magical power lines."

"Accurate," Zuba agreed. "It appears you must have some ley worm activity there in Atlanta if you're seeing new formations."

"Any idea what might cause a ley worm to do such a thing?" George asked.

"None whatsoever." Zuba leaned forward. "If school wasn't in session, I'd love to come investigate."

"We'll keep a close eye on things," George said. He reached for the phone and paused. "I do have another question. Are you familiar with demonicuses?"

"The correct plural is *demonicus*," Zuba said. "Yes, I have some cursory knowledge of them." He tapped a finger on his chin. "During World War Two, there was a Nazi cult that tried to raise an army of greater demons to help the Germans win the war." His eyes narrowed. "Hang on, let me find the text." Zuba vanished off screen.

"Are ley lines visible to the naked eye?" Tyler asked.

George shook his head. "No. They're also buried hundreds of feet below ground. The magical energy filters up through the earth, creating smaller veins of magic."

"This can't be coincidence," I said. "These new ley lines must serve a purpose."

"Agreed," Patrick said.

"Got it." Zuba walked back into view. "The cult was called the Children of Armageddon. They created a demonicus, but lacked the major ley lines necessary to summon a demon lord. Apparently, they raised a number of lessers and three demon knights, but the circuit collapsed and the demons devoured their souls."

My lips curled in disgust. "How lovely."

"That's what happens when you disturb powerful demons." Zuba clicked his tongue. "The cult still exists. Some reports claim the demon knights who were summoned took over the bodies of the cult members and are still around today."

"Demons corrode mortal flesh over time," Victoria said. "Even if they didn't, the bodies themselves are mortal and would perish."

"In this case, the knights might have had the power and the souls to maintain their presence." Zuba shrugged. "There are so many different kinds of demons that it's impossible to know the truth without proof one way or the other."

My heart fluttered anxiously. "In other words, some demons won't corrode their hosts?" The subject hit close to home because of Tyler.

"Absolutely," Zuba said. "Jacob Snelling is a perfect example. He made a deal with a demon to devour his soul because he didn't want to go to an afterlife, if one exists. The particular demon he dealt with is what demonlogists refer to as a jade spirit. This kind is very humanlike and closely related to the sapphire spirits."

"Do you call them jade and sapphire because of the color of their spirits?" I asked.

He nodded. "Yes, they're easily distinguished in spirit form by their color. Both are members of the symbiotic spirits. The worst ones are the caustic spirits—they tend to be a putrid yellow in color. They're far more common in history and legend thanks to their tendencies to possess people and wreak as much destruction as possible."

Immense relief swelled in me. *I knew there was something different about Tyler.*

"My natural form is jade in color," Tyler whispered in my ear. "That means I'm a jade spirit. I'm different than Barboar."

The happiness in his voice nearly brought a tear to my eye. "You're special, Tyler. You're good."

George raised an eyebrow at mine and Tyler's private conversation, but continued speaking to Zuba as if nothing had happened. "I wasn't aware you knew so much about demons," George said.

"I almost specialized in demonology," Zuba replied. "I changed my mind since there's so much negativity surrounding the subject."

"What do you know about Karak?" Victoria asked.

Zuba's eyes widened. "He's a demon lord with allegiance to the overlord Domathus." He tilted his head slightly. "Why?"

"Because he's in Eden in mortal form."

Zuba's face went pale. "I take it someone successfully used a demonicus to summon him?"

"Yes, and those responsible are here in the middle of Atlanta making another one," I said.

The professor stared blankly at me then shook his head. "If this is true, they must be stopped at all costs."

"Any word from the Templars?" Patrick asked George.

George nodded. "I'm afraid all resources are currently engaged in a major conflict with vampires."

Victoria's eyes hardened. "Do they know what's at stake?"

"It's not a matter of knowing," George said calmly. "It's a matter of having no spare soldiers to send to our aid."

"In other words," I said, "we have to stop an army of demons on our own."

Chapter 18

The silence greeting my proclamation lasted several seconds.

As usual, my mother was the one to end it. "No, we can't stop so many demons ourselves," she said. "At best, we can delay them."

"The pattern looked nearly complete," my father said. "If I had to take a wild guess, I'd say they plan to activate it tonight."

The idea of even more lessers and demon lords prowling the streets of Atlanta brought a queasy feeling to my stomach. I couldn't stop thinking about Barboar and his three associates. The more of their kind they had in this world, the harder it would be for us to capture them and banish them into the Abyss. I knew my reasoning was selfish, but after everything Tyler and I had been through, I didn't want to risk losing him as I'd almost lost him before.

"What if we sneaked inside and wiped away some of the lines in the pattern?" I asked.

Patrick shook his head. "It's not that simple. Patterns like this are magically etched into the surface and traced in blood. It's not the same as drawing a diagram to summon one demon."

I announced another solution. "We could pour paint over it."

"The lines still exist beneath the paint," George said. "Think of them as a magical circuit just as wiring conducts electricity."

"Except these won't short circuit unless there's a flaw in the pattern." Patrick pounded a fist into his palm. "You have to break the lines by force or magic."

Tyler got up and poured himself a glass of whiskey. "Would a sledgehammer work?"

"Sure, but we're talking about reinforced concrete," Patrick replied. "The lines in the pattern at the blood bank were nearly an inch deep."

John Corwin

"George and I have the strength to do it." Tyler straddled a chair and leaned on the table. "Two or three hits ought to do it."

Victoria clapped her hands slowly. "Brilliant. I suppose Karak and his minions will simply stand by and watch?" She arched her brow. "After they dispose of you, it will probably take them another day of work to patch the concrete and repair that part of the pattern."

"Actually, there's more to it than that." Professor Zuba reappeared in the holographic image hovering above the phone, holding up a book with a worn leather cover. "I located my first edition of Ezzek Moore's original demonomicon. He has a thorough description of constructing a demonicus, among other things."

George frowned. "Is this something a person could find in any demonomicon?"

"No, after the Demon Treatise of 12 BC, Ezzek Moore decreed that certain knowledge should be limited." Zuba gingerly turned the pages in his book. "This is perhaps the last remaining copy of his original work."

Victoria gave him a cross look. "Details, professor, details."

"Ah, yes." Zuba turned the book to display the illustration of a person creating a pattern. "Creating a demonicus is a very complex process. First, there must be an anointed—a person chosen who will seal the pattern with their blood and soul." He pointed a finger to the person. "The anointed person's blood is used to draw the pattern. After the circuit is completed, the anointed seals it with their touch, thus infusing the diagram with their soul."

I was aghast. "The process of creating the demonicus drains their soul?"

Zuba carefully set down the book. "It would appear so, yes."

"What does this mean for us if we want to destroy the pattern?" Tyler asked.

At this, the professor pressed his lips into a grim line. "Once a pattern is infused, it cannot be destroyed except with more soul essence."

"In other words, a sledgehammer isn't going to cut it."

"Precisely." Zuba looked at the book for a moment while the rest of us exchanged uneasy glances.

"I saw Kassus and Drang drawing the pattern," Patrick said. "I doubt they'd use their own soul essence to seal it."

"Agreed," George said. "I noticed a person with his hands inside a bucket while we were inside. In retrospect, I believe he was filling the buckets with his own blood."

"Can they use more than one anointed to infuse the diagram?" I asked.

Zuba shook his head. "No. The entire pattern would need to be retraced with the new person's blood and re-infused with their soul essence." He held up a finger to ward off another question and looked back at the book. "Ah, here it is. To destroy a demonicus, one must draw a counter pattern along any line of the demonicus and infuse it with their soul. This will disrupt the circuit."

"Show me this counter pattern," my mother demanded.

Zuba displayed a star inside a circle.

"A pentagram?" I asked. "I thought those were for summoning demons in the first place."

He tilted his head to the side and looked at me. "Actually, this is a pentacle."

"Is it holy?"

Zuba stared blankly at me for a moment. "You must watch a lot of nom movies."

My face grew warm. "Sorry about the interruption. Please proceed."

He shook his head and continued. "The diameter of the circle must be at least one cubit. The pentagram must be drawn in one continuous motion with blood, and all five points must extend slightly past the circle. This is how the infused soul essence is freed from the demonicus."

"How large is a cubit?" I asked.

Zuba displayed his forearm. "Traditionally from the tip of the elbow to the tip of the middle finger, or about forty-seven centimeters."

Tyler traced his finger on the table as if practicing. "Does it have to be perfect?"

"Not perfect, but reasonably symmetrical," Zuba replied.

"In blood?" I clarified.

"Yes. That's how you infuse it with soul essence." The professor rested his chin on a hand. "It's not difficult, but there is a catch."

"Of course there is." Victoria folded her hands on the table. "Well, what is it?"

Zuba bit his lower lip. "The book isn't very clear on this, but when you infuse the counter pattern and break the circuit, the infusion of soul essence must equal that within the demonicus."

My father's face grew grim. "In other words, whoever infuses it will probably die and perhaps lose their soul in the process."

"That would be my educated guess." He sounded pretty certain for someone making a guess.

I looked imploringly at the professor. "There must be some other way."

He sighed. "Perhaps, but I'll need to research." Zuba held up the book to display its thickness. "As you can see, the text is rather dense."

"We'll let you get to it," George said. "Please notify me the moment you find something."

"Of course, Mr. Walker." Professor Zuba nodded and his image flickered away.

George stood. "It appears there's only one way to stave off the inevitable."

"Choosing someone to sacrifice themselves?" Victoria said dryly.

"We must kill the anointed." He checked the time. "That might delay them long enough for the Templars to spare more soldiers."

Patrick nodded. "I agree. George and I will infiltrate the construction site and find a way to take out the anointed."

"You certainly aren't leaving me out," Victoria said. "Patrick, be a dear and fetch our weapons."

I jolted from my seat. "You're going into a demon hideout guns blazing?"

"Guns?" She pshawed. "I would never resort to something so vulgar."

"Your mother favors a bow," my father informed me.

I was too shocked to reply. By the time I recovered my wits, they were heading toward the elevator.

"You are not leaving us behind this time," I announced.

"As much as I'd like to baby you and tell you to stay here, I won't." Victoria punched the button for the lift and turned to face me.

"You led a sheltered life growing up, dear. I think it's time you gained more experience."

Heat radiated in my face. "Are you bloody serious? I sneaked into your little Exorcist church and rescued Tyler! I've helped George apprehend rogue vampires. How could you possibly think I have no experience?"

"You've had a spot of beginner's luck." The lift dinged and my mother boarded it. "Don't worry, child, it takes time. In a year or two, your inexperience won't endanger everyone around you."

I looked to my father for support, but the smirk on his face told me he found this amusing.

"I'll make sure she doesn't get anyone killed," Tyler said.

I blew out an exasperated breath and resisted the urge to kick him in the shin. It suddenly occurred to me that my mother was probably using sarcasm to make me realize I wasn't fit to accompany them. *She might be right.* I had no formal field training. I relied on others to protect me.

On the other hand, I had an ability that could help them sneak into the construction site and navigate it safely. In a way, glimpsing was rather like having supernatural radar.

I stiffened my spine and turned to my mother. "As it so happens, I can detect the possessed through solid walls. That ability might come in handy."

"True, it might." She didn't sound convinced. "If all goes well, I should be able to pierce the anointed through the heart with an arrow, after which we will make a hasty retreat."

"Why not use a rifle?" Tyler formed a pistol with his fingers and pretended to fire.

"Firearms are prohibited by the Overworld Conclave," Victoria replied.

He frowned. "Well, I hope the demons aren't using guns."

"Will they be able to detect that we're not possessed?" I asked.

Patrick shook his head. "Most demons can't detect if a person is possessed, but we have obfuscation charms we took from the Exorcists just in case."

When we exited the lift into the parking deck, Patrick walked to a black SUV and retrieved an ebony bow and two leather scabbards with sword hilts protruding from the top. George pulled a sheathed sword from the trunk of his car and strapped it over his back.

I rolled my eyes. "Do you plan to walk through the streets with swords and a bow?"

Patrick ran a hand along the leather. "The sheaths are charmed so most people won't even notice them."

Victoria sighed. "I look forward to you completing the Overworld Orientation, Emily."

"Good to see the Exorcists still recognize standard Templar protocols," George said. He looked at me. "The only reason you noticed the weapons is because you know about them. For those without direct knowledge, the charm encourages them to filter the weapons from their perception."

"Any way I could charm my hair on a bad hair day?" I hadn't really meant it seriously, but it gave me a better idea. "What if we use such a charm on ourselves?"

"You wouldn't want to charm a living being." George looked back in his trunk. "That's why we have camouflage armor." I expected him to produce said armor for all of us. Instead, he closed the trunk. "Unfortunately, I don't carry any with me."

I sighed loudly enough for all to hear. "Perhaps you could have flown away in your magical car and requisitioned some."

"I'll remember that for future engagements." He looked around at the group. "We should go."

"Do you have any weapons for us?" I motioned to Tyler and me.

George put a hand to his chin. "Do you have sword training?"

"I have martial arts training," Tyler said. "Nothing formal with a sword."

"What about one of those fancy dart shooters?" I asked.

George opened his trunk again, removed a short three-pronged sword, and gave it to Tyler. "This sai sword is all I have, I'm afraid. If our luck holds, we won't have to actually fight anyone." He took out a lancer and turned to me. "Hold out your wrist."

I did so. He strapped the leather armlet to it and slipped a band across my hand.

"How do trigger it?" I asked.

"Squeeze your hand and flick your wrist down." George pantomimed the movement. "Just be careful not to aim it at any of us." He held up my arm and pointed it toward a wall. "Give it a try."

I followed his example and was rewarded with a flash of silver and a zing as a dart streaked out and pinged off the wall. "Easy enough." *I just hope I have good aim.*

Victoria cleared her throat. "Are we quite ready?"

"Yes," I replied in my most imperious British tone. "Quite."

We set off down the street toward the fence. As the first few pedestrians passed us, I held my breath, fully expecting to hear a shout when someone spotted a sword, or the bow slung over my mother's back. Instead, everyone who looked our way seemed to feel an urge to look to the side or down at their shoes. One couple nearly fell over each other when the man glanced at Victoria and abruptly looked straight up. His feet tangled with his companion's and they stumbled forward, much to Tyler's amusement.

It occurred to me that with only half a block to go to the fence, I should probably scan the area for hostiles. I opened my senses fully. The muted heat from Tyler's presence washed over me, overwhelming everything else. I pressed my lips together to keep them from forming a scowl. *If I don't figure out how to filter Tyler, I'll be useless.* Another heat source pinged my mental radar.

I stopped and concentrated on it. Despite Tyler's vicinity, this new signal felt quite different. The emanations from Tyler felt comforting, like a wool blanket on a cold day. The new one felt hot and stifling, but didn't sicken me as Vatna and Xasha's presences had.

"I suppose," Victoria said. "Though it would be helpful if she'd say something."

It suddenly occurred to me that she was talking about me, and I'd missed most of the conversation. "I glimpsed a demonic presence." I pointed a finger south. "It feels like he or she will cross our path in a minute or two."

"Anything else?" George asked.

I shook my head. "Nothing in range."

"Perhaps we should take out their sentry," Patrick suggested.

"All of them," Victoria added. "It will make for an easier egress."

"Agreed." George tapped the lancer strapped to my arm. "It will be best if you incapacitate them, Miss Glass."

157

Tyler smirked. "Yeah, might look a little suspicious if we start conking people on the head."

"Won't it look strange if they drop unconscious to the sidewalk?" I nodded toward the other pedestrians.

"We'll do the old drunk friend routine," Patrick said.

"Drunk friend?" I asked.

Victoria nodded. "It's a very effective way to apprehend subjects in plain view."

"Sounds self-explanatory." Tyler looked up and down the sidewalk. "Where's our perp?"

I closed my eyes and detected the presence not far to my right. It took a matter of seconds for me to spot Astra on approach. "The short brunette in the dark red dress and knee-high boots."

"Use the bus stop as cover." Victoria leaned against the side of the small shelter. Patrick stood in front of her and gestured as if they were engaged in small talk. "When the possessed passes, Patrick and I will take positions on either side of her. You must knock her out quickly."

I gulped and nodded. *No pressure.*

Astra walked past the bus stop, eyes dull with boredom. She no longer exhibited the alertness I'd noticed earlier and barely seemed to notice us. Patrick and Victoria stepped out from the bus stop and paced just behind the possessed. Without really thinking about it, I walked behind them, aimed the lancer, and flicked my wrist.

A dart zinged. Astra slumped immediately, but my parents caught her. A couple walking in the opposite direction gave them an alarmed look.

"She really needs to stop drinking so much," I said in a loud voice. "I hope she doesn't puke again."

The woman gave me a knowing look, hugged her man's arm, and, most importantly, minded her own business. No one else seemed to have noticed the abduction and continued on past us, sparing only a brief glance for the drunk woman in the care of her friends.

"Let's take her back to my car," George said. "I can put her in sleep binders."

I nodded my head toward the bus shelter. "Tyler and I will wait here so I can detect the other sentries."

Victoria narrowed her eyes. "Do not engage anyone under any circumstance. Are we clear?"

"Yes." I failed to keep the exasperation out of my tone. *Does she think I'm an idiot?*

A bus pulled up to the curb and a stream of people disembarked. George and my parents went to the crosswalk and began to traverse the street. The bus pulled away, revealing a police car in the other lane. The officer stared at my parents and the unconscious Astra, his eyes full of suspicion. He gunned the engine and turned on his lights, screeching to a halt right next to the group.

Using the patrol car door as cover, he stepped out of the car and called to them. "Stop!"

Chapter 19

I stepped away from the bus shelter, but Tyler stopped me.

"Hang on. Don't let him see you." He tapped the lancer. "Get ready to use it."

"On an officer of the law?" I asked.

He chuckled. "Yep. It'll be fun."

"You're incorrigible." I took a few steps back and positioned myself where I could get an unobstructed angle on the officer.

George was the first to respond to the cop's demands. "May I help you, officer?"

"Not you." The policeman motioned George back toward the other side of the road. "I'm talking to the pair with the unconscious woman."

"Oh, of course." George backed away.

"Our friend had too much to drink," Victoria said in a twangy southern accent. "We're takin' her home."

"Identify yourselves," the officer said.

"I'm Terry Lee and this is Billy Joe." Victoria looked at the officer with wide innocent eyes. "I'm real sorry, sir. Jenny cain't hold her liquor worth a damn."

The cop frowned, and relaxed ever so slightly, though I noticed his hand on a stun gun. "I'll need to see some identification."

"Shore thang!" Victoria turned to Patrick. "Now, don't let her fall, Billy!"

"A'ight," my father said in a perfect imitation of a brain dead good old boy.

I felt warm hand press up on my chin and close my gaping mouth.

Tyler chuckled. "Never realized your parents were Broadway actors, huh?"

I was too enthralled with the scene to reply. Victoria leaned on the officer's car door, smiled at him, and carried on a conversation too quiet for us to hear. The cop burst into laughter at one point then looked into his hand as if he were examining an ID card. He made the motion of handing the invisible card back to my mother, laughed again, and drove off.

"Look at George," Tyler said.

I flicked my gaze toward the Custodian and caught a genuinely puzzled look on his face. "It appears my mother can surprise anyone."

George quickly recovered and rejoined Patrick. My mother caught my gaze and smiled knowingly.

"Mum can be annoying, but she's still impressive." I let my eyes wander to Tyler. "Now, if only she'd respect me."

"I think she just wants to keep you safe." Tyler wrapped an arm around my shoulders. "Give it some time to let her adjust to the idea of your new side job."

"Perhaps." I stiffened. "Good lord, I haven't been paying attention." *Don't bollox this, you ninny!*

"To more sentries?"

"Yes." Thankfully, there were no other nearby blips to be found. Somewhere on the other side of the fence, I felt the distant pressure of more demons. I closed my eyes and tried to differentiate the individuals from the crowd, but it was like trying to isolate a single, faraway voice in a roar of conversations.

Tyler squeezed my hand. "Anything?"

I shook my head. "Nothing nearby."

The others returned a few minutes later. "Welcome back Terry Lee and Billy Joe." My southern accent fell short of the excellent ones employed by my parents, but I tried anyway.

"Not bad," my mother said.

"How did you get the cop to think he had your ID card?" Tyler asked.

Victoria pointed to a ruby ring on her pinky. "This has a compulsion enchantment. It works best on noms."

"Handy." Tyler motioned to her other rings. "Are any of those enchanted?"

My mother offered him a sly smile. "Perhaps."

George held out a hand. "May I see the ring?"

161

Victoria raised an eyebrow but no objections and slipped off the ring.

"How does it work?" he asked.

"It's attuned to specific individuals," Victoria replied. "It would be of no use to you."

"I see." He handed it back to her. "I don't typically condone compulsion, but in this case, it was effectively used."

"Why, thank you, Agent Walker."

"You're most welcome, Mrs. Glass." George turned to me. "Are there other possessed patrolling the perimeter?"

"Not that I can detect." I waved toward the fence. "I sense about a dozen demons at least a hundred yards in that direction."

"I was hoping to thin the herd a little before we go inside," Patrick said.

Victoria pursed her lips and looked toward the fence. "Perhaps they have other sentries inside."

"Stay low and keep to cover," George said. "Let's move in." He went to the nearby gate and eased it open. Balling a fist, he peered inside before opening his hand and flicking it forward.

Concrete pylons offered concealment inside. Keeping my senses open, I followed George and the others behind piles of steel beams, mounds of dirt, and so forth until we reached the stairwell on the south side. George seemed to know where he was going, presumably because of the earlier recon mission with my parents.

He was just about to make for the stairs when I sensed movement and gripped his arm. I held up a finger and pointed it to the east. George nodded and my parents tensed. The possessed had been on the far side of the concrete skeleton towering in the middle of the site, so I hadn't felt him coming right away. Now it was obvious he was headed straight for us.

At the last minute, I felt inexplicably courageous and jumped out in front of the possessed. The startled face of Astra's male companion from earlier greeted me. My dart pierced his nose and his wide eyes fluttered shut.

George withdrew a strap and cuffed the man. "He'll sleep until these are removed." His eyes moved to mine. "That was a rather bold move, Miss Glass."

162

"It seemed the most expedient way to take him down." I knew it wasn't true, nor could I explain what precisely had possessed me to leap in front of so dangerous a being instead of simply standing to the side and hitting him in the shoulder when he passed.

"Perhaps you should let us be the bold ones, dear." Victoria focused me with her steely gaze. "We're lucky the chap didn't knock you senseless by sheer reflex."

"Apologies, *Victoria*." I reflected her glare right back at her. "I knew exactly where he was when I surprised him. If he'd tried anything, you and the others could have stopped him."

George put a finger to his mouth and spoke in a whisper. "Quiet, please. Let's move on." Without waiting for acknowledgement, he went down the stairs to the door. Bracing his hand on the frame, he gently tugged it open.

Concrete corridors ran in three directions from our location. Now within a close proximity, I glimpsed individual presences. "Ten possessed, two Arcanes," I whispered. I assumed the Arcanes were the battle mages, Kassus and Drang. Concentrating hard, I was able to sense the differences in the various demons.

"Locations?" George asked.

"One moment." I squeezed shut my eyes and let my senses do the wandering. "Two possessed to the left, maybe a hundred feet. Three to the right. Four of them are scattered more than a hundred feet away." I really had no idea how far they were, but my range wasn't much more than a couple hundred feet, and they felt far away. One throbbing presence grated against my senses as it had earlier when I'd first encountered Karak. "Karak is straight ahead near the two Arcanes."

"Looks like the left corridor is the safest," Patrick said.

"I hope Kassus and Drang didn't setup another crawler trap," Tyler said.

"What's the layout of this place?" I asked.

"The outer hallway runs the perimeter," George said. "The middle hall leads to a wide, open room about sixty feet away."

"The middle hall feels empty," I said. "The other demons are too far away to be in it."

"Are you certain?" Victoria asked.

I nodded. I wished to mute my senses so I could push Karak's unsettling aura away from me, but that would leave us open, so I dealt with the nauseating churn of my stomach and followed close behind my father. Tyler brought up the rear. A coppery odor tickled my nose and I made a face.

Tyler squeezed my shoulders as if to comfort me. With his enhanced sense of smell, he'd probably detected the smell of blood before most of us.

George halted at the corner then motioned us after him. We hugged the back wall and followed him behind a stack of discarded framing wood. Rounded columns supported the room all around the edges. Judging from the jagged remains jutting from the ceiling, Karak and his crew had destroyed the columns there to clear a space for the massive crimson diagram in the middle. I assumed they'd substituted magical means to support the concrete slab above, or perhaps they hoped it wouldn't collapse until after they completed their ritual.

Karak paced back and forth while the men I recognized as Zad Kassus and Martin Drang inspected the demonicus. The outer edges of the pattern were thirty feet away. It might be possible for one of us to draw the counter pattern before we were noticed if it came to desperate measures.

Patrick pointed to the corner on the opposite side of the room. A tall unnaturally pale man leaned against a column. He looked exhausted, and it was no wonder, I realized. That man had to be the anointed and the floor patterned with his lifeblood. The lines were so small and intricate I couldn't even begin to imagine how much blood it had required. One thing was certain—the anointed looked ready to collapse.

Victoria unslung her bow and knocked an arrow with a silver tip.

"It's ready," Drang announced in a deep rough voice. "The next one won't be so bad."

Karak turned to the pale man. "Your service is nearly at an end, faithful one. Your reward awaits."

"Gladly I give it all to thee, Lord Karak." The anointed raised his hands. "I exalt thee and those to come by the sacrifice of my lifeblood." He continued to offer praises while Karak's demeanor clearly indicated he was impatient for the fool to hurry up and kill himself.

I heard the creak of my mother's bow as she pulled back the knocked arrow. Karak shifted positions and suddenly his bulk was directly in the path of Victoria's aim.

"Bloody wanker," she hissed. Blue eyes darting about the room, she slowly released the tension on the bowstring. "I need a new position."

George pointed to a column several feet from the woodpile. "Will that do?"

"Only one way to find out." Remaining crouched, she swiftly made for the column while Patrick watched, face tense.

I felt the other possessed moving closer. Before my mother could take aim from her new position, people dressed in white robes entered the room from the right side and once again obstructed her aim. One group of people struggled as possessed dragged them into the demonicus. Others smiled serenely and took positions in the smaller patterns around the outer edges.

Victoria scurried back to us before the new arrivals made their way to our side of the pattern.

The anointed cried out something in a joyous voice. A chill spiked against my senses and faded into the background. I looked over the woodpile and saw Drang sling the body of the anointed over his shoulder and leave the room.

"We're too late," Victoria said. "We should have been here earlier."

George gave a tense nod. "I believe our best avenue is a hasty retreat."

"Too late," Patrick said. "Unless you want to fight our way out."

By now, robed people stood in all the outer patterns. They spoke excitedly with one another while others held their hands high as if entranced in prayer.

A woman stood in the center pattern, singing praises. "Oh, Lord Abaddon, how wondrous is this day! Soon you shall be among us and the stars will know their end!" She pranced in circles while possessed dragged screaming and crying men and women into the center with her. "I shall be a part of your greatness and pave the way for your rule!"

Karak watched the woman with an amused expression on his otherwise grim face. I had a feeling this woman was consigning herself to oblivion or worse.

The possessed herded the unwilling people into the center with the woman and bound them tightly around her with rope.

"I thought they had to be willing for a demon to consume their souls," I whispered.

Tyler's forehead pinched. "They do. I don't understand what they're doing."

Each of the slightly larger circles outside the center one held three people each. In most cases, there was one willing individual with two others hogtied tightly to them. I wondered how anyone could be so happy to let a demon eat their soul. The woman in the middle still sang her praises. Many white-robed people in the outer patterns looked at her with naked jealousy.

I thought back to the original demonicus. The people in the outer patterns would be possessed, not consumed, by lessers. Two of those in the middle patterns would be consumed while the third would be a host to a knight. Everyone in the core would have their soul consumed so the demon lord could keep his own corporeal form.

"I think I know how they plan to do it," Tyler whispered.

Victoria gave him a querying look.

"They're using the faithful as conduits." He pressed his hands together. "The reason they're tying them together is so they act like soul conductors."

Patrick scowled. "It doesn't seem possible, but you might be right."

"That would explain how they consumed the unwilling employees at the blood bank," George said, "and why they bound so many of them together."

"And why there were so many bodies at the scene." I peeked around the edge of the woodpile and watched the possessed leave the demonicus.

Karak, standing in the center, raised his hands and bellowed, "You are all here to serve a glorious purpose. For the willing, there will be infinite rewards and for the unwilling, the peace of utter oblivion."

"Praise thee, Lord Karak!" the woman in the middle proclaimed.

"For you, girl, the Chosen of Abaddon, you will become part of a greater whole. You will witness the power of his fiery spirit." Karak clapped his hands together. "Let the ritual begin. Let the second chapter of the uprising begin." He left the demonicus and stood between Kassus and Drang. "Armageddon awaits her horsemen!"

The battle mages rapped their staffs on the floor and began chanting. I couldn't hear much of what they said over the singing, screaming, and crying from the robed people.

"Looks like we'll get to witness something awful whether we want to or not," Patrick said. "I just hope we live to warn others."

"We could probably make a run for it," I said. "Surely, they won't chase us while they're in the middle of the ritual."

"I think we should stay and witness this." George sat with his back to the wood. "We can't stop it without using the counter pattern, and attempting that would possibly mean sacrificing all our lives."

"Use one of those fancy ASEs to record it," I said.

"I am." He motioned to a tiny silver sphere hovering just above the wood. "But if we leave and reveal our presence, they'll be sure to look for any form of surveillance."

"Better than getting us all killed." Before I could utter another word, I felt a deep uneasy churning in my stomach rivalling that of Karak himself and the room went deathly silent. I returned my attention to the ritual.

The demonicus glowed a sickly yellow color. The robed sacrifices stood stiff and still. The people in the outer circles began to foam at the mouths and shake violently. One by one, the patterns at their feet flashed different colors, from red, to yellow, to orange. Seconds after the flash, the people stopped shaking and looked around, smiles stretching their faces.

They're possessed.

When the outer circuit completed, the people in the middle patterns began to flop around violently. Two men who'd been unwilling participants unleashed horrific croaking noises. Grey smoke poured from their eyes and mouths and into the mouth of the willing host they were tied to. Tyler's theory had been correct.

I gagged and felt my gorge rising. These demons were forcing innocent people to give up their souls. Hatred burned into my veins. I didn't know what possessed me, but I grabbed my mother's bow. I wanted to kill Karak with all my being.

Strong arms gripped mine and held them tight. "What are you doing Em?" Tyler whispered in my ear.

I felt a tear trickle down my eye. "I want them dead," I whispered. "I want to kill them all."

"What's gotten into you?"

It took all my effort not to scream. My parents had raised me in the church. I believed in God. With all my heart, I knew what was happening here today was an abomination in His eyes. *Then why is He letting it happen?* "Oh, Father, who art in Heaven, hallowed be thy name."

Victoria pressed a hand over my mouth, eyes hard as diamonds. I directed my fury at her. It was her fault the anointed had finished the demonicus. If she'd been faster to aim and shoot, he'd be dead.

Howls of agony and despair rose behind me. I shook loose of Tyler and Victoria's grips and watched as the center pattern in the demonicus glowed a brilliant putrid yellow. The woman in the middle sucked in the soul essence of those bound to her.

Her body buckled, back bending at such an acute angle I thought it might break. She tried to scream, but it was as if the air were being vacuumed into her lungs, making her awful sucking cries even more horrendous. I could see by the look in her eyes that this was not what she had expected. The ground rumbled and a great deafening boom vibrated the air. Concrete dust drifted from the ceiling.

The woman's body turned violently inside out. Before her blood stained the ground, her innards burned to ash leaving a whirling cloud of souls. A fiery haze of orange glowed in the center of the claimed souls. Howling with despair, the wraiths wrapped around the demon's spirit form like a protective layer.

The sphere of souls morphed, at first into a great horned beast, and then shrinking into a blank humanoid template. Features chiseled themselves into the slab, as if an invisible sculptor were lovingly molding this horror into a work of art. The grey stone turned a peach color. Breasts swelled and red hair burst like a flame from the head.

The newly born woman looked down at her hands as if she couldn't believe they were real. A smile stretched her lips. She reared back her head and burst into a full-throated laugh.

Lord Abaddon had arrived.

Chapter 20

"I think we've seen enough," George said.

"I thought Abaddon was a man," I murmured.

A great roaring cheer went up around the room as seventeen new possessed celebrated their arrival on the mortal plane along with another demon lord.

George gripped my arm. "Miss Glass, it's time to go." He looked at the others. "Just act as though we're supposed to be here if anyone sees you."

With that wonderful advice, we sneaked out of our hiding spot, keeping as close to the back edge of the room as possible, and then went back through the doorway. Two men stood in the hallway smoking a joint.

"I'm so fucking happy that's over with." The first took a long drag and held it in.

"Hell yeah!" the second shouted. "Time to celebrate." He looked at our group, eyes calculating. "You part of the new group?"

"Yep," Victoria said

"Nice." He gave her a feral grin and turned it onto me. "We're hiring some hookers for a massive orgy going later." He licked his lips and looked me up and down. "I wouldn't mind fucking that body."

I bit my lower lip as if thoroughly entranced with him. "Get in line, baby."

He laughed. "Yeah, I will."

"How about a quicky?" the second possessed asked. "They haven't let us party for two days and my chubby aches like a motherfucker."

"We're going to orientation," George said. "Lord Karak's orders."

The two possessed backed off, hands up.

"Yeah, you go do that." The first shuddered. "I ain't gonna piss off Karak."

We passed by two more possessed who were too busy cooking heroin to bother with us. Finally, we reached the stairs to the outside. My heart fluttered like a hummingbird as I waited for someone to shout for us to halt, or for two demon lords to appear before us and devour our souls.

Our luck ran out the second we reached the top of the stairs.

"They finally done?" someone asked.

I looked up and saw a cloud of cigarette smoke vanish in the wind to reveal Xasha's face.

My father shifted his large frame to block the possessed's view of Tyler and me.

"What the fuck?"

I flicked my head toward the new voice and saw Vatna leaning against a concrete column. He pushed himself off and strode straight toward us.

I felt Tyler's arm tense where it touched mine. Freeing my hand from his grasp, I readied the lancer.

"Where did you get a bow and swords?" Vatna asked.

"Who has a bow and sword?" Xasha said.

Vatna pointed to Victoria. "Right in front of you, you blind idiot." His gaze shifted and found Tyler. "*You!*"

Before he could shout for help or do anything, I shot him in the throat with a dart. Xasha saw his friend fall and spun around. Before he went two feet, an arrow pierced his leg and he went down in a howl of agony. I raced up to him and shut him up with another dart.

"Won't be long before someone comes to investigate," George said.

"We need to take these two." I bent down and tried to lift Xasha, but failed to even budge him.

"Dragging a bloody unconscious person across the road to the condo is going to be a bit of a trick," Tyler said.

"Would you rather leave them on the loose?" I looked around furtively to make sure other possessed weren't coming up the stairs.

Tyler slung Xasha over his shoulder. "If anyone gets a picture of this, my company is toast."

"I have an idea." George motioned toward the other body. "Mr. Glass, please carry that one. I'll go get my car and fly it in here."

Patrick bent down and tossed Vatna over his shoulder. "I'm ready."

George raced away in a blur. The rest of us moved cautiously across the site, using cover whenever possible, until we reached the fence. George's car shimmered into view and the trunk popped open. Tyler and Patrick dumped the bodies into the spacious interior.

Once Tyler shut the trunk, the car rippled into invisibility. We arrived at the Gregorian a few minutes later and found George sitting in the car just outside the closed gates.

He got out and approached us. "I'll take the three possessed back to the Templar holding facility until we can properly exorcise them."

"We spoke of doing an Abyssal banishment," Patrick said.

George nodded. "Yes, Miss Glass spoke of her desire to make sure these demons never visited the mortal plane again." He scratched his arm and looked at my parents. "Are either of you familiar with the procedure?"

"Yes, but it's rather complex." My father ran a hand down his face. "At the moment, however, all I can think about is sleep. It's been a long, trying day."

"I know someone who needs sleep." My mother put an arm on my shoulder. "I was afraid you might reveal us when you took my bow and tried to shoot Karak."

I almost clenched my fists, but didn't want to accidentally discharge a lancer dart into my foot. "Of course I was upset. Abaddon devoured the souls of innocent people! Anyone who believes in God should be upset at such an abomination."

"I assure you, we are extremely upset." And yet, Victoria's face remained calm. "It isn't wise to lose control of your emotions during a mission, Emily. You nearly gave us away with your outburst."

"You don't feel what I feel," I spat back. "I glimpsed the true horror of this new demon lord. I felt her putrescence all over those innocent souls. I felt her sickening aura in my guts like nuclear radiation." I gagged just thinking about it. "Karak was bad enough, but now we have two highly powerful caustic demons loose in our world. How many more people need to lose their souls before we stop them?"

"Perhaps you shouldn't come on other missions until you learn to control your emotions." Victoria put a hand to her chin. "I believe that would be the best course of action. You're simply not ready for the field."

Tyler wrapped an arm around me. "I think if you could feel someone's soul being eaten, you might be a little more sympathetic, Victoria."

She shrugged. "Perhaps. Then again, I would learn to control it as I have my other emotions. It is an unfortunate but necessary part of being in the field."

My mother was right, but I was too angry and stubborn to admit it. I realized with a strange sense of detachment that I *had* led a sheltered life. There were horrors in this world I never could have imagined, and now there were plenty I had no problem imagining.

There was no point in arguing with my mother about this or anything else. She would always be right even if she wasn't. "Well, I'm glad you're at least taking an interest in my welfare now, Mother. Goodness knows you've rarely shown any until now." I knew it was a low blow, but it was also true. Though I hadn't realized the reason for my mother's long absences during my childhood, I now knew it was because she put her duties to the Exorcists first.

My mother's eyes went rock hard.

"I believe we all need some sleep," my father announced in a loud voice. He gave me a pointed look. "We'll be in touch." Before Victoria could say anything, he put an arm over her shoulder and guided her away.

George didn't look the least bit fazed by the family drama. "I'll speak with Professor Zuba about Abyssal banishments."

Tyler gave him a confused look. "Why wasn't he the first person you asked when we requested it a couple of days ago?"

"A Custodian I met in Colombia referred me to him, so today was the first chance I had to speak with him." George motioned to the lancer. "You may hold onto that, Miss Glass. Despite your sensory overload, you performed very well tonight."

"My mother is completely overbearing." If I'd hoped to hear a statement of sympathy from George, I was disappointed.

He simply nodded to each of us and said, "I'll be in touch." With that, he climbed into his car and drove away.

173

Tyler took my hand, opened the pedestrian gate, and led me into the lift and upstairs. "You and your mother are like oil and fire, aren't you?"

"Whatever made you think that?"

He chuckled. "I didn't really see it until tonight."

"Yes, well, I suppose we're too much alike." I tugged off my clothes and slipped into one of Tyler's T-shirts.

He pressed me to him and kissed the top of my head. "Do you feel like you have to make her proud of you?"

I drew in his scent and snuggled my head against his chest. "Sometimes, I just want her to tell me that I did something right. Instead, she always points out what I did wrong."

"I don't think that's true." Tyler lifted my chin and kissed me. "I'm pretty sure she complimented you at least once today. Maybe you tune into the negative too much."

"Maybe." I was willing to concede that small point. I really couldn't remember if Victoria had given me praise today or not. "On the bright side, we caught two of your tormentors."

A broad grin stretched his lovely lips. "Now we just have figure out when Barboar finds another host."

"I wish I hadn't killed him." I sighed. "Now it'll be doubly difficult to track find him again."

"Maybe." He traced a finger down my cheek. "Maybe Barboar will be compelled to join Karak's army when he finds another host."

I hadn't really considered that, but it made perfect sense. "What do you suppose Karak and Abaddon intend to do?"

Tyler bit his lip. "I'm not sure. Even with all those souls sustaining them, the mortal plane still holds a lot of risk for a demon lord. Domathus must have some ultimate goal in mind, but whatever it is, I don't know."

"Would he be after wealth or power?"

"Demon lords are always after power, but not the kind of earthly power men enjoy." He kissed my cheek and let me go so he could remove his shirt.

"The lesser demons like Barboar do enjoy earthly power, though," I said.

He nodded.

"Could a lesser demon become a demon lord?"

174

Tyler ran a hand down his chiseled abs. "You know, I'm not that familiar with how it works. Some demons have an insatiable lust for spiritual power, while others like myself don't care so much."

I couldn't stop staring at his lovely muscles. "Are the lustful ones caustic spirits?"

"As far as I know, yes." He tossed his shirt into the hamper. "Until Zuba classified the different types of spirits, I didn't even realize there was much variety. I just figured we were all identical except for the amount of power we accrued. I thought our colors had to do with power and not compatibility with mortals." His lips curled up. "I feel like I've got a new perspective on life, you know? I feel like I belong."

I ran a hand along his chest. "Maybe you're not really a demon but something else."

Tyler pulled me against him. "The only thing that matters to me is you."

"Aww." I kissed him. "You're such a sweet talker."

"Thank you, Em."

I leaned back. "For what?"

"After Barboar, I couldn't stop questioning myself." He ran a hand through my hair and gazed at me adoringly. "I thought maybe I was just as bad, that maybe my good phase was something temporary." His jade eyes locked onto mine. "You made me realize how wrong I was."

"I believe in you, Tyler." I pressed his hand to my cheek. "I love you."

"Without you, I wouldn't be the person I am now." He leaned down and hugged me. "You make me feel complete."

I felt tears burning my eyes and knew with all my heart he made me feel the same way. I never wanted us to be apart.

The next day at work seemed surreal. I had to sneak through a back door with the help of Jack to avoid the media lurking in the front of the building. Investigating who might be trying to destroy Tyler's business issues seemed trivial in comparison to the demonic menaces lurking in the city.

But it's still important.

"I planted more fake programs on my computer," Jack said. "Including a virus that will infect any computers used to open it." He took a sip of coffee and leaned back in the chair across from my desk.

"Mhm," I said absent-mindedly.

Jack raised an eyebrow. "Something on your mind?"

I shook myself from my musings and leaned forward. "I'm sorry. Late night. What were you saying about a virus?"

"I said, it will infect the host computer and send me information."

This piqued my interest. "We can spy on their computers?"

"Yep." Jack looked pretty pleased with himself.

I couldn't blame him. "Brilliant! Maybe we can track down the source of the cretins." Tyler's original assertion that Barboar and his gang were the culprits seemed less likely after witnessing how Karak ordered them about. They likely had little time for corporate espionage. That meant our instincts about someone like Brandon or Arianna seemed spot on.

Jack stood and stretched. "I'll let you know if anything happens. In the meantime, I've been doing the real work on my personal laptop."

"Excellent. Just don't let Hinkle or Jones see you doing it."

"I know." He grinned. "I've been using your old office as a hideout." He left and closed the door behind him, leaving me with my thoughts and little else to do.

Kevin and the other salespeople were out making the rounds, trying to woo new clients. I tried to focus on something productive, but a series of jaw-cracking yawns made me want to do nothing more than take a nap.

The day passed slowly, but I managed to make a few calls and set up some sales meetings for Kevin. I even tried my hand at espionage by keeping an eye on Jones and Hinkle. They seemed nervous, but didn't engage in another secret rendezvous.

George sent me a text as I prepared to leave the office. *Our guests are in the Templar holding facility. Zuba tells me the most efficient way to banish them is with the aid of a Daemos.*

The thought of using the services of a demon spawn intrigued and sent a twinge of anxiety spiraling into my stomach. *When can we do it?*

George replied a moment later. *I spoke with one who is willing. Will send you more information when I have it.*

I sneaked out of the building the way I'd come in and Joe delivered me safely back to Tyler's condo. While I waited for Tyler, I read the news on my phone. The investigation into the massacre at my apartment was still top news, and Tyler's name was on the lips of every reporter. Detective Long was quoted as saying, "We have mounting evidence pointing to a perpetrator and will make an announcement soon."

That sent a cold chill through my heart.

Tyler seemed to be his sole focus if my interrogation was anything to go by. I wondered if soon we might have police knocking on our door.

Chapter 21

When Tyler arrived, we had a quick bite to eat and returned to the Grotto for orientation, this time in a conventional car—though nothing else about the mystical place was the least bit conventional.

"Today we will learn about the Overworld Conclave and how it affects you," Desmond informed us once everyone was seated in the auditorium. He proceeded to show us an educational movie entitled, "The Overworld and You."

It was a long boring affair, explaining how vampires, Daemos, Arcanes, and other supers came together to protect the common good and keep their presence secret from the noms, as they repeatedly called our normal kin.

I found myself nodding off as a vampire in the movie explained how they were careful to keep their prey healthy, happy, and most importantly, clueless.

"I don't suspect they ever met Stephen," I whispered to Tyler. That vampire had wanted me dead.

Tyler chuckled. "I'm sure there are plenty of others like him."

"Desmond hasn't mentioned the vampire war in Colombia." I pursed my lips and looked at our robed teacher. "I wonder if he even knows."

Desmond concluded the class with instructions to meet the next day—as if we didn't know—and departed before I could corner him and ask him about the mysterious person with similar powers to mine he'd met in the Fairy Garden.

Angela and her friends, however, quickly surrounded us before we could leave, and I remembered my promise to her.

Once again, they gazed adoringly at Tyler and I had to take Angela by the arm and lead her away. I took her into the hallway and put a hand on her shoulder.

"Are you certain you don't want to be a vampire?" Never in my life had I thought I'd ask someone such a question.

She nodded rapidly. "Oh, yes, very certain. It really sucks when I look at my friends and can't think about anything but drinking their blood."

Already, I felt the parasitic cold inside her and couldn't help but grimace in disgust. "Okay. This will take a moment."

She tensed. "Will it hurt?"

"I don't think so, but you might feel weak afterward."

A tear pooled in her eye. "I'm ready."

"Okay. Let me concentrate." I opened my senses and touched her waist with both hands. Before long, the squirming cold became palpable. Gripping the invisible thing with my hands, I slowly slid it out of her.

She shrieked at the sight of the glowing white creature in my hands, stumbled, and fell as if her knees had grown too weak to support her. A rasping breath rattled from her throat and she clutched her stomach. Face so pale it had an almost greenish cast, she retched up a puddle of saliva.

The parasite thing dissolved in my hands, vanishing into the ether, leaving a cold wet feeling on my palms. I wiped them on my jeans and knelt next to her.

"Are you okay, Angela?"

She didn't speak for several seconds then finally nodded. "I felt terrible at first, but now I feel better." She touched her teeth, as if expecting to find fangs then smiled. "It's gone! I'm normal again!" Angela gripped me in a tight hug and squealed. "Thank you so much, Emily." Tears ran down her cheeks.

I helped her stand and brushed a bit of dust from her dress. "Remember, don't tell anyone. This is our secret."

Her eyes widened. "How will I explain to my friends that I'm not a vampire anymore?"

I shrugged. "Tell them an Arcane fixed you. I don't care, just don't tell them about me."

Angela hugged me again and whispered in my ear. "I won't. We're BFFs forever, now."

"Of course." I doubted I'd ever see her again after the class and hoped she could keep my secret.

We returned into the auditorium to find her friends swooning over Tyler as he regaled them with a story about running a business. It was a dry subject, but the girls didn't seem to care, so long as they could watch him talk. He stopped talking midsentence when he saw me walking toward him. The girls looked back at me, jealousy plain on their faces. Knowing this gorgeous man had eyes only for me made me feel special indeed.

The girls suddenly noticed Angela and seemed confused.

"Where did you go?" one asked.

"Just talked to Emily for a little bit about how to tell my parents I'm a vampire." Angela sighed. "I'm going to see an Arcane doctor soon. I heard it might be possible to fix me."

"Oh, really?" The other girl clapped her hands with delight. "That would be so awesome."

The other one chimed in. "Yeah, and you won't try to suck our blood anymore."

Tyler took my arm and led me away after I wished the girls a good evening.

"Enjoying the adoration of the ladies?" I asked.

His wolfish grin made an appearance. "Your adoration is all that matters to me." Tyler pecked a kiss on my nose. "Speaking of which, how did it go?"

"Rather well, if I do say so myself." We climbed into his car, an ordinary sedan the reporters hopefully wouldn't notice, and left.

"I just want you to know I admire you for helping that girl." Tyler stopped at a traffic light and rubbed a hand on my thigh. "You're a good person, Em."

I felt a blush creeping up my neck. "I try to be."

"I could tell from the look in her eyes, you just saved her life." He accelerated and turned onto the street to the condo. "I can't imagine how different my life would be without you."

"Yes, well, hopefully she learned a valuable life lesson." Tyler's praise made me feel giddy. I wondered if it was because of all the negativity from my mother, or perhaps I was simply an attention whore.

The media still stood watch over the entrance of the Gregorian, though there were fewer than earlier. Some of them tried to peer into the windows of the car but were thwarted by the dark tint.

I sniffed. "I wish they'd bugger off and bother someone else."

"They'll get tired of it sooner or later," he assured me.

I noticed two official-looking sedans parked in front, and put a hand on Tyler's wrist. "Those look like unmarked police cars."

He stopped the car at the corner of the building where the driveway curled around to the rear parking deck. "I saw the news. Detective Long seemed convinced he was close to an arrest."

"What if he's after you?"

"He doesn't have any hard evidence." Tyler pressed his lips together. "Then again, he seemed ready to railroad me no matter what."

"We shouldn't go in. What if they're waiting for you?"

Tyler drove around the back of the building where two more similar cars waited. He slapped the steering wheel. "Son of a—we need to get out of here." He made a right turn into the guest parking lot and stopped. "I don't understand what this Detective Long means to do. Unless he fabricated evidence, he doesn't have a case."

For some reason, it suddenly made perfect sense to me. "This must be related to the problems with your companies. What if this public relations nightmare is all some ploy to destroy your reputation? I remember seeing an unmarked police car in the guest parking lot even before the first time we met Detective Long. Remember how he went out of his way to investigate the gunshot?"

It didn't take Tyler long to connect the dots. "This must be their end game."

I took out my phone and browsed to a news site. *Officials Close to an Arrest* read the headline of the top story. I read it aloud. "Though no official announcement has been made, the lead investigator, Detective Long, appeared at the residence of Tyler Rock this evening. Reliable sources believe he is the target of this investigation." Anger swelled inside me. "This man is out to ruin you."

Tyler shook his head. "No, he's only a pawn. I'm sure if he arrests me, they'd hold me as long as they could before announcing a lack of evidence."

"He's already damaged your reputation."

"Seeing me arrested on live television would put a nail in the coffin." He growled deep in his throat. "Even if I was vindicated, it would take months to recover from the fallout."

"What do we do?"

"We go where they can't find us." He backed the car out of the parking lot and slowly drove back around the building and to the street.

Tension knotted my stomach. I waited for someone to shout at us, or for police cars to surround us at any moment. Thankfully, a sporty red Bentley pulled into the drive at that moment and drew away the gazes of the reporters.

We pulled into the street and drove away.

"Where won't they find us?" I asked. "The Grotto?"

"Seems like the best place."

An idea brightened in my mind. "I know who to ask." I called George.

"Yes, Miss Glass?" His voice sounded calm as ever.

I explained our troubles with the law and finished with a question. "Where can we stay?"

"This is very troubling," he said, not sounding the least bit troubled. "Who do you think is targeting you?"

"At first I thought it might be my former associates," Tyler said. "Now I think it might be unrelated to our demon problems."

"Well, we certainly can't have the mortal authorities arresting citizens of the Overworld."

George's statement surprised me. "We're citizens of the Overworld now?"

"Of course, Miss Glass." He sounded certain. "You both have supernatural attributes, and thus are subject to our laws."

"So the Custodians can help us?" I asked.

"Our main purpose is to cover up scandals perpetrated by supernaturals, though in this case, it sounds as though you are the victims." He paused. "Unfortunately, with resources spread so thin, we can't afford to do much at the moment."

"Lovely." I sighed. "Considering that hell is literally being unleashed on Earth right now, I'd say it's high time you hired more people, Agent Walker."

"Agreed, but that takes time. In the meantime, I will find you suitable accommodations to conceal you from the authorities." He said nothing for a moment and then continued. "Come to the Templar compound. I'll meet you there and discuss the options."

"Address?" Tyler asked.

"I will text it to you." He ended the call and forwarded the address. I entered it into the navigation system and pulled up directions.

Tyler laughed. "Fugitives again, huh, Em?"

I groaned. "When does it ever stop?"

"Sometimes being rich and powerful is a real pain in the ass." He shook his head. "Maybe we should just sell everything and travel the world."

I leaned against his shoulder. "That sounds pretty wonderful. No more demons, no more corporate worries. Just you, me, and wherever we find ourselves."

Tyler glanced at me. "Would you be happy living like that?"

"Are you kidding?" I giggled. "It sounds heavenly."

"Hmm." He stared at the road ahead. Nodded. "I'll talk to the accountants at my holdings company and see what they think we could squeeze out of everything."

"Do you think it's safe to go to work with the police looking for you?"

He shrugged. "I'll just call my people. I think we could get a few hundred million out of my enterprises. It might take some time to sell everything, but that shouldn't be a problem."

I thought of Jack and the others. "Could you keep OnTech? I really think your business model there will work, and I'd hate to see them soaked up by another big corporation."

"Sure. Maybe they can turn things around." Tyler looked at the car's navigation screen and took a left.

I studied him for a moment. "Are you certain you won't miss being a big-time businessman?"

He waggled a hand. "Maybe a little. I kind of liked seeing my companies succeed. I was thinking about adopting OnTech's workplace environment at a couple of other businesses just to see how it worked." Tyler pointed to a dirt road winding through pastures. "I think we're here."

Butterflies fluttered in my stomach as the tires rattled over a cattle guard and we entered the Templar compound. I somewhat expected a small army of people in black to stop us, but we were allowed to continue unmolested.

George stood outside the large barn next to a huge Husky. We stopped and got out.

"You may park in the underground garage," George said. "I've arranged for you to stay the night here if you'd like."

I went up to the Husky. "What a lovely dog. May I pet him?"

George's lips curled up faintly. "You might want to ask him directly. I don't think Ryland would appreciate it."

The dog yipped and then morphed into a large naked man with a wide grin on his face. "I don't reckon it would be appropriate," he said. "My lovely girlfriend might not take kindly to letting you rub my stomach."

Heat washed into my face. "Oh, lord. You're a lycan aren't you?" I was mortified.

Tyler burst into laughter.

I threw up my hands. "I can't even—I just can't!"

"I like you already," Tyler told the other man and held out his hand. "The name is Tyler Rock."

Ryland shook his hand. "What's your deal, Tyler?"

"I'm a demon." He shrugged. "I know it sounds bad, but I'm not that awful."

"Turns out I know a few good demon spawn, so I reckon you're not all bad." Ryland gave him a lopsided grin.

I finally recovered a bit and turned to look at the lycan, keeping my eyes well above his equator. "You realize you're completely naked, don't you?"

"Yep." Ryland crossed his arms. "It ain't easy wearing clothes in wolf form."

I pretended to look at something else. "Yes, I suppose you're right." With the shock fading, I sensed the lycan part of him as something wild, hot, and savage—the exact opposite of the vampires. Though he had what I'd consider a hot signal, it wasn't the same as what I glimpsed when around demons. They were a dry heat, while this was like sensing an explosion of hot blood in my mouth. I smacked my lips and looked back at Ryland.

He grinned.

Definitely an alpha wolf.

"Let's store your car below," George said. He turned to Ryland. "Good evening, and good hunting."

"Same to you." The lycan morphed back into a giant wolf and bounded away.

"He must terrify the horses," I said.

George climbed into the back seat of the car. "They're quite used to the goings on at this place."

Tyler and I slid back in and followed George's instructions to park the car. We got out and took a lift—levitator—down into the underground complex where our guide led us into a small room with a table.

"Please, have a seat." George sat at the head of the table. "Would you like tea, coffee, or water?"

I nodded. "Water, please."

"You have beer or wine?" Tyler asked.

"Not in here, I'm afraid." George reached into a cabinet and procured a bottled water, which he handed to me. "I brought you in here because I have good news."

I popped open the water. "Oh?"

"A Daemas has agreed to help us with the banishment and is on her way here tonight."

Tyler and I exchanged hopeful looks.

Part of this nightmare might be over in a few hours.

Chapter 22

"Are you certain?" I asked. "This seems very fast."

He nodded. "She's very concerned about the recent influx of demon lords and wants to interrogate them thoroughly."

"Finally, we're getting some help." I blew out a breath of relief.

Tyler looked a little uneasy. "What are these demon spawn like?"

"Something of a mixed bag," George replied. "Hopefully, this one won't have too many hidden agendas."

Hope glimmered in Tyler's eyes. "You really think she'll be able to banish them tonight?"

"That is the plan." George placed his hands on the table and gave us a steady look. "Let's talk about your other problems."

"With the police?" I threw up my hands. "Where do I begin?"

Tyler took the reins. "It all started with another company trying to hire away the best and the brightest from my holdings. During our investigations, we've found evidence of espionage and more." His fists tightened. "Barboar only added more fuel to the fire when he went to Emily's apartment in an attempt to track me down. He murdered her neighbors and gave whoever is trying to ruin me more ammunition."

"By publicly discrediting you," George said.

Tyler nodded. "Making me look bad makes investors lose confidence. Lack of faith in my leadership causes the value of the stocks to fall and makes it easier for someone to buy out my companies."

"Do they have to take over every company individually?" I asked.

Tyler shook his head. "The way Cyrus Rock structured mine and my siblings' businesses is by giving us each a holding firm. Mine is Tyler Rock Enterprises. If its stocks fall enough, another entity could buy it out and take over management for its subsidiary holdings."

"I won't pretend to understand how nom businesses work," George said. "It sounds purposefully complex to allow for subterfuge and money making. Trickery has worked so far for your anonymous opponent, but it might also work for you."

"I'm open to suggestions." Tyler sighed. "I thought of secretly spinning my holdings into a shell company, but Cyrus restricted how much we could do in the enterprise charter."

"I'm not suggesting anything businesswise." George clasped his hands. "I believe we could reconstruct the crime scene with solid evidence pointing to Barboar as the killer."

"I'm certain they already have evidence he was there," I said. "But whoever is pulling the strings has Detective Long pursuing Tyler first."

"It doesn't matter what they have," George said. "We have magic." He took out his phone and projected a hologram of Barboar. "I took several pictures of the demon's host body and used a spell to construct his image." He flicked the image and Barboar began walking and waving his arms. "I can make this do anything I want. With images of the inside of the apartment, I could remake the crime scene that shows Barboar murdering your neighbors."

I shivered. "That's awful."

"But it could work," Tyler said. "If we released a video like that on the internet, it'll make the police department look like fools."

I tried not to think about how gruesome it was to fake-murder my deceased neighbors and considered the idea. "We don't have any cameras in our apartment or the building."

"People use hidden cameras all the time," George said.

"Like a nanny cam hidden in a teddy bear," Tyler said. He clapped his hands. "This is great!"

"Yes." I grimaced. "Delightful."

"What do you need from me?" Tyler asked.

"Pictures of the apartment," George said. "Primarily of the main room."

"What about the other rooms?" I asked.

"Unnecessary," he replied. "A hidden camera would be static. I think showing Barboar drag your neighbors inside would be sufficient."

John Corwin

"Do you need pictures of them?" I asked, uncertain how I'd procure them.

"They're all over the news," Tyler said. "You can get their information from the internet."

"How am I supposed to get into the apartment unseen?" I asked. "Will I use your flying car to gain access?"

"Do the windows even open in your building?" Tyler asked. "I don't remember you having a balcony or anything."

I frowned. "You're right. I don't think I could get inside easily." I snapped my fingers. "But I know who could." I fired off a text to Isabel. *I need a favor, sis.*

Anything! Came her reply. The phone rang before I could text back, and I answered.

"Girl, are you doing okay?" Isabel sounded worried. "The news is just awful. They're dragging Tyler's name through the mud."

"We're fine," I assured her. "My other contacts gave us a place to stay."

George raised an eyebrow. "Does she know about the Overworld?"

I ignored him and got to the point. "I need your help with something."

"What is it?" she asked.

"I need pictures of the apartment."

Isabel gasped. "You want me to go inside—" She released a shuddering breath. "Okay, I'll do it."

"We only need a few pictures of the den."

"Make sure she takes them from an angle were there would be a shelf or something to support a camera," George instructed.

I relayed the information. "I hate to ask, but can you do it tonight?"

"Yes. Jack and I will go right away."

"You're the best, sis."

"You want me to email them to you once I have them?" she asked.

"That would be great." I felt a shiver of apprehension. "Please be careful."

"You know you don't have to tell me that." She laughed uneasily. "You owe me some drinks after this one."

188

"Name the time and place." I ended the call and looked hopefully at George. "I hope this works."

"If anything, it will convince the police to leave you alone," he assured me.

"Will they be able to tell it's a fake?" Tyler asked.

"The video itself will be quite real," George said. "I'll use a tablet to project the holographic images and play them forward. To anyone analyzing the video, it will appear authentic."

My heart beat a little easier at his confidence. "How long will it take to fabricate?"

"Perhaps a day." George's phone beeped. "Ah, our guest has arrived." He stood. "I'll be back momentarily."

Tyler got up and took a water from the cabinet then dropped back into his chair. "Interesting. This water is cold."

"I noticed. Must be some cooling spell in the cabinet."

He chuckled. "Sounds like you've accepted all the weirdness of the Overworld."

I flicked a hand. "Hardly. Having a dog turn into a naked man right before my eyes was rather unsettling."

"I thought your reaction was priceless." He sighed. "Wish I'd recorded it."

"Maybe when you get better using a smartphone, old man." I stuck out my tongue.

"I'm learning." He took a swig of water. "Maybe we'll swing by MagicSoft or Orange and grab one of those arcphones tomorrow after class."

"I wonder if they require a credit report."

George entered the room a few minutes later with a gorgeous blonde behind him. Her ice-blue eyes calmly regarded us as she pushed a silken tress of hair over her shoulder. She wore tight leather pants and an equally form-fitting shirt, both hugging her curves like an eager lover. Tyler noticed my reaction and grinned.

I stood and tried not to gawk at the woman. "Hello, I'm Emily."

The woman narrowed her eyes and looked from me to Tyler. Her full lips pursed into a rosebud. "I am Anae Vallaena Slade."

I wasn't sure what to do, so I held out a hand. "Pleased to meet you, Annie."

Laughter tinkled from her throat. "My name is not Annie, child. Anae is my title." She looked to George. "Do they know nothing of Daemos?"

"They are still in orientation, Anae Vallaena." George offered a faint smile. "You are the first Daemas they've had the honor of meeting."

"How interesting." She flashed pearly white teeth. "Then I will be gentle."

My stomach tightened. "What does Anae mean?"

"It is a designation of position in a house hierarchy," Vallaena said. "I am among the highest in House Slade." She waved a hand. "But let's dispense with the formalities. It would seem you've discovered something quite troubling. Agent Walker has explained some of it to me, but I must know more."

Tyler stood and turned to face her. "Easy enough." He didn't seem the least bit intimidated or entranced by her beauty.

"And you are?" The way she looked at him, it was evident his charms didn't affect her either.

"Tyler Rock." He didn't offer her his hand, but crossed his arms and leaned back against the table. "Technically, I'm a demon possessing a man's body."

She wrinkled her nose. "*Oh.*" Turning to George, she said, "I didn't realize Templars associated with such creatures."

"I'd like to think of us as one big happy demon family," Tyler said, his eyes harder than the tone of his voice. "I'm a jade spirit if that makes any difference."

She tilted her head slightly. "A jade?" She bowed her head slightly. "I apologize, Tyler. A jade is a rare spirit indeed."

Confusion flashed across his face. "Are we?"

Her lips curled up ever so slightly. "How old are you?"

"By mortal years maybe thirty or forty."

"Ah, then you are exceedingly young." She gave him an appraising look. "Who is your sire?"

"Baal."

Her eyes flashed with delight and she took his hand. "It would seem we are brother and sister. Daevadius will be so pleased."

"Who?"

"Perhaps you will meet him in due time." Vallaena's demeanor cooled once again. "He and I were sapphire spirits before giving up our place in Haedaemos to live among men. We joined our souls with those of humans to become the first Daemos."

"Honestly, I didn't even know about jade, sapphire, or caustic before yesterday," Tyler admitted. A wide, genuine grin spread across his face. "Wow, it feels weird knowing I have relatives on this side."

"You have a large family in Eden, Tyler." Vallaena walked around the other end of the table and sat. "But enough of small talk. Let us turn to important matters."

Tyler dropped into his chair, reached over and squeezed my hand. He was still smiling ear-to-ear. "A few days ago, two battle mages, Zad Kassus and Martin Drang, built a demonicus and summoned thirteen lesser demons, four greater demons, and a demon lord by the name of Karak."

Vallaena hissed. "Domathus is up to his old tricks again, I see."

"I wouldn't know about his old tricks, but from what little I know, Karak has always been the underling of Domathus." Tyler took a sip of water. "Last night, Kassus and Drang used another demonicus to summon Lord Abaddon."

"Abaddon is no lord," I said. "She's a woman. Shouldn't it be Lady Abaddon?"

"Demons don't differentiate," Tyler said.

Vallaena bit her lower lip. "This is very troubling. The last time Domathus tried to send his four demon lords to Eden was during the First Seraphim War."

"A war with angels?" I wasn't sure I'd heard correctly.

"The attempt failed." Vallaena's gaze wandered up, as if recalling something. "There were other attempts over the millennia, but Domathus lacked the souls to properly execute the demonicus."

"We think he's found a way around that," Tyler said. "They bound unwilling subjects to their human thralls. During the ritual, the thralls drew in the soul essence from the others."

Vallaena pounded the palm of her hand against the table. "Monstrous!" Blue eyes hard as diamonds she stared at Tyler. "You are certain of this?"

"We all witnessed it," George said. "I even have it recorded on an ASE."

John Corwin

"Why didn't you tell me this before?" Vallaena asked.

"I thought it would be best to discuss in private." George took out an ASE and rolled it in his fingers. "Would you like to see?"

She nodded. "I must."

We watched the entire affair again, but this time with the ability to pause and examine the scene from other angles. I noticed when the souls of the unwilling were being ripped from their bodies how the grey mist resembled a wraithlike skeleton. My bowels clenched at the absolute terror in their eyes.

Where is God in all this? Doesn't he care?

Vallaena seemed no more thrilled to watch it than me. "I have seen enough." Her lips peeled back from her teeth. "I believe Abaddon was not the last they will summon to Eden."

"You think they'll bring more demon lords?" I asked.

"There are many who follow demons, but very few who are absolutely willing to give up their souls." She shivered. "This limitation has long kept demon lords from this realm. Possessing a body is of little interest and great risk to them. By using souls to assume a corporeal form here, they are able to retain more power and assume less risk."

"You think since they found a workaround to take unwilling souls, Domathus will send more of his lords through?" Tyler said.

She nodded. "The question is why."

"The timing is highly suspect," George said. "Especially considering what else is happening."

"I do not know if Domathus wishes to capitalize on the instability in the Overworld, or if he has chosen a side." She met Tyler's gaze. "Let us see what little information we can squeeze from the prisoners before I banish them to the Abyss."

"Is it difficult to banish them?" I asked.

"It is tiring and time consuming." Vallaena stood and stretched her slender figure. "I would usually not consider lesser demons worth the bother, but I will make an exception for these." She walked around the table and put a hand on Tyler's shoulder. "After all, they are interfering with my brother."

Tyler stood. "Is there anything I can do to help?"

She shook her head. "No, but you are welcome to watch."

192

I wasn't sure I wanted to behold the interrogation or the banishment, but a morbid sense of curiosity crept up on me and I followed them out of the room.

George led us to the cells and showed us which ones had the culprits. "I'll leave you to it. Unfortunately, I must attend other duties, but everything will be recorded."

"Until next time, Agent Walker." Vallaena nodded at him.

"Until then, Anae Vallaena Slade." George returned the nod and left.

"Remain outside," Vallaena said. She touched the blacked-out glass on the first cell and turned it transparent from our side.

I saw the woman, Astra, on the other side. "She doesn't need to go to the Abyss," I said. "It's the other two we're worried about."

"Very well. I'll leave her for the Arcanes to handle." Vallaena touched the glass on the other cells where Xasha and Vatna waited. "These two are mine."

She entered Xasha's cell first. His eyes flashed when he saw her and he tried to bolt past her to the door. Vallaena easily caught him by the throat and threw him hard across the room. He tumbled over the table and smacked into the wall.

"Holy shit, she's strong." Tyler chuckled. "I think I might like my new sister."

"She is beyond gorgeous," I said. "I think I might have a girl crush."

"I don't know how I feel about that." His grin told another story.

"Where will the next demonicus be?" Vallaena asked Xasha as he rose unsteadily to his feet. Her words came through clearly as if there were no glass.

"Who the fuck are you, bitch?" Xasha wiped at blood trickling down his forehead. "I'm going to beat the shit out of you and fuck you to death."

"How quaint." Vallaena smiled. "I'd forgotten what it was like to deal with caustics. You're so base and unimaginative."

He roared and charged her once again. She gripped him by the throat and held his struggling form off the ground. He tried to tear her fingers from his throat, but she didn't even seem to notice. Choking and blue faced, Xasha's bloodshot eyes bugged from his head.

Vallaena casually tossed him across the room again. It took him a lot longer to recover this time. He eventually staggered drunkenly to his feet.

"Perhaps I should rip off your testicles and make you eat them," Vallaena said in a calm cold voice.

"What the hell are you?" Xasha asked.

"I am Daemos."

His eyes flew wide with fear. "W-what? Why are you here?"

"To get answers, you insignificant little bug." She strode forward. "Where will the next demonicus be?"

He shook his head. "I swear I don't know."

"Perhaps you'd like to meet my pet crawler. He does so enjoy demon souls."

"For fucks sake, lady, I'm a demon like you!" He backed up to the corner. "I don't know anything."

"You are nothing like me." Vallaena looked at the floor. It bubbled like black oil, forming a black ball. Legs sprouted, and the creature strained free from the tarlike substance around it.

Within seconds, a new monster was born.

Chapter 23

"Good lord, it's like that creature we saw at the blood bank," I said.

Tyler stared at it for a while. "She summoned it so easily. I wonder if that's something I can learn to do."

"Obviously, Daemos have no problems whatsoever."

The crawler shrieked and leapt at Xasha. He screamed and a dark wet stain formed at the crotch of his pants. The monster jerked short of the possessed, as if secured by an invisible rope.

"All I know is they plan on doing two more at the same time," he cried. "I swear, I don't know where!"

A very good question occurred to me. "If that thing eats him, it'll devour his soul, right?"

"I'm not entirely sure," Tyler said. "I know crawlers can eat human souls, but demons might be different."

Vallaena hurled more questions at Xasha, but he didn't seem to know much. "What was your next destination?"

"We were supposed to meet on the west side of town, but they hadn't given us directions yet." Snot poured from his nose. "If you let me go, I'll find out anything you want to know, I swear it, Mistress. I will be yours."

She seemed to consider his request while the crawler chittered and jerked on its invisible leash. "Perhaps." Vallaena left the room, leaving the crawler with the terrified possessed. She came to me. "Mr. Walker told me you could get this creature's true name. I'll need it to banish him."

"Why not let the crawler eat his soul?" I asked.

She tutted. "The crawler would devour the human and demon soul. Unless you wish to condemn the host, you will give me his true name so I can perform the banishment."

195

"Oh, I guess I didn't think of that." I didn't want to harm the host. "I'll need to touch him."

"That's it?" She raised an eyebrow. "Can you see my true name simply by touching me?"

I wasn't sure what I should tell her, so I left it unclear. "Something like that." I looked uneasily at the crawler. My skin crawled at the thought of going near the huge demon bug. "Will your pet hurt me?"

Vallaena shook her head. "I have it under control. Follow me in. I'll restrain him if need be."

Tyler put a hand on my shoulder. "Be careful."

"I will."

The Daemas looked from me to Tyler. "You are every bit as infected as my brother—*our* brother."

Tyler's forehead pinched. "Infected?"

She laughed. "With *love*." Vallaena's lips turned down. "I find duty is a far greater calling."

"Sorry, I'm just a weak male." Tyler looked deep into my eyes. "Life would be dull and meaningless without Emily."

I nearly giggled at the thrill he sent across my skin with that look.

"Daevadius says the same about his beloved Alysea." Vallaena let out a long sigh. "Come, Emily. Let's get this done."

I followed her into the room. Xasha cowered in the corner. He looked at me and his eyes burned with hate. "You're Grim's woman. Is he here?" His fear abruptly dissipated. "I'll tear out your beating heart, Grim!"

Vallaena blurred across the room. She lifted Xasha by his neck and slammed him against the wall. I skirted the crawler by walking along the opposite wall and touched Xasha's hand. He struggled and knocked me back. I stumbled and hit the window with a thud. Tyler appeared at my side and helped me up.

"You okay, babe?"

I nodded. "Yes."

"I'll kill you, Grim!" Xasha struggled. "Let me eat his heart!"

"You'll do no such thing," Vallaena replied in a calm voice and squeezed his neck.

He rasped in pain.

Gritting my teeth, I walked back over to Xasha and gripped his hand. A pattern blazed into my mind and with it, the name, *Xashabyullwt*. I turned to Vallaena and spoke the name with precise pronunciation.

The fear returned to Xasha's eyes. "How does she know my name? That's impossible!"

Vallaena slammed his head against the rock wall and dropped the senseless man to the ground. The ground around the crawler bubbled like tar and the creature melted back into it with a loud, protesting screech. She turned to Xasha, eyes glowing brightly azure.

Without saying a word, she lifted her hands. The ground beneath the woozy man turned inky black. Dozens of arms and hands rose from the tarlike ooze and lifted the man while simultaneously seeming to pull him down. Haunting wails rose from the dark pitch. Some of the extremities bore resemblances to claws, pincers, mouths, and other disgusting shapes. My legs backed me away of their own accord.

Xasha howled in agony. He struggled and tried to escape, but the hands had him. Yellow mist began to separate from the physical body, like peeling off a layer of grime from the man's skin. Xasha's cries of agony and despair never ceased until the final moment when something else came from the pool of pitch.

The creature had a humanoid torso, but its lower body was a dark vortex of sullenly glimmering energy. It had a glowing red light where an eye might be, but no other facial features. Even so, it spoke.

"You are not the one," the demon said, looking at Vallaena. Its voice was a collective of many voices, all speaking in monotone with deep timbre at the foundation.

She grew a bit pale. "The one?"

The demon ignored her and turned back to Xasha. "The Abyss awaits, Xashabyullwt." It wrapped its arms around the glowing yellow mist. "Welcome to your eternity." With a final ghostly shriek, the ground seemed to suck in the new demon, the groping hands, and the yellow mist that was Xasha's demon form. The host body dropped to the bare floor.

For the longest time, I couldn't move, couldn't think, and couldn't stop staring at the ordinary looking floor where that monster had manifested.

Vallaena stared suspiciously at the bare spot, then wearily sank into a chair. "I will need some time to recover."

"What was that thing?" Tyler asked.

"An Abyssal." She slumped.

"You actually summoned an Abyssal demon?" Tyler looked like a kid who'd just seen a cool skateboard trick. "That's amazing."

Vallaena offered a weak smile. "I didn't summon him. I held a bit of chum over a shark pit and waited for him to bite, though it took far less time than I'd imagined."

"What were the hands for?" I asked.

"Other demons trapped in the Abyss. Some believe they are trying to escape through the portal. Others claim they only want to drag other souls down with them." She motioned toward a water bottle. "Could someone fetch me a water, please?"

I obliged, removing one from the cooling cabinet, unscrewing the lid, and handing it to her. She gulped a third of the bottle and put it down. "I certainly hope the other demon knows more than this one."

"He said Karak planned to do two demonicus at the same time." Tyler rubbed his chin. "That's an awful lot of preparation, but with two demon lords, it won't be as difficult to pull off."

"This entire situation is unprecedented." Vallaena ran a finger down the bottle. "I'm not certain how powerful Karak and Abaddon will be with their new forms, but we must be very careful."

"We?" I raised an eyebrow. "Are you going to help us too?"

She nodded. "I must. The future is already dangerous enough without Domathus rallying his forces in Eden."

"You must be talking about Daelissa," I said.

Her lips quirked. "You believe in the threat the Seraphim pose?"

"Um, I don't know a lot about them, but yeah." I shrugged. "The Exorcists are following her now, so she must have a lot of clout."

"If I'm to prepare my nephew for the dangers ahead, I must do what I can to pull this weed before it grows any larger." She placed her hand over mine. "Your gift is truly remarkable. Do you have any supernatural strength or other attributes?"

I became distinctly aware of the low simmering heat of the demon presence inside her. She felt nearly identical to Tyler though her spiritual spark seemed to resonate at a different frequency. Her vibes were nothing like the putrid sensation from the caustic demons.

I abruptly realized she'd asked me a question and shook away thoughts. "No, aside from my ability to sense supernatural abilities and in some cases, remove them, I'm quite ordinary."

"This makes you very brave indeed." She kept her hand on mine and looked at Tyler. "I can understand your fascination with this one."

Tyler beamed. "She's pretty great, Anae Vallaena."

"Pssht." Vallaena backhanded the air. "When we are in private you may simply call me Vallaena. You have earned the right."

"Well, you've earned the right to call me Tyler, and her Emily." Tyler winked at me. "I'll admit I wasn't sure what to expect from a Daemos. I've heard a lot about your kind, but never met one until you."

"We have a simultaneous connection to this plane and Haedaemos. Our souls are both human and demon, bound into one." She drank more water. "It was a very difficult achievement, but well worth it."

"You intentionally bonded with humans?" Tyler looked confused.

"During the First Seraphim War, Baal saw the dangers the Seraphim presented." Her eyes seemed lost in the distant past. "Demons are masters of the spiritual world. Mortals are masters of the physical. Seraphim are masters of both. Baal surmised that by perfectly combining a human soul and a demon spirit, we would be as powerful as the Seraphim."

"Are you?" I asked.

Vallaena's gaze returned to the present. "Physically, yes, but demon magic does not translate well to this realm. We can connect to other spirits, namely, elementals, and gain their help. We can summon creatures from Haedaemos and control them. But we cannot compete with the Seraphim when they turn their destructive magic upon us."

Tyler leaned on his elbows, as if enjoying a good nighttime story. "Are they like Arcanes?"

"If you were to combine the might of a dozen Arcanes into one being, then yes." She turned her eyes on him. "Arcanes draw magical energy into an internal reservoir and cast spells. Seraphim channel the same energy directly from the source, giving them raw destructive power."

I grimaced. "No wonder you want to get rid of Karak first. Dealing with him and the Seraphim would be quite a nightmare."

"Especially if he were to join Daelissa."

Tyler's mouth hung open. "You really think demons would help Daelissa?"

"Domathus has long been Baal's greatest rival." A small smile touched Vallaena's lips. "There are many who would rejoice at his fall."

"Is Baal evil?" I asked.

She shrugged. "Who is to say? He does terrible things and he does wonderful things, but he does nothing without reason."

"You talk about him almost like he's a god."

"There are no gods, child." She finished the water and crumpled the bottle. "Only powerful entities who pull at the fabric of the universe and try to mold it into what they wish. Baal is one such being. So far, he has kept chaos and order in balance in Haedaemos. Otherwise, this world would be rife with caustics and possessions."

"I can agree to that," Tyler said. "Baal doesn't respect weaklings like me, but he also doesn't interfere much either. He's like the perfect absentee father."

"Daevadius feels much the same," Vallaena said. "Yet, I think it was no accident he found his cause here in the mortal realm."

Tyler met her gaze. "I'd like to meet him sometime."

"Soon, perhaps." She stood and drew in a deep breath. "He still has a role to play and I don't want him distracted."

"You must be Baal's number one daughter." I gave her a pointed look. "You seem to know what's coming, and you seem to know what Baal wants."

She met my statement with a smile and a shrug. "Let us just say I am very devoted to my duties—a trait my father admires." Vallaena walked out of the door and looked into the room where Vatna waited. "I feel much better now and would like to move to the next prisoner."

"Just let us know what you want us to do," Tyler said.

Vallaena entered the room and closed the door behind her. Vatna's eyes wandered up and down the woman's body. His lips stretched into a leer. "Well, well, well. I guess they sent me a little gift to enjoy." He walked to her and reached a hand toward her breasts.

"Unless you enjoy pain, you will control yourself." Vallaena's eyes glinted.

Vatna squeezed her breast. There was a flash of movement and the snap of bones. The possessed screamed and fell to the ground clutching his arm.

Tyler chuckled. "It's like watching a rerun."

"Were you like that when you hung out with Vatna and the others?" I asked.

"I mimicked them a lot." He blew out a breath. "I just wanted to be accepted and have lots of fun."

"You and every other adolescent in the world." I pressed my hand to his cheek. "I'm glad you grew up."

His hand covered mine. "You've helped me in that journey. Oh, by the way, the answer is yes." He winked.

I felt my brow arch. "Yes to what?"

"I think Vallaena has a thing for you. If you want to explore that a little, you have my blessing so long as I get to watch."

I pulled away my hand and crossed my arms. "Tyler Rock, don't make me slap you."

He snorted. "I'm just saying."

Truthfully, I did find myself a little drawn to Vallaena, though not because of a sexual attraction, but because she was a strong, purposeful woman. She reminded me a bit of my mother in some ways. I also admired how precisely she controlled her raw strength, as she now did by pressing Vatna face down on the table while he screamed insults at her.

"A warehouse in the west part of town!" Vatna shouted. "That's all I heard. Karak was going to lead us there."

"And the other location?" Vallaena asked calmly.

"He said something about the south."

"What were his precise words?"

"The cardinal points must be sanctified, south and west." Vatna squeezed his eyes closed. "Then something about a warehouse on the west side."

Vallaena leaned down. "What else?"

"Something like, the deep one will complete the circuit." Blood trickled from the corner of his mouth. "I don't know anything else."

Vallaena shoved him off the table then looked toward the window and motioned for us to come in.

"Who's out there?" Vatna's voice quavered with fear.

Tyler and I entered the room and the possessed man's demeanor erupted with anger.

"Grim, you piece of shit. I should've known you'd turn me into the authorities." He spat blood. "Then again, betraying your own kind is nothing new to you."

"I betrayed you?" Tyler belted a laugh. "After everything you forced me to do in this world and ours, you call me the betrayer?" He shook his head. "You deserved to be exorcised."

Vatna spat again. "Fine. Go ahead and exorcise me. I'll be back in a few months to make your life miserable, you sack of filth. I'll be more powerful than ever. I'm going to enjoy torturing you."

"Not this time." Tyler displayed a wide sarcastic grin. "This time, you're going to a very special place in hell."

The possessed's eyes narrowed. "Yeah? Like your secret hideout where you thought you were safe from us?" He sneered. "You'll never be safe from us."

"In this case, I believe you're wrong." Vallaena strode toward him. "Emily, if you'd be a dear." She flipped Vatna like a pancake and slammed him to the floor.

An agonizing cry tore from his throat. I touched his hand and gained what I needed to know.

"Vatnaphkkrryt." I didn't know how I was able to pronounce it, but it slid off my tongue easily.

"How?" Vatna shouted. "How does she know my name?"

Tyler knelt next to the prostrate man. "Have fun in the Abyss."

The other man's eyes bugged. "The Abyss? Please, no! Mercy! Mercy!"

"Just like the mercy you've always shown me?" Tyler shivered. "Like the time you and the others tortured my host body for a week and left me to die in the desert, all because it was fun?" His lips peeled into a snarl. "Or when you found me and Jalana in Haedaemos and tore her spirit to shreds just to laugh at my reaction?" Tears rolled down his cheeks.

Vatna snarled back. "You weak, stupid fuck. We tried to show you a good time, but you were too good for us."

A guttural roar burst from Tyler's lungs. "You and the others will have eternity to understand what a good time is." He leaned so close to the other man, their noses almost touched and whispered in a harsh

202

voice. "I hear the Abyssals love to play with their food before they eat it."

This set off another screaming frenzy from Vatna, which Vallaena ended by striking his head on the floor.

"Sounds as though you and Daevadius have a lot to talk about." She put a hand on Tyler's cheek. "You are a rare, special jade, but you are not alone when it comes to mistreatment." With that, she herded us away from Vatna's body and began the exorcism.

The Abyssal demon appeared more quickly this time, as though he'd been waiting for another sacrifice. Vatna awoke at the last minute, screaming and struggling, but the vortex creature ignored his pleas and turned his glowing red eye on us.

"In the darkness hangs a pinpoint of light." The demon began to sink into the floor. "The one will soon call me. I will be his salvation and he will be mine."

"Who are you talking about?" I asked.

"He brings salvation to all." The demon's many voices echoed briefly in the small room as he vanished into the pitch black.

Vatna's body flopped onto the bare floor.

"Very odd," Vallaena said. "In the several banishments I've performed, I've never seen the same Abyssal twice."

"You've done this a lot?" I asked.

"Many times." She frowned. "That one must be very powerful indeed."

I probably should have been worried about the Abyssal's strange prophecy, but all I felt was relief. Nearly all of Tyler's nemeses were gone from this world forever.

"I have the name of a final demon, but he is probably still in Haedaemos." I gave her Barboar's name. "Can you banish him as well?"

"Gladly," she said. "After I question the remaining demon."

Relief flooded me.

Soon, Tyler and I would be safe.

Chapter 24

Safety was a relative term in my mind and it didn't take long for me to remember that just because Tyler's tormenters were gone from this world it didn't mean we were truly safe. *Karak and Abaddon might have something to say about that.*

"I can't tell you how thankful we are," I told Vallaena.

The other woman stroked my hair. "You are two rare jewels, bound together for a reason I cannot discern." She frowned. "I am in the business of knowing everything. I've read foreseeances from every possible source so I could have some hint of the future." She narrowed her eyes. "Yet, I've had no inkling of you."

"Surprise." I smiled and tried to lighten the foreboding mood, but the Daemas was having none of it.

"This hearkens back to the first war. The mortals proclaimed that Heaven and Hell were invading their world." She absentmindedly stroked my cheek. "'Armageddon', they said. 'We are undone.'" Vallaena seemed to snap back into the present and lowered her hand. "We were all nearly undone, but the forces of Hell stopped the invasion of Heaven."

"It sounds like the Bible," Tyler said.

"Hell is the same by any name, though the description varies wildly."

My brow pinched. "What about Heaven?"

"Seraphina, they call it." Vallaena sighed. "I have never seen it, but many mortals were taken there during the Seraphim rule of mankind. I do not think it quite so wondrous as the legends would have us believe." She turned and left the room without another word, then stopped and stared at the female possessed who now huddled in the corner of her room.

"What will they do with Astra?" I asked.

"What do you sense about her, Emily?"

"She feels warm, like you and Tyler." I closed my eyes and tried to get more of a feel. With Vatna and Xasha gone, I no longer felt the nauseating sense associated with their caustic spirits. I opened my eyes as a realization hit me. "She's not a caustic."

Vallaena gave me a sideways glance. "Can you tell what sort she is?"

"I haven't seen color when I—" I tried to think back to what I'd seen when gathering true names.

Tyler nudged me. "When you what?"

I thought back to the patterns flashing in my head and realized there had been a color to them. "I need to touch her."

"Very well." Vallaena went into the room.

Astra stood, fear plain on her face. "Are you here to exorcise me?"

"Perhaps, but I have some questions for you first."

The possessed woman straightened. "I have a sworn allegiance to Lord Karak. I cannot break my oath under any threat."

Vallaena smiled. "You are no lesser." She walked over to the woman and inspected her. "Yet, you are not a lord. You must be a knight."

The woman nodded stiffly. "I am."

"Emily, please enter."

I walked inside. Astra's eyes widened. "You're the one Vatna and Xasha saw on the news. They wanted to rape you to death."

"Miserable caustics," Vallaena said. She motioned me toward her.

"It's not that simple," I said. "She needs to be in pain."

"Oh?" Vallaena raised an eyebrow. "You might have told me that earlier."

"It wasn't necessary," I replied. "Since the others were in a lot of pain."

Astra stiffened even more. "Even under duress, I will not betray my lord."

"I must apologize in advance," Vallaena said.

The possessed woman swung her arm at Vallaena. The Daemas blocked her and the two struggled for a moment before Vallaena pinned her to the floor.

"Now, Emily." She gripped the other woman's index finger and savagely twisted it.

I touched Astra's arm as she screamed. At first there was nothing, but then Vallaena slammed the possessed's head against the floor. A large pattern flashed bright red in my mind. *Astranamastia.*

I remembered her pattern as one of those in between those of Karak's and the lesser demons'. I jumped back as Astra flailed. Vallaena leapt back, her face red with exertion. "She is stronger than the others, but not quite my match."

"Astranamastia," I said in a bold voice. "You will be still."

Astra froze, eyes wide with terror. "How did you know my name?"

I turned to Vallaena. "Her pattern is red."

"Ah, a ruby spirit." She looked at the very still woman. "What does Karak plan?"

"I do not know much, and what little I do, I will not tell you." She pushed herself up, favoring her broken finger. "You may have my true name, but you will not have my honor."

"Can't we force her to tell us?" I asked.

"A true name gives you power over a demon in spirit form, but even then, that power is limited." Vallaena folded her arms and looked at Astra. "I would so hate to send you to the Abyss as I did Vatna and Xasha."

Astra blanched. "Do your worst."

I couldn't help but admire her. "Why are you so loyal?"

"Karak has been my mentor for thousands of years. He has helped me thrive." Her lips trembled. "I cannot betray him."

"Can you at least tell me if he intends to do harm to Eden?" Vallaena asked.

"He proceeds by the order of Domathus," she replied. "I do not know if the master shared his designs for Eden with the others."

Tyler asked a question I hadn't thought of. "Do you know about Daelissa?"

At this, Astra gave away the merest hint of a flinch. "I will say no more."

Looks like she knows something. Unfortunately, I wasn't a mind reader.

Vallaena pursed her lips and regarded the woman. "Well, we can't have you in Eden. I see no choice but to send you back from whence you came."

"Not to the Abyss?" Astra's voice sounded a hopeful note.

"I think not." The Daemas shook her head slowly. "You will, of course, lose a great deal of power from the exorcism. Perhaps not enough to keep you from Eden, but enough to make your next incarnation less powerful." She seemed hesitant, but after a long moment, her shoulders stiffened with resolve. "You are admirable in your loyalty. I pray it isn't misplaced."

"Misplaced or not, I will not waver from my duty." Astra pushed herself up and faced Vallaena defiantly. "I am ready."

Without further delay, the floor at her feet turned to pitch. Like tentacles grasping their prey, oily tendrils crept up Astra's legs and pulled at her. She tried to maintain her brave façade, but a scream tore from her throat at the last moment. Brilliant red mist poured from her eyes and mouth, forming humanoid shape. With one last wraithlike rattle, the hell portal drew her demon form into the ground and the woman's body slumped to the floor. Two grey shapes flitted into the air above her and vanished into the stone ceiling. I stared for a long moment, wondering if I'd truly seen them or not.

"Those other souls must have been bound to her spirit," Vallaena said, proving I hadn't imagined it. "No wonder she was so strong."

"Well, there will be three very confused people when they wake up," Tyler commented dryly as he regarded the unconscious woman. "How do the Custodians handle them?"

"The hosts will likely have no memories of their possession." Vallaena knelt and touched the woman's throat. "She and the others will be taken somewhere and left, I imagine."

"Too bad we don't know much more than before all this." I sighed and dropped into a chair. "At least there are three fewer demons walking around in human form."

"Granted, it is not much," Vallaena said, "but it's a start."

I noticed several new emails on my phone and opened them. Isabel had attached pictures of the apartment for George to use. I saved them to my phone and was able to forward them to George despite the weak internet signal while Tyler talked with Vallaena about their brother.

"Baal's children are legion," Vallaena noted dryly. "I wonder if we share a common mother."

Tyler chuckled. "There's no telling."

"What color demon is Baal?" I asked.

"I believe he was originally onyx," Vallaena said. "Though some claim he was ruby. He's absorbed so many other demons over the millennia, he can appear in just about any color."

"I'd never thought much about demonic colors until Professor Zuba told me I was a jade." Tyler leaned on his elbows. "How many colors are there, and what do they mean?"

"I don't think there is much meaning in the colors, only in the demons themselves." Vallaena stifled a yawn. "Caustics are not always born a sickly yellow. A demon can start out as one thing and become something entirely different."

Tyler frowned. "You mean, a jade could become a caustic?"

"Oh, yes. It is up to each individual to make decisions and ultimately decide their fate." She touched her forehead as if warding off a headache. "You are looking for simple explanations about demon behavior when none exist." Looking at the slumbering form of Astra, she sighed. "I must go and rest. This has been a very taxing evening and I still have much planning to do if my nephew is to be properly guided."

"You mentioned this nephew before. Who is he?" I asked.

"His name is Justin Slade."

Tyler and I looked at each other. I spoke first. "Was he rescued from the vampires who captured him in Colombia?"

Vallaena smiled proudly. "Yes, and then he led Templar forces back inside and overthrew a small vampire army."

Tyler chuckled. "He's a busy guy."

"Indeed." Vallaena's smile faded. "I'm afraid this is only the beginning for him." She walked toward the door. "If you would be so kind as to inform Mr. Walker that he has noms to attend to, I will let myself out." She stopped and grasped one of my hands in both of hers. "I will be sure to banish Barboar after I have rested. I assume you do not need to witness it?"

Tyler chuckled. "Just tell him bon voyage for me, okay?"

She nodded. "Of course. Should either of you need me, inform Agent Walker and he can contact me."

I found myself entranced by the way her silky hair cascaded down her shoulders when she turned her head. "What hair products do you use?"

She raised an eyebrow, but a smile touched her lips. "Nothing special. My demon side keeps my hair looking lustrous no matter how I mistreat it."

Tyler chuckled. "How do you think I keep my majestic mane so thick and shiny?"

Vallaena nodded at Tyler and left the room. I texted George and told him about the host bodies.

Agents on the way. He replied. *I have an illusionist working on your fake video as well.*

Twenty minutes later, three people in tight black unitards appeared and hauled away the sleeping people. George showed up shortly after that and took us down another level to private quarters about the size and layout of a hotel room.

"This will be cramped compared to what you're used to," he said, "but it will do for now."

"I can't get the internet," I complained. "We're too far underground."

George held up a finger. "One moment, please." He returned moments later with a thin tablet computer. "This arctablet will do everything your nom mobile phone does, and also accepts verbal commands."

"Excellent." I pressed a button on the top and the screen lit up.

"I suggest you lay low until we sort things out with the nom authorities," George said to Tyler."

"What about me?" I asked. "Can I go to work?"

"Why would you want to?" Tyler gave me a quizzical look.

"Because Jack has been working on tracking down the people behind this mess." I put the tablet on the table behind me. "The sooner we put a stop to this nonsense, the faster we can concentrate on what really matters."

"I wouldn't recommend you go to work, Miss Glass." George held his calm gaze on me. "If they can't find Mr. Rock, it's likely they'd use you to track him. I can't have you leading police here. It would make for a very messy situation."

John Corwin

Admittedly, I hadn't really thought it through and George made far too much sense to ignore. "I'll just text Jack for updates."

"Excellent idea." George turned halfway toward the door and stopped. "Breakfast starts at six AM in the mess hall on level one—straight down the corridor from the levitator and you'll see it on your right." He nodded at each of us. "Goodnight."

After he left, Tyler and I decided to go to bed. It was nearly midnight and had been an exhausting day. Unfortunately—or perhaps fortunately—we had no clothes to sleep in. I was more than happy to snuggle up next to my naked Adonis.

"Do you suppose they have surveillance in this room?" I asked Tyler.

He snorted. "Doubtful."

Questions lingered in my mind about some of our earlier conversations. "When you said I've helped you grow, were you being serious?"

He nodded. "When I was so uncertain about what sort of demon I was, you convinced me I was different—better."

"I suppose finding out you're a jade spirit helped."

"It did, but you saw the good in me—that I'm not like Barboar or the other caustics." Tyler caressed my cheek, his eyes welled with emotion. "Em, you are my anchor to this world. You help me see things about myself I never would have considered." A tear trickled down his cheek. "A life without you isn't worth living."

Emotion overcame me and I wrapped my arms around him. "I feel the same way, Tyler. I never want this to end."

He kissed me gently on the forehead. "Neither do I."

The next morning, Tyler and I enjoyed a hearty breakfast with a group of excited Templars who were talking about vampires.

"Next thing I knew, the whole place lit up like New Year's Eve," one man said to Tyler as he recounted the previous night's events. "When we ran in to help with the cleanup, we found out all the vampires had lost their powers."

"How?" I asked.

"Some huge spell is what I heard," a woman replied.

210

"I hope this means the vampire war is over." The first man jabbed a fried egg with his fork. "Colombia was a nightmare. Thought for sure we'd lost Commander Borathen."

"I hope it's over too, but we're gonna be on cleanup duty for months." The woman looked us over. "So why are you two here?"

"We're with the Custodians," I said. "We didn't see any action in Colombia though."

"Sounds like you guys have had your hands full with demons." The woman finished her grits and stood up, tray in hand. "Take care. My squad has to hunt down runners and vamplings today."

"Vamplings?" I asked.

Another Templar answered. "Vampire zombies."

The woman made a face. "If a young vampire tries to turn a human, it usually fails and turns them into the walking, hissing, blood-sucking dead."

With that pleasant thought, the other Templars rose and left, leaving Tyler and me alone in the mess hall.

"Well, it sounds like things aren't calming down much for the Templars." I stirred the grits with my spoon and contemplated eating them.

"From the way Vallaena was talking, I think the vampires are the least of their worries." Tyler had already cleaned his tray and looked at the food left on mine. "What are we going to do today?"

I set the tablet George had given me on the table. "I'm going to do some research."

"I need to stretch my legs." He stood and picked up his tray. "Want to take a walk?"

"Sure." Spending some down time with my love sounded wonderful. I took a bite of grits and discovered they were quite tasty. After finishing them, we stacked our trays with the others.

I grabbed the tablet then Tyler and I took the levitator to ground level and stepped outside. Cool air greeted my lungs while gray clouds threatened rain.

"We need more clothes," I said, wishing I had a sweater to pull around me.

"Yeah, but we can't exactly go back to the condo and get some." Tyler stopped walking and looked toward the barn. "Maybe George would let me borrow his car again."

211

John Corwin

"Doubtful." I started walking toward the white fences in the distance where I presumed lay a horse pasture. I handed Tyler the arctablet and took out my phone to send George a text. *We need more clothes. Can we use your car to sneak into the condo?*

While I waited on his reply, I sent Jack a text as well. *Find anything new?*

Jack replied quickly. *Someone at Trax Worldwide opened the program. Looking into it now.*

I sent him a reply. *Great! Tyler and I are in hiding so I won't be at work until this blows over.*

Isabel told me. Be careful.

George sent me a reply seconds later. *We'll go by the condo later this afternoon before your orientation class.*

I let Tyler read it.

"Ugh, I can't stand this," he said. "I feel trapped."

"We're not trapped, just limited." I took his hand. "I'm sure George's people will have that video ready soon, and we can go back to our normal lives.

He barked a laugh. "*Normal.*"

"Yes, well, our new normal."

We reached the pasture where a majestic white horse grazed next to a palomino sporting a rich chocolate coat. Tyler leaned against the fence and looked at them. "They're beautiful."

"Yes, they are." I wondered if we could ride them.

Tyler climbed to the top of the tall fence and sat on it, then helped me up. The boards were wide enough to offer a comfortable roost. We enjoyed the sight for a few minutes, then I took out the tablet and pulled up a map of the city.

"Does this have something to do with the research you wanted to do?" Tyler asked.

"I'm trying to figure out where the demons will go next." I pointed out the markers I'd placed for the first two demonicus. "What do you think? They plan to do two more demonicus very soon."

"Probably tonight, considering how quickly they pulled off the second one." Tyler stared at the points on the map. "We know for a fact they'll be west and south, but there's a ton of ground to cover."

"I know." I rested my forehead on a hand. "And we have no idea how to find them."

212

Chapter 25

I texted my father and told him about the previous night's activities with Vallaena. I hoped he might offer a brilliant way to track down the locations of the next two demonicus, but he had nothing of use.

George invited us to the Templar compound to speak with some people there about employment, he texted.

When my parents arrived at the compound that evening, Tyler and I gathered with them and George in a conference room. Mr. Sticks showed up a moment later, a stolid look on his face. It was already growing late, and I felt the clock ticking away.

I told them what little we'd discovered from our former captives.

"The deep one?" Patrick scratched his chin. "What sort of circuit could he be completing?"

"I have an idea," Tyler said. "Can you display the map of the ley lines again?"

My father produced his arcphone and displayed a map. The magical conduits we'd noticed earlier had grown in length.

"How up to date is this map?" I asked.

"The spell sends out a pulse along the ley lines and sends back an up-to-date image." Patrick traced a finger along the two new ones, which now stretched to two new points.

"Oh, my," I breathed. "I think I see the circuit."

Everyone else saw it too, judging from their looks. The new ley lines formed a nearly complete circle encompassing the middle of Atlanta and stretching all the way to the west and south sides where they intersected other major lines.

"Notice how even the distribution is," Victoria said. "They're not just creating two new demonicus at those locations."

"They're using a ley worm to connect the ley lines and construct a massive pattern all across the city." Tyler's words brought a long silence as we all contemplated the meaning of this new information.

"The question is why?" my father asked. "The two ley lines the new ones intersect are already large enough to support more demonicus. Why go through the trouble of connecting them all?"

"Let me contact Zuba." George took out his phone and displayed the professor's image above the table.

"Greetings, all," Zuba said. "How can I be of service?"

"What do you make of this?" George said.

The professor's wide eyes foretold of something bad. "They're creating a daemonculus."

"A what?" My mind fumbled with this new term.

"Once they complete the last two demonicus, they'll be able to create a single massive pattern and summon something truly monstrous." Zuba picked up his ancient book and turned the pages. He displayed a pattern that stretched across two pages. "They'll need precisely thirty-three souls for the ritual."

"Won't be a problem with the loophole they found," Patrick said.

"It'll be a bloody disaster if they complete this." Victoria leaned on the table. "What do you propose we do?"

"Two countersigns on opposite sides of the daemonculus." Zuba's jaw tightened. "It will surely mean death for those who do it."

"Will they lose their souls?" I asked, chest tight with worry.

"I assume the same rules apply as with the demonicus." Zuba shrugged. "I really can't say for sure."

"They'll still be dead either way." Tyler said.

Zuba nodded grimly. "Undoubtedly."

"What if we break one of the demonicus?" I asked.

"It might delay their efforts, but they can repair those patterns. If the daemonculus is broken, it will create a massive feedback loop that will destroy the patterns." Zuba pointed to a passage in his tome. "There is no precedence for this, so all I have to go on is what's written here."

"In other words, we have no guarantees," my mother said. "People who make the countersign will die whether they do it on the smaller patterns or the large ones."

"We're overlooking something," I said. "We know where the smaller patterns will be, but we have no clue about the location of the final pattern."

"That should be easy enough to calculate." Zuba motioned to the pattern of ley lines. "Notice that large circuit crossing the center."

"I see it," Patrick said. He traced his finger along the outer circle, highlighting it. "Phone, calculate the center of this circle."

"Calculating," said a monotone voice.

A bright dot formed in the middle right over the ley line bisecting the circle.

Patrick zoomed the image and changed it to show a satellite view. Westview Cemetery occupied the spot.

"How appropriate," Victoria said.

"There are tombstones all over the place," Tyler said. "How will they fit a pattern there?"

Patrick zoomed in further. "That particular spot is just grass and trees." He blew out a breath. "I can't imagine how much planning it took to make this happen."

"Why Atlanta?" I looked away from the image. "Why not in the middle of the desert where there's nothing?"

"Atlanta is particularly rich in ley lines and it's much easier to kidnap people in a large city," Zuba replied. "Your city has also been the center of a great deal of activity as of late."

"Yes, it has," George agreed. "Everything that's happened has been for a reason."

"And it all comes down to this." Tyler hissed a breath between his teeth. "Guess I'll mention the elephant in the room." He gave us a dramatic look. "Who will be the sacrificial lambs?"

Silence gathered. George finally spoke. "I will be the first volunteer. I believe Mr. Sticks will be the second."

The other man's expression never wavered as he nodded in assent.

"No, George!" I slapped my hand on the table. "There has to be another way."

"It is my duty and obligation," he said. "We are sworn to protect Eden, and if this is all we can do, then we have no choice."

"I don't like this at all." Tyler frowned. "Look, I'm a demon. I can do it and if it frees my soul, I'll simply return to Haedaemos. Just keep my body alive, and I can eventually return."

"Absolutely not." I frantically gripped his arm, terrified at the thought of losing him, and immensely proud he was willing to make such a noble sacrifice. "We don't know if your soul will survive or not. Zuba only guessed it might."

"Well, it's better than letting two people who definitely can't come back sacrifice their lives." He displayed a confident grin. "I know it'll work."

Mr. Stick's eyes focused on him with something bordering on respect, but as usual, he said nothing.

"A very noble offer," George said. "But this is our duty."

"It's still my fight," Tyler declared.

"Wait!" I said. "Let's ask Vallaena. She knows a lot." I knew I was grasping at straws, but I liked George, and would die before letting Tyler throw himself on the demon sword. "Perhaps she can suggest alternatives."

George pursed his lips. "I'm willing to entertain other options."

"Can we contact her now?" I asked.

"Yes." George looked at Zuba. "If you come up with any other information, please let me know."

"Of course." Zuba nodded. "Good luck."

George ended the call and picked up his phone. He contacted Vallaena and projected her image over the table, then told her everything we knew.

"This is extremely troubling." Her eyes flashed. "Unfortunately, I know little more than Zuba when it comes this daemonculus." Vallaena's eyes grew distant for a moment. Finally, she spoke. "We have no choice but to stop them tonight."

"We have no reinforcements," George said. "The Templars are still tracking down rogue vampire elements and have no one to spare."

"I will bring my people. The possessed will have no chance against us." She looked at something not in view of the camera and nodded. "All we must do is stop them from creating one of the two demonicus. I believe we can reach the one to the west—a soccer field at Baskin Elementary School—more swiftly."

"Agreed." George checked his watch. "If the demons are keeping to the same tight schedule they used when summoning Abaddon, we don't have much time to stop them. How soon can you be there?"

"Thirty minutes." Vallaena looked down as if consulting something. We should meet in the vacant cul-de-sac to the north."

George scrolled the map and highlighted an unfinished part of a subdivision. "Here?"

"Yes." Vallaena gave us a tense look. "We'll see you there." She ended the call.

"Let's get everyone outfitted, shall we?" George motioned for us to follow him and took us down a level to a room with a window in a large wall. A man in a tight black uniform sat behind it.

"Yes, Agent Walker?"

"I need six sets of Nightingale armor complete with lancers," George said. He looked at my parents. "Any preference on weapons?"

"We brought our own," my mother said.

I really wanted a sword, or perhaps a shotgun, but felt certain I would receive neither. Tyler procured a set of nun chucks.

"Are you really planning to fight with those?" I asked. He nodded. "These are the best non-lethal weapons. After all, we don't want to kill the possessed hosts."

I really hadn't thought of that. "I suppose you're right, but can we afford to spare them?"

"If at all possible, Miss Glass." George slid a sword into a sheath on his back. "But we will do what is necessary."

Mr. Sticks banged the butt of his staff on the floor as if to underscore the point.

The man behind the window returned shortly with strips of black cloth and the other equipment.

I took a strip of the cloth and stared at it for a moment. "What are we supposed to do with these?"

"Place the belt around your bare waist," George instructed.

I lifted my shirt a fraction and wrapped the cloth around it. The ends seamlessly joined.

Tyler ran a hand along it. "Cool."

"Now, pinch the upper hem and give it a slight pull up," George said.

The second I did, the cloth literally grew up my torso. I squeaked and jumped back, as if that would remove the strange sensation crawling up my skin.

George smiled. "Do the same for the sleeves, gloves, legs and boots."

"Good lord, that's a lot of tugging." I bit back a multitude of questions and did as instructed until my entire body except for my head was covered in the material.

George took off his business suit to reveal a black uniform patterned with thin honeycombed ridges. "Remove your street clothes and leave them here."

Tyler removed his clothes. The tight armor highlighted every nuance of his muscular physique. He gave me a curious look when I hesitated to remove my clothes. "Something wrong?"

"Of course." I pinched my belly. "Every little bulge of fat is going to look horrid in this thing."

Tyler pressed his lips together, but couldn't repress a snort. "Em, you are too much." He pressed his hand to my stomach. "Your body is perfect, and it'll look just as perfect in the uniform."

"This material protects against many forms of physical and magical harm," George said. "It will also help us approach undetected, whereas your regular clothes are a bit bright for the job."

I sighed and removed my clothes. Patrick looked positively monstrous while my mother presented a shapely and lithe figure. Mr. Sticks looked odd without his suit and bowler, but no less menacing than usual.

George handed me a small dagger and a sheath. "I don't want to leave you completely without, Miss Glass, but use this only if necessary."

I tightened the belt of the sheath around my waist. "You can wager I'll avoid a sword fight at all costs."

We went to the garage, climbed into George's flying car, and flew off into the night sky. Though we were on the opposite side of town from the elementary school, it didn't take long to traverse the distance.

Torches flickered from the ground below, offering barely enough light to make out a pattern etched into the dirt below.

I couldn't tell how much was done. "Just to be clear, once the pattern is anointed, even digging up the ground won't get rid of it?"

"Correct," George said. "The pattern is then invisibly held together by the soul." He steered the car north to the empty cul-de-sac mentioned by Vallaena.

A dozen black-clad figures melted out of the forest around the street. One of them lowered a hood and a blonde ponytail spilled out, quickly identifying her as Vallaena.

"How shall we proceed?" she asked.

"Stealth," George replied. "Incapacitate the patrols first and then move inward." He knelt and drew an oval in the dirt. "They have six sentries in these locations." He put a dot at the locations. "I suggest your people approach from the south and west. We'll infiltrate from the north and east. Try to remain undetected as long as possible."

She nodded. "By incapacitate, I assume you do not want anyone killed?"

"The hosts are innocent. Any demon lord present is a different manner." He frowned. "How do you suggest we handle him?"

Vallaena remained silent for a moment. "I had hoped you might know. Perhaps I can banish him." She turned to me. "For that, I'll need his true name."

"I hope we're strong enough to hurt him," Tyler said.

She pulled the hood back over her head. "As do I." She turned to her followers. "We go." With that, the Daemos blurred into the night.

"Man, they're fast." Tyler stared intently after them, as if he might see them in the dark.

"Move out," George commanded and jogged toward the woods separating us from the soccer field.

Patrick incapacitated the first sentry on the north side of the field. George put the man in sleeper cuffs and hid him beneath a bush. We went to the edge of the trees and surveyed the area. Torches around the pattern flickered fitfully in the breeze, making it difficult to see how many people were in the middle of the field. Trees offered cover on all sides of the track, which would make it easier to sneak round the perimeter.

George turned to me. "Miss Glass, how many demons do you detect?"

I'd opened my senses already and had a number for him. "Thirty-seven regular possessed." The encounter with Astra had taught me what the demon knights felt like. I was barely close enough to make them out. "Five demon knights, and one demon lord." Karak was the easiest to discern, like an inferno bound in a bottle.

"Very precise, Miss Glass." George looked impressed. "You improve every day."

I felt a blush creeping up my cheeks. "I try."

Victoria touched my arm. "Remarkable, dear. Could you place each of them?" I blinked a couple of times, unsure if my mother had actually complimented me. My heart dared flutter with excitement, but I tried not to let it show.

I knelt and drew an oval in the dirt then pinpointed their approximate locations. The sentries were the easiest to place. I sensed the presence of two Arcanes as well.

My forehead wrinkled with confusion. "For some reason, I think Kassus and Drang are both here." I looked up. "Shouldn't one of them be drawing the other demonicus?"

"Perhaps they already completed the other one," Patrick suggested.

A bush rustled and I nearly jumped out of my skin as Mr. Sticks appeared with a bundle over either shoulder. He dumped two possessed onto the ground and George secured them with sleeper cuffs.

He pointed to my diagram. "Let's see how many we can capture before someone notices."

Sticks nodded and vanished into the dark.

Patrick put a hand on my shoulder as I stood. "Honey, you should wait here."

"I agree," Tyler said before I could protest. "Just be ready to come glimpse Karak's true name."

I glanced at my parents. "You don't have supernatural strength."

My mother turned her gaze on me. "Yes, but we have lancers and weapons, and we're trained to use them."

I decided not to mention how I'd taken out the three possessed at the construction site and simply shrugged. "I'll be here."

The words were hardly out of my mouth before the others had vanished into the trees. George and Sticks returned first, followed shortly by Tyler. We soon had a respectable number of unconscious people lying in a row on the forest floor as each member of our party returned with new guests. Many of them weren't possessed, I realized.

Demonicus

Some of these must be potential hosts.

I was just about to congratulate myself on how well things were going when I heard shouts followed by brilliant flashes of light. I ran to the edge of the trees and saw bolts of lightning crackling into the trees on the eastern side of the soccer field. Two figures with staffs stood at the center of the field, hurling magical destruction.

Two large glowballs shot high into the air, illuminating everything like daylight and revealing at least fifty people remaining on the soccer field. The demons had brought along plenty of humans, I realized.

Karak walked up behind Kassus. "I know someone is there," he boomed in a deep voice. "Give yourselves up and you won't be harmed."

George stepped out from behind a tree to the west of the field, hands in the air.

"What the bloody hell are you doing?" I said to myself. *They clearly outnumber us.*

"I represent the Templars," George said. "We're here to stop you from completing this demonicus."

"I understand," Karak said. "Unfortunately, I cannot comply."

Kassus raised a fist and shouted, "The Children of Armageddon will not submit!"

Karak motioned the man to silence.

"We also cannot give you a choice in the matter." George pointed to the large patches of yellowing grass in the field. "Do you see what effect your presence has on this world? We cannot allow you to summon Domathus with the daemonculus."

Even from this distance, I saw the surprise flash on Karak's face. "You're very well informed, Templar."

"We do our best," George said. "Now, if you'll kindly cease and desist, then remove yourself back to Haedaemos, I will consider the matter closed."

Karak shook his head. "Eden is diseased, Templar. The mortals have metastasized like a cancer, infecting it and making it ripe for conquest." His form seemed to grow slightly in size. "Soon this world will be overrun by Seraphim as it nearly was thousands of years ago." His voice deepened as he spoke. "If Eden is conquered, Haedaemos will be vulnerable."

221

I dared feel a spark of hope. If the demons were here to help, that couldn't be all bad, right?

"We gladly accept your help in the defense of Eden," George said. "But devouring the souls of the innocent to do so is unconscionable. Despite this, perhaps we can work out an arrangement to allow you to remain until the dangers to Eden are pushed back."

Karak laughed. "You misunderstand me, Templar. We alone will push back the Seraphim hordes should they dare encroach this realm again. First, we will possess all of humanity itself. Eden will be ours."

Chapter 26

That was most definitely not what I expected. I peered across the field in a vain attempt to see if Vallaena or the others were moving on the demons just yet.

"A most ambitious plan," George said. He scratched his neck. "I assume Atlanta is just the first city. Once the daemonculus is in place, it will allow Domathus to drain hundreds of souls."

"He will consume thousands," Karak said. "There will be no rival to his might."

Chilling horror consumed every last shred of doubt in my mind. We had to stop these creatures no matter the cost. Even if we had to kill every last host body, this couldn't be allowed to happen.

I felt something tingling in the distance. Something supernatural lingering at the edge of my vision. Try as I might, I couldn't glimpse it.

"Then I'm afraid this ends tonight." George ran a hand through his hair.

Dark figures blurred from the south. Mr. Sticks, Tyler, and my parents appeared at George's side.

Zad Kassus laughed. "You're gonna need a lot more Templars to take us on."

"That armor won't protect you for long." Martin Drang lifted his staff. "How'd you like a taste of hellfire?"

A black arrow whizzed through the air and pierced Drang's hand. He screamed and dropped the staff. Before his staff hit the ground, another arrow streaked toward Kassus. He spun his staff and the arrow glanced off a shimmering shield. He snarled and fired a searing bolt of energy back at my mother.

She threw up her arm as if to ward off the blast. I would have screamed if my heart hadn't choked me with fear. Miraculously, the deadly spell splashed around Victoria and dissipated harmlessly into the air, probably thanks to the armor. I ran from the cover of the trees and stared at my mother, hardly able to believe she was still alive.

Meanwhile, the possessed gathered in the middle of the field, lining up like a small army to protect their precious demonicus. Just as they braced themselves, the Daemos reached them. Vallaena leapt high through the air, casting her hood away and leaving only the sleek black outfit. Her body morphed, doubling in size. Horns sprouted from her head, curling up and her skin turned azure blue. A long tail with a pointed end lashed out behind her and brilliant flames flickered in her eyes.

My knees buckled. The sight filled me with terror and awe. Vallaeana was the loveliest monster I had ever seen.

When she and the other Daemos fell upon the enemy, they were no longer completely human, but part demon as well. I was so entranced, I almost didn't sense possessed coming from my side. I spun and saw a short man speeding toward me.

He must have seen me emerge from the trees.

I fired a lancer dart, but it flew wide. I dove to the side. His hand grabbed my foot and jerked me up short. I screamed, but he towered over me.

I felt the nauseating sensation of the demon's caustic nature before he even sneered at me. Thankfully, the martial arts training Tyler had forced me to endure activated a learned reflex. My foot swung hard and popped into the man's crotch. He howled and released my foot. I probably should have run, but Tyler and the others were busy fighting and I knew this man would catch me.

Before the attacker recovered, I rolled to my feet, grabbed the back of his head, and smacked it hard against my knee. His pattern and true name flash into my mind. Something wet sprayed my face. Blood pouring down his mouth, the possessed snarled and lunged.

"Gingrichkchta, you will halt!" Either my command worked, or the demon was so surprised to hear his true name, he tripped over his own feet and fell.

I used the opportunity to do what I should have done before kneeing him in the face, and pierced his neck with a lancer. He moaned and went down.

Panting with fear and relief, I turned toward the shouts of battle. Many possessed lay prone, but Karak and the two battle mages were holding their own. I spotted the unmoving demonic forms of at least four Daemos.

Vallaena drove her fist into the ground. A massive flaming hand sprung up and engulfed a screaming possessed. The hand simultaneously squashed and roasted the man. The other Daemos followed suit. Stone hands ripped from the earth, killing and maiming the possessed. My mother's arm was a blur as she fired arrows toward the enemies. Possessed and humans alike fell as her precision strikes hit them in the chest and throat. George had obviously decided saving Eden outweighed preserving the possessed hosts.

Victoria had little luck against the battle mages. Kassus and Drang took turns shielding each other and firing their deadly attacks at the Daemos. Patrick fought off possessed as they tried to reach my mother.

I looked desperately for Tyler and finally found him battling alongside Mr. Sticks. The pair dispatched several possessed in a matter of seconds.

Kassus slammed his staff into the ground and shouted a word. A brilliant meteor streaked through the night sky and slammed into earth. Daemos bodies flew in all directions. Kassus sneered. "You think Daemos can defeat battle mages?"

Only Karak, the two battle mages, and four possessed remained. The possessed, however, were demon knights. Judging from Vallaena's struggle to subdue Astra, these would be far more difficult to handle.

My mother had only a handful of arrows left. My father stood next to her, a bloody sword in his hand, and bodies at his feet. My father was apparently no one to be trifled with. Impressive as it was, I still felt a bit sick at the sight. *I can't believe he's so good at killing.*

The Daemos engaged the demon knights. Kassus and Drang ceased their attacks, obviously afraid to hit their own people.

Karak unleashed a primal roar and waded into the conflict. His body swelled and a nimbus of orange flames flickered around him, burning his clothes to ash. He gripped a Daemos by the horns and hurled him away. His flaming fist caught another in the face, and the Daemos's skull erupted in blood and brains.

225

Vallaena snapped the neck of her opponent and turned toward Karak.

A shriek from the very bowels of Hell erupted from her throat. Her body surged in height and mass. Shredded clothing fell away revealing scaled flesh and massive black-clawed hands. She dwarfed her fellow Daemos who immediately retreated when she achieved this new form.

"Bloody hell," I whispered. Was there no limit to this woman's ability to surprise me? I had a feeling Karak was about to meet his match. "Kick his ass, Vallaena."

A demon knight flew at her. He met a swipe of her claws and his head rolled to the ground. Karak roared and lunged. Vallaena rammed her horns into him, but he seemed unfazed. She slashed him, but his cuts refused to bleed. It was then I remembered how Abaddon had bound himself with the souls of mortals. *How can you hurt something that is mostly soul essence?*

A van drove onto the clay track encircling the soccer field. The side door slid open and a man in a white robe stumbled out of it. As he raced for the soccer field, I realized he wore the robe of the anointed. The demons had so far protected the pattern from damage. No one but me could stop the anointed from sealing the demonicus.

I ran toward him, firing lancers, but my accuracy from such a distance was awful. Eyes wide, he dove for the pattern. I reached the outer edge and thought about trying to break the line, but it was more like a small trench painted with blood.

I can't break the pattern before he seals it.

The man reached the diagram, dropped to his knees, and pressed a thumb against it. I slammed into him. He rolled backward. Before he could recover, I jumped on his chest and pounded his face with my fists. He struggled weakly, probably because so much of his blood was on the demonicus. I aimed the lancer at him and fired. Nothing happened. *Oh no! What a time to be out of darts!*

The man squirmed and turned onto his belly. His outstretched arm reached for the pattern. Using both fists, I pounded him in the back of the head until he stopped moving. Panting, I stood, vaguely aware of other people shouting somewhere behind me.

When I turned toward the noise, I saw other white-robed people leaping from the van and running my way. I had seconds to do

226

something and it left me with no alternative. Gritting my teeth, I drew the dagger George had given me and held it above the unconscious man.

I have no choice.

I plunged the knife into the man's chest and felt it slide with sickening efficiency inside him. Blood welled. The man jerked and gasped, but didn't seem to be dying quickly enough. I couldn't chance leaving him.

"God forgive me!" I cried, and slashed his throat. Blood sprayed and his cries turned to horrific gurgles. The other people were nearly upon me. I jumped up and ran, crazed zealots close behind.

Tyler flashed past me and rammed into my pursuers, bowling them over. Before they could stand, his whirling nun chucks cracked against their skulls and sent them right back down again. Eyes burning with rage, Tyler savagely twisted each of their necks. The air echoed with the sound of crunching bones.

I winced at every crackle.

Many of the demon knights were down. Kassus and Drang had fled. But the battle between Karak and Vallaena raged on. Though their strength seemed evenly matched, Karak showed no sign of slowing despite Vallaena's vicious attacks.

I had to learn his true name. It was the only way for her to banish him.

"I need to touch Karak," I told Tyler.

"No!" He slashed the air with a hand. "You can't risk it! He's not even in pain."

"I've got to do something or we lose." I raced toward the melee.

My parents and the others slew the last of the demon knights then stood helplessly by as they watched the fight.

"Pin him to the ground!" I shouted.

Vallaena didn't seem to hear me over her roars of pure rage, so I continued to shout at her. Finally, she seemed to register my words. She gripped Karak's arm and twisted him around. Grabbed the back of his head and slammed it into the turf.

I stumbled forward and touched his arm.

A nauseating feeling overwhelmed me and I nearly lost consciousness. George and Sticks appeared at my side and plunged blades deep into the demon lord.

Finally, he bellowed in pain.

A large pattern flashed in my head—the same one at the center of the original demonicus. The name thundered through my consciousness.

Karak-ta-thul-shrokcanthuliostomentoman.

Karak's arm shifted and for an instant, I was airborne. The ground jarred my shoulder so hard it popped loose from the socket. I rolled and tumbled, crying with agony at every bump. Blackness overcame me like the blink of an eye. I drew in a ragged breath and felt arms gently caress me. I looked up into Tyler's face. Lips pulled back in a snarl of rage, skin crimson, he cuddled me in his arms like a babe.

"Em, are you okay?" A tear coalesced in his eye and tumbled down his cheek.

I nodded weakly. "I have the name."

Shouts echoed and Tyler spun. Pinpricks of heat touched my senses and I glimpsed another demon-possessed horde coming our way.

The others seemed to see it as well.

"Retreat!" George boomed. "Retreat!"

Tyler cradled me in his arms and we plunged through the forest. The pain in my shoulder stabbed relentlessly like a knife in the wound. I felt leather beneath me, heard car doors slam. Gravity tugged on me as George's car took flight.

I passed in and out of consciousness. Lights flashed overhead. I heard voices murmuring and peeled open my eyes. A woman stood over me, a concerned look on her face.

"You're going to be fine," she said, and waved a wand over my face.

Darkness fell.

I woke up feeling rather sprightly. Sitting up didn't hurt in the least and neither did rotating my shoulder. The room, a rather white and spartan affair, evoked memories of a hospital room. When I turned and faced the door, I saw the rock wall in the corridor and knew I was in the Templar compound.

A figure slumbering in a corner chair turned out to be Tyler when I tugged the blanket down off his face. He mumbled something about bran muffins and jerked awake. Not a word was out of my mouth before he held me tight in his arms and then just as abruptly apologized and backed off.

"Sorry, babe, I forgot about your shoulder. How is it?"

"It feels perfect." I raised my arm above my shoulder and lowered it. "Whatever that woman did to me, it worked."

"Magical healers." Tyler grinned and assaulted me with hugs and kisses. "Please don't ever try to take on a demon lord again, babe."

I savored every second of his attention until grim memories intruded. "Tyler, what happened last night after I glimpsed Karak's true name?"

"He got reinforcements." Tyler sat back down, pulling me into his lap in the process. "The other demons must have finished their demonicus, because they had a whole lot of people with them."

"I felt them coming." Closing my eyes, I recalled the sensation. "Abaddon was there with another demon lord." I squeezed my eyes tighter but couldn't recall any other details.

"Vallaena lost most of her people." Tyler's voice was grim. "George, Sticks, and your parents all needed healing. They were pretty banged up."

"How is Vallaena?"

"I don't know." His eyes looked into the distance. "That creature she transformed into was so incredibly strong, and even then she could barely contain Karak."

"Why didn't the rest of the Daemos turn into demon beasts?" I asked.

"You'll have to ask her." He ran a hand down his face and shook his head. "The bottom line doesn't look good."

He didn't have to say what he meant. We'd lost last night, even if by the narrowest of margins. If someone as powerful as Vallaena couldn't handle Karak, how in the world would we handle Domathus?

Chapter 27

Thousands of souls.

I couldn't stop thinking about how many people would perish if Domathus were allowed to come into this realm.

Tyler and I found George and Sticks in the conference room. They spoke with a man whose stiff posture and stern countenance immediately gave the impression he was in charge. His eyes lit on me the moment I stepped into the room.

"Miss Glass, I'm Commander Thomas Borathen." He shook my hand. His eyes seemed less friendly when they settled on Tyler, but he offered a curt nod. "Mr. Rock."

"Commander." Tyler seemed to switch into business mode. "I hear you've been busy."

"The same could be said of you." Thomas turned back to George. "I have thirty soldiers I can spare. From what you've told me, they can handle the normal possessed, but the demon lords are going to be the problem."

"Sir, a fully manifested Daemas was barely able to fight him." George took out an ASE and played back the battle.

"Do you record everything?" I asked.

He didn't reply.

Watching a replay was almost an out-of-body experience. The point of view hovered just above the tree line. I saw Kassus and Drang retreat when the demon knights began to fall. I hadn't seen them run because right then, I saw myself dash toward the man in the white robes. I didn't want to watch the next part, but couldn't help it.

Tyler hissed when he saw me plunge the dagger into the man's chest. His hand tightened on mine when I slashed the anointed's throat. In the recording, Tyler was already racing to my aid. I turned away when he broke my pursuer's necks. I squeezed my eyes closed for a moment. *The anointed chose their path,* I reminded myself.

Thomas didn't seem the least bit fazed by the violence. When it was over, he regarded me appraisingly. "You've had no formal training, Miss Glass?"

"Emily, please, and no, sir." I nodded my head at George. "Agent Walker has taught me a few things about protocol."

"You performed well."

"Agreed," my mother said from behind me. She entered the room with my father. "I'm very proud of her."

Her appearance and praise caught me off guard and I stumbled back a step. From the proud gleam in her eye, her words were genuine. I repressed the gleeful smile that tugged on the corners of my lips.

"Miss Glass exceeded expectations," George said. "Though her attempt to gain Karak's name was ill-advised, I cannot fault her for trying."

Emily, you are the cock of the walk today. I handed them another nugget of pure gold. "I have his name." My words caught the attention of everyone in the room. "Unfortunately, with two more demon lords in this realm, I don't know what good it will do to banish one."

"It might do more good than you realize," Victoria said. "When a demon's true name is used to exorcise him, it also invokes his pattern."

That didn't sound right to me. "I didn't see a pattern when Vallaena exorcised Astra and the other demons."

"It is drawn from the very soul essence of the demon itself," she replied. "It is invisible, but it is there."

"I fail to see the relevance of the pattern," Thomas said. "Why does it matter if the pattern is there or not?"

"Two summoning patterns cannot occupy the same place," Victoria said. "The newer will break the older."

Tyler snapped his fingers. "You want to exorcise Karak on top of the daemonculus."

My mother rewarded him with a rare smile. "There will be no need for a counter-pattern. Transposing Karak's soul-infused diagram on the one intended to summon Domathus should cause a feedback loop severe enough to break the entire daemonculus."

231

Corwin

"In other words, we only need to start the exorcism for it to cause the break?" George asked.

"It won't be immediate," she replied. "From the moment a demon's true name is used, it takes several seconds for the pattern to complete."

"I think we're overlooking something." I looked at the paused image of last night's conflict. "We disrupted their demonicus last night. All we have to do is keep them from using it. Surely we can spare people to guard it."

George's lips flattened. "I'm afraid they completed it last night, Miss Glass."

My mouth dropped open. "But we killed all their sacrifices!"

"The Children of Armageddon have plenty of willing souls, I'm afraid." He took out another ASE and played it. "Shortly after we retreated, Kassus and Drang returned and used the blood of another anointed."

Sure enough, not thirty minutes after we'd fled for our lives, the two battle mages reappeared in the recording with buckets and began tracing the diagram with fresh blood.

"They must be milking the anointed for blood in advance," Victoria said. "That would explain how they've been so efficient with their time."

We continued to watch the video.

After the two Arcanes finished the blooding, a woman appeared and pressed her thumb to it. A split second later, she dropped dead. The demons dragged more bound people onto the field while humans in white robes took positions in the outer diagrams. The entire process took perhaps two hours. The man in the center diagram shouted with glee until the awful moment when he realized with horror that he wasn't to be a part of the great Lord Belhor, our newest unwelcome demon lord in Eden.

Now all Karak and the demon lords had to do was complete the daemonculus to summon their overlord, Domathus.

Thomas's jaw tightened. "I'll see if I can spare a hundred soldiers. The vampire conflict cost us dearly, and we're still dealing with the fallout." He blew out a breath. "We've also discovered the Templar forces still loyal to the Synod are treating us as defectors."

"A Templar civil war?" Victoria said.

"The Templar Synod isn't happy with Commander Borathen's decision to disavow the Divinity." George handed Thomas an ASE. "As a Custodian, I cannot vow loyalty to any one Templar commander or legion. I believe in the prosperity of a whole and hope that this information will help you prepare for what may come."

"You are a true and faithful Templar," Thomas replied. "I will get you as many soldiers as possible. I hope it's enough."

George pressed a hand over his chest. "We won't fail, Commander."

Thomas turned to my parents. "Agent Walker informed me of your service to the Exorcists and to the Templar cause of protecting Eden. I'd like to extend invitations for you to join our order."

My mother lifted an eyebrow. "Without the Divinity, we would be without enhanced strength or speed."

"I realize that, but we are not all about fighting." Thomas turned his gaze on me. "Your family is remarkably talented and I believe there's a place in the Templars for all of you." He gave us a curt nod. "Please consider it." Commander Borathen left the room.

I turned to the group. "I don't mean to be overly negative, but even if we have a hundred Templars, will that be enough to defeat four demon lords?"

George deactivated the ASE recording and set it on the table. "I am hopeful Vallaena will be able to help." He retrieved a thumb drive. "On another subject, here is the forged video, which should vindicate Tyler."

I took it. "Excellent, but what do we do with it?"

"You need to disseminate it to news organizations."

I wasn't sure how to do that, but knew who to contact. "I'm going topside."

"You already sound like a Templar," Tyler said with a smirk. He had an old-fashioned paper map on the table. Red circles indicated where each demonicus was located, and a red X covered the spot for the final pattern. Next to it he'd written, *Grand finale.*

I chuckled. "These fancy electronic gadgets too much for you to handle?"

He folded the map and stuck it in his back pocket. "I like the feel of something physical in my hands." Tyler stood and motioned his head to the door. "I'll go topside with you."

"I'd like a moment with Emily if you don't mind." Victoria didn't wait for Tyler to answer and guided me into the hallway. She took my hands and managed a smile.

"I haven't seen you do that in a while," I said.

"Things have been a bit tense between us lately, dear." Her smile faded. "It worries me when my untrained daughter throws herself in the way of rogue demon lords."

"I have an ability that can really help people, Victoria." I squeezed her hands. "Sure, I'm going to bollox things, but I'm trying."

"No, you're not trying." She met my eyes. "You're *doing*, and doing amazingly well." Mother smiled again. "I'm proud of you. What you did last night to Karak was incredibly brave."

Tears stung my eyes. "You don't think I was being stupid?"

She laughed. "What you did was foolish and dangerous, but you did your duty. It made me realize that you are like me when I was your age. If I survived, then so can you."

My lips trembled and I couldn't hold back anymore. I squeezed Mum in a tight hug while tears rolled down my cheeks. "I love you."

"And I love you, Emily." She pulled back and wiped away tears of her own. "There's something I need to tell you."

"Yes?"

"Your Aunt Lydia and I were adopted."

A cold shock of surprise froze me in place. "Why are you telling me this now?"

"I've withheld too many secrets from you—the Exorcists, the Overworld, and this. It's well past time I told you."

"Did you have another premonition?" I asked.

Victoria nodded. "It felt even worse than my last one. Unfortunately, I have never been able to focus my enhanced intuition. Sometimes I get a feeling moments before an event, or months."

"Who is your real mother?"

She sighed. "Lydia and I don't know. After this is over, I think you and I need to find out."

The thought of embarking on a family adventure appealed to me. It would give me more time to get to know my mother and hopefully draw us even closer together.

Tyler stepped out of the doorway. "Ready, Em?"

I looked long and hard at my mother. "Once I get back from sending Jack this video, we're going to talk about this with Dad."

She nodded. "I'll wait for you."

On the way up the levitator, I told Tyler all about Mom's revelation. I was so excited by my newfound relationship with my mother, I could barely contain myself.

Tyler couldn't stop grinning. "I love seeing you so happy."

"Does it make you happy?" I asked.

"Seeing you like this is the best feeling in the world." He kissed me. "You're so adorable."

I giggled, but Karak's awful face flashed into my mind and stole some of my joy. "I can't let a bunch of demon lords take away my happy family reunion."

"That's why we're fighting them, Em." Tyler put a hand over my heart. "For you, for me, for family."

I felt a tear sting my eye. "Do you think of me like family?"

He wiped the tear away with a thumb. "You *are* my family."

Even Armageddon couldn't steal the happiness swelling in my chest. *We're going to win.*

The levitator stopped at barn level and we walked outside. Light rain speckled my hands and face, but I didn't mind. It was good to be alive after laying hands on a demon lord.

I dialed the number of the person I knew could handle this video. "Jack, it's Emily. I have a video from a nanny-cam in the apartment that I need to get out there. It vindicates Tyler."

"You do? Now I know why Isabel wanted to go to the apartment so badly yesterday." He grunted. "I can't believe the cops didn't find it."

"I don't think they were looking very hard for the real perpetrator."

"Why didn't she just give it to me?" he asked.

"I wanted to take a look at it first." I didn't really want to come up with an elaborate lie and hoped he just accepted it.

"All right. Just email it to me if it's not too large."

I didn't actually know how large it was. George had been kind enough to put it on a thumb drive, but I didn't have a computer to check it on. "I'll just bring it to you myself."

"Is that wise?" he asked.

"Don't worry. I can get in without the police seeing me." I ended the call and turned to Tyler. "I hope George is willing to lend us his car again."

Tyler grinned. "Already taken care of. I told him we needed fresh clothes, so he said to take the car if I needed it."

"Excellent idea." I looked at my soiled armor. "Fresh clothes would be delightful."

Tyler flew George's car to the Gregorian and parked it next to the balcony railing. We went to the bedroom, grabbed a couple of duffle bags, and dumped clothes in them. It took us a moment to figure out how to remove my Templar armor. Apparently, touching the seams in order retracted each section until only a cloth belt remained around my waist.

"Wish we had time for some fun," Tyler said, as he finished disrobing so he could change.

"Maybe we do." I tried on a mischievous grin and was rewarded by his soldier standing at attention. I was about to turn and say something sexy when I noticed something strange in the upper corner of the room. At first, I thought it was an insect. Instead, I realized it was a bug. I pointed to it. "Tyler, that's a camera!"

His eyes flashed. "Get dressed!"

I heard a banging on the door. "Too late!"

Whoever was watching the condo was already here.

Chapter 28

Tyler grabbed the duffle bags. "Get in the car!"

My boobs bouncing and his privates flapping, we ran naked through the house.

Just as we rounded the corner into the kitchen, I heard the front door swing open. Tyler tossed the suitcases into the open car door and then helped me inside as footsteps tapped down the hallway. He climbed in and eased shut the car door as plainclothes police burst into the kitchen.

"Check all the rooms," someone shouted.

"Could they have gone to the roof?" Detective Long stepped into view.

A man dressed in black slacks and a white shirt shook his head. "They would've shown up on the elevator camera."

"How in the hell did they get in without us seeing them in the elevator?" The detective glared at the other man.

"I have no idea."

Tyler shifted the suitcases to the back seat, a wide grin never leaving his face. "I wonder if they enjoyed the show."

I should have been mortified. Instead, I found the entire episode rather hilarious and had to hold my mouth shut to keep giggles from bursting out. "I never in my life thought I'd be running naked from the cops and jumping into an invisible flying car."

Detective Long came outside and glared at the cityscape. "Where the fuck did they go?"

The man was practically staring into the rear passenger window and didn't even know it. I repressed the urge to roll down the window and punch him in the face.

The man in the white shirt reappeared. "Sir, aside from the messed up bed and a pile of clothes, the place is clean."

"Son of a bitch!" Long balled his hands as if he wanted to punch someone.

Tyler stuck out his tongue at the man and shifted the car sideways, just enough to bump Detective Long and send him falling on his ass. We sped away in the invisible car, howling with laughter at our little prank and went to OnTech. Once there, Tyler parked on the roof.

I grabbed fresh clothes for both of us and we slipped into them.

The roof door was locked, so I called Jack and asked him to come unlock it.

"How in the hell did you get on the roof?" I heard him snap his fingers. "Ah, a helicopter."

I didn't correct him. "We'll be waiting."

He showed up with a laptop in his hand and didn't look the least bit surprised to see Tyler there with me. "Whatcha got for me?"

I handed him the thumb drive. He set his laptop on an air conditioning unit and played back the video. Though the image wasn't high definition, there was little doubt the man entering the apartment wasn't Tyler. The intruder, Barboar, put away a set of lock picking tools and shut the door then snooped around the den.

A knock sounded on the door. He opened it to reveal my neighbors. Before they could say anything, he slammed their heads against the doorframe until they dropped to the floor. He dragged their unconscious forms through the den and out of sight down the hallway. A moment later, Barboar returned and took a large butcher knife from the kitchen. He tested the edge and grinned before returning down the hallway.

Awful screams and the chopping of the cleaver echoed down the hall.

Jack gagged and stopped the video. "Holy shit, that's awful." He looked up at me. "This is a slam dunk, though. I'll make sure the news gets it."

I gave him the contact information for David Cornwall. "That's the chap who interviewed me for the BBC. Be sure he gets a copy too."

"I'll send it to him first." Jack emailed David and then switched to another screen. "Tyler, I've got another present for you."

"Oh yeah?" Tyler watched with interest as Jack pulled up another file.

"I tapped into the webcams on the computers that opened the virus I created."

"Virus?" Technology wasn't Tyler's strong suit.

"Yeah, I planted fake programs on my work computer so the people monitoring the spyware on my computer would think those programs were something I was working on." Jack spoke as if he were instructing a kindergartener. "When they opened the files, they infected their computer with a virus that gives me control of their computer."

"Ah, okay." Tyler took no issue with Jack's tone and actually seemed to appreciate it. "I'll get better with this stuff one day."

Jack grinned. "Job security."

"So what did you find?" I asked.

"Let's just say I wasn't surprised by the person I found on the other end of the webcam this morning." He clicked the file. "Their computer was just infected this morning."

A leather chair appeared on the screen. Jack fast-forwarded the video and soon the torso of someone dressed in an expensive business suit appeared. The man sat down. Jack paused the image of Brandon Rock and crossed his arms.

Tyler glanced at me. "Just as we thought."

I was sad it had taken us so long to prove it.

"Does this video have sound?" Tyler asked.

"Sure." Jack turned off the video and flicked to another window that showed a spreadsheet. The mouse seemed to move by itself. "This is also a live image of Brandon's desktop. As you can see, he's looking over the fake financial report he stole from Kevin's computer."

"Look, he's activating a video conference call," I said as the mouse pointer clicked on the program.

Detective Long's face appeared on the screen and moved his lips, though no sound emerged from the laptop. Brandon's image took up the top right corner of the screen. Jack adjusted something and the audio sprang to life.

"Tyler was here. I even have the camera footage," Long said. "From what we can tell, he and his little bitch ran out to the balcony and vanished."

"What did they use, *parachutes*?" Brandon snarled. "I paid you for results, not excuses."

"Look, the evidence is planted, and everything points to your brother," Long said. "He can't run forever."

"I need him arrested *today*." Brandon looked at his watch. "All the pawns are in place but the king is missing."

"Are all your plants keeping an eye out for him?" Long asked.

"Detective, do I look like a fool? Of course they are." Brandon bared his teeth. "You have twenty-four hours before I find someone else who can do the job right."

"I'll find him," Detective Long said.

Brandon ended the call without another word.

"Please tell me we recorded that," I said.

Jack chuckled. "Everything is being recorded. We've got that asshole dead to rights."

Wicked delight brought a smile to my face. "Let's email that to the news as well."

Tyler held out his hand. "Can I use your phone, Jack?"

"Sure."

"I need you to look up the number to my stock broker." Tyler motioned to the computer and gave Jack a name.

A moment later, Tyler placed a call. "Hey, Milt, I—yep, I know they're looking for me." He chuckled. "Everything is about to turn around in a huge way, though, and I want you to be ready for it." He paused to let that sink in. "I want you to put a watch on the stock for Brandon's holding company. When you think it's bottomed out, I want you to snap it up, okay?" Tyler grinned again. "Don't worry—it'll happen." He ended the call.

"Turning the tables, eh?" I said.

He bared his teeth. "You know it." He turned back to Jack. "If you find anything else, don't be afraid to post it as well. Just don't let anyone know it's coming from us."

"You got it." Jack pumped a fist into the air. "Victory!"

"Brandon obviously has spies at all the offices," Tyler said. "Let's go stir things up a bit to really make him worry."

"You mean, you're going to show yourself to Jones or Hinkle?"

"Exactly, Jack." Tyler shifted his predatory gaze to me. "Let's have some fun, Em."

We went downstairs to the office and took a stroll.

Sandra looked particularly shocked. "Mr. Rock, please tell me what they're saying on the news is false."

"You should start seeing some new evidence today that exonerates me." He flashed her a confident smile. "Don't worry, OnTech is about to recover in a big way."

"I certainly hope so." She dropped into her seat and fanned herself. "This week has been very stressful."

"I'm sorry, Sandra. I promise things will be better soon." We headed down the hallway to the sales department.

Thomas Jones tripped and spilled his coffee when he saw Tyler coming. "Careful there, Jones. Don't want you burning yourself."

It took everything I had not to burst into laughter at the comical look on the man's face.

"B-but—the cops are looking for you," he sputtered.

"Are they?" Tyler winked at him and kept on going to the programming department.

We stopped by Hinkle's cubicle. Tyler popped his head over the side and said, "Good afternoon."

Hinkle fell over backwards in his chair and a sprinkle-covered donut rolled away from his grasp.

"Careful, there." Tyler scooped up the donut and put it on Hinkle's desk. "That looks too tasty to go to waste."

We left the shocked man floundering like an overturned turtle and sneaked back to the stairwell. After making our way back up to the roof, we boarded the invisible car. Tyler flew us across town to a warehousing company he owned. We stepped inside, greeted a few people, and kept a sharp eye out for anyone who looked too surprised.

Tyler gave a short speech about how he planned to invest a million dollars in the warehouse, but asked the employees not to tell anyone. After we got back into the car, he told me that was to help him pinpoint the moles.

We visited his last business in the Atlanta area, a restaurant supply company where he planted a story about a possible multi-million dollar contract with a large restaurant chain.

Once finished, we got back into the car.

Tyler ran a hand through his hair. "Hopefully the moles will contact Brandon and Jack can figure out who they are." He drove the car down a side street, looked around, and activated the camouflage before taking off and heading back to Templar headquarters.

I kept an eye on the BBC's U.S. website and wondered if Jack's videos had reached the press yet. Tyler was parking the car when the top headline changed. A picture showing Barboar entering the apartment bore the headline: *New Evidence May Clear Tyler Rock.*

Beneath that was another headline: *Was Tyler Rock Set up? New evidence points to conspiracy.*

I pumped my fist. "Yes! Look, Tyler." I showed him my phone.

"I love the smell of victory." He kissed me hard and pulled away. "Too bad we can't properly celebrate here."

I giggled. "George wouldn't appreciate the odor of sex in his car."

He barked a laugh. "We could leave the windows down."

We rode the levitator down to the housing level and dropped off our bags, then rode back up to the conference room level. There we found my parents and George poring over the map where the daemonculus was probably being blooded into the ground this very moment.

Tyler reached for his back pocket and felt around. "What did I do with my map?"

I thought back and remembered him putting it—"Tyler, it was in your jeans pocket. Did you put those in the duffel bag?"

He bit his lip and narrowed his eyes. "Yeah, I think so. I'll go grab it in a minute."

I rolled my eyes. "I really don't think you need it."

A tall man whose olive skin tone and almond-shaped eyes hinted at an Asian-Caucasian heritage entered the room. His dark blue cloak tapered tightly at the waist and ended with a stylish flare near the hem. Judging from the way he carried himself, his attire would prove no hindrance should he need to fight.

Even Mr. Sticks gazed at the new arrival with respect.

"It's good to see you, Master Kanaan," George said.

"A pleasure," the man replied.

The rest of the conversation faded away as I thought about the brutal fight ahead. If Karak and the others summoned Domathus to

242

Eden, nothing else would matter. Thousands would lose their souls, and the city would literally become Hell on Earth.

I texted Isabel. *You and Jack need to get out of town tonight. Don't come back unless you hear from me.*

Her response was almost immediate. *What's happening?*

A lot of people might die. Massive demon from Hell might be coming to town.

Holy shit! Please tell me you're leaving too.

I swallowed a lump. *I can't. Have to stop this. Get out of town.*

Isabel didn't reply for a long moment. *I know I can't talk you out of it. I love you, sis. Please don't die!*

My parents are with me. We WILL win. Love you too. I put away the phone and watched George erase his latest battle plan from the map. Even he looked a bit frustrated.

"They know we're coming, don't they?" I said.

George nodded. "The only element of surprise will be Karak's true name."

"Then it is fortunate you have us." Vallaena entered the room in dramatic fashion. Behind her came a handsome man with thick black hair, a swagger in his walk, and a cocky smile.

He looked around the room and rubbed his hands together. "Sounds like we're having a demon roast tonight. Did anyone bring s'mores?"

"Is this your—our brother?" Tyler asked.

My parents flinched at the announcement, and I realized I hadn't told them.

"This is Daevadius," Vallaena replied.

"David Slade," the Daemos said, and held out his hand.

Tyler shook it. "Tyler Rock."

"Wow, a jade spirit." He shook his head slowly and looked at Vallaena. "I didn't think old Baal had it in him." David released Tyler's hand. "Good to meet you. Hopefully we don't all die tonight."

Tyler chuckled. "Last night was close enough for me."

Vallaena released a long sigh. "Enough with the banter. We must plan."

I took the chance to ask her a question. "Why didn't the other Daemos turn into the huge demon form you used last night?"

John Corwin

David answered for her. "There are very few Daemos who can manifest into full demon form and maintain control." He waggled his finger between him and his sister. "We're the only two in House Slade who can reliably do it. Anyone else risks going on a mindless rampage, destroying everything in their path until they die or run out of juice."

"It may come down to that." Vallaena slowly shook her head. "I would rather risk that than allow Domathus to wreak havoc on Eden."

"Well, I could've asked my lovely fiancé to join us." David smirked.

Vallaena's lips curled back. "Kassallandra would certainly take this more seriously than you."

He shrugged. "Well my wife probably wouldn't want me working too closely with my future wife anyway."

Tyler and I looked at each other in confusion.

David belted a laugh. "Kassallandra doesn't even have to manifest to be scary."

Tyler's eyes brightened. "Can I learn how to manifest, and to summon crawlers?"

David gave him a regretful look. "As Daemos, the demon part of our soul resides in Haedaemos while the human part is in Eden. We have a window in our souls, so to speak, that allows us to remain in constant contact with the other side." He patted Tyler on the shoulder. "You, on the other hand, are inside this body, completely inside Eden."

"Are you saying I'll never be able to do the things Daemos can?" His voice sounded so dejected, it made my eyes mist.

"I'm just saying your circumstances are a lot different." David shrugged. "Thousands of years ago, we figured out how to conjoin our demon souls with human souls. We think it's because we're sapphire spirits. It might be easier for a jade spirit than it was for us."

"I like the body he's in," I said. "Unfortunately, the previous owner died right when Tyler took control."

Vallaena pursed her lips. "Interesting. Is that not what Kassallandra did?"

"It's exactly what she did," David said. "Mainly because the human souls couldn't survive the process with her."

"Is she a sapphire spirit?" I asked.

244

David barked a laugh. "Hell no. She's a ruby spirit."

Tyler's eyes narrowed. "Like Astra?"

"Precisely," Vallaena said. "Kassallandra somehow devised a way to maintain the link to Haedaemos even though she possessed an empty body."

"She's not the nicest person in the world." David rolled his eyes. "But if you go see her, maybe she'll help you out."

"For the time being, maybe we should get back to planning." I wasn't sure how I felt about Tyler becoming a Daemos—if it were even possible.

Vallaena turned to George. "We bring thirty Daemos to battle—nearly everyone we have available in Atlanta."

"That's a very generous number," George said, "though I'm surprised House Slade doesn't have more people in the area."

"We are stretched thin, preparing for other great threats to the realm." Rather than elaborate, Vallaena inspected the map. "I hired noms who specialize in covert demolitions to destroy the earth at the cemetery last night in the hopes it might delay the demons."

"You used noms in a supernatural operation?" George said.

"They have been to the orientation," she said. "They know the dangers."

That reminded me about our orientation. Surely, preventing the destruction of Atlanta qualified as a reason to miss class tonight.

"Did they report any people on site?" George asked.

She nodded. "A dozen men were using heavy construction equipment to flatten the earth and remove stumps and other obstacles to drawing the pattern."

"Noms or possessed?"

She shrugged. "I did not ask. My people were, unfortunately, unable to do their work, as more workers arrived and began deploying nom weapons around the perimeter."

"They've also warded the area with an obfuscation spells," George said, displaying a live feed of the area. "As you can see, the grassy field in the southwest quadrant of Westview Cemetery looks unaltered."

"Is it an illusion spell?" I asked.

George nodded. "Our scouts are attempting to break through the wards."

I posed another question. "How long do we have before they complete the pattern?"

"It should take them several hours," George said. "They will probably have it ready by the time night falls."

Kanaan spoke. "The enemy is prepared, motivated, and ruthless." His voice was low and rough, but confident. "I believe we have even less time."

Tiny worry lines appeared on George's forehead. "I'll have a live feed of the area in a few minutes, Master Kanaan. Then we'll have a better idea."

Those few minutes passed slowly. Finally, George's phone rang. He projected a large image above the middle of the table.

A person covered from head to foot in Templar armor appeared. "Sir, we're in position."

"Very good, Agent Beamis," George replied. "We're ready to see what's inside."

She nodded. "The ASE is in position. We're falling back before we're discovered." The image blinked to an overhead view, displaying a wide barren patch of orange-red clay. Dozens of yellow construction vehicles lined the edges of the lot heaping piles of grass, trees, and other debris into a long barrier. Hundreds of people moved about the area, with many putting what looked like the final touches on a huge circular pattern. Nearly half of the etched lines gleamed crimson with the blood of the anointed.

"I was wrong," Kanaan said. "We have no time left at all."

Chapter 29

"Smart enemies are a pain in the ass," David said. "Maybe we should just kick down their front door and beat the shit out of them."

"The direct path of the aggressor may be the shortcut to defeat." Kanaan shook his head.

David rolled his eyes. "Smart allies are also a pain in the ass."

Kanaan ignored him. "They have wards to bar direct line of sight from outside the perimeter. This protects them from a remote assault. They barricaded the north with construction vehicles and debris." He marked a red line on the north side of the area. "Open fields with only tombstones for cover would make an eastern approach dangerous." Once again, he drew a red line. "The south and west offer the concealment of the forest. I prefer the west, because the sun will be in their eyes by the time we attack."

"I agree with Master Kanaan," Vallaena said. "But we might need a diversion."

"How about dropping explosives from a flying car?" Tyler asked.

"Their obfuscation wards make an aerial assault difficult," George said. He pointed out four circles near the edge of the property. "These are nom machine gun emplacements. Anything in the air would be shot down before it even got through their wards."

"Not to mention anything on the ground," Tyler said.

People offered various ideas, but none seemed practical.

My half-hearted suggestion was using fighter jets and bombs. George didn't even entertain the idea, and instead held up a hand to draw attention back to himself. "I'm afraid we'll have to proceed without a diversion."

"What if we planted explosives on the construction vehicles as if we were trying to break through there?" I said.

He paused and looked at Vallaena. "Can your specialists get the job ready in an hour?"

"I think so." She took out an arcphone and made a call.

George turned back to me. "Excellent idea, Miss Glass."

I caught a smile from my mother. It filled me with delight and reminded me that she and I still had something to discuss.

"If the demons complete the pattern and it is sealed by the anointed, we will first try to lure one of the demon lords onto the pattern so Vallaena can banish them."

"We're gonna need the true names first," David said.

"I have Karak's." I tapped a finger on my chin. "If we could get him on the pattern, Vallaena could exorcise him."

"I won't be able to do so without complete protection," Vallaena said. "Somehow, we must hold off the other demon lords."

"We'll need to thin the herd before we exorcise Karak," David said. "Once we wipe out the lessers and the knights, that should make it a lot easier for Vallaena to do her thing."

George folded his arms over his chest and nodded. "Agreed. If we fail to break the pattern by exorcism, Mr. Sticks and I will use the counter-patterns to end it."

"Hang on." I raised a hand. "If any pattern will break the daemonculus, why don't we just exorcise a lesser on it?"

"A lesser's pattern is far too weak to override the daemonculus," Vallaena said. "Not even a knight would suffice. Only a demon lord's pattern is powerful enough to overwrite it."

A Templar entered the room. "Agent Walker, I'm Lieutenant Reed. Commander Borathen sent me with a hundred soldiers to help you."

"Excellent, Lieutenant. We're almost ready to move out." George drew a final battle plan on the map and gave us our assignments. Kanaan, my parents, and Tyler were in my group.

"What are you a master of?" Tyler asked Kanaan as we put on our Templar armor and weapons.

Kanaan had no bladed weapons I could see. Instead, two sheathed wands clung about thigh-high to the sides of his robe, and two compact staffs dangled from holsters at his waist. "I do not profess mastery of anything, only proficiency," he said. "I am here by the order of Captain Takei of the Blue Cloaks along with ten of our best battle mages."

"Blue Cloaks?" That was another faction I hadn't heard of.

"The militarized arm of the Arcanes." Kanaan regarded me. "It is my duty to get you close to the demon lords so you can learn their true names. Even if Vallaena can banish Karak on the pattern and break it, we will still need to banish the other demon lords."

"Is that why George put you with us?" Tyler stepped in front of me and shook his head at Kanaan. "There's no way I'm letting her near those monsters."

"Your reluctance is understandable, but our duty is unavoidable." Kanaan stepped closer to Tyler. "You will be her bearer. It is your responsibility to stay close to me and bring Emily close to the demon lords so she can touch them."

At this, Tyler's forehead furrowed. "How am I supposed to do that? Give her a piggyback ride?"

"A flying carpet would be preferable, but impractical in this case." Kanaan put a fist to his chin as if thinking it over. Finally, he nodded. "Yes, a piggyback ride might work best."

"You must be bloody kidding," I said.

"Perhaps you should practice before we deploy." Kanaan looked quite serious.

"Well, if you say so." Tyler still looked uncertain, but if I had to rely on his supernatural speed and strength to get me around, riding on his back sounded easier than him cradling me or balancing me on his shoulders.

"Maybe pulling me in a little red wagon would be better," I suggested.

He didn't laugh.

"Our transports are ready," George said. "Everyone assemble in the garage."

As the room emptied, I went to my parents and stopped them from leaving. "We need to finish our conversation."

My father nodded. "Your mother told me. Unfortunately, we don't know much more."

I gave them an imploring look. "You don't know who my real grandparents are?"

"We can find them together after this is over." Mum took my hands. "I know we haven't been a real family in a long time, Emily. Perhaps this will give me a chance to know the woman my little girl has grown into."

I felt tears well in my eyes.

"Can I speak to you for a moment?" Tyler said to Patrick.

"Sure." The pair walked away.

I squeezed Mum in a tight hug. "I can't wait. We can take a vacation and do some genealogy research."

"Sounds delightful." She kissed my forehead. "I'm certain that together we can find answers."

"Do you think Lydia will help?" I asked.

Mother's eyes grew troubled. "It's hard to say. Your aunt seems content to let the past remain firmly in the past. I tried piquing her interest, but she always refused—calmly and meekly, of course."

I chuckled. "I'll bet you wanted to punch her."

Mum laughed. "More times than you can imagine, dear. She can be very trying."

Tyler and my father returned, both smiling.

"You two must have kissed and become friends," I said dryly.

"It took some time, but after learning a bit more about jade spirits and seeing Tyler in action, I have to admit he's a good guy." Dad shrugged. "I figured it was time to let go of past prejudices and get over my issues."

Tyler's grin was so wide, he almost looked giddy. He kissed my cheek. "I was going to wait for a better time, but considering the odds we're facing, I didn't want to wait another minute."

I laughed. "To become friends with my father?"

He dropped to a knee and opened a box with a brilliant diamond ring inside. "Emily Glass, you are the most precious person in this world to me. You're my best friend, my lover, and my trusted companion. Being with you has taught me things about myself I never would have discovered on my own. I can't envision a future without you in it." A nervous smile lingered on his lips. "Em, will you marry me?"

I couldn't speak. Tears of joy blurred my vision and I laughed with delight. "Yes, yes, and again, yes!" I rubbed the moisture from my eyes.

Tyler slid the ring onto my finger, took me in his arms, and kissed me long and hard. "Love you, Em."

"I love you, Tyler." I wrapped my arms around his neck and kissed him again. When we at last pulled away, I saw Mum wrapped in Dad's big arms.

"Well, I suppose we should get this unpleasantness over with," Mum said, wiping at her red eyes. "I, for one, am ready to enjoy a vacation."

Dad chuckled. "It's been way too long."

It was time to go.

Tyler practiced giving me a piggyback ride by running down the hall to the levitators while my parents hurried to keep up. So long as I wrapped my legs around his waist, it worked remarkably well.

We met George's small army in the garage where everyone piled into large metal boxes.

George pointed to one such box where Kanaan sat. "You'll take that slider."

I didn't have a chance to ask him why they were called sliders.

Once everyone was situated, George signaled for us to depart. The outward appearance of the boxes flickered and suddenly they resembled large helicopters, complete with spinning blades, though they made no sound. They lifted off and slid quickly up the ramp, out of the barn and into the air. The pilot touched a button and the slider emitted a loud whumping noise, much like a normal helicopter.

"So many toys, so little time," Tyler mused.

We traversed the city quickly. My nerves fluttered one moment then tightened into a knot so hard, I could barely breathe. I wondered how many would be killed in this little war. I wondered if tomorrow the dawn might greet a demon overlord and a destroyed city.

Before I could give it much more thought, the slider's artificial sounds went silent and we flew low over houses and past a tract of crumbling red brick warehouses. Moments later, the transport reached a clearing near a small asphalt road. I noticed we were the only transport to set down in this location. The pilot touched a button and the outside of the slider went invisible, much like George's car.

We disembarked and gathered next to Kanaan who seemed to be our de-facto team leader.

"We wait for the Templars to engage the enemy from the east, then we will approach from the south," he said.

That explains where the others went.

I had more to ask him when I noticed a low-flying chopper—a real one—zip overhead and toward the cemetery. Sirens wailed in the distance.

A voice emanated from the pendant Kanaan wore on his collar. "This is Agent Walker. Nom police forces are entering the combat zone."

Explosions boomed in the distance, presumably as Vallaena's people destroyed the construction vehicles.

"Why are the police here?" I said. "Did they see through the obfuscation spell?"

"Oh, shit." Tyler gave me an open-mouthed look. "They must have found my map."

I wasn't entirely upset. If the police were firing on the demon forces, we might have a chance with the extra manpower. "Detective Long is in for quite a surprise."

"It would appear we have double the diversion," Kanaan said. "It's time to move out."

My mother unslung her bow and my father unsheathed a large sword. Kanaan jogged toward the forest, and we followed him toward battle.

From outside the obfuscation zone, the cemetery looked utterly peaceful. From the sounds of gunfire, shouts, and the whumping of at least two helicopters, it sounded as though all hell was breaking loose.

Well, not just yet, if we can help it.

Stepping through the warded perimeter was like entering a gateway to another dimension.

Black SWAT vans lay smoking on their sides while armored police with automatic weapons fired on the horde of encroaching demon forces who fired back with weapons of their own, including the machine-gun emplacements. There were so many people, I couldn't fathom where Karak and the others had found them. Surely, they couldn't all be possessed.

My senses told me otherwise. So many of the people here were controlled by infernal spirits, the sensation nearly overwhelmed me.

The presences of Karak, Abaddon, Belhor, and the unknown fourth demon lord bloated in my mind like rotting corpses.

I spotted Karak's large form to our right. He watched Kassus and Drang blood the final parts of the pattern.

"If we can take out those two, the pattern won't be completed," I said.

Kanaan looked at the enemies between us and them and nodded. "Agreed."

It didn't take long before a group of possessed saw us coming across the barren earth and came at us. Victoria's bow twanged, and most of them fell with arrows in their throats. Those that reached us fell to my father's sword.

Mum tugged the arrows from the fallen, tearing the gruesome wounds even wider. I grimaced as she wiped the blood, gristle, and flesh from the sharp tips onto the clothing of the deceased.

"Never waste good arrows," she said.

It occurred to me I didn't know my mother well at all. But I couldn't help but admire her. She was certainly a warrior.

A group of four enemies approached, this time more cautiously and with automatic guns. I prayed the Templar armor worked as advertised. Shots rang out. I flinched and waited for impact. Instead, the air before us rippled and warped slugs fell harmlessly to the ground. Kanaan held a staff before him, eyes steady with concentration.

The possessed seemed to realize the guns were no good and instead drew swords. Kanaan released the magic shield, compacted his staff, and slid it into a holster. He drew the two wands and waited for the enemy to reach him.

I came to my senses and identified our new opponents. "Those are demon knights," I warned him.

Arrows sang through the air, but the knights swatted them easily with their swords. In an instant, they were upon us. Tyler caught a sword slash meant for me and my father deflected a thrust aimed my mother.

Kanaan flipped over a swinging blade and jammed a wand into the ear of a knight. The man's skin glowed with an inner light. He screamed, and his eyes exploded from his skull. Before the next knight could defend himself, Kanaan shouted a word, and searing beams of light cleaved the enemy's head from his shoulders.

The other two knights fell back, eyes wide with fear. Kanaan offered them no respite. Ducking, dodging, and weaving between their thrusts, he cast glowing ropes of energy around their feet and jerked them out from beneath them. No sooner had they hit the ground than Kanaan flipped through the air. He landed gracefully on one knee between them and simultaneously stabbed his wands into their eyes.

Gouts of fire poured from demon knights' mouths and their host bodies died, screaming in agony.

Gray souls unwrapped from the corpses and wailed away into the sky.

Mum nocked another arrow and sent it flying at Kassus. Karak leapt in the way and the arrow plunged into his chest. He didn't so much as wince. The demon lord jerked the shaft from his body and bared his teeth. Not a single drop of blood stained his shirt.

"I will give no quarter to the enemies of Domathus," he bellowed. "Flee now, or forfeit your lives."

"You master's plans for Eden will destroy it," Kanaan said in a calm voice. "We cannot allow that to happen."

"This world is already laid waste by the mortals," Karak said. "Man preys upon man and slaughters the beasts of the land until they are gone. Mankind has grown ever more imperfect, ever more cancerous, ever more expendable. The Seraphim will destroy these weak people and then all the realms will fall."

"We're stronger than you think!" I shouted back. "We will defend Eden. If you complete your plans, you will make it easier for the Seraphim to win!"

Karak strode closer and closer. "Mankind will be perfected under the yoke of Domathus."

Tyler gripped me and pulled me back. My father and mother paced backward with us. Only Kanaan stood fast.

"Now we hear the truth," I shouted. "Domathus doesn't want to save us. He wants to rule us like the Seraphim."

The demon lord blurred toward Kanaan. The Blue Cloak dodged, spun, and stabbed his wands into him. Energy crackled along Karak's body, but he showed no pain. He drove a fist toward Kanaan, but the man easily dodged it and continued his attacks. Their dance of death turned to a blur of movement.

"We've got to do something," Mum said.

"Our physical attacks don't do anything to him," I said.

Tyler stared at the fight. "We need Vallaena."

I suddenly remembered our objective. "We've got to stop Kassus and Drang while Kanaan has Karak busy." I saw the two battle mages stand up and inspect the pattern.

Mum loosed an arrow. Her targets, apparently thinking Karak had us occupied didn't see it coming. Kassus went down with a shaft protruding from his back. Drang spun and saw the second arrow in flight. He shielded himself and it ricocheted into the ground.

"You fucking bitch!" He shouted, and unleashed a volley of energy discs. I tried to duck, but my feet tangled. A dark figure in my peripheral vision rammed into me, sending me tumbling to the ground. I looked up and saw Tyler dodge to the side. He blurred forward and slashed down with his sword. Drang's hand came off at the wrist. The mage screamed and fell to his knees, blood spurting from the wound.

Another quick slash parted the man's head from his neck and it thudded to the ground.

An agonized roar rose next to me. I turned and saw Dad, cradling Mum's limp body in his arms. My legs turned to jelly and I nearly fell to the ground. She'd saved me and taken the brunt of Drang's attack.

"No," I whimpered. "No!" I crawled to her on my knees.

Blood poured from large gashes in my mother's armor. I pressed my hands to one, vainly trying to stop the blood. Her hand reached feebly to my cheek. She smiled. "You make me very proud, Emily." She choked and coughed up blood.

"Somebody help!" Dad roared. "Help!"

But there was no one to help.

"Patrick…" Mum coughed weakly. "Always love you." Her body sagged.

My mother was gone.

"The demonculus!" Tyler yelled.

I couldn't move. My mind couldn't grasp what had just happened. Numbly, I turned and saw a man in white robes touch the diagram and fall to the ground dead.

The pattern was complete.

People in white robes herded dozens of bound people into the center while the battle raged all around the pattern. Police fired their weapons. A helicopter smashed into the trees in a ball of fire. Vallaena and David in full demon form battled the demon lords in a futile effort to stop the summoning about to happen. I saw a man in a robe similar to the ones Kassus and Drang wore, raise his staff and chant.

Somewhere deep inside me emerged an immense burning anger. Hatred poured into me, but there was nothing I could do. I was a weak mortal who could do nothing to save her world.

Chapter 30

"No!" I rose to my feet and turned toward Karak. *I am not weak! I am not powerless!* I ran toward the battling Karak and Kanaan.

Tyler grabbed my arm. "What are you doing?"

I jerked free. "The only thing I can do." I ran closer and shouted at Kanaan. "Get him into the pattern!"

"Emily, no!" Tyler shouted behind me.

The Blue Cloak dove free of Karak. In one smooth movement, he sheathed his wands and unholstered his staffs, flicking them out to full length. He pounded them to the ground and a web of energy shot toward the demon lord.

Karak threw up an arm to shield himself, but the web caught him and flung him into the pattern. I ran after him and leapt atop his chest. He reared back a fist, which would surely kill me in one blow.

"Karak-ta-thul-shrokcanthuliostomentoman, you are mine!" I felt his nauseating power flooding against my senses. I let it wash over me, drilling my consciousness deep into him. The demon lord seemed unable to move. I didn't know if it was from the shock of hearing his name, or if I actually had control. I couldn't afford the time to think it through.

My senses wormed through a morass of bound souls and found what they protected—his demon spirit. I grasped the bucking, swirling energy with all my might and shouted his name once more.

"Karak-ta-thul-shrokcanthuliostomentoman, I command you back to Haedaemos." My senses gripped his spirit tighter. "I command you to return!"

He bucked and bellowed, but his limbs seemed frozen. His physical form began to lose cohesion, gray energy twisting and turning like snakes seeking escape. I felt the bound souls. Felt their struggle. Felt their intense fear.

"You are free," I said, and pulled with all my might.

A great glowing orange mist pulled loose, and the souls howled away, shrieking like banshees even as the glow from the pattern grew brighter and brighter around me. I heard a deep rumbling growl that made the very earth tremble. I looked up and saw a massive creature rising from the depths in the center of the pattern. Hot wind howled around me, whipping my hair against my face. Lightning exploded against the ground. Tornadoes ripped the earth, spinning it into a cloud of dust and debris.

I was almost out of time.

Holding onto the shifting spirit of the demon lord, I spoke once again. "Karak-ta-thul-shrokcanthuliostomentoman, I command you *home*."

His howl of outrage echoed inside my head. The pattern beneath me tore open and I looked into a burning maw. It sucked the orange mist inside, tearing it from my grasp. I felt myself being drawn after it and clawed desperately at the red earth. My nails dug gouges into the dirt, but my body slid inexorably toward the portal.

Strong arms grasped my arms and suddenly, I was ripped free of Hell's grasp. Tyler raced for the edge of the pattern, dragging me behind him. We reached the outside of the circle and fell free of the consuming gravity.

I turned onto my back and saw the spirit form of Overlord Domathus raise his clawed hands to the sky. He bellowed, empty sockets in his horned head burning with outrage. The portal to Haedaemos crashed shut. The pattern exploded in light and a vortex of ash and flame sucked Domathus back into his world.

Thunder exploded. The shockwave hurled me backwards. I rolled to a stop, face down in the dirt.

The world seemed to pause.

I rolled over and saw souls unraveling themselves from the demon lords they'd sustained. The gray forms streaked into the sky and vanished. The glowing spirits held their humanoid forms for a moment before the earth swallowed them whole, leaving us with only the echoes of their cries.

The surviving possessed fell to the ground as their demon spirits suffered the same fates as their lords.

The battle was over.

I climbed wearily to my feet and noticed Tyler, covered in blood, rising from the ground. His armor bore rips and tears, and blood welled from a cut on his arm.

"Are you okay, Em?" he asked.

I looked at the still form of my mother. At the tears in my father's eyes.

I shook my head. "No, I'm not." And then I lost all control. Tears flooded my eyes as I ran to my fallen mother. I buried my head in Dad's chest and let the sorrow take me.

"I'm so sorry, baby," Tyler said, running a hand through my hair.

I heard a ragged, tired voice speak. "Tyler Rock, you're under arrest."

Looking up, I saw Detective Long in a torn business suit, looking at us with haunted eyes and a pistol aimed our way. He looked like a man trying to rationalize everything he'd witnessed, and yet here he was trying to carry out his false duty. He was a bloody fool.

Tyler raised an eyebrow and walked over to him. "Am I?"

The detective trained the gun on him and his resolve seemed to settle. "Turn around—"

Tyler blurred past him, chopped the man's wrist and knocked the gun to the ground. He held the detective by his collar. "Tell my brother, Brandon, he can go to hell." With that, he punched the Detective Long in the face with a loud crunch. He released him, and the man dropped bonelessly to the ground.

A grin spread on Tyler's face. It quickly vanished when he looked back at me. His face sagged with worry. There were no words to be said.

My heart shattered. The shards lodged like knives in my chest.

It felt as though I sat with my mother and father for hours, hot tears streaming down my face in an endless river. *She died for me. She died for me.*

Guilt clawed at my heart.

More Custodians arrived and took the surviving police into custody while Templars removed the surviving host bodies. A team of healers placed Mum under a preservation spell and left her where she was while they did the same for the other casualties.

George spoke with a group of Custodians. He looked at me several times and walked over after finishing with them. "I am truly sorry for your loss, Miss Glass." He bore a number of cuts and bruises, and a section of his hair looked as though it had been burnt down to the scalp.

I wiped the tears from my face. *I am my mother's daughter.* Somehow, I found the willpower to temporarily cope with the loss. I had seen the souls bound by the demons fly away into the sky. Surely, they'd gone to a better place. Surely, my mother was there now.

I took a deep breath and nodded. "How many people did we lose?"

"Five Daemos, eighteen Templars." George looked at the smoking wreckage of the police helicopter. "Twelve police officers are dead, and we took another eight into custody."

"How do you plan to deal with them?"

"We'll perform some minor memory alterations and stage a scene."

The area looked as though it had been hit by a bomb. "Why not just use memory alteration all the time instead of making people go to orientation?"

"Don't confuse alteration with a mind wipe." A healer stepped next to George and began examining his wounds. "We will take small parts of their memories about today and alter them ever so slightly so they can rationalize what happened. We've had far more success with such procedures than mind wipes, which tend to raise more questions. Police are typically far more inquisitive than their civilian counterparts, and if this entire group lost the past few hours' worth of memories, some would never stop looking until they found answers."

A slider floated in and landed nearby. "That is your transport to the Templar compound, Miss Glass. I thought you might like to ride with your mother and father."

My throat constricted as reality once again set in. "Thank you, George." I couldn't stop the tears.

George touched my shoulder. "You're very welcome, *Emily*." He cleared his throat and turned back to the healer.

Tyler and Dad loaded the stretcher with Mum's body into the slider. We slid onto the bench seats, the two men on either side of me. Dad's eyes were red, but he seemed to have cried himself out.

"Your mother was one of a kind, Emily." His voice was low and gruff. "I don't know why she chose me. I don't know what I did to deserve her."

"She was just as lucky to have you, Dad." I leaned on his shoulder. "I'm lucky to still have you."

"Luck had nothing to do with what you did to Karak," Tyler said. "You're the bravest woman I know, Emily."

Pain gripped my heart. "I'm not braver than Mum."

"Wherever she is, she is so proud of you," Dad said. "You're every bit the woman she was."

I didn't care what they said. I just wanted Mum back.

We held Mum's funeral a week later in England.

The official word to the rest of the family was that she'd died in a car accident. George and Mr. Sticks attended the service but stayed unobtrusively in the back.

"I c-can't believe it." My brother, Phillip, stared at the casket, eyes red. He attended Oxford and hadn't seen our parents very much over the past several months, though they'd spoken on the phone. "She was supposed to come visit me next week." Tears pooled in his big blue eyes.

I wrapped my arms around him and leaned against his chest. He was nearly as tall as Dad, though not quite as burly. "I know," was the only reply I could muster without bursting into tears again.

Aunt Lydia came to me just after the service. Seeing my mother's twin sister filled me with longing. My father kept his eyes averted when she was around. I couldn't imagine how painful it was to see the shadow of his wife in her sister's face.

Aside from appearances, however, Victoria and Lydia were nothing alike. Mother was bossy and headstrong, while Lydia was meek and wouldn't defend herself if her life depended on it.

"I'm sorry, dear." Lydia kissed my forehead and led me a distance from the others. "She died in the line of duty."

I wiped tears from my eyes. "A car accident isn't exactly the line of duty."

She gave me a very solemn look and shook her head. "I saw how she died, dear. I touched her and witnessed her last moments." She smiled at my confusion and rested a hand on my cheek. "I also see you're special. I've known for a long time, but now I see how."

"You can see the past by touching someone?"

"Sometimes." She rubbed the top of my hand. "Your mother had a gift of her own, though she refused to discuss it with me. She never told me what she did with her life, but when she came to visit me, I touched her and was able to relive her adventures."

I gripped her hand. "You never told her about your gift?"

"I didn't want her to pull me into that dangerous world she loved." Lydia sighed. "I'm afraid you will suffer a similar fate."

I shook my head. "It won't stop me. I know this work is dangerous, but I can make a difference."

"I wasn't cautioning you to be careful, dear." Her lips turned down. "I was simply saying you'll soon be dead."

My heart froze. "Why would you say—can you see the future?"

"Yes, sweet thing. It's very rare I see anything, but when I first touched you this time, I saw you lying pale and dead in a coffin."

"How do you know it will be soon?"

"Someone next to me at your funeral was checking their phone, and I saw the date." Tears sparkled in her eyes. "I'm afraid you have only a few months to live."

I had to know everything. "What's the date?"

"October sixth, though, keep in mind, this was the funeral."

I tried to keep calm. "Where is the funeral?"

"I can't say for sure." She sighed. "I wish I knew more."

"Is there anything else in the vision? Other people you recognized?"

She nodded. "Tyler was there."

"Dad too?"

She closed her eyes. "I'm sorry, but I didn't see him."

What in the hell was going to happen to me a few months from now? At least it gave me time to complete one more journey—finding my real grandparents. I wondered if searching for them was how I'd end up dying. Then again, I could get hit by a bus crossing the street. There were too many possibilities to contemplate. "If you think of any other details, let me know immediately."

Lydia nodded. "Certainly."

Tyler approached us. "Everyone is heading back to the house."

262

Demonicus

"Okay, I'll be there in just a moment." I looked at my aunt. "We're almost done talking."

"Sure thing." Tyler kissed my cheek and walked away.

I turned back to Lydia. "Mum told me you two were adopted. She said she doesn't know who your real parents are."

"Yes, it's always been a mystery." She smoothed a stray lock of hair from her face. "I still have the original basket we were found in."

"Someone dumped you at an orphanage?" I asked.

She shook her head. "We were left with our adoptive parents."

"How odd." I wondered if the choice had been random or intentional.

"Yes, though you couldn't ask for better parents."

"Or grandparents," I added. "I need to talk to them. Maybe they know something about our past."

"They won't be able to help." Lydia pulled her coat tight about her as a chilly breeze passed through. "Believe me, your mother and I interrogated them many times."

My heart sank, but I refused to give up hope. I would discover the truth. Victoria's real parents needed to know what kind of woman she'd been.

I hugged my aunt tight. "Thank you, Aunt Lydia." Though my aunt and I had never been close, I promised myself that I would keep in touch with her.

She gave me a puzzled look. "You thank me even though I told you about your death?"

I nodded. "Especially because you told me. Now that I know death plans to pay me a visit, I'll be ready." Discovering the Overworld had brought with it many questions about life, and doubts about my faith. Did God exist or were we fleeting specks in an infinite universe? After freeing the bound souls from the demons and seeing them fly free, I had to believe they went somewhere else—somewhere better.

I might be small in the grand scheme of things, but I planned to do as much as possible before I died. I wanted to be larger than life like my mother. I wanted to make a difference. I would not squander my gifts.

I would change the world.

263

John Corwin

I hope you enjoyed reading this book. Reviews are very important in helping other readers decide what to read next. Would you please take a few seconds to rate this book?

For the latest on new releases, free ebooks, and more, join John Corwin's Newsletter at www.johncorwin.net!

Meet The Author

John Corwin is the bestselling author of the Overworld Chronicles. He enjoys long walks on the beach and is a firm believer in puppies and kittens.

After years of getting into trouble thanks to his overactive imagination, John abandoned his male modeling career to write books.

He resides in Atlanta.

Connect with John Corwin online:
Facebook: http://www.facebook.com/johnhcorwinauthor
Website: http://www.johncorwin.net
Twitter: http://twitter.com/#!/John_Corwin

www.ingramcontent.com/pod-product-compliance
Lightning Source LLC
Chambersburg PA
CBHW050402260626
47156CB00003B/843